THE
LUMBERJACK

ERIK MARTIN WILLÉN

OPEN WINDOW

Livonia, Michigan

Published by Open Window
an imprint of BHC Press

Library of Congress Control Number:
2017952308

ISBN: 978-1-946848-61-1

Visit the publisher:
www.bhcpress.com

Also available in trade softcover and ebook

Death…
The Final Frontier.
~ Erik Martin Willén ~

There is a pleasure in pathless woods,
There is a rapture on the lonely shore,
There is society where none intrudes,
By the deep Sea, and music in its roar:
I love not Man less, but Nature more,
From these our interviews, in which I steal
From all I may be, or have been before,
To mingle with the Universe, and Feel
What I can ne'er express, yet cannot all conceal.
Roll on, thou deep and dark blue Ocean-roll!
Ten thousand fleets sweep over thee in vain;
Man marks the earth with ruin—his control
Stops with the shore;—upon the watery plain
The wrecks are all thy deed, nor doth remain
A shadow of man's ravage, save own,
When for moment, like drop of rain,
He sinks into thy depths with bubbling groan,
Without a grave, unknelled, uncoffined, and unknown.
His steps are not upon thy paths,—thy fields
Are not a spoil for him,—thou dost arise
And shake him from thee; the vile strength he wields
For earth's destruction thou dost all despise,
Spurning him from thy bosom to the skies,
And send'st him, shivering in thy playful spray
And howling, to his gods, where haply lies
His petty hope in some near port or bay,
And dashest him again to earth:—there let him lay.

George Gordon Lord Byron
1788–1824

THE
LUMBERJACK

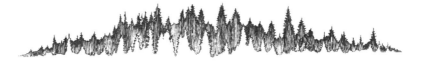

PROLOGUE

The truck came to a stop at the head of the hill, on the landing zone. Paul Harris parked it near the cable yarder, ignoring the safety regulations; after all, this was *his* site. He was the foreman, the man in charge. He looked over the situation, and saw that the spider web, with its guidelines made of thick steel cables, was intact. They should have removed the 90-foot-long steel tower, but the storm had hit them too fast. He was happy to see that nothing major had been damaged yet.

He got out of the truck and walked to the edge of the road to look down into the valley. The morning fog was thick, impenetrable to his eyes more than 20 feet out; all he could see were the two wires attached to the yarder coming up from the fog in two dark lines. It looked unnatural, wrong, somehow. He cursed when he realized that his crew had forgotten to secure the skidder at the top—that the darn thing was still at the bottom of the hill. That's when he really noticed the faint hum of the diesel engine; he'd gotten so used to it that he hadn't paid any attention to it when he arrived. He looked around, but he couldn't see any other trucks parked in the parking area. He cursed; if the morons on his crew had left the engine for the cable yarder on all night, there would be hell to pay…and apparently the idiots had.

Sighing, Paul got into the cab of the cable yarder and turned it on. He prayed that the choker setters had fixed the wires and not left them attached to a log. If they had, then he would have to climb down and get them lose. All he wanted to do was to secure the stupid thing and get back home before the storm picked up again. According to the weatherman, they were in the eye of the storm, and it would return in its fury within the hour. He had to be quick.

The old diesel engine thundered away, tugging against some sort of resistance; the wires seemed to be stuck. Paul kept his calm and eased on the throttle, and again he forced the engine to max, pulling at the thick wires. Finally, it gave way, and Paul let out a sigh as he went for the cigarette package in his left breast pocket. He stuck a Marlboro between his lips and then he looked for his lighter. He found it in his right jeans pocket. "Darn it to hell," he cursed as he dropped the lighter on the floor. He bent to pick it up, and was just about to light his first cigarette of the day when his mouth went wide; for a second, the cigarette hung from his bottom lip before it fell to the deck of the cab, and soon the lighter followed.

A sudden fear struck Paul like an electric shock, and his skin tingled into goose bumps. Emerging slowly through the thick dense fog came the skidder carriage, and hanging upside down from one of the wires was what looked like a dead body.

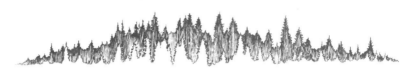

ONE

She held back her tears and swallowed hard. There had been tears enough in her last relationship, and she had finally learned to know when it was time to walk away; and so she had, from the one man who had meant everything to her. She thought back on her life, re-evaluating it, wondering what had gone wrong.

A voice from the intercom interrupted her thoughts as the pilot warned about the final approach before landing, and asked for everyone to fasten the seatbelts. For the first time since she had gotten on the plane, she looked out the window. It was a sunny, beautiful day; and below, on the ground, were giant, glistening white fangs challenging heaven. The dark green of thick, old-growth forest cloaked the lower slopes of the snow-capped peaks, and filled in the landscape between them. For a moment she forgot her misery, instead observing and enjoying the beauty as the plane hurtled downward, the ground rushing towards her with surprising speed. The wind caught the wings of the plane and shook it violently for a few seconds. This was the part she hated most about flying, along with the take-off: the landing. Without noticing, she held her breath until the plane touched the ground, followed by a brief jolt. She started to breathe normally again; and a sudden and childlike expectation rushed through her, just as it always did whenever she traveled to a new place.

As she waited for everyone to get off before her, she grabbed the small backpack that she used as a carry-on and dug through it for her standard disguise: a pair of large round sunglasses, definitely not a fashion statement by any means, and her old baseball cap. She braided her long hair sloppily and tied it up in knot. So far, she didn't think anyone on the plane had recognized her. Then again, it was mostly old people onboard, and the only crew were the pilot and co-pilot.

Finally, everyone was off but her. She flashed the crew a smile before exiting the plane, then stopped for a moment at the top of the ramp to view the surroundings. The air was fresh and clean, despite the jet-fuel smell of the hot engines. She saw that they had landed in a valley surrounded by large mountains. Everything looked very different than it had from above. She liked what she saw, but then she looked in the direction from which she had flown; and in the far distance, on the horizon, she noticed thick, dark gray clouds girding for battle. A chill went down her spine when she realized the cloud formation was moving swiftly towards her location.

She noted that there were several hangars with smaller private planes stretched out on both sides of the small airport—or perhaps "airfield" was the proper description. A building further down had large red letters on the roof that stood out: *Skull Creek Sightseeing & Rescue*. There was something morbidly humorous about the name that made her shake her head. She saw one helicopter on a helipad, and another that took off heading towards one of the mountain ranges.

A sudden gust of wind made her grab her cap. *Not much for flight regulations here*, she thought as a plane flew very close over the departing passengers, very near the plane she had arrived on. She could see the pilot smiling and waving behind a pair of typical black sunglasses—Ray

Bans, she guessed. She turned around and saw the crew of her plane waving back, laughing.

Suddenly, she felt someone lightly pushing on her shoulder while clearing her throat; and to her surprise, she looked down at a tiny old lady. She would have bet that she had been the last of the passengers to leave, but apparently, she was wrong. The little old woman nodded her head forward, and she wasn't smiling. Christina whispered "Sorry," but before she had a chance to move forward, the old woman pushed her aside and moved swiftly down the stairway. Christina was completely taken back as she observed the old lady, who by now was cursing the world, as she hurried towards an old man who was waiting for her, holding his hat and looking scared. She couldn't help heaving a short sigh while shaking her head.

"Don't mind that old bat," a confident voice said behind her.

She looked back into a perfect set of brilliant white teeth on one of the crew, possibly the co-pilot. She gave him a dry smile and nod, then hurried down the stair, heading toward the small terminal building, trying not to smile when she passed the old hag lecturing the waiting man while she swung her index finger in the air like a sword.

For once, it only took a few minutes of waiting to gather her luggage. No one seemed to recognize her, thank goodness; in fact, no one seemed to pay her any attention at all, and that was always good. Then again, there were fewer than a dozen people at the airport, most of them very old, and all of them seemed to be in a hurry to get away from the place. Plus, her outfit didn't stand out; she was wearing plain denim jeans and a dark T-shirt with a pair of comfortable sandals; definitely not a fashion statement, but practical whenever one had to get through airline security nowadays. Perhaps she wasn't as famous as she thought she was, she thought dryly.

She grabbed her suitcase and backpack and headed outside, taking in a deep breath; and again she noticed how fresh and clean the air was. For a moment she felt confused; normally there was someone there to meet her and pick her up, like her agent, a production assistant, or in the best and rarest scenario, her boyfriend. Well, now her ex.

The thought of him immediately put her back in a somber mood.

She watched as the last pickup truck in the lot took off, leaving a cloud of dust in its wake. But there *was* supposed to be someone here to pick her up; what was his name again? She checked her pants pocket for the note, found it, and crumpled it open. Not her agent but her private attorney, Mr. Thom Welles Billing—whom she trusted more than any-one else these days—had made the arrangements for her secret get-away. He would never call and bother her unless there was a family emergency, unlike her agent, whom she suspected had a crush on her. If that ever proved to be right, then she would fire him. Never mix business with pleasure or personal life; that was something her parents had taught her and her brothers as they grew up.

A Mr. Hancock was supposed to be here to pick her up, accord-ing to the note. There was a number next to the name, and Christina went for her cell phone in her purse. She called twice, but only got a voice-mailbox for something called Hancock Tool Supply. She searched for a cab company in the area—and of course, that's when her phone's battery died. Christina sighed and put it away.

A sudden cold breath of wind swept over her, making her skin prickle with goose bumps. She peered into the far distance, following the road as it bent past a few hills, and at the very edge of her vision she could make out what looked like the beginning of a town hid-den among the tree-covered bluffs. It was the church tower that gave it away.

Christina considered the long walk ahead and then looked down at her naked feet in her comfortable and ugly sandals. Definitely not the right footwear for a long hike. She thought of the sneakers packed in her suitcase, and decided against unpacking them. She looked around for a cab but saw none. She thought of going back to the terminal and asking someone about a shuttle or cab, but decided against it. Instead, she be-gan the long walk towards town; she was in good shape and didn't mind some extra exercise. The only bad part was that she had her old suitcase that didn't draw attention. Its biggest drawback was that it didn't come with any wheels, so she had to carry it, changing it from the right to the left hand every so often. She smiled as she thought, *If only my fans could see me now.*

Christina put in her earplugs and turned on some music. That would make the long walk easier, she thought; and then she realized again that the smartphone's battery had died. Sighing, she rolled up her earplugs and placed them, along with her useless phone, in her carry-on. She walked on the left side on the road towards traffic, not too concerned about any cars coming from the rear. It would be a cold day in hell before she would hitchhike.

The wind was picking up, though, so she increased her speed. She looked towards the sky and noticed the thick, dark clouds in the distance, fighting for dominance against the blue as they approached the valley; with them came a cold wind from the north. A helicopter flew by in the distance, towards the airport, and a truck came up fast towards her. She stepped to the side, by the ditch, hoping it was her ride. It wasn't; the truck flew by, leaving her coughing in a dust cloud. Redneck bastard! Now she wished that she'd gotten some water to take with her, as she tasted the gritty dust in her mouth and try to spit it out. Sighing, she grabbed her suitcase and started to walk again; now the darn thing felt heavier. Maybe she needed to get back to a gym and do some heavy lifting?

A flash and sudden explosion from above, followed by another flicker of lightning in the far distance, made her stop. She was surrounded by fields and bluffs; definitely not a good place to be when there was a thunderstorm approaching. She took a firmer grip on her suitcase and began hurrying her steps—only to have the handle snap off. Cursing, she realized that she couldn't fix the darn thing here, so she picked up the suitcase and hugged it while walking. After a short distance, having had to make several stops to rest, she had to stop to swallow her tears. She bit down and refused to give up, pushing forward, knowing that it was only a matter of time before the rain would come.

Just as she finished that thought, Mother Nature dropped all her rain at once, in a deluge that instantly converted the dust of the poorly-maintained road to mud. Tempting fate, she muttered, "What else can go wrong?" The strong wind hit her hard, and the rain was icy-cold, but Christina decided to go on—and that's when she slipped, falling face-down into the muddy ditch. "That's it!" she shouted out loud, sitting in a mud puddle, staring at a broken sandal. Shit—that was her favorite pair!

She gave it a quick inspection and realized that it could probably be fixed if she could find a cobbler. She wasn't going to toss them away; she was too fond of them. She removed her other sandal and tucked them both in her backpack with her sunglasses; no need for them now. She looked down at her naked feet, giving them a wry smile. *So much for that last-minute pedicure the day before I left*, she thought, knowing full well her feet were as soft as a baby's butt and definitely not made for walking on a gravelly dirt road. But by now Christina saw this ordeal as a challenge, and giving up was something she had *never* done, so she pushed on.

She soon reached an intersection with four stop signs, though she didn't see any of the cars or trucks passing through the intersection actually stop. She was surprised by how busy the intersection was. Most of the trucks that came from town or from the opposite side of the intersection turned into a road leading away from town, heading through a thick forest. Many were loaded down with huge logs.

The closer she got to town, the darker it became, and the more the storm intensified. She guessed she'd been walking for an hour, but her watch was in her backpack, and she couldn't care less what time it was. No one had bothered to stop for her; so much for small-town friendliness. By now Christina was very close to town, but she was exhausted; not so much from walking, but from having to carry her suitcase. She paused briefly and closed her eyes while stretching her back. Several cars or trucks honked their horns, and she thought it was at her. Instinct told her to open her eyes, and when she did, she was showered by muddy water as a red convertible with the top down swirled by her on the wrong side of the road as it passed a large eighteen-wheeler, turning back to the right side of the road in the nick of time, almost colliding with oncoming traffic. The soaked driver just honked his horn and gave everyone the bird.

A second wave of muddy water hit Christina when the oncoming traffic—another large truck—hit the same stupid puddle. Several trucks and cars passed her, some honking their horns, while some guys wolf-whistled. Many large trucks hauling timber flew by her, and no one seemed to care about the speed limit. More than once mud showered her, but by then she didn't care. She held her suitcase hard towards her chest, ignoring all the disgusting offers and cheeky remarks as the traffic slowed down nearer to town. Too bad her hands were tied up carrying the luggage or she would have gladly waved back to all of them; and to a few, she would have waved with both middle fingers.

When she reached the city limits, she paused at the city sign: *Welcome to Skull Creek—home to 4,021 hardy souls.* Some comedian had drawn a poorly made picture of a human skull next to the text. Yuk, yuk. Not too far from where she stood was a large gas station. She finally reached the station and walked inside, where she found several people congregated, most dressed like typical rednecks or loggers; all of them stank of dirt, diesel, and sweat. *The scent of real men,* she thought sarcastically. The moment she entered the building, everyone stopped what they were doing, and silence reigned.

There were several stares, and Christina realized she had forgotten to maintain her disguise; but when she noticed her own image in a mirror she gave herself a wry smile. She didn't even recognize herself. She noticed an old cuckoo clock on the wall; it suddenly let out a strange sound, and instead of a bird coming out of it, a naked female figure emerged in a running pose, followed by a lumberjack with an ax who chased her, moving the ax up and down. Classy.

She smiled at the morbid clock and decided that she wanted to buy it. But not now; she had to take the initiative, and she did. "Can anyone tell me how I can find Hancock Tool Supply?" she said in a strong voice.

There were some murmurs, and then a young man behind the counter said, "Follow Main Street straight on, and you'll see it about a quarter a mile up ahead. Now, if you don't mind," he pointed at a sign by the door that said No Shirt No Shoes No Service, "You're kinda dirtying the floor." He gestured towards the floor and the exit. Christina looked down at the dirty puddle she stood in. Instead of arguing, she just nodded to the asshole and stepped back outside into the rain and the dark evening.

"Now that was one dirty old hag," someone said, followed by laughter.

"Yeah, must be one of them mountain folks, all of 'em dirty and shoeless."

"Wouldn't make it as nickel and dime hooker."

"Damn hobo."

Christina ignored the mean remarks. She was actually happy that none of them realized she was a famous film star—perhaps a falling star, but still famous. Of course, she had no make-up on and that did alter her appearance, and she was short, something most people never realized until they met her. They were still a flock of assholes, and she was rethinking buying the clock.

She passed what seemed to be a large biker bar; *Harley or Death* flashed on a sign. Outside were several large motorcycles, some under covers while others were not. The owners apparently didn't mind if their bikes got wet. On the far side of the main building a drunk lay passed out in the rain, while another biker held one man by his neck and beat the crap out of him. Christina hurried away and eventually reached the town proper. She passed several buildings, and the street lights flashed disturbingly in the storm. Thunder crashed and echoed down the street, and in the distance she heard the sound of one or more emergency vehicles; probably cops, she thought. She passed a few restaurants, and was a bit surprised when she noticed that most of them were filled with people. Typical country music spilled out. Between the restaurants were large parking areas filled with pickup trucks and a few cars. For a supposedly small, "quiet" town, this was anything but. Had Tom been wrong when he recommended this place? After all, she'd planned to stay for several months, if she liked it.

So far it looked like she wouldn't.

Finally, she reached Hancock Tool Supply. It proved to be a log building that didn't look too big from the front. She walked up three steps to the covered porch. There were a few rocking chairs there, moving in the wind, as if they had invisible ghosts sitting in them. There was a second sign hanging down from the porch ceiling, and it swayed back and forth in the strong wind with a rusty creak; it reminded her of something from an old western movie. As of a matter of fact, the entire town reminded her of that.

Just as she headed for the entrance, the door opened and a person ran straight into her. Her suitcase hit the ground, together with a few of his bags. "Watch it, you filthy shit!" shouted the person who had run into her.

Christina almost fell back into the street, and stumbled down the steps on the porch, only to sink her bare feet into mud. She gathered herself and was just about to launch into a rage and let the brute have it, but all she could do was stutter like a little school girl. The big man just gave her a quick glance as he picked up his bags from the ground, before heading to a waiting truck. Christina watch, shocked, as the man pulled out and drove away. It had been a very long time since anyone had treated her like that. Was everyone in this town an asshole? A bit flabbergasted, she stared at the taillights on the truck, trying to remember the man's face.

Sighing, she opened the door; and at that moment there came an explosion as lightning struck a power transformer, immediately plunging the surrounding area into darkness. She stood in the doorway, staring into a large black room as another lightning flash strobed. A woman screamed at the top of her lungs, and that made Christina scream too.

"Oh my God," came a woman's voice. "Sorry, you scared the living crap out of me. If you aren't coming in, please shut the door, and if you're coming in, please shut the door, but hurry, we're closing soon. Be with you in a moment, hon."

There was some rustling in a drawer and a moment after, the flash of a match-strike. A kerosene lamp soon lit up part of the place. Christina awoke from her trance and hurried in, making sure she shut the door; but then she remembered what had happened at the gas station and stopped, looking at the spotless, shiny floor.

"Now where did he lay the darn flashlight?" the old woman complained, and then noticed Christina still standing in the doorway, shaking, looking less-than-presentable.

"Oh my, what's happened to you?" the old woman asked, holding the lamp high.

Christina stuttered at bit before she found the words. "I'm looking for a Mr. Hancock. He was supposed to pick me up at the airport. I've rented one of his log homes for the next two months."

The woman behind the large counter—which filled one side of the wall—opened a hatch and hurried through towards Christina, looking very concerned. "You poor thing, what happened to you?" She eyed Christina from head to toe, shaking her head,

Christina repeated, "Mr. Hancock was supposed to pick me up at the airport, but…"

"By golly, I'm gonna have his hide for that. What a maroon! FRANK!" the old woman screamed. "FRANK, YOU GET YOUR OLD LAZY ASS DOWN HERE RIGHT NOW!"

Mumbling protests came from a staircase in the back, followed by footsteps as an older man in his late sixties hurried down the stairs.

"Frank, anything slip your mind this afternoon?" the old woman said sweetly.

With a deer-in-the-headlights look, the old man said, "Not that I know of…" trailing off as he saw Christina's bedraggled form.

"You only forgot about our new tenant, Frank! Our *famous* tenant!" the old woman said bitterly as he joined them.

The old man looked like a bit ashamed, like a puppy who'd had an accident on the rug, as he looked Christina over. Before she knew it, she was wrapped in a large, warm blanket.

Frank tried to defend himself. "But she was supposed to call…" He trailed off again when he saw his wife's stare.

"I did. Left a message on your voicemail," said Christina.

Now Frank looked even guiltier. "Oh. Uh. Well, I have trouble figgerin' that system out."

"I suggest you learn," Christina said icily.

"Well, don't just stand there, help me get the lights back on or something," his wife ordered, then said sweetly to Christina, "and you, dear, need to get into a nice hot shower before you catch a cold."

Christina was too tired to object.

Five minutes later, the sound of an engine kicking in was followed by the lights flickering back on.

"Nothing like a backup power source. Told ya the new generator would be useful, Claire," Frank rumbled; and just as he was heading towards the garage, he noticed the dirty track from Christina's feet leading into the kitchen and through the store.

"I'm so sorry." Christina said. "I…"

The old woman, apparently Claire, said comfortably, "Don't you worry about it, honey, I'll take care of it later."

From the glance exchanged between husband and wife, Christina knew who would be the one cleaning the floor.

There was some sort of commotion from above, and some barking. Frank shouted, "Silence!" and the barking stopped.

Christina let herself be led into back of the store, into a private area. She realized that the building must be much bigger than it had looked from the outside. The back of the house was large and comfortable, with a nice spicy smell from the logs comprising the walls. Claire took her to a guest suite with a private bathroom, where she placed a white plastic basket on the floor for Christina's dirty clothes, and several towels on a counter. There were soap and shampoo and a conditioner of unknown origin. After a long, hot shower, Christina dried herself; and then it dawned on her that all her clothes were still in her broken suitcase. She got out of the shower and almost slipped, not because of the wet floor—it had a rug—but because she suddenly felt very tired. On a small pallet nearby lay some new clean clothes; shorts, a white T-shirt, and a thick gray morning robe.

Soon, Christina sat in a comfortable armchair with her feet propped up on an ottoman in a large family room, facing a huge fireplace while sipping hot cocoa, still wrapped up in the blanket like a mummy—Claire had insisted on it. She inspected the damages, including the loss of her latest pedicure—it had been a pure torture having one done, because of her sensitive feet, and she didn't know why she had bothered. She frowned and shook her head at her own vanity.

She had stopped trembling, and the towel covering her head was very wet. It had taken Christina some time to calm everyone down, assuring them that she wasn't mad and that she was all right. Frank had given her more than one thankful expression behind his wife's back. Despite Christina's movie parts, in which she usually played the part of a tough, outgoing badass, she was the direct opposite in real life: shy and rather quiet. So she listened more than she spoke to her new landlords.

Claire placed a large plate with an egg sandwich and some pickles with sour cream for dip on the table next to her. Christina had a ravenous appetite from her ordeal, and attacked the plate with no manners whatsoever. Claire looked on like a proud mother while Frank, still blushing, looked down at his boots. Christina was very tired and had difficulty listening to conversation.

"You're welcome to stay here tonight," Claire said at one point.

"Thank you, Claire, but if it's not too much to ask, I'd like to get to the cabin and get settled in as soon as possible."

"That's a nasty storm out there. Think you can take her there now, Frank?"

"Ha, this little breeze? 'Course I can. I'm gonna get the truck ready."

"And I have to lock up the store. You okay, hon?"

Christina nodded with a friendly smile.

After a while Frank came back into the large living room and said loudly, "Well, I'm ready."

"Shhh," warned his wife, and nodded over towards Christina, who was dead asleep in the big, comfortable armchair with her feet propped up. The only sound came from the burning logs in the fireplace. Frank and Claire both smiled at the sight.

"Guess I'll take her in the morning, then." Frank embraced his wife from the side, and they exchanged warm smiles.

Christina slept like a baby through the night, and she had a wonderful dream; but suddenly, the dream shattered into a million pieces, and she woke up instantly, screaming and laughing. Something cold and wet had slithered across the naked soft soles of her feet, and her reaction had been immediate, just as it sometimes was whenever she had a pedicure: she kicked the air and quickly rolled up into a ball in the big chair. The ottoman had tipped over, and Christina stared at the villain who had so abruptly ruined a wonderful dream—not that she remembered it anymore. Breathing heavily, with his long tongue hanging out, a stocky British bulldog stared at her in an amused but demanding manner. He began breathing heavily as he tried to climb up into the chair. Christina sensed someone to her right, and she turned her head, letting out another frightened shout. Facing her, only an inch away, was a huge Rhodesian Ridgeback, its large tail sweeping the floor. A long tongue gave her a morning kiss, followed by an eager stare.

A sudden loud bark from the opposite side made her jump a third time. On her left side stood yet another dog: a big black pit-bull, its tail whipping the air, demanding her attention. Still in shock and a bit confused by the wakeup call, Christina tried to gather herself. She felt something like a paw touching her left foot, and she quickly pulled it under the blanket. The bulldog had decided to join her in the chair; however, it couldn't make it all the way up, and let her know it with a loud bark—and that set off the entire orchestra.

"You all right, hon?" A worried Claire charged inside the living room from the adjacent kitchen. "SILENCE!"

The dogs immediately stopped barking, but the bulldog kept struggling to conquer Mt. Chairverest.

"I, I think so," Christina shuddered, giving the smiling dogs a toothy smile in return.

"Oh, you met our babies! That's Nugget to your right and Hunter to your left, and of course the alpha of the pack, Winston. I believe Winston wants his armchair back. Frank must have let them inside. I think they like you, and old Winston don't like many."

When Christina tried to get up, Winston pushed his head against her left leg and looked up at her with an innocent expression. Christina melted instantly. He jumped up on his back legs, leaning his front legs on the armchair. He turned his beautiful, innocent dog face to her, giving Christina a questioning expression: *What are you waiting for? Help me up, lady.*

"You might want to give him a nudge. Don't worry, they're harmless when we're around. We use them to guard our store and home—well, not Winston, he's too old and lazy. *Someone* keeps feeding him goodies when I'm not looking."

Claire gave Frank a glare as he entered the room. Christina got up from the chair, and at first she hesitated, but a quick bark reminded her of her duty to the Prime Minister. She helped the determined dog onto his armchair; he immediately turned a series of circles before settling down with a satisfied grunt and looking up at Christina expectantly.

"Oh, he likes you! Now he wants to be scratched behind the ears."

Christina hesitated at first, but then she gathered herself. After all, she loved animals, she thought as she scratched Winston while making silly baby talk to him. A nudge from the side, and Hunter demanded his time with the stranger, and so did Nugget. Christina, now kneeling, petted both dogs, but Winston wouldn't have it and barked right in her face. That made her fall on her ass in surprise, and soon the melee began. It was literally impossible for her to get up as the dogs welcomed her to their home; and since she was lying on the floor, it was obviously time to play. They scrubbed her with their tongues and Christina started to laugh and cry for help.

Frank whistled, loud and short, and as sudden as the dogs had jumped her, they backed away to sit a few feet away in silence...except for Winston, who apparently didn't give a damn. He remained in the chair and demanded Christina's attention, woofing again in his deep voice.

"Can't tame them all, now can we?" Frank stated, while reaching out with his large hand to help Christina to her feet. Despite his age—Christina guessed he was in his late sixties or early seventies—Frank's hand was firm as a rock, followed by a huge forearm corded with muscle. She felt as if she was almost flying to her feet as he tugged on her. "Sorry if the dogs gave you a fright; didn't mean to wake you like that."

Christina felt a little sorry for Frank, because so far all she'd heard from him since they'd met had been apologies. She gave him a friendly embrace and laughed.

"Breakfast," Claire said loudly.

The dogs got on their feet and rushed into the kitchen, and Winston apparently got his superpowers back, having no problem jumping to the floor and racing after the other dogs while barking loudly, making sure they knew who was the alpha.

The large kitchen table was loaded with food, and with minimal fanfare they sat down and started to eat. Christina, who normally watched her diet, decided not to do so today, and tried a little bit of almost everything. The dogs each had their own bowls away from each other, but when Winston had finished his own, he decided that the others were his, too. Poor Nugget and Hunter moved aside reluctantly while Winston slobbered away, and hurried up to the table, sitting next to Frank, who once in a while slipped them a treat.

Clair cleared her throat more than once; this seemed to be a casual ritual among them. At one point, Christina dropped her sandwich when a sneeze attack overcame her. When she reached for it on the floor, all she saw was a happy Hunter licking his lips. A large paw landed on her lap on the opposite side, and there was Nugget, demanding his share. Christina quickly smuggled some cheese to him, and all of a sudden she had two friends for life. Needless to say, Winston noticed what was going on; he barked loudly, making the other dogs whimper a bit while muscling in on the new guest, demanding his own treat.

"LEAVE!" Clair ordered.

All the dogs hurried back into the living room…well, Winston walked reluctantly, and when he reached the threshold, he turned his head and snarled, making sure he had the last word. Christina could have sworn that Claire had smuggled a treat to Winston when he passed her.

She looked around the kitchen of the log home, and liked the open plan and high ceiling. She hadn't spent much time noticing it when she'd arrived. It was very homey, this home of Frank and Claire Hancock. They had been the perfect hosts; almost instantly she had felt welcome, as if she had known them for years. Tom Billing hadn't lied about his friends; they were very nice indeed.

"Um, where's my stuff?" Christina asked, after she'd had her fill.

Claire nodded her head to the side. They'd placed Christina's suitcase on a counter. Next to it lay her clothes from the trip, all neatly folded and cleaned. Frank got up and eyed the case's broken handle; he fumbled for his glasses in his left breast pocket, and with them on the tip of his nose, inspected the damage. "Nothing that I can't fix, but it'll take a little while."

Christina opened the suitcase, only to discover that most of its contents were wet. She went through her things and placed her sneakers on the counter. "Oh my, if I'd known everything was wet I would have cleaned them too, but I'd never go through someone else's things," Claire said a bit defensively.

"No worries—you've been the perfect hosts. I should have gotten a newer and better suitcase before I left. It's just that whenever I go on a trip that isn't work-related, I use this old thing. No big deal. The handle broke, and I'll have to get a new one anyway."

Frank looked at the sneakers and gave them a disapproving glance. "One moment. I'll be right back."

When he returned, he had some thick socks and a brand-new pair of black boots; they looked military. "These are Original S.W.A.T. CLASSIC 9 boots," he told her. "They're real soft, so you won't be getting any blisters from them, and they're perfect for hiking…unlike your other footwear. I placed some insoles in them, because these are our smallest size."

He handed her the socks and boots. Christina put them on; they were very comfortable. A little too big, but she could always wear one more pair of socks. As if Frank could read her mind, he placed another three packs of socks on the counter, two of them extra-thick. He also laid a large military-style duffle bag next to her.

"It can get cold in the mountains, Miss, and fall has just begun," he said, and then he left the kitchen.

"Wait! What do I owe you?"

Frank ignored the question and moved on.

Claire answered for him. "Nothing, dear, it's my absent-minded husband's way of apologizing."

"Well, thank you," Christina said, a little flustered.

"Mr. Billing said if you liked it here, you might stay for a while, and would get whatever you needed eventually anyway."

Christina gave Claire a friendly smile. "Only if you let me pay for whatever I purchase in the future, if I want to stay."

Claire smiled back. "You'll stay, if you're looking for a nice, beautiful, quiet place."

"There was quite a bit of commotion on the road."

"That's the loggers and miners. They've descended on us like a plague of locusts recently. For what it's worth, Skull Creek is a really nice place with friendly folks. Business is booming these days. Our beautiful town had almost died, but now that business is increasing, the economy's better."

Christina smiled at the sales pitch, and hid her thoughts while finishing her hot, black coffee. The start of her getaway had been a nightmare, but she really liked her new hosts, and decided to leave her long walk from the airport behind her where it belonged.

Christina also received a care package from Claire: a basket loaded with food. When she stepped outside, she got a better look at her surroundings. The night before, she hadn't cared about the sights; she only wanted to get to the store and meet her new landlords. For a moment, she felt as if she had stepped back in time. The entire town, from what she could see, still reminded her of the Old West—with the exception of all the cars and trucks, naturally. She remembered a job she'd had in Deadwood, South Dakota; it was a lot like this, but this place seemed smaller.

Later, Frank drove Christina through town in a shiny blue Dodge King Cab pickup truck. Nugget and Hunter had joined them, while Winston stayed with Claire at the store. While driving, Frank gave her the nickel tour, pointed out the various locales and sights, warning her about some business owners, and so on.

"So," he finally asked, "what brings someone with your background to our little community?"

There was a moment of uncomfortable silence.

"Oh, don't worry, Claire and I promised Mr. Billing to keep your stay a secret, and we think we understand why. Sorry if I'm a bit nosey. It's just that I thought being a famous movie star and all, you'd would want to go to a five-star hotel on a beach somewhere."

Christina chuckled. "Oh, that sounds nice, but no…staying in a hotel on a beach is the *last* thing I want right now. I do love beaches and the ocean for occasional visits, and back in California I live near the beach, so that's something I can see whenever I'm home. No, I want to see real nature, just like this." She made a gesture with her right arm towards the surroundings as they left the town in the background, heading up into the mountains on a narrow but paved road.

"You do realize that most parts of this region are wilderness, and we do have a lot of wild and sometime dangerous animals around here," Frank cautioned. "Mountain lions, lynx, the occasional bear. Even grizzlies every once in a while."

"That might not help your sales pitch," Christina joked.

"Well, selling this property is important, and being honest about it is even more important. A lot of folks watch those reality shows about the wilderness and gold miners on television, and get caught up with the romantic side…but the truth is that it's a lot less romantic than it looks. For the most part, it means work—hard physical labor, mind you—and sometimes it can get dangerous. Not that I'm saying you're not up for it. I'm just saying."

"Thank you for the heads-up, Frank, but I think you've only made me more interested in this place than I was before."

Both of them laughed, and that triggered the dogs to start barking. Nugget and Hunter were fighting and playing each other for the standing place between the driver and passenger. Once in a while, Christina petted whoever managed to get his head near her.

They passed a large warning sign bearing the words SLOW DOWN! DEADMAN'S CURVE.

"By the way, we're entering a tricky part of this road," Frank noted. "If you look over here on the left, you'll see a vertical cliff. Right here it can get treacherous, because there's a blind bend in the road here. Always drive slow here, it's called…"

"Deadman's Curve, I saw the sign," Christina said, concentrating on the road.

Frank pointed at the cliffside on the sharp turn. "This straight road will become a serpentine road in order to get up the mountain after this hellish curve, so be *especially* cautious when driving at night. Too many good people have died here."

Christina turned her head to the right and noticed that several trees bore scars as if they had been hit by something, probably cars, before they fell into the valley below.

Suddenly, another truck came at them at full-speed, driving too fast, and Frank had to make a hard right to the side of the road, almost driving off it and down into that valley. He hit the brakes, then the horn. "What did I just say?" he grumbled. "Look at that fool! You all right, Christina?"

Christina, having lived part of her life in L.A. and having become used to the mad traffic there, barely lifted her eyebrows. "I'm fine, but that idiot shouldn't have a driver's license."

Frank nodded in agreement.

Christina noticed that Frank never seemed to curse. Nor did he take his eyes off the road like most people—like she herself—would have done whenever they met an idiot behind the wheel. Frank continued on in his calm voice, like nothing had happened, informing her about the last survey of the land while pointing once in a while, but Christina only listened with one ear, because she'd begun to think about her own life, and why she'd ended up here.

After having failed to be cast in three major motion pictures that she would have killed to be a part of—*Should have brought my kneepads to the bloody auditions*, she thought morbidly—the death of one of her parents had sent her into a deep depression, unlike anything she'd experienced previously. The icing on the cake had been the break-up with her long-time boyfriend, which had occurred almost at the same time. *Typical; when you need someone the most, suddenly it's over.* Christina had fallen deeper into depression.

Through sheer strength of will, and without a single headshrinker's help, she had pulled herself out of it. She had a degree in psychology, and it would be a cold day in hell if she ever spent a dime on one. However, she desperately needed to recharge her batteries before she took another run at life. She also had to get away from all the glamour, and the fake lifestyle that she had lived most of her life.

But thinking that made her feel guilty and fake herself, because that lifestyle had once been a dream, an opportunity for her to succeed where countless others had failed. She had never become an Ivy League star, but she had been close. Now the thought of being a has-been seemed like a nightmare. She was mentally exhausted, and knew she had to pull herself up out of the gutter once and for all.

Hollywood had been great to her as a child star; and unlike most child actors, she had been able to find work almost constantly as she grew up. She realized that some nude, provocative, and sexy scenes in a few movies, once she had matured, had helped her career as she learned the ropes in Hollywood. In the beginning, it had been fun and games, doing something millions could only dream about. The parties had been wild, her friends crazy, most of them young actors too. She had been strong enough to stay away from the heavy drugs, and that helped her stay sane. But after a friend and fellow actor had committed suicide, nothing had been the same. A part of her had died that day along with him.

Even though the death of her friend had been a long time ago now, it had been the beginning of the end. Fewer good parts came her way. Now she worked as little as possible, because even though she had some wealth, she was by no means financially independent.

This journey had started out badly, but perhaps now there was some light at the end of the tunnel…or so she hoped. If she decided to buy this home and land, it would be a steal. She almost felt guilty about it when she thought of her nice landlords. Business might be booming in the small town, but the real-estate market was pretty much dead all over the country; it was definitely a buyers' market.

An hour after they had set out on the journey, after taking some extra side-roads—Frank had insisted on showing Christina some "short-cuts" and rest areas—they turned onto a small, unpaved road that wound up towards a clearing on a plateau. The dogs' whining fast, heavy breathing, and typical eager, nervous behavior made Christina smile, since it indicated that the road trip would soon come to an end.

Frank parked outside what looked like a small lodge, not at all like the pictures she had seen; it was bigger than she expected. She had finally arrived at her new home, and if she liked it, she would stay here for several months, perhaps longer. Who knew? She might even purchase the place. She knew that was what Claire and Frank hoped for. Apparently, they had had the place up for sale for over two years, with no takers for some reason. When Christina had seen the pictures of the home and landscape, she had instantly fallen in love with them; however, while a picture might say a thousand words, that meant nothing until you experienced the real thing.

The log home had two buildings near it: a detached garage, and large storage building that almost looked like a barn, similar in build to the main house, using the same type of cedar logs. The rustic appeal was very strong, and almost provocatively beautiful. With the buildings came hundred acres of land, including a stretch of a wide river, as well as several creeks with waterfalls and two small lakes. Otherwise, the mountainous terrain was covered with trees. There were valleys with a few small grassy fields at the bottom. Christina hadn't paid much attention to most of the pictures, because there had been so many of them; she just needed a new place to start her life all over.

Now she thought that maybe, just maybe, she'd found the perfect place.

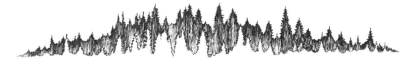

Two

Brooke ran for her life, and death followed after. She could hear the sound of the beast behind her, as it pursued her like a predator craving a kill. She tried to scream again, but she was exhausted and in shock. Whatever had attacked her boyfriend earlier was coming up fast from behind, gunning for her life.

She cried and kept running from the danger, until finally she couldn't hear anything from behind anymore. She made a quick stop and turned her head, searching her surroundings as far as she could see, but the deep, dense forest was silent. Not even the birds sang. She was sweating profusely, and her heavy breathing was the only thing she could hear except for the wind. Her lungs ached badly, like a thousand needles were piercing them.

She turned again, and hurried on at a slower pace, trying to catch her breath and locate the sound of her pursuer—and that's when she heard the truck engine. The new sound gave her hope, and immediately a new surge of power went through her tired body. She headed towards the sound, hoping for safety, dashing up a rough hillside studded with large rocks and trees. Branches whipped at her body and face, leaving bruises and cuts as she stormed through the thick brush. She didn't care; all she wanted was to be safe.

She stopped just in time, teetering back and forth on the edge of the 50 foot drop above the road, until she fell back on her rear to temporary safety. She looked around in desperation for a place to descend… just as she heard a twig snap behind her. She trembled, and started to run along the cliffside in search for a place where she could get down onto the road: an animal path, a notch, a slight slope, anything. She turned her head and listened for the engine sound from the vehicle she had heard before, but there was nothing.

Brooke had to slow her pace, because the terrain was too treacherous. The sound of another vehicle approaching made her stop completely, and there it was: a shining blue Dodge King Cab pickup. She saw a clearing a few hundred yards away where she ought to be able to climb down almost to the road; and then, hanging from the ledge, she could jump or simply fall to the road. As she hurried toward it, she realized she wasn't going to make it before the truck vanished. The truck was just below her, not going very fast, and she could see two people in the cab: a man sitting in the driver's seat, pointing at something on the side of the road to a woman sitting on the passenger side. She waved desperately, her hands over her head, and jumped up and down while screaming at the top of her lungs. Tears covered her dirty face, and she screamed again, louder and more desperately now, as she realized her safety was driving away without having noticed her.

Suddenly, a realization cut through her panic mode: if she kept this up, she would attract the monster chasing her. She turned in a slow circle on the spot, trying to locate her pursuer, but she could see no one.

There was a sudden change in the wind, thought, and with it came the foul odor of death. That's when Brooke sensed something behind and below her; she felt a razor-sharp cut into her left ankle, made by a paw with deadly claws, the very same that had torn Diego to shreds. She jumped and screamed even louder, then threw herself towards safety at the clearing below. The blue truck had passed, but she didn't care. The road was her safe haven, all she had.

She turned her head and saw something dark behind her, something that made her run again, faster than she ever had in her life. Inevitably, given the uneven terrain and her sheer terror, Brooke tripped and fell, scraping her knees badly, the pain instantly shot through to her spine; but the pure, raw fear kept her crawling on all fours until she got on her feet again, limping and wobbling. Blood poured from several gashes on her left ankle, but she didn't care; she was far too afraid to feel the wound. Her tears had made a muddy mask of her face.

Just as she reached the clearing, where there was only about a ten-foot fall to safety, another truck came from the opposite direction of the Dodge, this one a dirty old Ford. Instead of climbing down and then dropping onto the road, she lunged over the side of the cliff toward safety, because there was no time left; and as she fell, she saw something large, dark, and hairy where she'd just been. The ground came at her fast, and she hit it hard, losing her breath as she landed on her back. She blinked her eyes rapidly while trying to regain her breath, until finally she begin panting again; and that's when she saw the monster just standing there on the cliff's edge, staring at her with dead eyes.

She didn't understand what it was. She slowly got to her feet, never taking her eyes off the beast, which did nothing but stand and stare at her. A sharp pain from her right ankle told her there would be no more running. Completely helpless, she turned away from the beast, knowing she was beaten.

She looked up, the last thing she would ever do in her life.

Donny Hill drove the company truck with his knees while texting on his phone. He wasn't supposed to do that, but he had important business to take care of. From the speaker boomed the Charlie Daniels Band, burning through *The Devil Went Down to Georgia*. More than once, he cursed out loud at the bad reception on his dumbass smartphone.

The sound of a honking horn got his attention, and at the last moment he swung back to his side on the road, barely looking at it. He missed the blue truck with only an inch or so to spare, and completely ignored the other driver, who almost went off the side of the road and down into the valley. He didn't even look in his rearview mirror to see if the other driver was okay. Instead, he went back to more important matters. Donny wasn't going to let his girlfriend have the last word, no sir.

"Stupid bitch don't know what's coming—Ima slap the shit outta her once I see 'er again!" he shouted himself while finishing the text. He hit the accelerator with the rhythm from the song and increased his speed; after all, he knew this road like the back of his hand. There would be only one more sharp turn, and then the road would go straighter than his dick on a Saturday night. He was just about to hit the Send button when, suddenly, his truck hit something very hard. He looked up from his phone just as the window shattered into thousands of crumbs, and something shot through the newly empty space, striking Donny right in his face. He felt something break with a sick, wet *crack*, and then everything went black.

The beat-up Ford didn't even leave a skid mark on the asphalt; the driver never hit the brakes at all. Instead, it accelerated and shot over the side of the road into the valley. It struck a large pine tree dead on, which made it twirl around, and kept falling down into the valley, hitting the slope and rolling several time until it landed right-side up on a ledge, next to a bunch of car parts from previous accidents.

With the exception of a large strip of bark that had been torn from the pine tree, and a few twigs and branches that had been snapped off from the impact, everything looked pretty much the same after the accident as it had before.

From the cliff edge above, two dead eyes surveyed the scene, searching for its prey. The woman was dead, though. So was the truck driver, what was left of one arm lolling out of the shattered windshield. The beast snarled and turned, facing the forest. Winter was around the corner, and it could sense it. There would only be so much time left for it to still its hunger before going into hibernation.

It needed more.

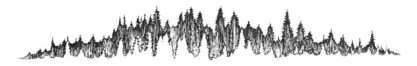

THREE

Christina stepped out of the truck and was rudely pushed to the side as Nugget made his way out and away, not having the time to wait for some dang slowpoke human. Both Hunter and Nugget ran all over the yard, afterward sniffing the ground. Once in while they attacked and chased each other, like two very large puppies, as happy as any child—until Frank's hoarse voice ordered, "Search and protect!"

Instantly the two dogs snarled and darted towards what looked like a small path leading into the forest, still arguing, as only dogs can, over who should go first.

Noticing the puzzled expression on Christina's face, Frank smiled and said, "I've trained them to move over the property nearby and check for any intruders or predators, like wolves, bears, what have ya. Don't worry, they'll be back soon. They'll only follow the electric fence."

"Electric fence?"

"Over here, let me show you."

Frank took Christina to the gate entrance. She had missed the gate when they drove through; now she saw that between the wooden planks of the fence, there were four metal wires. The fence was about six feet high.

"The wires keep the animals away from the house, but the fence only encloses about an acre near the house. If you notice, there's no barbed wire here, though there use to be. I had it removed—I think it's inhumane."

"Can I touch them?"

"Sure," Frank said, smiling.

She did, only to jerk her hand back instantly. "Ouch! That hurt."

"Yep, told you they were electrical. Won't kill anything, but it sure will give them a reminder, right? 'Specially if one of them male wolves tries to mark his territory!" He guffawed, bringing a smile to her face.

"What powers them?" Christina wondered, sucking on the index finger that had been jolted by the fence.

Frank gestured for her to follow, then pointed at one of the poles that had some type of dark but shiny plate on top of it. "Solar power. If you look over there, you'll see most of the trees are cut down near the house, and there are a lot of these little solar cells spread out all over, enough to power the fence. There's also a backup battery that gets its power from the sun. I'll tell you all about it later, along with the back-up generators and everything else you need to know while you live here, and if there's any problem, just give me a call. We're about 40 or 45 minutes from the store. You have your own water well with very fresh, clean water, and of course the purifiers."

Frank walked towards the main building, fishing in his pocket for the keys to the house. Christina started to follow, but then she noticed an opening between the buildings and headed in that direction. There was a large stone only a few feet high, and she stepped gently onto it. She realized she was standing on a plateau over a drop-off, and when she looked over the view, she instantly fell in love with what she saw. It was a majestic vista over an enormous valley dressed in green, and far below in the distance was the river, the one she owned a part of now. From somewhere in the distance, the sound of an eagle's scream echoed through the valley. Smaller birds sang, and the wind caught Christina's long, dark hair. She was completely taken aback by the mesmerizing surroundings. She didn't even notice the tear rolling down her cheek.

It was beautiful.

Frank cleared his throat from behind her. "Pretty, isn't it?"

Christina was too overwhelmed to speak, and could only nod her head in agreement. They just stood there for a while, enjoying the moment. "You should see it at dusk," Frank said after a moment. "Nothing like sitting on a porch with a cold one and taking in the setting of the sun," he said dreamily, gazing towards the western horizon.

Later, he took Christina on a tour around the immediate vicinity of the property near the main house. "Everything you see here was built by the best people in the trade; a company out of British Columbia in Canada. This home is one of its best, a one-of-a-kind original."

"Who had it built?"

"I don't know their names, and I never met them. It was a wealthy young couple from the Big Apple who came out a few years back. But as far as I know, they only came here once to inspect the progress on the build. Then something must have gone wrong, because eventually the bank put it up for executive sale, and it was purchased by someone else—but it turned out that idiot didn't have sufficient funds for it. Because Claire and I had the second highest bid—and I don't mind telling you it was far less than the bidder who failed to make the payment—we got it pretty cheap." He looked at her sharply. "Well, crap, maybe I shouldn't have said that." Christina laughed. "Let me guess: Claire takes care of the family budget?"

"Why of course, dear, and that's why we have a happy marriage," Frank joked, but at the same time he looked a bit somber. "We had to put quite a bit into the house and land to finish it up, I don't mind telling you. Everything is pretty much finished but for the basement."

Christina surveyed the land, thinking that most of the surroundings almost looked like a park; and then she realized that the garden, with all its trees, reminded her of a fairy tale, with neatly trimmed grass, trees, and bushes intermingling with the thick green, brown, and gray mosses on the ground. Birdsong filled the air, and she could hear a strident cheeping coming from a nest visible in a nearby tree. The air smelled incredibly fresh, as if it had just been created by the world, with just a tang of resin from the conifers surrounding her; it almost smelled odd to her city-attuned nose. Looking around the garden, she saw a few manmade paths, lined with sawdust, meandering among the plants. There was the sound of falling water coming from somewhere nearby.

"Anyway," Frank said, oblivious to her immersion in the natural world, "the entire home is self-sufficient energy-wise. It has its own power sources, from the sun and the air." He pointed at a windmill on top of a low cliff that Christina had missed earlier. It also had solar panels below it, tilted toward the sun, and there were more panels on the roofs on all the buildings. Frank continued, "I'd planned to try out a paddlewheel generator on one of the rivers, but couldn't get a permit. Still, what we've got's good enough."

The closer they got to the lodge, the more she realized just how big it was. She had to wonder: Was it *too* big for her? The house included a wraparound covered patio and a carport, and it looked like there was some type of tower in the back.

Frank unlocked the door to the airlock entry and mud room. The door was a heavy security model made of solid metal, clad in wood paneling to match the rest of the home. That Christina liked, having had her fair share of stalkers in her life. None of her exes had been stalkers, but some of her fans had been, and it was still sometimes a problem. *The price of fame*, she thought, even if she *was* something of a falling star.

"This here is a security door," Frank said, "and all the windows on the first floor and the basement have bulletproof glass. Third floor has storm windows, and they can take a heavy punch too. If you noticed, there are shutters by the windows; even they were made by a security company, and can be tightly closed and locked. I'll show you how in a bit."

"Seems like whoever built this place took their privacy very seriously," Christina noted. "Almost seems a bit paranoid."

"Well, having bulletproof windows, that's not so unusual nowadays. People want to secure their privacy. Lots of strange folks rooming around everywhere, even in quaint little towns like ours."

"You're right. Same thing back in L.A., I have to admit."

"Let me give you the grand tour," Frank offered. He removed his cowboy boots, and took a pair of new slippers from a bench in the mudroom; and Christina followed his example. Suddenly Hunter and Nugget popped up at the door, demanding to come inside.

"Stay," Frank ordered. "Stop right there, you two. Paw patrol!"

Both dogs stopped in their tracks, simultaneously lifting their right paws. Frank removed a towel from a hook and dried off all four of each dog's paws, one at a time. When they sat down, paws clean, he then unlocked the next door, a normal door with a glass insert. The dogs remained seated until he called out, "Secure!" With that command, the dogs raced inside the home, searching it for any intruders.

Now Christina was really impressed. "Wow! You do know how to control those dogs, don't you? Is it really necessary to check the house?"

"Well, it's not so much about control as it is training and discipline. The most important thing when it comes to training any dog is to be kind and relaxed. If you're tense, they will be too. There's a lot of psychology involved, and most time, it's up to the owner and not the dog. Hunter is an American Staffordshire Terrier, what most people call a pit bull. The majority of people have misunderstood that breed of dog. Most of the time he's completely harmless, but he won't say no to a fight when challenged. And to answer your second question, it's more for the dogs than it is necessary to check for any intruders. But even though this home has a very good security system, it never hurts." He gave Christina a reassuring and friendly smile.

"Nugget, he's an African dog, right? Ridgeback?"

"Yes, his breed originated in Rhodesia, and they were trained to hunt lions. It's the perfect dog for a family, and he seldom barks…unlike Hunter, or as you know, Winston."

Frank smiled and Christina laughed when thinking about the grumpy bulldog. "Winston is one of the few dogs I haven't been able to train very well," Frank confided.

"I thought he obeyed you fine."

"Nah, only when he wants something, that lazy ogre. Old Winston has a mind of his own. You should see when Claire takes him for a *roll*, if you can call it that. More like him taking her for a walk."

Frank gestured for Christina to take the lead, so she could get the first look at her hopefully future home. He knew the house was breathtaking. She entered, and was instantly taken aback by the beautiful interior, which had been created by some of the best craftsmen in the business. There was a large family tree in the center, and two more large tree trunks throughout the open plan interior, acting as support beams. The fresh aromas of cedar and a clean house filled her nostrils.

Nugget and Hunter returned and sat immediately by Frank's feet, breathing heavily with their tongues hanging out, while their tails swept the shining hardwood floor. He gave them each a treat that he had in a pocket of his vest. He nodded his head, and the two beautiful dogs moved away.

Christina walked over to the main center window in the great room, and again she was astonished by the view towards south and west. There was a large patio outside, and she couldn't help letting out a cheerful cry when she saw the hot tub. There was a huge open fireplace both inside and outside in the large room. The place was beautiful, and she loved it! She walked alone through the house while Frank went to the kitchen and put on some coffee. He didn't want to behave as a real estate agent, not at this point. Eventually he would go through the entire house again with Christina, showing her everything she needed to know.

The scent of freshly brewed coffee soon filled the house.

Christina returned after about ten minutes. "Where did you learn so much about training dogs?" asked curiously, not revealing her thoughts about the house.

There was a brief pause as Frank took a deep breath. Then he said, "In another life, ages ago it seems today, I was a police officer in Chicago. One day, I decided I wanted to become a K-9 officer, and eventually I did." Frank look a bit sad as he told Christina about his background. She realized she had touched a sore subject, and was just about to change it when Frank continued.

"I got my first dog, a female German Shepherd. Gosh, I loved that dog. We trained forever, it seemed at the time, and eventually we graduated. Of course, she lived at home with me that whole time. That's how it works. You bond that way." Again he quieted down, and moved slowly through the open plan of the first floor, which combined the great room with the kitchen, dining, and breakfast nook. When he reached the breakfast nook, he looked out the center window -— there were three of them, and just as Christina had thought, it was part of a wooden tower—and watched the horizon in the distance. Christina followed Frank, impressed again by the beautiful woodwork combined with the custom-made furniture; everything fit perfectly.

She began, "If you don't want to talk about it, then…"

Frank motioned with his hand for her to be silent. "No. She deserves to be remembered."

"It was our first day on duty. I worked nights back then because of my young age—most rookies did. Even if you'd been on the force a couple of years, you were still considered fresh meat. We got a call about some trouble and took off. Someone had attacked an old woman in her early eighties. She had been mugged and raped. It was in a park, and Betsy—that was her name—got on the perp's trail instantly. We caught up to him, and that's when I…messed up. It was a young man, and he was about to climb over a fence, so I let Betsy have a go at him. I regret that to this day. Betsy got his leg and dragged him to the ground. I hurried after her, but I tripped and dropped my gun. By the time I found it, the perp and Betsy was fighting pretty hard. There was a lot of growling from Betsy and screams from the perp. I got the gun and aimed while shouting to Betsy, who instantly stopped her aggression and backed off, still barking. I lay there and had a clear shot, and that's when everything went bad. I was just about to order the perp to lay down on the ground, so I could cuff him, but my sergeant called me on the darn radio. I took my eyes away for a second while I looked for my radio, and that's when I heard the most horrible sound I had ever heard—a kind of yelping moan. It was Betsy; she had been stabbed by that ba- by that awful man."

There was a moment of silence before Frank continued his story.

"I was paralyzed. In shock, I guess you could call it. She died before I got to her. Bled out."

"What happened to the guy you chased?" Christina asked gently.

"He got away," was Frank's flat reply.

"I'm so sorry. I—"

"I looked for the perp for days. I wanted vengeance, but eventually I came to the realization that what I was doing was wrong, and I was no longer fit to be a police officer…so I resigned."

Christina looked at him, concerned.

Frank noticed Christina's reaction from the corner of his eye and said in a kind voice, "No, dear, I didn't hurt or kill the perp. There was a time when I wanted to, but that was my emotions talking back then. The perp really did get away."

Frank dried his eyes, and then swung his long, powerful arms in a sweeping and friendly gesture while his warm smile returned. "It's all in the past, but boy, I do miss that dog. Only bad thing about owning a dog is they only live for so long. Winston's close to 15—probably has a year or two left, while these two monsters have a bit more."

After giving Christina his tour of the house—that took about half an hour—they moved back the kitchen. On the kitchen island were three folders with information about the house, and how to run things; there was a list of phone numbers, and general recommendations on several contractors. There was also a very good map of the entire parcel of land that came with the house, and another larger map depicting the local roads and nearby towns. Everything was marked well, and every minute,

Christina realized she liked the place more and more. Frank gestured towards the coffee brewer, and Christina nodded. He turned it on again, and while the wonderful aroma of fresh-brewed coffee filled the room, he continued informing her about the house's do and don'ts, and what she should or shouldn't do if she ventured into the forest.

"Like I said before, everything is finished in this home but for the basement. Be careful when you go down there—you saw the mess."

"I doubt I'll be spending any time down there soon," she admitted.

"Good. Then all we need to do is sign a few documents…"

Suddenly, both Nugget and Hunter rushed to the main door, growling almost silently but still very threateningly.

"Aha, I guess we got company," Frank said, while looking for the documents, his glasses perched on the tip of his nose. He seemed content to wait until whoever it was actually came to the door.

Less than two minutes later, the front doorbell rang. Hunter and Nugget lay by the second door, silently staring, focused 100% on the door. Frank removed a remote from one of the drawers in the kitchen island and pushed a button. A painting with an ornate frame on the wall in the kitchen transformed into a CCTV screen, displaying four camera views. He scrolled through several images, displaying various views on the plot outside and a few rooms inside, including the garage and the utility room. The doorbell rang again, and the view from the outside entrance came in view on the screen, displaying the door outside and a tall man waiting patiently to be let in.

"The place has its own surveillance system?" Christina gasped. "I didn't see any cameras on the way here or outside!"

"Guess we have a few things more to go over," Frank joked.

"This is getting better and better. You don't by any chance happen to have a robot that can cook and clean, do you?"

"Sure do. Name's Claire. I'll have the little missy come up and do that for you anytime you want," Frank said smiling.

He laughed to his own joke while trying to figure out the remote, his tongue sticking out between his lips. He was completely concentrated on an instruction manual for the thing. Christina laughed out loud, knowing Frank wouldn't dare refer to Claire as a robot in her presence, and promised herself never to mention it to anyone.

Frank finally hit the right button on the remote, and the man outside opened the door and walked in. There was a minor commotion when whoever it was changed his footwear to slippers in the airlock entry. Then the door opened, and a good-looking middle-aged man walked in. He looked at the dogs that lay on either side by the door in silence, guarding silently, patiently but still alert. They only stared at him, and neither was breathing heavily. When they recognized him, they got up and charged him, showering him with slobbery dog-kisses, barking and growling happily. Frank came to his rescue while Christina kept back, as always being suspicious and shy whenever meeting someone new.

"Robert, good to see you again," Frank said while shaking his hand. Nugget and Hunter moved away and sat down.

"May I?" asked Robert, removing a large bone from his denim pants pocket.

"By all means, get them out of the house."

Robert tossed the bone outside, but neither dog moved; instead, they stretched their necks toward Frank, waiting patiently. He nodded his head in consent, smacking his tongue, and the two beasts went for the catch of the day. Frank hit the button on the remote, and the front door closed, leaving the sounds of two arguing dogs outside.

A horrified Christina almost shouted, "Won't they fight over it?"

"Nope, they'll just chase each other and eventually lie down and share the bone, believe it or not." Frank gestured for Christina to move closer. "Christina, allow me to introduce a very dear friend to Claire and me. This is Robert Joffry, the caretaker of all our properties. He's also the best lumberjack and precision tree-cutter in history."

Robert blushed from the introduction and looked down at his somewhat tight slippers. *He's shy,* Christina thought as she reluctantly advanced, stopping a bit too far away from him while extending her hand. She had to bend forward to reach his, because he didn't approach her whatsoever. He had a firm and strong grip, and to her surprise, a soft hand with perfect cuticles. His three days' worth of stubble, mixed with dirt and dust, enhanced his sharp, clear blue eyes. He wore blue, washed-out and well-worn denim jeans that sat tight on his muscular legs, and a red-and-blue plaid flannel shirt with the sleeves rolled up. Typical lumberjack attire.

His muscular forearms were tight, but the shirt hung loose—concealing a picture-perfect body, Christina suspected. He wore a large scuba watch turned to the inside of his right wrist, but otherwise no jewelry and no ring, or any markings from a ring. In his hand he held a dirty baseball cap—typical Southern manners—that was just about worn-out.

When he looked up into Christina's eyes, her heart seemed to somersault in her chest, and suddenly she lost her train of thought and didn't hear what he said. She blushed like a schoolgirl as he said, "It's nice to meet you, ma'am."

After a moment, Robert looked at Frank for help, because obviously the woman holding his hand was mute.

Christina was used to being in control of her life, and was very experienced at meeting fans, producers, and strangers in general. She almost always felt she had the upper hand, given her vast range of experience due to her work. Well, all that experience just went out the window with Robert. Her knees felt weak as rubber, and there were a bunch of stupid butterflies rattling around in her stomach. Finally, she stuttered, "N-nice, nice to meet me too…um, I mean, to meet *you*. Sorry!"

Frank came to the rescue and laid his arm over Robert's shoulder. "How 'bout some coffee, buddy?"

Robert and Christina, both feeling awkward and uncomfortable for some reason, nodded their heads in unison.

Christina let the two men take the lead, not so much to be ladylike as because it gave her the opportunity to check out Robert's rear end. It was perfect. *Dude must be gay,* she thought. *Straight guys don't come like this.* She smiled at the thought, and just then the bastard had to turn around, saying something that, of course, she didn't hear due to her acute lack of concentration. Christina blushed again as she realized that she'd been standing there staring at Robert's ass with a grin on her face, and he had seen it. Oh, crap!

Again, Robert had to repeat himself. "So, what do you think of this place, ma'am?"

Completely at a loss for words, Christina just smiled widely and nodded her head. Again, Frank came to the rescue. "Christina how do you want your coffee?"

"Black. Black will be fine."

"Great—my kinda gal! The only way to drink this magical brew." He knew that was how she liked it, having served her earlier, but someone had to rescue this train wreck of a conversation before it derailed. "How's the work going at River Crossing?" he asked Robert.

"Almost finished, but I won't be going back today with the storm coming."

"Yeah, I heard about that. Nasty weather this time of year."

"Storm?" Christina asked.

"What you experienced last night was just the beginning, Christina," Frank replied. "Weatherman's been all over the news warning us about it. Don't worry—this place is like a fortress, and if you need help, me or Robert are almost around the corner."

There was an awkward silence in the room. Through the kitchen window Christina could see the dogs tearing by, Hunter chasing his "brother," but even though they were obviously barking there were no sound to be heard from them. The house was very well-built, more or less soundproof. When Frank saw her looking, he asked, "Would you like for me to leave one or both of my dogs?"

"I couldn't. Shouldn't they be guarding your shop?"

"Oh, don't worry about that. We always got good old Winston."

Robert let out a quiet laugh.

"What?" Frank sounded hurt, but then he smiled.

Frank did most of the talking after that, while Robert nodded his head and Christina only-half listened as she tried to make eye contact with the silent man next to Frank. He didn't say much. Maybe he was mostly mute after all.

Half an hour later, Christina watched as Frank drove away in his blue truck, followed by Robert in his older, more beat-up white truck, with what look like a giant box in the rear with several small doors. Robert stopped by the gate and closed it; he didn't look back, which she had hoped for.

She stood there a long time after they had left, just staring and dreaming; and then she came to the realization that she had made an ass of herself in front of Robert. She blushed and shook her head at her own stupidity. What was it her mother used to say over and over when she was a child? Ah, yes: "You only get one chance to make a good first impression." Boy, if only she had listened to her mother…

Oh well, they should be back tomorrow to show her the lay of the land. She'd had enough for one day; besides, she'd felt completely naked without any make-up whatsoever when she'd met Robert. Normally she wouldn't care, but now, for some reason, she did. Not too much make-up, mind you; just the perfect amount to bring out her best features, her cheeks and nose. Yes, tomorrow, Saturday, would be better.

She looked at the sky and dark clouds now covering it. She felt some drizzle wafting in under the eaves, but decided that it wasn't too bad for now. Her walk into town had been far worse. She went around the compound near the house, garage, and storage building. Perhaps the storage building could be turned into a stable? It more or less looked like one already.

Everything was very well-built and perfectly organized. She would have to get her own wheels, but it could wait till Monday. This weekend, she would stay at her new place and relax. Having decided that, she walked towards the back of the house, stepped onto the enormous porch, and looked towards the horizon. Bad weather or not, the view was striking. She could literally see for miles. A valley with a large river lay far below, surrounded by more trees she ever had seen in one place before.

A kayak with two people fighting the currents and rapids with their flashing paddles caught her attention. They were very far away at first, but approached at a very fast speed. She wished she had a pair of binoculars. Definitely professionals, she thought, observing the way they handled the kayak with ease, avoiding jagged and dangerous rocks. As they approached, she momentarily lost sight of them. She stepped closer to the edge of the wooden fence on the porch, which protected anyone from falling down the cliffside some three hundred feet below into the cold river. Now she could see and hear them; sounded like a man and a woman from their shouting and laughing. She looked at them a bit jealously.

The drizzle turned into rain, so Christina went back toward the door. She had many things to do in terms of settling in before she hit the sack; maybe she'd open one of the bottle of wines that lay in the gift basket on the kitchen counter, and read a book or just watch the setting of the sun. After all, she did have the best seat in the house.

Then a sudden gust of wind brought with a foul, awful stench. The birds stopped singing, and a creepy silence fell over the lodge, except for the eerie sigh the wind made while moving through the forest. Thicker, darker clouds had moved in, casting the area into darkness. Christina stood with her arms crossed, leaning on one of the wooden columns of the carport, still daydreaming and planning her future.

Without any warning, the strange sensation that she was being watched came over her. She could feel the goosebumps prickle on her forearms, and a chill went down her spine, just as it had the other day when she had observed the clouds. Suddenly she felt very alone and vulnerable, and she immediately regretted not taking Frank up on the offer to keep one or both dogs with her. She immediately went inside the house and locked the door.

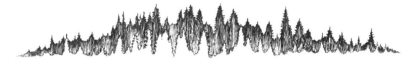

FOUR

Lightning tore through the dark sky, followed immediately by rumbling thunder. Mother Nature opened the clouds and broadsided the entire region with rain, and She didn't hold back. The rain hit the ground hard, quickly churning the soil into a mud bath with droplets the size of cherries. Not long after, hailstones the size of golf balls began falling as well. The powerful wind sounded like a battle cry, protesting what humans had done to their world for centuries.

This storm wasn't taking any prisoners. Bushes and branches swayed and bent in the wind, and here and there trees broke or were pulled from the sodden ground, roots and all. Some branches flew long distances in the straight-line winds, turning the forest into a natural battleground.

When the door opened, the powerful wind outside took hold of it and rammed it hard against a new guest hurrying inside the watering hole called The Lumberjack. As he stood there in the entrance, rubbing his nose, the sound of Billy Ray Cyrus's classic *Achy Breaky Heart* wailed from the speakers. As the song hit its famous musical bridge, the big man everyone referred to as Little Noise charged through the entrance toward the storm like a bulldozer, pissed beyond belief, cursing up a storm, using all of his somewhat limited vocabulary in surprisingly inventive curs-es. The unfortunate man who had just survived the heavy door was still running a hand over his face, checking for damage, so he didn't see the bulldozer storming out the door. The 6'10", 300-pound figure charged straight ahead, as relentless as a ballistic missile, and for a second time in seconds the other man was rammed by a powerful force. He stumbled backwards through the door, off the porch, and onto the muddy ground. There he lay in the muck while the rain pounded him. Two young wom-en holding newspapers over their heads—which protected them from the wet about as well as a surfboard does a surfer—scuttled towards the en-trance so they could escape the hideous weather ruining their war-paint and skimpy outfits. However, the interaction between the two men did catch their attention.

It took Joseph a few moments to realize the humiliating damage he'd just suffered, and it didn't help that the bouncers were laughing; and to make matters worse, the girls were giggling as they dug in their purses for their IDs. Snarling, Joseph got to his feet and cursed the mo-ron who had pushed him out the door. He wiped at the mud still on his face as he rose, vowing to end the fat bastard's life. After all, the girls were both very attractive; time to save some face. When Joseph finished cleaning the mud from his eyes, he looked down at his brand-new den-im jeans and his once-polished cowboy boots, which only compounded his anger. But when he saw his Stetson lying in a puddle, he became in-furiated. His new shirt and jacket had been ruined, not to mention his watch, the one he only used when he dressed up.

He clenched his fist, psyching himself up to annihilate the fat-ass that had done him wrong. Trembling with rage, Joseph, who considered himself unnaturally intelligent, said the most degrading thing one could ever say to any lumberjack anywhere. He didn't know if this idiot *was* one, but he suspected it from the stink that caught in his nostrils, an aroma concocted of sweat, dust, diesel, and tree sap.

"You fucking brush ape!" he snarled.

Of all the bad things one could label a lumberjack, that was just about the worse. Joseph saw a pair of large boots appear in front of him; and, his head still pointed down, he slowly raising his gaze, staring coldly, in a way he had practiced in front of his bathroom mirror thousands of times, at the thug facing him. When he reached the waistline of the "fat bastard," something inside Joseph suggested he be a tad cautious. When he reached the man's breast, he expected to meet a face, so he could stare down a pair of eyes and then punch the living shit out of them, but the problem was there was no head there; so Joseph had to raise his neck even further—and that's when he realize that he faced a giant of a man.

His anger transformed to concern, all in an instant—or was it fear? Staring back at him through the pouring rain was a huge, scarred face with tiny dark eyes that displayed absolutely no intelligence whatsoever, framed by thick, messy, long dark-grayish hair and a long beard, all in desperate need of a good trimming. The giant's forearms were twice as thick as Joseph's legs, and they were hairier than a musk ox in heat. He had found the Abominable Snowman.

This Yeti reeked of alcohol and that indefinable lumberjack smell. Joseph swallowed hard, his facial muscles spasming uncontrollably. He tried a faint smile, but the only result was that his feet left the ground as a big fist knotted in the collar of his muddy jacket, and there, finally, they were facing each other man to man. Joseph now had absolutely no desire to fight this missing link whatsoever. The giant had lifted him about a foot in the air with just one hand. The pull from the collar of his jacket prevented Joseph from uttering a word. With his other hand, the giant raised a coffee cup, taking a sip while giving Joseph a stare and chewing his tobacco.

Suddenly, the Yeti pulled him closer. His breath reeked like a garbage can with a dead animal in it that hadn't been emptied in a month or two. He grunted something, and then he mumbled, "Hey. Urban cowboy. Watch where yer goin'."

With that said, the yeti spat a stream of black juice in Joseph's face, giving him a broken-toothed smile before he tossed Joseph over his shoulder like a rag, sipping on his coffee without spilling a drop. Joseph flew straight towards the entrance, where one bouncer was bent down while he struggled with the door, colliding headfirst with the two pretty young women and another bouncer, who was checking their IDs. The bouncer struggling with the door finally, with a happy shout, managed to shut the entrance with a loud bang.

Little Noise had already forgotten about the minor obstacle that had hindered his path, and was now moving against the powerful wind towards his beloved pick-'em-up truck, an elderly Dodge. He got in the beat-up truck, still pissed that he had to go back up to the landing and check on the cable yarder. Had he shut off the engine or not? This was the disturbing question tumbling around in his somewhat empty brain. Well, no matter; he had made up his mind to go back and check on it. Better do it before the boss man, Paul Harris, found out. Little Noise didn't want to get fired again. So he placed his coffee cup next to his spit cup and turned on the ignition. The truck might be an old one, but it started up like a snarling cat. A blue-black cloud left the exhaust pipe as Noise hit the accelerator. He drove by some more youths, both boys and girls, all dressed up and scrambling for the doors to get away from the rain.

Noise could have slowed down when he saw the large puddle next to them, but he did not; instead, he increased his speed and a wave of dirty water splashed the kids, covering them with mud. He guffawed as he checked his latest feat in the rearview mirror. Dumbass kids. He looked around for his chewing tobacco, and there it was: his good old Redman package. He already had a nice handful of chew in his mouth, but its strength had diminished, and half of it he had already swallowed or spat out. Steering with his knees, he offloaded a large chunk of new chewing tobacco and showed it into his mouth. Once he had given it a few chews, he packed it with the old tobacco inside his right cheek, making it pop out like an enormous pimple that was about to burst. He grabbed his spit cup with his right hand while he was steering his beloved truck with his left, and spat out a long, dark gob into it; then he grabbed his coffee cup, so he could finish his coffee. *Nothing like the mix of fresh coffee and chew*, he thought. He gulped down everything and swallowed it in a flash.

Noise's eyes became the size of dinner plates when he realized he'd grabbed the wrong cup and swallowed his own spit. Coughing and cursing, he slammed on the brakes. Opening the driver's side door and leaning out, he vomited a black stream of repulsive crap onto the road.

A sports car drove by, and a bunch of kids screamed, "Amateur night, you old bastard! Go home and take a shit!"

A flood wave of water from another puddle hit Noise in his face, making it even uglier. He looked after the young assholes as dirty rainwater dribbled down his beard, and decided that whatever he had planned on doing could wait. 'Sides, he'd already forgotten what it was. He slammed the door shut, made a three-point turn, and headed after the kids. An eye for an eye, the little fuckers.

Just as he had predicted, the kids were headed for the bar. Noise hit the accelerator and pulled up next to them. When he had the driver's attention, he pointed his finger at him and then he slid it over his own neck, showing the shitheads what was coming. He saw the fear in the eyes of the driver, and he smiled at the scared little fucker. But then the kid's expression changed into a mischievous smile as he pointed ahead—and that's when Noise noticed the lights of another car heading straight at him.

The last he saw of the kids was the driver flipping him the bird—something kids learn right after birth nowadays. No matter; Noise hit the brakes and pulled his car to the right behind the sports car. His truck aquaplaned from the heavy downpour, though, and Noise lost complete control when he hit the brakes and slammed down into the ditch. His pick-'em-up hit the bottom of the ditch very hard, and the air went out of him from the impact. The oncoming vehicle zoomed past with blue lights flashing. He checked around for more oncoming traffic; in the distance were the taillights of the sport car, slowing down as it approached the bar with its large neon sign in the far distance. No matter. It was time to whoop some ass. Who in the hell dared to run him and his beloved pick-'em-up truck into the ditch?

The sparse brain cells in the middle of his huge head made a sudden pause, then sent a signal to the enormous body: crusher time. Noise was just about to exit the truck when blue lights flashed again, illuminating the dark night. It took a moment before Noise realized what he had done; he had almost hit a goddamn cop car. Noise wasn't very bright, but he did understand that almost hitting a police car while speeding down the wrong side of the road was *not* a good thing to do. Yeah, well, the two six packs he had inhaled with his steak dinner weren't improving his situation either.

Hell, as long as it weren't that illegal alien sheriff from Mexico, or worse the new blackie sheriff, then he might be able to talk 'im out of this one. Oh wait, the new sheriff hadn't got here yet—it was still that damn Mexican. Or was it?

"Bwaha! It's just a dern woman," he said aloud when he noticed the short figure struggling with a raincoat against the powerful wind, and the long hair blowing to the side like a flag. The lady cop held her hat tight and limped against the strong wind towards his truck. She knocked on the window. "Are you okay, sir?" she had to shout over the sound of the wind. Turned out she was a very attractive girl in her mid-twenties, with dark hair and a slight accent.

Noise had absolutely no idea how to handle the broad. If she booked him he would be in trouble, having a rap list as thick as the Bible. He cranked down his filthy window and held up his thumb, trying to give the female cop a seductive smile while winking one of his eyes, as what was left of his chew clogged his mouth.

She gave him a suspicious look and lifted her eyebrows; and just as she was about to say something, a call on her radio ordered her to report to HQ ASAP.

"Do you need paramedics, sir?"

Noise shook his head no.

"I'll call for a tow truck for you. Do you need someone to pick you up?

Noise found his tongue and said, "No, we're near town. I'll just walk back, miss."

He wasn't going to ask the miniature porker for a ride. The only time pigs would give you a ride was when you were going to the slammer. Besides, his brain cells had started to work again, and he realized he needed another ride to get to the logging site on the mountain ridge. He got out of the truck, standing in the rain, watching the cop car drive away.

BBB was the solution to his problem. She lived nearby, less than a mile away. Just had to follow this road until he got to a small three-way intersection, and there'd be an old dirt road leading to her home. *Best hurry, 'fore she goes to work at the bar, or worse, she decides to get drunk at one of them bars,* Noise thought as he hurried toward BBB's home. He knew these parts like the back of his hand, and decided to take a shortcut through the woods once he reached the next intersection.

The wind picked up, but he completely ignored it, marching on like he had a purpose, which he kinda did. The street lights flickered, and when he reached the outskirts of town, the road pretty much turned dark. He moved fast, though, and made sure he walked against the traffic; he knew that many drivers would be drunk or wouldn't know how to drive in a storm, and the last thing he wanted was to get hit by one of them idjits. He saw the intersection where he had to turn left; then he could take the shortcut through the forest.

There was only one light at the intersection, right by the city limits sign, and next to it stood someone. At first, Noise didn't care; but as he came closer he saw there was something odd about this person, and a sudden prickling surge went down his spine like a jolt of 'lectricity. Was that fear? He wasn't used to that. Something was wrong here. He stopped about one hundred feet away and peered at the person, and that's when he realized that the "person" had fur. "Crap! A dern bear this close to town," he muttered. "Or *is* that a bear? Could be one o' them bigfoots. What da fuck." He squinted to get a better look, but then the creature was gone. Huh. He reluctantly moved towards the intersection, and looked in the direction of the sign and light.

More than once, he tripped and cursed as he hurried through the forest. Damn undergrowth. Whose idea was all them stickers and briars? The storm intensified, so Noise hurried some more. A faint light between the trees gave him hope, knowing he was almost there. The trees grew sparser the closer he got to BBB's house. A root lay in his way, and because he was focused on the light, he didn't pay any attention to his footing and fell headfirst into a small sinkhole. Instantly the light from the house vanished behind a small bluff. He rolled around like a fool, spitting out some mud—and suddenly he stopped. As the rain poured down like a shower and sudden lightning lit up the region, followed by a thundering explosion, Noise felt someone near him. Having spent most of his life either in the slammer or in the woods, he was experienced with the feeling, so he slowly turned to his side, looking behind him from the spot where he had fallen.

He didn't know what the hell he was looking at, but it stank and it was big. *Bigfoot!* he thought. *Ever'one what sees 'em says they smell real bad!* When another lightning strike lit up the world, he looked closer at the enormous beast, but it only sat or stood there very oddly. The thing was just thirty feet from him, having the high ground. The beast tilted its head, just observing him. Noise froze, and decided that pretending to be dead was the best thing to do. With a theatrical groan, he fell back and lay still. Despite the cold, he started to sweat. After a few terrifying moments, he opened his eyes—but there was nothing there. *Musta been what I saw at the intersection*, he thought. *Maybe a bear after all?*

Noise was scared shitless, though he'd never admit it. No man ever had or could scare Noise, but a Bigfoot or a big grizzly would definitely do the trick. Or whatever this was. He slowly began crawling up and away. When he reached the top of the bluff, he got up and ran for his life towards the light of BBB's house.

THE DOOR shook from the earthquake-like bouncing, fast and loud, and it really pissed off the owner. BBB knew it wasn't the damn storm, but some asshole wanting to get in. Typical—she was just about to have her weekly shower and then head on down to her favorite bar, Harley or Death. The knocking intensified, and the door trembled on its hinges.

"You hit that door one more goddamn time and I'ma shoot ya!" she shouted over the noise of the storm. It wasn't an idle threat, either. She pulled an ancient sawed-off shotgun from the old umbrella stand, and pumped it just like they do in the movies. A shell ejected and bounced off the wall. She opened the door slowly, the chain still attached.

"BBB, it's me, open the goldamn door!"

"Noise, what you doin' showing yourself here like this?"

After some more begging from Noise, BBB finally opened the door. She stepped aside and watched the giant charge inside. Then, to her surprise, Noise slammed the door shut and even locked it. Something big was up, she reckoned.

"What's gotten into you, Noise? You look like shit."

"Got in a accident with my truck, so I come over here, and then a damn grizzly or a Bigfoot or somethin' started chasin' me through the woods. It's right outside, I reckon."

"Yeah, right, no bears come this close to town. Ain't been no grizzlies in these parts for years, an there ain't no such thing as no bigfoot, just idjits with size 20 clodhoppers like you. Tell me the truth."

"Woman, I'm…! Boss man tole me I had to go check on the cable yarder, see if it was locked down."

"Why didn't you guys do it while you were up there?"

"Well, see, that's the problem. I cain't remember if we did shut it down, and since Donny ain't here, boss man put me in charge."

"So where the hell is Donny, and why don't ya just call him?"

"I did. He ain't been seen since he took off this morning, trouble with his woman or somethin', no one's heard from him all day, and I think boss man's gonna fire him and make me the second boss."

"Haha, he'll never fire his own nephew, ya dumb bastard. Now tell me truth—why're you here on my only day off this week? *My* boss makes everyone work extra before the gold and lumber season is over, and all the faggots go back home."

"I'm telling you the truth," Noise said angrily.

BBB looked out the window, but saw nothing, "Don't you worry about nothing, you big lug, me and old Betsy here'll take care of your shit." She patted the shotgun in the crook of her arm, then raised it into the air and pumped it again—just like they do in the movies. Another shell ejected, hitting Noise in the face. Well, *that* never happened in the movies.

BBB opened the door, ignoring Noise's protest, and stepped out on the porch with her shotgun ready. The porch roof protected her somewhat from the storm and rain. The light by the door blinked a few times as she squinted into the darkness. "Where'd you see this teddy hear, Noise? I don't mind me a new fur coat!" BBB laughed loud and yelled into the storm, "Come on, now, you furry piece of shit! Come and get some from old Beatrice and Betsy!"

Again she pumped the shotgun—like they do in the movies—and she surveyed the forest edge. The wind caught something, and there was a loud noise from behind her pick-up truck, and it made her jump. She aimed in the air and pulled the trigger in an attempt to chase off who- or whatever was lurking out there, but nothing happened. She tried to fire again, but nothing happened this time either. Well, shit. Her shotgun was plugged, damn game warden made her do it, so it only held three shells…and all that pumping like they do in the movies had ejected them all. Cursing, she hurried back inside to the hallway, and looked around. On a shelf above the umbrella stand lay an opened box with more 12-gauge shells for the gun. She grabbed a few and hurriedly loaded the weapon. There was another sound from outside, sounded like something broke, which made her hurry some more.

"You mighta been right, something's definitely out there," She locked and loaded again, but when she did she still had her finger on the trigger—and the shotgun went off, blowing a hole in the wall next to Noise, who ducked and hit the ground for shelter.

Beatrice, being so worked up by now, only gave the hole in the wall a quick glance before she charged outside and fired two rounds into the darkness. Nothing happened. When she was satisfied, she went back inside.

"Yeah well, whoever was out there must be gone by now, I think. 'Sides, I didn't see shit out there. Could be one of them vagabond gold miners lurking around. They's all over the place, damn nigra sher'ff ought to do something about that shit, with all the break-ins and all."

Beatrice stomped into the kitchen, and slammed the shotgun down on the kitchen table. Opening the fridge, she grabbed two beer cans and handed one to Noise. After opening hers, she took a large sip and then burped loudly.

"The sheriff ain't a nigra, he's one of them spics…wetback, I think," Noise rumbled.

Beatrice gave Noise a stare, and said, "Potayto, potahto."

"Yeah, well, you heard the sounds outside, din't ya?"

"Don't matter. What'd you want?"

"I need t' borry that truck of yours."

"Kiss my ass."

"That can be done." Noise gave her his most mischievous expression. "Look here, I'll take you anywhere you need to go, and then go up the mountain, be back in a couple hours, and then I'll join you. How's that? Drinks on me, I'll even fill her up for ya." He moved closer to her and placed his large hands on her large shoulders. Beatrice blushed. "What do you say? I'll even toss in a big bonus."

Before BBB knew it, she was whisked off the floor by the giant— Beatrice herself, who normally would need four paramedics to carry her on a stretcher—and was tossed on her own bed, giggling like a drunken schoolgirl.

"No, no, NO you big lug, not there… WRONG HOLE, WRONG HOLE, WRONG HOLE!"

"Potayto, potahtoes! Yee-ha!"

(SLAP!)

"You crazy bastard!"

OUTSIDE IN the rain, below the bedroom window, crouched a hulking dark shadow, listening to the love-making couple. It bled from a couple of minor wounds made by the pellets from a 12-gauge shotgun blast.

It had been injured, and now it was furious.

FIVE

Christina slept like a baby in the huge, super king-size bed, completely bare, and hogged it all to herself. She woke up slowly and sighed, yawning while she stretched. For a second, she felt like she was being observed, and grabbed one of the thick blankets, covering herself. She sat up, looking around confusedly, not recognizing the place. Then she smiled as she remembered where she was.

Again, the irritating feeling of being watched came over her. She looked around, and to her astonishment, she stared into a pair of eyes. It was a huge owl, sitting on a tree branch outside the window. Its head turned almost 180 degrees away from her, followed by several howls.

She smiled at the owl, and then ran her fingers through her long, dark hair. She shook her head and rolled around in bed, relaxing. For the first time in a long time, she was feeling good about herself. The loss of her parent still lay in the back of her mind, and that feeling would never go away, she knew that. But in time she would learn to live with it, as everyone must do, to go on with her life.

She rolled over on her back and stretched out spread-eagled, not worried about the winged peeping tom. She closed her eyes, and after a while opened one slowly and glanced towards the owl on the trunk; and how right she was. The bird had turned back its head facing her. She wrapped herself in a blanket, got out of bed, stuck her tongue out at the peeping tom, and closed the blind on the window.

"Henceforth, thy name shall be *The Peeping Owl.* Yep, definitely a dude," she said about the curious bird.

She went into the gigantic master bathroom to take a shower, but changed her mind. When she looked out the window, she noticed that the storm from last night had eased; it wasn't raining anymore. Maybe she'd go jogging first. She looked out the bathroom window at the large hot tub and the view. A hot tub indoors and another one outdoors—what a place!

She returned to the bedroom and put on a T-shirt and shorts, then she walked barefoot into the open loft. Again, she was taken aback by the rustic beauty of her soon-to-be new home. That decision she had made almost instantly, but kept to herself. She hadn't decided when she was going to break the news to Claire and Frank. She had to call Tom Billing and have him make all the arrangements. She had a million and one things going through her mind in the meantime. She definitely needed more furniture, and Frank had mentioned a company that custom-made it to buyer specifications. She also had to plan the move from L.A to her new place, and keep her new address a secret for as long as possible. That included not mentioning it to her agent, at least not for now.

SHE WENT downstairs into the kitchen and put on some coffee. While it brewed, she checked the refrigerator. It was stocked with fresh food; clearly, she wouldn't have to go to the store anytime soon. There was also the gift basket filled with fruit, wine, champagne, cheese, chocolate, and several dry sausages and some nice crackers and bread. The second picnic basket Claire had given her was also full of food; most of it she had put in the fridge. She made a mental note to return the basket; it looked a bit old, and Claire probably wanted it back.

She drank some orange juice and ate a banana before taking her piping-hot coffee to the family room area, where she sat down in a nice, comfortable arm chair while sipping on the hot liquid and taking in the view outside. She couldn't get enough of it. After her coffee break, she cleaned the kitchen, then ran upstairs to her bedroom where she changed clothes: a pair of old and unsexy underwear, old gray sweats, and plain white tube socks. She took out her sneakers and checked the soles; they were clean, so she put them on and stood to stretch her arms and legs.

Just before she left, she jogged into the kitchen and opened a drawer; inside was a nice box. She opened it, and took out a high-tech watch. It belonged with the property, as it happened, and not only was it a watch, it was a smart-watch, with all the features of a smart-phone, plus one major addition: It was also hooked up to the property's alarm system.

She locked the doors as she left her soon-to-be new home. There were branches scattered across the front yard, courtesy of the storm. She would clean up the area later on, she decided. It was still drizzling a bit, but she decided that she would still go for a run.

At first, she just walked along the sawdust path, which was still quite wet. She saw that despite the near-hurricane last night, the sawdust remained, for most part, where it had been laid. After walking for a few hundred yards, she started to jog slowly, until she'd built up her speed a good bit. She regretted not having any music to listen to while she ran, but today she wanted to learn about the lay of the land without any distractions. The air smelled fresh after the previous night's rain, though branches, both dead and green, were strewn all over—including on the roof of the lodge—not just in the front yard. The storm had noticeably damaged the forest, and it was going to take a serious clean-up effort to clear the branches. Well, she had months to do it. She idly wondered if she could buy or rent a chipper, to make more sawdust for the garden paths, and maybe some compost. That sounded interesting.

Christina trotted faster down a hill into a small valley, and then onward into an open, grassy field. The morning dew glistened in the sun as it started to emerge above the mountains. But there were still some thick, dark clouds in the sky, and the sun had to struggle to retain its dominion.

The fresh scent of the rain, intermingled with the green, resiny scent of the ravaged forest, was wonderful, almost intoxicating, and Christina took several deep breaths.

She ran following a series of white circles painted on trees, space about fifty yards apart. The training round had been marked by the first owners, and the paint had begun to fade, but it was bright enough for her to see it. Eventually, she would learn the lay of her land. She had promised Frank not to venture out too far for now, not that she couldn't take care of herself; it was just that some parts of the forest were very dense, he said, and it was easy to get lost. Frank had told her several stories how about people who had lived there for years had gotten lost, as well as tourists, not to mention the latest problem—the gold miners. Game wardens, police, and park rangers had ventured numerous times into the forest, looking for lost people. Almost everyone had been found, but not all, and some had suffered bad luck. Many had hurt themselves and some had even been attacked by animals. A few had died while river rafting or fishing, having gotten caught in the strong, swift current of the local river, which people called Skull Creek—hence the name of the town. Where Christina was from, anything that wide was a river, period.

For now, she kept inside the fence line and trusted that the electric fence worked as advertised. She increased her speed a bit as the trail started to go uphill; and at the moment, she wasn't paying much attention to the surroundings as opposed to her running. Christina did, however, notice that the ground wasn't as dry as she had hoped; here and there, there were mud puddles, and those she would definitely avoid, having had more than enough mud experience in this county. The water from some of the puddles did splash on her face now and then, but she didn't care; by now, the drizzle had already soaked her hair. She would take a shower when she got back.

She reached the top of the hill and followed a large turn, going towards the thundering river, which was swollen from the rain. She followed it upstream, now running on a natural stone surface. After a time, Christina stopped and bent over, hands on her knees, catching her breath. When she'd recovered, she stretched back and raised her head towards the sky. Foam and water droplets from the raging stream splashed her face—and she loved it. With her hands on her hips, she looked around the area.

She saw the white markings on trees up ahead, leading up toward a higher hill and back towards the house. But she wasn't tired; she wanted to work out some more, so she headed in the direction opposite the one from which she had come, and saw a large tree with several large branches hanging near the ground. She walked over to one branch and jumped up, grabbing hold of it, and slowly did pull-ups until her arms ached. Then she dropped back to the ground and caught her breath again, before leaping up to do more pullups, until the lactic acid burned in her muscles from the strain.

After resting, she looked around on the ground until she found a large, thick, newly-fractured branch; from here, it looked like oak. She rolled it over, and saw scores of bugs congregated beneath. Christina tested the weight of the old branch, and decided it was durable; it was heavy, even though it had begun to rot. She removed her sweatsuit jacket and brushed off most of the dirt and bugs on the branch. Then lifted it over her shoulders and started doing squats. After forty reps, she rested, then lay down on the damp ground and begun doing crunches till her stomach muscles ached. She jumped up and did another forty squats, and when that was done, she finished off with more crunches. When she finished, she just lay in the grass grasping for air.

Great, more rain coming, she thought, looking up into the sky at the fat, dark clouds. She'd probably overdone her training, and definitely hadn't stretched enough before she had begun. A hot bath was looking good about now. Of course, she was too tired to do any more stretching after her workout, though according to some trainer or other, it was equally important to stretch afterward. Oh, well—no instructor around here. She was a big girl, and could do as she wanted.

She was thirsty, though, and realized suddenly that she hadn't brought any water with her. The river sounded inviting, increasing her thirst; but she wasn't *that* much of a wood elf, though she had played one once in a Peter Jackson film. She'd looked so exotic with pointed ears she almost wished she had kept them. She decided to head back to the house and get something to drink there—and the word "breakfast" also came to mind.

A rumbling thunder in the distance warned that the storm was returning, and she'd better be indoors by the time it did.

She got back onto the trail and continued her run, going up a hill and down into a valley and so on for a while. The trees were very dense on this stretch of the trail and kept most of the sunlight away, which made it almost evening-dark. The trail looked a bit morbid and gloomy for a while. The sound of birds singing made Christina smile, though; it wasn't something she was used to hearing in the morning. More like honking and cursing drivers.

The more she ran, the more she thought about getting a dog. Maybe she would take Frank up on his offer, but what about him and Claire? They obviously loved their dogs…

Her thought was interrupted by the buzzing of her security watch. She stopped; a small yellow light blinked and a tiny screen popped up, showing the camera at the gate. The picture was very poor, but she could make out a square box on a truck. Christina's heart made a sudden leap and the blood started to pump faster, and suddenly the butterflies were back in her sadly empty stomach, which decided to protest with a loud growl right then, reminding her that she was hungry for food…though if she was honest, that wasn't the only thing her body hungered for. She licked her lips and smiled, mischievous and confident. Her expression faded when she realized that, again, she wasn't wearing her "face"; instead she was sweaty and probably looked like a scarecrow.

"Oh crap! Should I hide?" she asked herself, then continued with her conversation. "Don't be silly, it's only a man…and like all men, he'll crave a hot Hollywood star…yeah, I'm gonna stop talking to myself now and just hurry on home and make that boy do as he's told… And soon I'll have him smiling like there's no tomorrow. Yeah, definitely going to shut up now."

Christina licked her lips and increased her speed. The more she thought of Robert, the more interesting images flashed in front of her, and the faster she ran. She no longer cared about her make-up; after all, she *had* been working out. She slowed down and thought about another approach; she didn't want him to think that she was desperate. Then again, she kind of was. The more arrogant *pretending-not-to-see-him* approach would probably be the best. Christina decided that was what she was going to do: just jog to the house and act surprised when she saw him. Yeah, that would definitely do it.

She rounded a corner at the top of a bluff and could see the house. The rain had intensified, and the distant thunder was coming closer. Between the trees she spied something white: Robert's truck, she imagined. She ran down the hill into the small dip below, and now she had only one more bluff before she came to the edge of her front yard. Something caught her eye as she ran up the bluff, and then came the sound of howling.

"Oh hi there, you horny little Peeping Tom, you," she muttered out loud.

She lost her concentration and realized she wasn't paying enough attention to her footing; if she wasn't careful, a branch on the path would soon ruin her day. She kept running, ignoring Robert, who waved to her from where he was standing near the main entrance. She put on her most arrogant look, but remained too ignorant of her footing, running faster—until suddenly she face-planted right into a mud puddle.

Her mouth full of muck, she just laid where she had fallen—not helpless, mind you, but completely humiliated. She heard Robert's footsteps as he ran towards her, not saying anything or calling her name or asking if she was okay—what a heartless bastard! Christina decided to pout, and buried her head even deeper into the mud. *What else can go wrong?* she asked herself.

Never, ever ask yourself that, or the universe will answer.

Robert's strong hands grabbed her shoulders, gently but firmly; however, Christina wasn't going to let him think he was Prince Charming saving her in his wet, shining armor, oh no. She scrambled to all fours and raised her head very quickly…a bit *too* quickly. She hit something rock-hard with the back of her head and it made her see stars. She squinted her eyes, trying not to shout any unladylike curse words. "Ouch!" would do and it did, more than once.

Her head hurt like hell now, and she was starting to feel woozy — like when you hit your head on a cupboard—but that didn't make her as woozy as the scenario facing her. Robert now lay on his back on the muddy ground, eyes blissfully closed. Christina stared in disbelief at the hunk on the ground. She must have knocked him out when she got up!

"And *that's* what can go wrong… Oh, crap, *now* what have I done?" she asked herself, confused.

She kneeled next to Robert's head, and touched it gently. Good; at least he was breathing. She softly called his name, but currently there was no one home. She looked at this perfect male specimen, and again touched his face gently with her dirty but soft fingers. She realized she had just smeared mud on his face, and that made her giggle. Again she looked him over, as her imagination undressed him.

Christina got serious, and shook her head in an attempt to think a bit more rationally, and let her hand gently massage his forehead, his nose, cheeks, and chin. His few days' worth of bristles tickled her hand. She normally liked her guys clean-shaven, but on this specimen the stubble only enhanced the rugged image. She lay his head in her lap, not sure what to do, and kept touching his face and short, thick, messy hair.

She surveyed the situation, and suddenly a mischievous smile covered her face. "The things I could do to you now, cowboy…ride 'em, cowgirl…yeah, I'm gonna shut up now."

She was leaning over to Robert, trying to assess the damage she had inflicted, when he suddenly started to move. That caught her off guard. "You'll be riding what?" he muttered.

Crap, he heard me, she thought as her eyes widened, and then everything turned black as Robert suddenly sat up very fast, holding his head with his left hand—and this time it was his turn to knock out Christina.

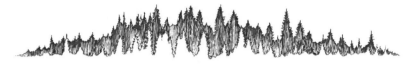

SIX

Carlos da Silva—whose name was often confused with a famous Brazilian soccer player, Roberto Carlos da Silva—leaned back in his office chair. He placed his leather Ropers on the morning paper on his desk, enjoying his third cup of strong black coffee this morning. He yawned and looked tiredly towards the window on the second store. The storm was coming back, and with it, he sensed problems. He liked to be in early—before the circus started, so to speak—not that there was ever complete silence in *his* building. It was a small precinct, with only seven deputies, and more than once this last year, ever since the Gold Rush started, he'd had to borrow help from either the highway patrol or the police departments in other, larger cities miles away.

Before, when there were pretty much only lumberjacks and the folks who supported them living in Skull Creek, they could be dealt with; but ever since this ridiculous new Gold Rush had started, he knew he'd have to make some serious changes. He would need twice the number of deputies, that was one thing for sure. How he would handle the county commissioners and the mayor he hadn't the faintest idea right now. They had, somewhat reluctantly, agreed that he could hire one more person this year as his chief deputy: Malik. Then again, that one person was as good as three, given his fearsome reputation.

For now, his mind was on a warm beach in the Caribbean with his wife and kids. Their annual trip would take place in December and would last a full month. He always looked forward traveling to his wife's home on the island of Saint Thomas. Malik Washington would take over the office when he was gone. Malik was an experienced police officer he'd worked with on numerous cases, a former sheriff in a neighboring county who had some differences with the local politicians and had gladly accepted a position on Carlos's force as his SIC. They more or less held the same rank, but Carlos was the older and therefore the senior of the two.

Malik's nickname was *The Enforcer*, and he was respected and borderline-feared by anyone who knew him—an untouchable straight-shooter who had grown up in the worse slum in L.A. and worked himself up from there. He would be the first black deputy on this force. Carlos himself was half-Mexican and half-Irish, but the latter not many knew; they simply judged him for being a border runner from Mexico, just another privileged Latino.

There were two more Latinos working with him; Diego and Adrianna. Diego was a former Miami SWAT man who had also worked in L.A. as an instructor. Carlos had brought Diego with him when he became the local Sheriff three years back. In this town, the Sheriff was appointed, not elected. Adrianna had been with the force for less than a month, having replaced a deputy who'd retired and moved to Florida. She had an impressive résumé and was a retired Marine, having been injured three times on two tours of duty.

It wasn't Carlos's intention to bring in more ethnic people, as he had been accused of a few times. His want-list when hiring was very simple. He wanted the very best he could get, and he didn't care about gender or skin color. Though perhaps he might have been a bit hasty with Adrianna. She was a bit short and petite, and definitely too good-looking for her own good. He had more than once heard wolf-whistles when she walked by—something he frowned upon. Thus far she had done an outstanding job, but he hadn't seen her in any physical action to this day. He was a bit concerned, because what the average joe didn't know was that people who work in the forest industry, especially lumberjacks —who normally created more than half the trouble in these parts—have one thing in common: they are all exceptionally strong.

But he wasn't going to get rid of her for now, anyway, being short-handed as it was. The other officers were all good, old-fashioned white boys, which was normal in a typical redneck county like this one. Lucy was the second female officer, and she liked women as much as any man. Then there was Dex, a young know-it-all bodybuilder. Bard, the old-fashioned giant cop, was also a lumberjack who sometimes helped his younger brother's crew. Whitney from New York Police and also a K-9 officer. One of his best but least-liked officers in town was Takoda. He was a Lakota Sioux, and the irony with that was that his name meant *friend to anyone*. The reason he was less liked was because he would never, ever bend any rules whatsoever for anyone, adult or child. He knew the book inside out and he never made mistakes. He also held a master's degree in criminal justice and a Ph.D. in psychology. Why someone with his background wanted to work as a police officer remained a mystery to everyone, and it wasn't a popular subject. Last there was Montana, named after the state—a former park ranger who had decided to re-saddle and become a police officer. Montana had been a cowboy in his youth, and he loved going hunting, fishing, and camping. He wasn't from this region but had lived here for well over fifteen years, and he knew the lay of the land best.

Overall, Carlos's force was small, but tight and loyal. Then again, the crimes in this county were mostly domestic violence and fights, especially on payday Fridays. Overall, it was a pretty quiet place, and Carlos intended to keep it that way.

He heard the sound of a cane striking the floor outside his office, followed by someone banging on his door with that very same cane. Carlos knew instantly who it was: his secretary, the one he had inherited from the previous sheriff, who had probably inherited her from the one before, and maybe the one before that. The morning routine had begun. *Woman must have lived during the Civil War era,* he thought. Aloud, he called, "It's open. Come on in, Ruth."

Nothing happened, but the knocking on the door intensified, a bit angrier this time. He knew the drill; rolling his eyes, he got on his feet. He put his coffee cup on the desk, and went and opened the door. A very old, slightly bent woman entered the room, ignoring him and going straight to his desk, where she placed a folder; then she stumped over to the windows and opened the blinds, followed by opening one of the windows. Without a word, she walked out; and as she passed his desk, she took the coffee cup.

"Hey, now, I hadn't finished that…"

Carlos could only shake his head and smile as he watched the old woman moving through the room, towards her desk and its ancient typewriter. She sank down in an ancient chair, patched with enough duct tape to keep a Navy cruiser afloat. When he had insisted on replacing it with a new and better one, she had refused and given him *The Stare,* which everyone in the department knew to avoid as often as possible. The chair was probably as old as she was.

She started to type very slowly, and once in a while she scratched her chin. Her white hair she kept in a prim bun on the top of her head. Carlos shrugged and went back into his office. He'd look at the folder, containing reports from last night's events, but not until he got another cup of coffee. He walked by her desk and opened the main office door; the top half glass, with his name on it in gold paint.

"People are concerned about that new Negro Terminator fella."

Carlos stopped dead in his tracks at the sound of the creaky old voice, completely at a loss for words and more or less in shock, still holding the door handle, not really knowing how to react or respond.

"Folks think he's be gonna replacing you, they do."

He turned around quickly, about to give the old woman a piece of his mind, but she completely ignored his body language and kept staring at the letter she was typing painfully slow when she continued, "Don't go off half-cocked, now, Sher'ff. You know 'Negro' ain't no racist word, like nigger or kaffir."

"But why use it?" he demanded.

"He's black, ain't he?"

"Well yes, but…"

"So that makes him a Negro, don't it?"

"Yes, I suppose it does. You could call him African-American, though."

"That's some PC bull hockey right there, Sher'ff. Man ain't no African no more than I'm a Polack 'cause my granddaddy came from Poland. We're both Americans."

"What does that make me, then? I really am from Mexico." He gave her a flattering smile, curious how she would respond to that one. On the inside, Carlos was preparing to erupt. He was too upset to think, so he headed back into his office just to sit down and rest. He wouldn't slam his door shut and let the old bag get the better of him.

"A CILM," she said thoughtfully as he was about to sit down.

"Say what?"

"A Confused Irish-Latino Man."

Carlos eyes widened at her cheeky remark, surprised she knew his mother was Irish. Normally, this was as many words as Ruth would use in a month, and for that he had been grateful. Perhaps he needed to look for the *shut-the-hell-up* switch on the little old lady.

He almost fell back into his own chair. He calmed down and grabbed after his coffee cup, and then came to the realization it wasn't there anymore. Dammit. He knew, or *thought* he knew, that Ruth wasn't a racist, but sometimes she did say the most awkward things. Carlos decided to let the conversation go; he never held any grudges anyway.

He got back on his feet and headed towards the coffee maker downstairs. Sometime in the near future he was going to get his own coffee maker in his own office. *One of those Keurig thingies. They sell 'em at Walmart over in Elkton,* he thought as he left the upstairs office, heading downstairs to a much larger, more typical police office landscape.

He walked into the kitchen and looked sadly at the empty carafe; to his dismay, he had to make more coffee, and no one liked his coffee. Hell, he didn't even like it much. Cutting way back on the amount of grounds he usually used, he waited patiently. When it finished, he poured a rich-tasting cup. Not bad this time!

He was just about to take a second sip when the alarm went off in the speakers, shattering the silence. From the speaker came the voice of Betty Cramer—the receptionist who took all calls during the day shift.

"Sheriff, 10-67 at Paul Harris camp! Urgent!"

Carlos put down the coffee cup on the kitchen counter, cold fingers running down his spine. Goddammit. A death report was always top priority. *Probably another lumberjack accident,* he thought, sighing. Sadly, it would be the third this year alone, and he was glad the lumbering season would soon be over. But the damn storm was back, and that could be a problem. Those logging roads were hellish in these conditions. Normally, he'd send someone else on something like this, but he was still frustrated from having to deal with Ruth. He decided some fresh air was better than anything here at the station.

He walked calmly into the open office space, and saw Diego typing on his computer, while Betty sat at her desk opposite the counter where visitors normally stood. She looked very concerned, and listened to the call intently.

"Who's out there?" Diego asked.

"Lucy's on her way back from finishing her night shift, and Bard has already gone home. I was just about to go on this one."

Betty turned around in her seat and held her hand over the microphone attached to her head set. "He says it's a *murder*. Paul says it's a *murder*," she said, shocked.

"So Mr. Harris thinks he's a coroner now, does he?" Carlos muttered to himself out loud as he headed towards the entrance with Diego in tow.

Betty looked at the receiver, concerned, and hung up. "He sounded very shook up, Sheriff. He said that the body is hanging on something, and then the call was cut off."

"Could be the storm. Try and reach him again while Diego and I get up there. Separate cars, Diego—and Betty, keep a lid on this one. Also, I want you to call in the next two deputies on your list. Something tells me we're going to need them. Diego, no lights or sirens, *comprende?* If the man is dead, he's dead."

Just as he spoke the words, an ambulance flew by outside on the main road, with lights flashing and sirens wailing, followed by not one but two Highway Patrol cars.

In the first car he recognized a girl named D'Lancy, an Asian woman he wanted to hire; behind her was her boss, a true redneck who should never have been allowed to carry a badge: Ethan Jones, old and very experienced, as well as a good old-fashioned bigot and proud of it.

Betty informed him, "The paramedics are on their way, and so's the Highway Patrol. Since the base camp is off one of the mountain roads, I thought…"

Carlos felt very tired all of a sudden, watching and hearing his plan of stealth going up in smoke. *Great, before we even get to the place, the entire town will know about it.* He said in a calm voice, "Okay, Betty, but please don't send anyone else for now. The storm is back, and it's only going to get worse."

With those words, a large fire rescue truck thundered by, also with lights flashing and sirens wailing.

"Um… I didn't call *them,*" Betty cringed.

Soon Carlos and Diego were following the circus with their own vehicles, both with flashing lights and sirens, because by now some civilians in their person vehicles had decided to tag along. They had to zigzag between a few cars and trucks while honking their horns. Carlos almost rear-ended Diego more than once. Suddenly, a Lincoln Town Car passed them on the wrong side.

"Great, that's all we need—the stupid newspaper reporter," Carlos muttered, watching the black Lincoln keep driving on the wrong side, trying to cut in line. He reached for the radio microphone. "Diego, see what you can do to get that crazy reporter off the road," Carlos ordered through the police radio.

"Will do."

He saw Diego speed up, turning onto the wrong side of the road, chasing the black Lincoln with lights flashing.

The rain intensified, and so did the storm. Dark clouds rolled like giant waves over the sky, and the wind showed no mercy. The tree tops swayed in unison, like a ghost army on the march. Branches, mud and dirt flew in the wind, mercilessly battering anyone and anything in their path. The rumble of thunder echoed in the sky as lighting exploded along the enormous mountain ridges.

The visibility was very poor, and Carlos slowed down, watching all the others vanishing into the rain. "Fools," he muttered; and as he eased on his brakes, his car started to aquaplane and skid towards the left lane. He immediately put the car in neutral and carefully eased it back onto the right land, just as an eighteen-wheeler flashed past, loaded with timber and loudly honking its horn. He regretted having ordered Diego to go after the reporter at that moment. He just knew, with a certainty born of experience, that something bad was going to happen.

A call over the radio from Diego answered his paranoia, "Accident at Deadman's Curve, acci…"

The radio went silent but for the static.

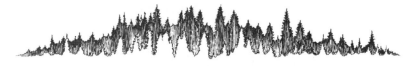

SEVEN

"Wakey, wakey, Miss Cowgirl…you all right?" Slap, slap. Christina's eyes opened and went wide. *He* did *hear me, that bastard*. "Did you just slap my cheek?" she snarled.

"Had to wake you up, miss."

Christina sat up in the mud, furious, and exclaimed, "You don't hit a girl like that to wake her up!"

"Worked, didn't it?"

That said, he picked up his cowboy hat from the ground, stood up, and walked over to the house while brushing it off.

Christina just sat there in disbelief. *What an ass*, she thought, while getting up with what little dignity she could muster. *Playing hard to get, is he? I'll show him hard to get.*

She trotted after him with her nose in the air, marching straight by him to turn off the outside alarm, then opened the door and turned off the inside alarm. There was a third alarm behind the second door inside the house, but she hadn't bothered with that one; she had a limit when it came to paranoia. She kicked off her sneakers and walked into the great room, wet socks leaving a trail of footprints behind her. Robert didn't bother to remove his wet boots; he just marched inside. Christina heard his boots echoing on the shiny wooden floor and stopped in her tracks, then turned facing him with her clenched fists on her waist, mouth set in a hard line, staring at him surprise and disbelief.

What she might have said he never learned, because at that instant they both heard sirens wailing on the main road as emergency vehicles of some kind approached. Robert hurried over to one of the windows and looked outside. The woods between them and the road were thick, but he saw the flashing lights of at least one Highway Patrol car. He ignored it and turned around, facing a furious girl.

"Frank should be here any moment," he said.

"Imagine that."

Robert wrinkled his forehead, looking at Christina and then at what she was looking at: his muddy footprints.

"Oops, sorry. I wasn't thinking. Head's till spinning, you know. I'll take care of it."

His calm, confident voice calmed Christina. "Don't worry about it," she said grudgingly. "I'll take care of it. It's just stone, not like it'll stain. Coffee?"

"Sure."

They went into the kitchen, and Christina made a fresh pot, then filled two cups. She took one, leaving the other on the counter with the cream and sweetener. He smiled and went to grab it—and when he did, his shoulder brushed her chest accidentally. Christina enjoyed the moment, but stepped away from him, keeping safe on the opposite side of the kitchen island. "So what's on today's agenda?" she wanted to know.

"Frank wants to show you the lay of the land on the house's plot, and wanted me to assist, I guess."

"You mean hold his hand?"

Robert smirked at the remark. "Over a hundred acres is quite a bit of land, and I think he's concerned you might wander off…and before you give me that look of yours, I meant no offense. Even the most experienced of us can get lost in this neck of the woods."

"So, what'll keep me safe?"

"Keep to the river, and once in a while turn around and survey your surrounding and look for recognizable markings, like a huge rock or unusual tree, or a distinctive dip in the land and so on. We'll show you, and if you ever want to go river rafting, a friend of mine has a kayak and rafting service on the river behind you." He nodded towards a back window, where both of them knew that the river lay far below. "They also take tourists on sightseeing tours and a few hunting tours. Or you can do some of this from the air, with Skull Creek Sightseeing & Rescue."

"I think I saw their sign at the airport."

"That's them, all right."

"What about you?"

"What about me?"

"Do you give any sightseeing tours?" Christina looked at him mischievously, then took the last sip from her cup, covering her face, while staring at him intently, as if she were looking for trouble. But he didn't even seem to notice, to her frustration.

"No, I don't do sightseeing," he answered seriously. "I used to help my friend sometimes, but it's not really my cup of tea."

"So what *is* your cup of tea then?"

He snorted and finished his own cup of coffee, playing with his hat on the counter. "Peace and quiet, I guess," he said after a long moment.

No ring or the markings of one on his ring-finger, and to top it off, he had the most beautiful hands, with perfect cuticles. She placed her own left hand on the counter, hoping he would notice that she didn't have any ring either. The things one had to do to get into a guy's pants! This was ridiculous; she was a famous actress, with men (and women, for that matter) lining up to have their way with her—but this one, not so much. It then dawned on Christina that perhaps he didn't know what she did for a living. Could she really be that self-centered, and expect *everyone* to know about her?

Her own thoughts betrayed her, and suddenly she blushed and quickly removed her hand. Jeez, what had happened to her? She needed a new rule to live by; no boys. Well, not for a while at least… Then again, it had already been a while. She sighed at her thoughts, and to her horror noticed that he was observing her with his deep blue eyes; and yes, they were perfect too. Defensively, she said, "You don't say much about yourself, do you?"

Robert just smiled back.

"When it comes to your work, *then* you talk; but you never say anything about yourself. Why?"

Robert just kept looking at her, and now his expression was neutral. She gave him a suspicious look. "What type of wood is the fence made of?" she demanded suddenly.

"For most part it's oak, and then there's…"

"Aha, gotcha! It *does* speak only about its profession, now doesn't it?"

Silence.

"Unbelievable. It's a programmed robot," she cried, pushing away from the counter and walking away.

"Well now, Ms. Cowgirl…"

She stopped in her tracks, then turned to face him; and to her surprise, he stood just behind her, very close. She found herself facing a blue denim shirt, which caught her off guard. With his boots on, he was unfairly tall.

"So, how much did you hear and for how long did you pretend to be out?"

"Honestly?"

"We can do honest for now."

"The moment your fingers touched my face."

"But why? Why didn't you…?"

"It felt nice."

"And you heard me?" She moved closer.

"Some of it."

"You heard all of it, didn't you?"

By now she was on her tiptoes, about to close her eyes. It was the perfect moment, that moment that's actually better than the kiss; the moment just before.

Then a terrible screaming sound made Christina's eyes open wide. Again the sound came, and it was clear it came from his breast pocket; it was the sound of a donkey braying. Immediately he turned 180 degrees and fished for his cell phone. He sounded very curt and serious when he answered. Christina looked at his perfect back and ass—but when she heard the word *accident,* she immediately got serious. Robert put on his hat, turned around, and marched towards the door.

"Wait what's going on?"

"Accident."

"Frank! Oh no, is he okay? WAIT!"

She intercepted him, stepping into the doorway and blocking his way out. "Hold on, now, what's going on?"

"Gotta go. People need me."

"Well, I'm coming with you."

"No."

"Yes."

"No."

"YES!" She stamped her right foot.

"I said NO."

He found himself facing two burning furnaces, the likes of which he'd never seen before. Christina gave the bonehead *The Stare,* the one imbedded in every woman's chromosomes—the one that, to this day, remains a horrifying mystery to all men.

He looked her over and shook his head. "You can't go like that anyway."

She moved swiftly, like a snake, one step closer to him. Again, there was less than an inch between them, and she could feel his breath on her face. It smelled like mint. She gave him a wide smile and winked to get him off guard, and it worked. She forced her hand into the right pock-et of his jeans—she had seen him put his truck keys there before—and though she felt something more than the keys, that had to wait. She pulled out the keys, dangling the keychain in his face and then snapping them away before he could get them back. She ducked away from his arm as he tried to stop her.

"Hey, wait, it's serious! I really gotta go!"

"I'll be right back. Time me—less than two minutes," Christina shouted as she raced upstairs.

Before Robert could protest, she was gone; and in less than two minutes, he heard her running back down the stairs on her tiny bare feet. She was back, wearing old denim overalls with only one shoulder strap buttoned, with the same damp T-shirt underneath. "You're going barefoot?" he demanded.

Heart pumping fast, Christina grabbed her sneakers and got down on the floor, forcing them back on her feet; but they were still damp and she had to do some struggling and stamping, with her tongue stuck out between her teeth and her long, messy hair covering her eyes. Robert was saying something, but she ignored him. When she was done, she jumped up and clapped her hands. "Ready!"

He looked at his watch. "You're late."

They hurried to his truck, and when they got inside he placed his right hand in front of her face. "Keys."

"Sorry. Here they are."

He drove very well, not too fast or sloppily but definitely in a hurry. By now, the rain was pouring down, and the wind was very powerful. The windshield wipers had to work overtime to clear the glass. The truck was old but clean, she noticed, something Christina liked. There were no trinkets hanging from the rear mirror, like that awful green tree some people used that stank something horrid. There was the typical gunrack in the back window, but no weapons. She put her long thick hair up in a loose knot back of her head while humming a tune. She decided to start a conversation to break the man's shell. "So, what do you do for fun around here?"

Silence.

"Have you lived here long?"

Silence.

"When you work in the forest, do you have a dog with you?"

"No."

"Don't you like dogs?"

"I do."

"But you don't have one?"

Silence.

"Don't you feel lonely when you work in the forest?"

"No, and most times I have a partner."

Silence.

"Dogs die."

There was something sad in his answer, and Christina decided to back off. This guy didn't put on a show for her; he was sincere, and she respected that, and liked him more for being himself. They drove for a while in silence, and when they came to the first four-way intersection they had to slow down and pull to the side of the road. Two ambulances with sirens wailing and lights flashing came in from the right road but to both Christina's and Robert's surprise one went up on the road they had come down, while the other turned the direction they were heading.

"That was odd," Robert said. "Could have sworn Frank said that the accident was down by Deadman's Curve."

"Maybe there's been more than one accident, or something else happened?" Christina suggested.

"Maybe, but those two ambulances are from the next county, and the way they came from is a very long detour."

He was about to speed up when two police cars came from the same direction the paramedics had—and also split up. "Something's definitely up, that's for sure," Christina said.

They drove in silence, no music or conversation, passing two more intersections. When they came to the last one, there were warning flares on the ground, and a police vehicle stopped in the road. A police woman wearing a ridiculously large yellow raincoat signaled them to stop. Robert lowered the driver's side window, and the woman leaned forward.

"Sorry, road closed, there's been an accident. You have to turn around."

Robert pulled down his visor to reveal several thick rubber bands holding down a series of cards. He removed a plastic one with his picture on it, and handed it to the police woman, who eyed it suspiciously. "You don't have a blue light?"

"No, I still haven't gotten one."

"But you do have a yellow light on the roof. May I suggest you use it? And what about her?"

"My little personal assistant," he said confidently, patting Christina on the top of her head…a very furious head indeed, with an open mouth and an *I-can't-believe-he-just-did-that* expression.

The policewoman handed back the card, and they drove on slowly, with the yellow-orange light on top of the truck flashing. Neither said a word, and Christina sat with her arms folded over her chest. She was not a happy camper; in fact, she was a bit concerned that this would turn into some big brother/friend fiasco rather than what she'd hoped for. Meanwhile, Robert focused on the crappy road ahead. It was no surprise that there had been an accident. Or accidents, since the emergency vehicles headed up the road were clearly rushing to the scene of another emergency.

When they reached the accident, they were greeted by a scene straight out of a modern-day Hieronymus Bosch's worst nightmare of Hell. Instantly, Christina regretted that she'd been so head-strong about tagging along. It was more than an accident: it looked like a war zone.

EIGHT

The first thing they noticed was the fire truck lying on the treetops, balanced precariously over the cliff's edge, supported by no more than a few broken branches. The twisted remains of a black Lincoln with its entire front end totaled was crammed against the high cliff on the opposite side of the road. A body was stuck halfway through the windshield, while firemen and paramedics trying to extricate him and treat his injuries. Thick black smoke swirled through the scene, occasionally reducing the visibility to zero.

On top of all that, a police car lay in a ditch with tree branches thrust through the window, while an eighteen-wheeler had tipped over nearby, huge logs scattered all over the place. A group of firemen fought a fire in a civilian car, while a few tried to take care of the fuel spill on the road. The fire was spreading rapidly, and the rain from the storm didn't seem to be helping much.

Rescue vehicles were spread out across the area, taking up most of the space on the cramped road. There were two large fire-rescue trucks and one smaller truck on the scene, along with three ambulances; as they watched, one of them took off toward town with lights and sirens blaring. Rescue personnel moved careful around the debris, doing their jobs professionally; no one seemed to be panicking, though Christina was on the verge. Shouts and screams from at least two people could be heard over the howling wind.

They parked behind a large green truck with electric signs on top, indicating that oncoming traffic should detour around the scene. Two men stood at the back, gathering equipment and struggling with some sort of short, thick ladder. The younger of the two, about the same age as Robert, glanced at Robert's truck with a scowl. He was handsome in a way, but looked too dour for Christina's taste.

Christina noticed that Robert eyed the other man with equal dislike. When she turned her head, she could barely see what was going on below the bend in the road from where she sat, but she did see two police cars blocking it, and many civilian trucks and a few cars parked along the road, stretching back quite a ways. There seemed to be a problem with crowd control. Out of the blue, a photographer crossed the cordon and strode swiftly around the scene, taking pictures of the wreckage and carnage. *The bloodier and more morbid the better,* Christina thought with disgust. She'd had her share of paparazzi, and photographers like this one were worse. Like most famous people, she thought of them as *stalkerazzi*, or photo-terrorists, and in the past they'd made her life a living hell. Today, she would make sure she kept away from him and anyone else with a camera.

A fireman took off after the photographer, and suddenly he got help from a huge police officer, who caught the bastard and forced him away under wild protest. *Idiot's probably screaming about his rights,* Christina thought. She smiled when she saw how roughly the police treated the vulture. Served him right.

Like a shadow, a big man moved through the smoke, and when he came closer Christina recognized the serious face of Frank. He wore the typical fireman's helmet and an unbuttoned fireman's jacket. On one of the patches on his chest were his name and the word *Volunteer*. He nodded to the two electricians and exchanged a few words with them, then pointed at one of the electrical poles on the side of the road. He walked over to Robert's side of the truck and greeted them with a nod.

"Robert, Christina." He touched the tip of his helmet when greeting Christina, and if he was surprised to see her, he didn't show it.

"What happened?" Robert asked.

"Not sure, but we need you over there by Diego's patrol car, and you need to bring your special kit and saw. Once you're done there, you might want to get into your monkey straps and see what you can do about that mess with the fire engine hanging over the cliff there." He motioned with his left thumb over his shoulder towards the truck, which was still stuck in the trees.

"But that's not the worst thing," the old man sighed. "A school bus filled with boy scouts went over the cliff over there." He pointed at a small opening between the large trees. There were a few broken branches visible, but it didn't look like an entire bus had gone through there. The guard rail that was supposed to prevent vehicles from going over the cliff was just plain gone. In some places, there were a few pieces of the twisted metal and support posts still intact, leaning drunkenly.

Christina remembered Frank warning her about this part of the road, and that the guard rail was poorly maintained because of the many accidents that occurred here. "Scouts on the road on a Saturday morning?" Christina asked.

"They were supposed to camp all weekend, but they canceled after the storm last night, and decided to go home early this morning. Should have canceled yesterday, if you ask me."

"Casualties?"

"Afraid so, Robert. The bus driver and one of the scout instructors, I think. Kids seem mostly all right. Anyway, get saddled up; right now the chief wants you to help Diego. He's got a tree branch in his chest, and it's bent something awful and look like it's under a lot of pressure."

"Shouldn't we help the kids first?"

"Chief had a few firemen and paramedics rappel down there to help the worse injured, but the problem is that the firetruck stuck in the trees there could fall at any time on the bus, which is pretty far below. Some parents are causing a problem, and the police have their hands tied. Diego won't make it if we can't rush him to the hospital ASAP."

An explosion erupted from one of the utility poles, and several downed wires spewed out wicked blue electrical arcs, whipping around mercilessly.

"Crap, that's my cue, gotta go, hurry up!"

ROBERT SLAMMED the door and rushed to the back of his truck to open the box contained his rescue gear. He removed his denim shirt and grabbed a rescue jacket, and suddenly he sensed someone standing next to him. He removed his leather cowboy hat and looked for a place to put it; It landed on Christina's head, sideways. He smirked when he saw her surprised expression. The hat was too big for her, and if it hadn't been for her hair bun, it would have covered her head and face completely. "Sure are nosy, aren't ya?" he grumbled.

Robert kicked off his cowboy boots, and pulled down his pants—no shyness whatsoever. He wore boxers. *Yeah, there'll be no big brother/ friend BS here, and that's that,* she decided as he put on some awful-looking thick black pants with sawdust on them, followed by equally ugly safety workboots the color of fresh rust. They looked heavy. With only a tight white T-shirt over his muscular torso, he put on the jacket.

The wind picked up, and with it the rain intensified. "Won't you catch a cold wearing only that?" Christina wondered. Robert just smiled, and unexpectedly wrapped his denim shirt around her like a real gentleman. It was far too large for her, but felt oddly comfortable. She leaned her head over and smelled the collar, scenting a musty, sweaty and yet clean odor that she liked very much.

"Try not to get it dirty," Robert told her.

So much for being a gentleman, she thought.

He put on a bright yellow warning vest with reflectors on it, and tossed one to Christina too. "Wear this just in case someone asks about you. Tell them you're with me." He then grabbed a typical orange lumberjack's hard hat with black ear protection attached and a black grill to protect his face. He closed the hatch to that compartment, then opened another, bigger one at the back of the truck.

He took out a Husqvarna fuel can. It looked practical and very robust, with accessories for both fuel and lubricants. Many different tools were attached on both sides by the handle. There were several chain-saws stacked neatly in the new compartment; some were small, while others were much bigger. He grabbed two of them, and a bag with more tools. He also took out a huge, circular backpack—it looked extremely heavy - and tossed the tool bag on top. Robert then placed the fuel can around his neck with the help of a leather strap attached to the handle. He kneeled and took a chain-saw in each hand, then got up and got moving. He'd only walked a few yards before he stopped and turned around, the muscles in his arms tensed. "Stay here with the truck. Please."

Christina nodded and said, "Be careful, please."

He gave her a puzzled look, then he entered the melee.

As Christina waited in the truck, each minute felt like an hour. When she finally looked at the clock on the dashboard, she rolled her eyes; Robert had only been gone for twenty minutes. She was frustrated at not being able to help; she hated feeling useless, but knew she would only be in the way. She was tired of sitting, though, and needed to stretch her legs.

Out of nowhere, Robert showed up with the fuel can. She got out and met up with him on her side of the truck. He opened a compartment with a warning label and a painted flame on it; and inside stood two large plastic containers, one red and the other blue. He used attachments to refill his fuel and lubricant. "How goes it?" she asked.

"It's pretty bad," he said in a somewhat discouraged tone. "That's what happens when someone drives like an idiot, I guess."

"The cop, were you able to save him?"

"Diego. I got him loose from a branch that had penetrated his abdomen and nailed him to the seat, if that's you mean. It's up to the doctors now."

He stopped in his tracks, and suddenly he looked Christina over from head to toe, very intently. Christina didn't know what to think.

"How much do you wei…nah, never mind." He grabbed her arms in a firm grip, forced them along her body, and then lifted her a foot off the ground with no effort, like she weighed nothing. He put her back down, and stood there thinking for a moment before he decided, "No, too dangerous, and the chief probably won't let me do it."

"Do what exactly?" she demanded.

"We need someone light to attach a pulley far up in a tree and thread a line through it."

"Okay."

"Do you have any experience climbing trees, wearing a harness, and rappelling of any sort—and can you tie a real knot?"

Christina gave him a shy smile. "I have some training in rock climbing, so yes, I'm familiar with climbing and rappelling. I'm also experienced with harnesses and hanging strung up in all kind of weird positions, sometimes for hours. So yeah, I've been tied up many times, and I'm very familiar with knots."

She wasn't thinking about what it sounded like until Robert gave her a puzzled look. She started to stutter—something she did whenever nervous—and tried to say something about a green screen, which made no sense to Robert.

"What are you? A dominatrix?"

There was an awkward silence between them, before she blurted, "Not so much, but if that's what it takes," and then clapped her hands over her mouth when she realized she had said it out loud.

Christina noticed his hesitation. She saw a harness on the truck bed. She grabbed it and put it on, demonstrating that she knew what she was doing, but suddenly she removed it. She then, to his surprise, grabbed some rope and measured it up about eight feet. "Got a medium or large snap link?"

He nodded to a compartment, and Christina picked out one medium link. Then she tied a reserve harness around her legs and waist, attached the snap link, squatted down, and secured the line while it was flexed—something most military people knew about, but most civilians didn't.

Maybe she's been in the military, Robert thought.

She adjusted the harness and its shoulder strap, climbed in the openings, and fasten it like a seatbelt. It had a more modern snap link already attached.

Robert nodded thoughtfully. "Okay, then. But if the chief says no, then don't argue. Just come back here, all right?"

She looked up into his face and gave him a sloppy salute.

"You'll need a helmet too."

He looked around and handed her what looked like a black baseball batting helmet, similar to the ones the SWAT team used. He changed the inside to small, removed his cowboy hat from her head, and replaced it with the black safety helmet. He pulled the chin strap tight. Never once did he look into her eyes.

He explained what she had to do; the firetruck that lay on top of the trees over the cliff edge remained where it was because of one gigantic tree. "I've tried several different ways of getting a line around it, as far up as possible, but failed. The only way is either to climb up from below or get on the tree from above with the help of a crane, but you have to get into the tree and climb down right there," he said, pointing at a location high on the tree. "We need a smaller person who can climb from the top and about a quarter of the way down. There are too many branches, and most are too small to climb from the ground."

Christina listened, focused, and nodded as she looked at the giant tree. The tree leaned over the cliff edge at about a 45-degree angle.

When they reached the group of men around the tree, there was more than one suspicious glance aimed at Christina. *What are they feeding these people when they're kids? All the men are giants,* Christina thought.

"Who's the kid?" the fire rescue chief, Nolan, demanded, staring at Christina, who tried to take cover behind Robert.

"I say we wait for Adrianna," Bard insisted, after looking Christina over.

"What if there's an accident, and the tree shifts or the cliff gives way?" someone asked.

"Emergency action supersedes that," Frank intervened. "Besides, we'll soon have a thunderstorm right above us, and we have to do something *now*."

Nolan looked at Christina. "You sure you're up for this?"

Christina gave him *The Stare*. He had seen it before, so Nolan shook his head and motioned "Okay" with his shoulders. Frank stepped up to Christina. "Sure you know what you're doing? I don't like this."

"I know what I'm doing, and I really want to help."

Frank winked eye at her, smiling.

Robert escorted Christina to a large firetruck he called the Tower; it included a crane with several ladders and a basket. Inside the basket waited a fireman. The crane shook violently as they took off, then ascended smoothly towards heaven. The fireman was nice and calm, and handled the controls on the dashboard with obvious experience. They went quite high, and Christina could see the accident entire spread out far below them.

"We have to hurry," the fireman shouted over the sound of the storm. "It's only a matter of time before the storm's on top of us. Once we're up, you have to rappel down and get through the branches to attach the line and pulley to the trunk. When you're done, just kick off at the trunk, and hang on. I'll lower you to safety."

It all sounded easy, but it wasn't.

Once they reached the desired elevation, the fireman opened a gate. He doubled-checked the lines on Christina's harness and the spare safety line attached to the harness she had roped herself. He looked up, impressed, and smiled at her. He noticed that they had forgotten to give her gloves, so he handed Christina his own. He had to shout over the raging storm, "You're good to go. Remember, there are no safety lines that can break your fall from below."

"This one is all I need," she said confidently, patting the one on her harness. She backed up to the edge, checking her lines. *Don't look down, don't look down,* she thought, and then she looked down. *Crap.*

She lowered herself slowly, and far below, a small crowd looked on. She didn't see the photographer taking hundreds of pictures in the distance, where the rest of a civilian crowd had gathered behind the police lines.

The wind caught her, and she let out a small cry, but she gathered herself and kept moving down. She had some minor problems because her gloves were too big. She stopped to assess her position, and again she looked down.

She could see all the way below to the ground; it was more than three hundred feet to the bottom, and the school bus lay far below. It seemed the size of a broken toy. She could see at least three fire rescue workers, and one of them had begun to climb up with the help of a rope. She turned her head and saw the fire engine with a line attached to it, helping pull the climber up.

A wind gust caught her, and she spun around; and now she saw part of another vehicle, lying by a bend on the cliff on what looked like a small outcropping of rock. There was an arm sticking out onto the white hood or back of the truck; she couldn't tell which. They hadn't told her about that vehicle. Did they even know about it?

When she got a few feet above the desired location on the tree, she had to swing to get closer. The firefighter above noticed her dilemma, and slowly eased her closer to the trunk. She faced many branches thick with needles and cones, standing like a wall against her. She grabbed one and pulled herself closer. A branch whipped her hard in her face, and for a moment she lost her concentration; then she fell towards the ground.

The people below gasped in fright as they observed the little monkey-like figure doing all kinds of aerial acrobatics. She jerked to a stop after a fall of a couple of feet by pulling on her brake line; then she vanished into the thick brush, and for a long moment nothing happened but for two gloves falling down toward the ground. Now the onlookers nearest her were more concerned.

Christina had been terrified, but had gained control over her own fear and what could have been a fatal moment. She bit down on the ends of the stupid gloves and pulled them off with her teeth, letting them fall where they might. She had her legs wrapped around the trunk. It was covered with a gooey greenish sap, and she could smell turpentine. Robert had warned her about that, and had explained why the fire engine was a major priority. A thick layer of white foam covered part of the road and the fire engine. She got the sticky crap all over her body and face, but this was no time to think about herself. She tied a timber hitch, then swiftly attached the pulley and the rope. She checked her work, and everything seemed fine. She then tossed out the line for the people below, but it got tangled in some branches. She stopped for a moment, catching her breath; but a sudden explosion of thunder from a lightning strike nearby launched her back into action. She pushed against the trunk with her legs, going after the rope. She got it, but at the same time she had forgotten the brake line, and again then she fell along the edge of the tree canopy.

The watchers below shouted loud warnings, and there were many concerned expressions, especially on two of them.

Christina pulled the brake line, and the fireman above moved the crane away from the tree. She signaled to him that she had finished and all was okay. Slowly, she was lowered to safety, hanging like a piñata and hoping no one would have a baseball bat waiting for her below.

Many strong arms and hands reached into the sky, helping the grubby little woman to safety. She received more than one hard pat on her back. She felt satisfied with herself, and a bit tired.

"Take care of that, or it'll leave a scar."

It was the electrician who had stared at Robert, looking her face over closely. He then turned his back and walked away. He was very handsome in a tragic way, she thought.

"That was one hell of a job you did up there, boy," Nolan praised Christina.

"I'm a girl," she answered somewhat groggily, while scratching her face and smearing the sticky sap and foam even worse than she had already.

Not looking at Christina but at some of the rescue workers, Nolan said, "Of course you are. Don't worry, son, I don't judge or discriminate against anyone."

Christina lunged forward to punch the inbred idiot, but large hands grabbed her shoulders and pulled her back. Robert whispered, "Calm down, Christina, he didn't mean nothing by it."

With his back turned, Nolan continued, "My nephew is a transvestite, too, and despite that he turned out pretty okay, if you ask me." Nolan began walking away, talking into his walkie-talkie, and Christina launched herself at his back again, this time determined to whip some ass. Suddenly she was lifted bodily into the air, and to her embarrassment found herself carried away kicking and screaming.

"Put me down, Robert, or I'll turn you into a eunuch, you bastard!"

She got her footing back, and that's when she realized it had been Frank who had grabbed her so roughly. Robert stood next to them, a big grin on his face. Shaking his head, still smiling, he walked towards the big tree, inspecting the line attached to the winch that was attached, in the distance, to another three pulleys fitted on an equal number of large trees. A firefighter had already begun cranking the huge winch; slowly, the tree extending over the cliff bent dangerously toward the road. Robert saw another large tree underneath, an oak. Now he understood why the heavy fire engine could lay the way it did. "The oak shouldn't be any problems," he said aloud, and hoped. He prepared his chainsaw to make the final cut.

"OOPS, SORRY, Frank…" Christina said to her landlord, feeling chagrinned.

"No, I'm the one sorry for not introducing you before; but there was no time, and I do remember Mr. Billing's very strict instructions about not mentioning your name to anyone."

She realized that he was right and calmed herself down, as both headed over toward Robert's truck.

"So, what now?"

"We'll stay here and watch the master at work. He'll soon have that big oak down, and the tow trucks on either side down the road will help pull the firetruck back on the road—on its right side we hope. We need to get clear of those thick wires."

"When will he make the cut?"

"Once the chief—your favorite fireman—gives him the go ahead. The last kids are up and safe, but there are two more rescue workers. We don't want anyone below, in case something bad happens and the firetruck falls off the cliff."

Christina thought for a moment about the white vehicle and the arm she'd seen while hanging like a piñata. "But what about the person in the white truck down there?"

Frank turned his head with a frightened expression. "What white truck? There wasn't a white truck involved in this accident, far's we know."

Quickly Christina explained what she had seen, and Frank got on his radio, sending a coded message that immediately made everyone stop what they were doing. A frustrated Nolan hurried to them, followed by Carlos da Silva, the police chief. Frank explained what Christina had said.

"Jack, hold on, are you and Tim still below?" Nolan barked into his walkie-talkie.

"We're about to climb up, chief."

"Hold that thought. I want you to move to…" He looked at Christina.

She pointed in the direction of the white truck. "It's on some sort of ledge; it looks almost like one of those shelf funguses growing on a tree."

Nolan knew instantly where to direct his people. They waited for what seemed to take forever, and then came the call. *"White pickup truck, markings from one of the lumber companies, not sure which one yet. There's at least one body, possibly two…and from the looks of it must have happened a day or two ago."*

Deputy Bard had joined them by Robert's truck, and so had several more people, including Robert and the electrician; one had to be blind not to notice the hostility hanging in the air between them. They all swore under their breaths.

"Harris's team reported a truck missing yesterday evening," Bard said in thundering voice.

Carlos remembered not having had time to read last night's report; now he cursed himself in silence for not doing so. He should have read it; if he had, the first thing he would have done would have been to check out this curve, since Harris used this road to get to and from their logging site. He turned angrily towards Bard. "If it was one of Harris's trucks, why didn't you or someone check this murder turn?"

A somber Bard answered reluctantly. Wanting to avoid an argument with his boss, he leaned forward and whispered, "I did, Chief, it's in the report, but I saw nothing then. You know, bad weather and all."

Carlos calmed down and said, "Thank you, Bard."

Without thinking, Christina removed her helmet, unknotted her long dark hair, and shook it out in the wind. Her hair flew like a flag. A sudden silence fell, and when she noticed it she turned around.

"What?"

Half a dozen giants stared at her while Frank squinted his eyes and said, "Crap."

The big men and some of the flabbergasted onlookers recognized her; her beauty was unmistakable, after all. No one said anything. Robert came to her rescue, and so did Frank. Robert leaned inside his truck and quickly slapped his hat on her head. A surprised Christina looked up at him with the brim over her eyes; she had to lean her head back to see him, "What?" Then her eyes went wide; she covered her mouth with her hands as she realized what she had done.

"You ain't no boy," Nolan muttered.

"Sure ain't, you big oaf," she spat back.

Nolan, a bit confused, said, "But, but what are ya then?"

Robert kneeled down, putting a new chain on one of his chainsaws. She patted him on top of his head and said, "Why, I'm his kinky dominatrix, slick!"

More than one set of eyes widened, but none as much as Robert's. Christina just rolled her eyes, and with the cowboy hat still covering most of her head and face, she walked over to the back of the truck to remove the harness. Someone whistled. She could hear them talking about her, and poor Frank had to put on a charade.

Bard scratched his chin and said, thinking aloud, "Swear I seen her before. Isn't she that famous…?"

"She ain't nobody special. Now let's get back to work—we still got plenty to do," Frank insisted.

Carlos gave him a suspicious glare, then looked at the chief and said, "Frank is right. We should finish up here as soon as possible, and thanks to Robert's dominatrix, looks like we have some more work to do."

Bard leaned over towards Robert. "Where does a man get one of them pretty little thingies?"

"Kinda the other way around. The thingie gets *you*."

The hostile electrician also observed Christina interestedly, eyeing her from head to toe, before he joined the others.

Frank gave Carlos a friendly smile, and Carlos whispered something to Frank. The two men walked up to Christina, and Frank said, "Sorry, Christina, but Carlos here does need your full name for his report."

So much for living here secretly. Oh well; her star had begun falling a while back anyway.

Everyone was interrupted by an excited voice on the radio, warning that the tree had to be taken down ASAP before the weather situation got worse. The many onlookers watched on nervously as Robert vanished into the brush alone. A moment later his voice came over the radio: *"Making the cut in one minute."*

They heard the sound of a chainsaw revving, then working its way into a tree; then there was silence. The tree seemed, at first, as if it was going to fall into the valley below, taking the fire engine with it; the people watching held their breath. And then came the collective *Wow!* as, suddenly, it altered direction. The wire and lines stretched to the limit… and suddenly the tree leaned back towards the road and fell sideways. The truck slid on its side down onto the road surprisingly gently, having only been a few feet away, and then, to everyone's horror, the giant tree started to fall in the same direction, like it was going to crush the fire engine. But the attached ropes and wires altered the tree's direction, and it came crashing down along the road inches from the fire truck. The two tow trucks pulled on the fire engine, and shortly it was back on an even keel. Firefighters hurried up to the vehicle and continued drowning the tree and fire truck with foam; they knew that there was a chance that the tree had natural turpentine in the greenish sap along the trunk, and it could ignite if they didn't take precautions.

Clapping, bull whistles, and joyful cheers could be heard over the noise of the storm, and many hands patted Robert on the back as he emerged from the darkness.

Meanwhile, Carlos had collected Christina's personal information; and just when he was about to return to the melee, two police vehicles—a highway patrol car and one of his own police SUVs—pulled up by the barricade. Takoda approached him, followed by D'Lancy Tanaka from the Highway Patrol.

"Some folks have reported a bear over near town," Takoda reported. "Might be a grizzly."

"Whereabouts?"

Takoda took a folded map from his breast pocket and pointed on an area. "Want me to check it out, chief?"

"No, have one of the park rangers do it—we're short-staffed as it is, and this is a friggin' mess. Have there been any reports of aggressive behavior or attacks?"

"None. Some parent called it in. Their kids claimed they seen one."

D'Lancy cleared her throat. Her face held a friendly smile, but there was an element of distress to it. "Um, Sheriff, Mr. Jones is very upset and wonders why you haven't answered any of his calls. So here I am, promoted to his personal courier."

Carlos—frustrated, wet, and tired—answered with an angry sweeping gesture of his right hand, indicating the mess behind him. D'Lancy's eyes widened. "Damn, heard about an accident over the radio, but I had no idea."

"You do now. I'll get to Ethan when I have the time."

D'Lancy knew full well about the hostility between her own boss—whom she despised—and Carlos, and made sure she kept out of it. "Sorry, sir."

"Come on, don't make this day any worse, use my name." She smiled at him as he continued, "When are you going to come and work for me instead of that Grand Lizard of the KKK?"

"Doubt he's really a member. Anyway..."

"Problems?"

She just nodded, and then she said a word that anyone in law enforcement dreads: "Homicide."

Carlos closed his eyes, in a desperate hope it was all a dream; but when he opened them, it wasn't. He removed his rescue helmet and walked away from them, motioning with his hand for them to leave him alone. Both D'Lancy and Takoda kept their distance.

Carlos closed his eyes, raised his head towards the sky, and let the rain pour over it. He combed his hair back with his hand—and suddenly, with a shift of the wind, there came a foul odor. He tasted the air with his tongue, eyes still shut. He opened them and stared dead ahead, then squinted, staring towards the cliffside in the far distance. *That smell, that smell...I recognize it,* he thought. Chills went down his spine and goosebumps tickled his skin. Terror fell over him like a dark shadow. He felt observed. His head moved side to side, slowly, and he stared along the cliff edge; and there, by a large bush in front of the tree line, he thought he saw something. He closed his eyes from the strain after staring intently, and when he opened them again, he couldn't see anything amiss.

Takoda approached on Carlos's right side while D'Lancy walked up on his left, both looking the same direction. "Something wrong, sir?" D'Lancy asked.

Carlos didn't answer; instead, he stared more intently.

Takoda repeated D'Lancy's question, as she gently placed her hand on his left forearm. Carlos moved his head quickly to either side; first he stared at Takoda, and then at D'Lancy.

"Sir, what is it?" Takoda demanded.

Carlos turned his head back towards the cliffs. "Up there. Do you so anything?"

Both D'Lancy and Takoda looked in the same direction as Carlos. Neither saw anything. "What did you see?" Takoda asked.

"Not sure, but there was something, I think."

"Maybe a curious onlooker," D'Lancy suggested.

"You think? Up there?"

"Do you want me to check it out, sheriff?" Takoda asked.

"No, the last thing I need is another one of my deputies in the hospital from climbing a cliff in the rain. It's probably nothing. Now, let's go on up to the lumber camp. After all, we mustn't keep the Grand Lizard waiting," Carlos said shakily, trying to brush aside his earlier emotions.

D'Lancy and Takoda were experienced officers, having met thousands of people, victims as well as villains—and they knew when someone was scared to death. Both looked at Carlos, concerned.

IT WAITED on the cliff edge in the distance, above the accident scene, patiently observing the weak two-legged creatures below. It searched for its primary prey, peering down on a group of three people. *She sure looks pretty in that hat,* the beast thought. It licked its lips and tapped its deadly claws on the rocky surface, then lowered the binoculars.

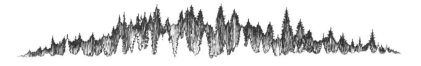

NINE

Takoda parked his police SUV alongside the narrow dirt road behind D'Lancy's highway patrol car. Carlos sat on the passenger side—his vehicle had been parked on the opposite side of the accident and therefore he couldn't use it—thinking it was a miracle that eighteen-wheelers could manage to drive up and down this dangerous path at all.

He was embarrassed over his behavior earlier in front of his colleagues, but he couldn't help it. It wasn't what he thought he had seen that had terrified him; after all, that could have been an animal or just a curious person. It had been the strange, foul smell. Somewhere in his mind, a hidden memory of some sort had generated a *déjà vu* moment. Possibly. He wasn't sure, because he couldn't remember. Maybe it had touched on a memory from his past he had chosen to forget. As a lawman, he'd seen some gruesome sights. Whatever it was, it had troubled his mind greatly, and he didn't like it at all.

There were very few vehicles at the camp; only Paul Harris's truck, the paramedics, another highway patrol car, and a pickup truck parked on the road about a hundred yards away from the scene. There had been one person standing in the rain there, smoking a cigarette.

Dressed in a long yellow raincoat and rainhat, a slim man in his early sixties observed them in silence. Next to him stood Paul Harris; his breath smelled like he'd just been sick. He was smoking nervously, and as Carlos watched, he lit a new cigarette from the stub of the last. Kneeling on the ground were the two paramedics; also on the ground lay a black body bag, and inside was the victim. Carlos and Ethan Jones exchanged salutes, tipping their hats to each other. Jones didn't even glance at Takoda or D'Lancy.

"You want to look at this." Jones gave Carlos his smart-phone. While Carlos went over several pictures of the dead person hanging from cables, Jones continued, "There's a video there, too, from when I got here and we took the victim down. He was dangling something awful, and I was concerned that if there was evidence on the body, it might get ruined by the weather."

Carlos was well aware that Ethan Jones had crossed the line in interfering in his investigation, but he had done the right thing because of the horrid weather conditions, so he only nodded while watching the short film. In a very soft voice nonetheless filled with arrogance, Jones said, "D'Lancy took some better pictures with another camera; I'll have her send them to your office." He deigned to look at the woman. "By the way, since you're just standing there, why don't you amble on down the road and take care of crowd control." He grinned sarcastically while nodding towards the single man still standing in the rain by his truck.

D'Lancy's expression betrayed nothing, and without a word, she left them to take care of the "crowd." Takoda gave her a supportive smile as she passed him and, then without moving his head, shifted his body to stare down the smiling Ethan Jones. Jones lost his smile, then cleared his throat and pursed his lips in a self-satisfied smirk.

Meanwhile, Paul Harris tossed his latest cigarette butt on the ground and started puffing the next coffin nail. After some prompting, he reluctantly told his story to Carlos, stuttering and going through several cigarettes in the process.

"Have you had any trucks hauling timber this morning?" Carlos asked when he wound down.

Taken aback by the question, since it didn't seem to involve the dead person, both Harris and Jones looked at each other, confused, and then at Carlos. "No, none of my trucks or any of my people should be working today," Paul said. "Gave everyone the day off, not that it matters, it's the weekend --it's just that the weatherman warned about the storm. I had a double-shift working, taking down as many logs as they could the other day to the mill. If you saw any trucks, it must be from another crew. I know some of the young pups don't care about the weather and the danger it brings with it, and only focus on the damn quota. There are four more crews in this region, but all are on different locations."

Carlos knew full well how many logging crews there were in his jurisdiction, but he let the man talk; what he talked about might be helpful. "Do we know who the victim is?"

"One John E. Clement, we think...or at least that's what Mr. Harris claims," Jones drawled.

"You *think*?" Carlos shot Paul a questioning glance.

Paul got even more nervous, and flicked away his cigarette—still only half smoked—before immediately lighting another one, cupping his hands to protect the lighter's flame from the rain that was still pouring down. "Well, from the size of him and the tattoos, I'm pretty darn sure it's Noise."

"You mean that big bastard they call Little Noise? Damn, I should've remembered his real name, considering all the time he's spent in my lock up."

Harris just nodded.

"Want me to take a closer look, sir?" asked Takoda.

Carlos had hoped it wouldn't come to that, having just seen the pictures, but he knew that Takoda was an expert on animal attacks— and they needed as many answers they could get. When Paul Harris saw Carlos motioning to one of the paramedics to open up the body bag, he turned around and puked his guts out.

Carlos didn't change expressions. He'd seen horrors like this before; not so much in this county, but when he had worked in the larger cities. He already knew that the head was missing, having seen the pictures and the video. He walked away against the wind, closer to the edge of the rise, and looked down at the hundreds of giant logs laying all over the steep hill, looking like scattered Lincoln Logs at this remove. He figured it was maybe nine hundred feet to the bottom. The entire region looked like a huge square had been trimmed down almost to the ground, with only the stubble of occasional stumps remaining. There wasn't even any brush left. Typical clearcutting. At least the surviving roots would control the erosion.

Takoda kneeled and pulled back the cover on the body bag, then reeled backward because the body stank something fierce. He looked at Carlos, and immediately envied him for standing a bit away against the wind, not having to smell this shit. And some of the smell *was* shit, the body's bowels having loosened, mixed with piss, BO, the coppery stink of blood—and something else, something rank and animalistic. The dead man was indeed a giant. There were several lacerations and tear marks from what could only be claws. *Most likely a bear*, he thought.

"Any ideas?" Ethan Jones asked in a neutral tone.

"From having seen the pictures and now the markings and bruises, so far I'd say he went a round or two with a grizzly. But..."

Jones finished his sentence "...but a bear don't chop off someone's head that neatly, and they definitely don't string up bodies on a wire."

"Could the body have gotten tangled up in on the hooks accidentally?" Takoda asked.

"No, not the way they were tied. You can see it on the pictures better."

"Damn. It'd be hard tying these thick wires."

"Weren't tied with a knot. They used hook and wire like a noose, just the way they do when bringing up logs, but someone did add some rope too. Making sure the body wouldn't slip, I guess."

"To intimidate, or frighten," Carlos thought out loud, still standing a bit away.

"Or vengeance, who knows. Maybe some crazy fucker found him dead from a grizzly, then did the rest to him for some twisted reasons of their own. But he was definitely left that way to scare people, and apparently it worked." Jones nodded at Paul Harris.

Carlos asked Jones, "Has anyone been down there looking for any more evidence—established the actual crime scene?"

"In this weather, no, it's suicide with all the wet logs and branches. It's simply too slippery, not to mention the undergrowth. I wouldn't go down there for a million bucks."

Jones was right, and Carlos didn't like it. Not that he was right, but because there could be some important evidence, like a murder weapon, or whatever was used to behead Noise and so on, but the weather was just getting worse.

"We need to get down there and check for more evidence, but I guess it has to wait until tomorrow…depending on the weather. Either that, or this place will be shut down. I don't want anyone up here or down there," he pointed down valley. "I doubt we'll find much once we can conduct a better investigation, but still, no one can be here till I say so. You hear me, Harris?"

"Sure, sure, just find the bastard who did this."

"We have to do something to block off the road and keep people away from here. I can't afford to send one of my deputies to guard this place."

"If you want, Sheriff, I can have Mike Hudson drop a few logs over the road. He's down there by his truck, talking with D'Lancy."

"Yeah, I can see the big crowd." He glared at Jones and then asked, "What's he doing here, by the way?"

Looking a bit ashamed, Paul Harris said, "I called him. Sorry."

"Well, let's try and keep a lid on this for as long as possible, okay?"

In the background, Takoda gestured to the paramedics. "Bag him, please, and take the body to the coroner's office."

Just then there was a change in the wind—and with it came a foul, horrible stench. Carlos froze. Ethan Jones noticed Carlos's reaction, and said calmly, "It's from the body. Not sure what to make of that, though. Guess that bear might have taken a piss on him."

Jones laughed at his own joke while heading towards his car; Takoda observed the idiot from behind as he brushed by, and then he turned towards Carlos—and that's when he saw the change from concern to fear in his boss's eyes.

MIKE HUDSON sweated profusely from being so worked up, and he drove his pickup truck well beyond the allowed speed limit. More than a few times, other drivers honked their horns at him, and some of the less happy ones shot him the bird. He ignored all of them, staring dead ahead, but he wasn't focused on his driving. He had more important things going on in his head; he was thinking up the best story for his drinking buddies at the Last Post. This was big time, big news—big old Noise slaughtered! Go figure. Boy, was he going to be the center of attention! People would listen to and respect him. Now he'd seen it all, he knew, as he reached towards the glove compartment for a bottle of bourbon. He took a big chug, and then another, drifting over to the other side off the road. He saw a flash of movement and realized he'd almost hit a shiny blue Dodge pickup. He reacted fast, though, and with both hands he turned the steering wheel hard right. Realizing that he'd used both hands and the bottle was lying on his lap with the remaining contents pouring out, he cursed prolifically.

It took him almost two hours to reach The Last Post, due to an enormous accident at Deadman's Curve. The pigs had only one lane open while road workers rebuilt the guardrail, and they checked all the cars for some reason; probably the murder, he guessed. He had been lucky, noticing the long line of cars, and have taken the long detour at the intersection before the accident. Otherwise they'd have arrested him for sure, given the reek of whiskey all over his cab.

His truck came to a sudden stop in the Post's parking lot, splashing muddy water all over. He had his story straight by now, and he couldn't wait to get inside, because he needed a few more drinks. Maybe he should have the others pay for them in exchange for telling his tale, which by now had far more details and information than even the investigators had managed to glean so far.

"I TELL ya, all those motherfucking foreigners are taking over this fucking place," she muttered, ignoring the facts that her own mother had been born in Germany and she hadn't a speck of Native American blood.

BBB waved her fat arm in the air, trying to get the bartender's attention for a refill. The weather-beaten old man calmly walked over to her and filled up her glass without saying a word. From the speakers came the sound of country music. "They need to build that wall the Pres'dent promised, dammit, and they need to do it in a hurry. Goddamn invasion is what it is," she muttered. "Shoulda done it two hunnert years ago."

BBB looked around the dingy barroom at a dozen or so onlookers, who stood by the bar a bit away from her or sat in chairs next to small, round tables. The establishment reminded her of a scene taken from an old Western movie, with the exception of the more modern clothes on the guests. Four men completely ignored her while playing poker, using matches for wagers in the event the long arm of the law popped up; they would be transformed into dollar bills in the men's room later on. When she saw the poker players, she became furious and cursed loudly. One of the players raised his hand and shot her the bird. BBB's eyes widened, and she struggled her way off the bar stool. "I'ma whip your ass, you disrespectful fucker!"

She stopped dead in her tracks when the man slid his jacket open, revealing the butt of a large revolver tucked into the waistband of his pants. He never moved his head an inch; the only thing that really concerned him was the game.

"Yeah, well, you're probably a fuckin' Muslim too, faggot!"

She crawled back onto her barstool, gesturing to the bartender for a fill up. Somehow her damn glass had gotten empty again. The shut opened suddenly, letting a cold, wet wind inside, while outside the rain came down hard and the storm thundered away. Mike Hudson, pale as a corpse—due to proper hydration, no doubt—charged to the bar shouting for a bourbon and a beer. He took one shot after another, and downed several beers in just a few minutes. He drank like a champ, like he wanted to impress everyone.

"Boy oh boy do I have news you gonna wanna hear," he shouted after a while, "but first I need another drink. BARTENDER!"

The bartender walked over to Mike with another beer, maintaining a neutral expression.

BBB replied, "Yeah, well, with the new pres'dent in office there's gonna be some changes, mark my words! Enough of all them foreign students comin' here and behaving like they know it all, I'm glad he won the fucking election, YOU HEAR ME, YA BASTARDS?"

An older man with a white mustache and beard and bloodshot eyes turned to BBB. "The president never won that election, you know."

BBB's eyes grew large, "You fuckin' stupid old man, if he didn't win, then what the fuck's he doing as the motherfucking president, you fucking inbreed!" She slammed her glass down hard, ordering another drink and cursing some more.

"He didn't win 'cause what happened was that all the professional politicians lost, people being tired of all their bullshit. Hell, Big Beatrice Butt-Slammer or whatever you call yourself, if you'd run for office, you'd a been elected too."

People laughed at what the old man said while BBB was thinking hard—too hard. She knew he had said something good...she thought. All her brain cells were completely immobile and miswired by this late in the day. So she just smiled and thought out loud, smiling like an idiot, dreaming as she looked up at the ceiling, "Me as president!"

Someone shouted, "Hey, can you turn it up?"

The bartender walked over to the stereo controls on the wall and turned up the volume. There was a jukebox in the establishment, and he would turn it on later when there were more customers, so they could spend their money. He walked away, cleaning a glass with a dirty rag.

The country music echoed a little bit louder from the speakers, and BBB liked the rhythm.

"Man, this is some good shit, I tell you, this is some music with culture and shit. Man, I never heard this one before, who the fuck is it, and don't tell me it's that Miley horn-bitch Cyrus…I ain't stupid, because I can hear it's a real manly man singing. Well, bartender, who the fuck is it?"

The bartender just shrugged, and then someone shouted, "It's Miley Cyrus after her operation! She's a man now, Big Beatrice Buttfucker."

The room exploded with laughter, and even the somber bartender smiled.

"Fuck you, faggot, may a Muslim shove his dick up your ass!"

"You should know."

More laughter. BBB was furious, and was ready to kick some serious ass again. She got up from her seat a little too quick, and wobbled around, looking for the bar for support; eventually, she hit the floor hard.

Even more laughter from everyone but for Mike, because he was too mad—the fat bitch had upstaged him! He knew better than to interrupt BBB; after all, the late Little Noise was one of her lovers…and then his face lit up.

An older biker walked over to BBB and helped her to her feet. She reached to his chest and she looked up, smiling something horrible at him. The biker gave her a mischievous smile and said, "The name of the singer is Simon Andersson."

"Never hear of the fella, but he's good. So why don't a stud like you get me another drink and tell me some more."

The old biker leaned over the bar, grabbed a bottle, and poured up two glasses. BBB did everything she could to smile at the gentleman who had helped her from the dirty floor.

"The name of the song is *Crazy*."

"I like crazy. Now, that's some good name on a song."

The biker smiled winked one eye at BBB and said, "And he's from Sweden."

BBB's eyes grew big while she took in the information. At first she only sputtered, and then she exploded. "Didn't I tell you all that we're being invaded? Shit and fuck, that's it! Now the foreigners are stealing our fucking music too? They better start building a fucking wall in New York too, bet that's were all them fucker are invadin'!"

More laughter, but one of the patrons shouted back at BBB from a table in a corner of the room, "BBB, be careful stepping on the Scandinavians, because half of this town has relatives from there."

BBB turned around in her seat while the biker, laughing, walked over to some friends. She stared at the man in the corner. "Fuck you! They should build a wall around you too."

She then turned around, and facing her was a younger bartender from India, wearing a turban, his white teeth sparkling as they contrasted against his dark skin. With that odd but still beautiful accent, he addressed BBB: "Perhaps my lady would like to slow down on her drinking for a while."

BBB could not believe her eyes, "What the --! What fucking bottle did you pop up from, genie?"

More laughter in the background, and Mike Hudson realized he just had to wait his turn.

"Oh ho, that is very funny. I am Akash, the new bartender. Old Joe over there needed some extra help, so…"

"Joe, you fuckin' traitor, you got yourself a fuckin' Muslim here?"

"Actually, ma'am, I am a Hindu, and…"

"Fuck! You're what I tell you you are, terrorist!"

"ENOUGH, BBB!"

She turned towards the bartender, and she knew that he only gave one warning; but she was still thirsty, and by now a bit drunk. She decided to retreat into the ladies' room; she was there for quite some time, being in no hurry. She realized after a while that the music had stopped, and there was silence. When she finally emerged from the ladies' room she walked back to the bar, but there was a near-complete silence, as everyone listened intently to Mike Hudson. Even the poker players had stopped playing, and now leaned over their chairs, listening.

"So that's what happened. I saw it all, man. It's a bloody mess, I tell you."

The old biker said, "You sure it was Little Noise?"

BBB sobered up a bit when she heard the name.

"Sure as I'm standing here. His head was gone, but I recognized them tattoos of his…and the Sheriff, he knew. They all knew. Noise was murdered, and it was bad."

A sudden shriek from BBB made everyone turn around as she hit the floor in a dead faint.

CARLOS WENT in through the back, feeling very tired. A major car accident and a homicide, Diego in critical condition, and the weather still wasn't letting up. He was quiet as he walked up the stairs, avoiding his colleagues as the evening shift was gearing up. He opened the first door, and saw the standard envelope containing the day's events on Ruth's desk. He opened the envelope and eyed the few notes and phone messages. The last was a call from Malik. He walked into his office and was reaching for the desk phone when the intercom in his office came to life. It was the night shift receptionist, Manny.

"Sir, we have an urgent call from the Last Post."

"We'll have one of our patrols go by there and break up the fight or whatever it is."

"There have been gunshots, sir."

CARLOS PULLED in right after Adrianna; Lucy's car was already parked outside with lights flashing. He listened to the radio as Lucy asked for paramedics and a K-9 unit. The rain poured down, and once in a while the lightning lit up the entire region, followed by booming thunder. He could distinctly hear gunshots from the back of the building, and he wished Diego could've been there. Well, time to see what Adrianna was made of.

"Your orders, sir?" she asked now.

"Cover my back."

Both drew their guns and headed inside. There were a few people there, all looking scared and talking nervously. Nothing they said made any sense.

Someone asked, "Is it true about a grizzly killing Noise and eating his head?"

Carlos stopped in his tracks and turned towards the voice; he didn't recognize the man who had asked, but he did, however, recognize the person standing behind him trying to hide: Mike Hudson. He gave Mike a withering glare, but he had more urgent business for now. *Great. Before breakfast, everyone will know about the murder.*

Adrianna and Carlos headed to the back entrance; outside were a few overturned garbage bins, with their content stinking up the alley. Carlos was grateful that there was a patio cover keeping the rain off. The backyard behind the bar had a porch with a tall wooden fence built around it. There was a large entrance there made up of two gates for delivery trucks; both were wide open. The rear parking for the employees was outside the fence. On the ground lay the fat woman everyone called BBB, bleeding; a few patrons leaned over her, trying to help. A new kid he didn't recognize, wearing a turban, held her head tenderly in his lap; there was blood splashed on his white apron and headdress. A number of people were talking at the same time, their conversation a confusing babble. Next to BBB stood old Joe, the bartender; he was trying to calm down the guy with the turban.

"I believe you, Akash, all right? Now relax. That's why we have an enclosure—we don't want any animals going through the garbage, like bears and such. Must have broken open the old gate somehow in search for food."

"But it is my fault! I left her here!"

"Stop it. If there's anyone to blame, it's me, I should have gotten her a goddamn cab and sent her home, all right? But I didn't. You only followed my orders to bring her out her so she could sober up some. Got tired of hearing her shit on you, Akash."

Carlos listened, and painted a quick picture of what had happened. The bear reported earlier this day had probably looked for food, gotten in, and attacked. He relaxed some, hoping that was the scenario; but when he kneeled down and looked at BBB, he could smell the same fetid odor as he had earlier that day, and at the Harris site.

A hidden memory from his past flashed through his mind, but he didn't understand it.

Shaken, Carlos turned on his radio. "Lucy, report."

"I'm behind the parking lot by the edge of the woods, Chief. Got a little problem with some gun-happy locals."

Carlos glanced at Joe and the young man still holding BBB. In a quiet but sympathetic voice, he said, "You can let her go now, son, she's dead. Joe, gather up inside everyone, and make sure no one leaves."

Joey nodded to Carlos, and then he led Akash, still upset and trembling, back inside.

Carlos joined Lucy and several armed customers from the bar, who were surveying the area beyond the back lot. None of the customers tried to conceal their weapons; he ignored the scofflaws for now, but he did memorize them, and he knew them all. Everyone just stared in the direction of the tree line on the hill above the lot.

What really caught his attention and set his blood to boiling was a man leaning over two pit bulls, whipping them with a leash while cursing them. The dogs just lay there, whining, refusing to move. He grabbed the man's wrist from behind and yanked it down hard, still keeping his eyes on the two dogs in the event they decided to attack him. He quickly subdued the man and Lucy had her cuffs on him in an instant.

"Don't move, motherfucker!" said a clear, high voice.

He turned around and saw a large biker with a bowie knife standing right behind him; next to him stood Adrianna, with her pistol's barrel at his ear. She got him on his knees and cuffed him too, finished with a kick to the man's back that sent him face-first to the ground. Lucy nodded and did the same thing with the other guy. *Not bad,* Carlos thought, winking at her.

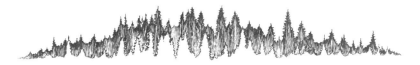

TEN

"You look concerned, Frank."

Frank smiled back at Christina as he turned off his cell phone. "I have to take a raincheck on that coffee, ma'am, the Sheriff needs my help. You're sure you'll be fine by yourself?"

"I'm a big girl."

He smiled agreeing, "Yep, that you are. Any plans on how you're going to get around?"

"I planned on going shopping for a nice pickup truck on Monday or Tuesday, and I still have a lot of food you guys sent me, so I'll be okay till then."

"Let me know your plans, and if you need any help getting around in the meantime."

"Sounds like a plan."

An exhausted Christina answered Frank's goodbye by the closed gate before he got into his truck and drove away. She had hoped Robert would drive her home, but he had to stay at the accident site and do some clean-up work. She hadn't even had time to say goodbye to him.

She kicked off her sneakers and walked upstairs, straight into the master bathroom, and let her dirty clothes fall to the floor. While she was in town, she'd have to pick up a basket for dirty laundry, she thought. The floor would do for now, though. She turned on the shower, and soon a foggy steam filled the room, and damp mist covered the windows. She really had to struggle to get that sticky green—by now, black—sap from her face and arms, but at least she had a rough loofah to work with. Reluctantly, she stopped after a while; she wasn't going to get everything cleaned off right now anyway, and besides, even though she was tired, she was starving even more. She'd been up for well over twelve hours, and all she'd had was her meager breakfast, and then a long workout on top of that. Someone had brought the rescue workers some sandwiches and coffee, but she had missed that, because she'd been playing the part of a living piñata during that time. *Nothing like soda and popcorn while being entertained,* she thought wryly.

After drying off with one of the fluffy towels in the bathroom cabinet, she put on a pair of sweatpants, a sweatshirt, and socks. She kept the towel wrapped around her head as she walked downstairs to the kitchen. Her stomach reminded her that she needed to hurry. She opened the fridge and looked at a large pot with a sticker on it labeled *Hunter Stew.* She removed the lid, and a savory aroma rose from the contents. She took a spoon and stirred it a bit; it consisted of thick brown gravy, meats of different kinds, carrots, potatoes, onions, and some other stuff she couldn't identify.

Christina found a deep plate and scooped some of the stew into it, then put the plate in the microwave for a few minutes. While her food heated, steamed, and popped, she took some *pain riche* and grilled it in the oven. She then grabbed a bottle of Chianti Rosso—the one with the basket, a cheap but tasty wine. While the food was warming, she walked to one of the walls and pushed what looked like a small wooden peg. A hatch opened, revealing a state-of-the-art stereo system. Her previous boyfriend had one just like it, so she knew how to work it. She scrolled through several lists of songs and albums of purchased music, and was glad that there were many she liked. She wanted to listen to something calm and soothing. Debussy's *Clair de Lune* was a nice start for the evening.

She wished she had a candle or two, and placed them on her mental "to buy" list. After retrieving her edibles, Christina sat down at the kitchen table, which provided a beautiful view of the outdoors. The storm had not yet abated, and the lightning display was awesome in the far distance as it raced from cloud-to-cloud, occasionally stabbing down to the Earth. Where she was, there was only strong wind and rain. She knew that having the lights on wasn't the way to go when there was lightning, but she figured it was far away; and if it got closer, she would turn hers off.

She ate not one but two plates of the tasty stew, and drank half the wine. She was still thirsty after supper, so she had a large glass of water. She didn't feel tired, strangely enough, so she walked over to the huge fireplace and started a nice fire. She took the rest of the wine and what was left of the bread, and lay down on a huge couch. She stripped off her socks and pulled down a blanket from the back of the couch, and half sat and half laid there very comfortably, listening to the classical music in the background, nibbling the bread while sipping her wine. Yep, she was getting a bit tipsy.

"What a Saturday night... all alone in the most romantic place on the planet. No, wrong," she corrected herself, "it's not the place, it's the person you're with that makes it romantic."

She sighed. She knew the wine could have a depressive effect and put her to sleep if she wasn't careful. Even though she felt exhausted from the rescue effort, her mind was alert, and she wasn't tired, having gained new strength after her meal. But she didn't want to be, or at least to *feel*, alone right now. Being alone was something she was very used to because of her profession, so she decided to call and bother her best friend, Tammy.

She ran upstairs and got her phone, returned to her place in front of the fire, and called, letting heat from the fireplace warm her feet. On her second try, a cheerful voice demanded, "WHAT!"

"If you're on top of him right now, call back when you're finished," Christina replied.

"Christina, what a nice surprise! And no, I'm not doing that anymore. Not at the moment."

Christina knew that there would be the usual warm-up chat about something that was taboo, because they didn't speak with each other as often as they used to. "Anymore? What you're doing then?"

"Surfing. Well, I just got back, and I'm supposed to have a blind date tonight, so I was going to get ready for that. Though to be perfectly honest, I'll rather be on top of a wave than a guy right now."

"Wait a minute, what about Mark?"

"I gave him the pink slip. Got too controlling—and I guess some guys have problem when their girlfriend is more successful than they are. Puts a dent in their pride. Besides, I never got over the feeling that he used me to get closer to you…you know, like half my exes."

Christina sighed, "Sorry. Guess it's the price you pay for knowing me." She felt sad, because she had lost most of her girlfriends for that very reason.

"No, I'm the one who should be sorry. I apologize for bringing it up, should never have mentioned it. It came out wrong."

Christina decided to brush it off. "And here I thought you two had the perfect relationship."

"Look who's talking. You, on the other hand, really seemed to have had one."

"Yeah, well, he left me when his star rose over mine, go figure, and now he's with a much more famous star…a blonde one." Christina sounded sarcastic.

"Hey! No blonde jokes. You seem a bit down… hang on, I gotta make a quick call."

After a couple of minutes, Tammy returned.

"And so that date's over, fired his ass too."

"You didn't have to do that. Who was he?"

"I wanted to, and I have no idea who it was. Called the person who set it up and told her I had more important things to do. Besides, when a sister sounds down, then I'd rather cheer her up."

"Thank you. How's your work?"

"My what…? If you're going to ask me about that, then we might as well talk about the weather. Work is going very well…wait a minute, is that classical music in the background? Let me guess: you started off with Debussy. Yeah, you definitely need to get some."

"That obvious, huh?"

"I know you like I know my vibrators, girl."

They laughed.

"Just grab the one I got you for your last birthday, when Prince Charming left for that long film production that eventually led to you guys' demise."

"Are you kidding? Bring that thing with me on the plane and get embarrassed again? No thank you. Been there, done that."

"Ha, you mean what happened in Canada?"

"No, before. The one that happened during the security check at the airport in L.A."

"Fucking bastard had to hold *it* up so everyone could see!"

"Yeah, he wasn't a fan, I bet."

"Use a fucking cucumber."

"All out. Got hungry and ate them all."

There was a brief silence.

"You've met someone, haven't you?"

Again there was a brief and awkward silence between them, before Christina said slowly, "I don't know yet."

"What do you mean, you don't know yet? You either have or you haven't!"

"It's complicated."

"It's always complicated with you. Get on your knees and uncomplicate the fucker!"

Christina couldn't help laughing at Tammy, knowing her friend was the best, and a bit crazy, while being outspoken like no one else she knew. That's why she loved her: she was so very honest.

"So, do you like the place?"

"I love it."

"Good, I can hear it in your voice. Hate to see you move, though."

"What are you talking about? Ever since your promotion a year back, you've lived in San Diego!"

"Yeah, but still. We should see each other more often."

"You're welcome anytime."

"That does it! I'll check my schedule on Monday and then I'll call you back, but it might be a week before I can go. How's that, and will you survive without me till then?"

"I'm sure I will. Besides, I need to get settled in before I have any visitors. You'll love it here. Anna would have loved it, too."

Both were silent for a while, then: "Life isn't fair."

"You got that one right, Tammy. Sorry for mentioning it."

"Don't be, she'll always be part of us. Remember the three hottest beach *señoritas*? That was what we were. So you love it there, huh? Is it a nice place?"

"Yeah, but that's not what I was referring to."

"Then what? ...fucking nature?"

"The male species. Seems most of the men I meet here are giants, very tall and strong. Not sure what the heck their mothers fed them, but it sure did the trick."

"Yeah, well, do they have any brains? Nah, never mind, don't answer that. No man on this planet has one anyway. Not above the waist."

"Be nice."

"*Now* I know why you want to live in the deep, dark forest. You're on the prowl, chasing your own big sexy lumberjack, aren't you? So you'll have your own boy-toy to ravish now and then."

"In your dreams."

"Well, yeah. I'll get up there and visit you as soon as I can, and don't you worry about your lack of vibrators. I'll get you a new inventory, because I don't give a shit about airport security. If anyone tries to embarrass my ass, I'll fucking show them how to use the little fuckers, right there in front of everyone, and then we'll see who's fucking embarrassed. Fucking men!"

"And what if it's a woman?"

"I'll show her too!"

"Didn't know you liked that."

"You're telling me you've never done it with a woman before?"

"Nope, never."

"Huh. Should I give you a couple of titles of the *movies* you've been in?"

"Not fair. That doesn't count. Wasn't real."

"Come to think of it, after all these years we've known each other, we never talked about that."

"Because we're straight. Well, *you* might be a little confused."

"Maybe I'll do you, then."

"Or I'll do you."

"Money talks, bullshit walks. Yeah, well, let's shut up about that, or I'll regret not going on that date."

"You might still have time."

In a more serious voice Tammy said, "No, I *don't* have the time, because you need my time, and I also need yours."

They talked for another hour about more serious topics, until suddenly Christina felt as if a shadow fell over her; and with it, she became very sleepy. They said goodbye to each other, swearing holy oaths that all men were pigs and that they would start their own nunnery soon, and so on. Or at least a male brothel.

When the conversation was over, Christina checked the fireplace; there were only a few embers and ashes left. She secured the glass cover over it, and left the wine glass, bottle, and the plate with the leftover bread on the nicely carved table in the family room, being too tired (or lazy) to clean it up right then. Her bed was calling her name. She staggered upstairs, checked a security monitor, and then crawled into the bed and got under the blankets. Moments later, she was dreaming of Robert.

ELEVEN

Frank parked in the back of the store and went inside, where Claire meet him with a friendly smile. Nugget and Hunter rushed Frank, demanding his attention; and when he embraced Claire, both barked and tried to push him away. "I never got them to stop doing that," he said regretfully.

"Too bad we can never dance when they're around, they probably think we're hurting each other," Claire joked, and then she continued, handing Frank a plastic bag, "I made you a couple of ham and cheese sandwiches and some fresh coffee, and if you're back in time we'll have the chicken pot pie."

"Where's Winston?"

"Where do you think he is? He's in the kitchen guarding the pie."

Frank leaned over the kitchen counter, and there sat Winston, staring into the oven, very focused. "Hey, boy."

Winston turned his head and barked loudly. *Get away from my pie, human.*

Claire and Frank shook their heads, used to the old dog, but at the same time still amused by his behavior and odd habits. "That one you never managed to train."

"And I'm glad I didn't. Some animals just have too much personality."

"Will you take Hunter, too?"

Frank looked at Hunter, who looked back expectantly.

"No, I want him here with you."

"But I have Winston."

"Please."

He gave his wife a peck on the cheek. Hunter looked less happy, and lay down where he had stood, whining some. Frank turned around and said, "Protect," pointing at Claire, and suddenly Hunter got up on his feet, having received an order. "That should keep him happy for a while."

"I was going to take the dogs out for a walk…well, not Winston."

"Please don't take Hunter for a walk. Stay in the house. We might have a grizzly loose, like I told you on the phone."

"But it's so unusual to have any bears near town."

"I know. Must've been, what? Ten years now?"

Frank opened the passenger door on his king cab truck, and Nugget jumped in easily. By the time he seated himself in the driver's seat, Nugget was already sitting in the passenger seat, staring dead ahead, pretending Frank wasn't there. "Haven't got control over you either, huh? Bad influence, that Winston fella."

Frank waved at Claire, who stood in the kitchen window waving back at him. He took a pickle and chowed down, and his stomach let out a purr. He opened the bag with the sandwiches, took one out, and closed the bag. He took two big bites, then placed the sandwich on the console in the center of the bench seat, poured some fresh coffee into a cup, took a few sips, and placed the cup in a holder. Then he got the truck in gear and slowly drove away. Frank turned and made one last wave to his wife as he pulled out. He reached for his sandwich…but of course, nothing was there. He quickly and angrily turned his head towards Nugget, who pretended to ignore him while staring dead ahead, licking his lips. Frank saw a few bread crumbs on Nugget's mustache, and then he had to laugh at his own stupidity and pat Nugget on his head. You can't trust a dog with your food.

He arrived at the crime scene, and parked his truck a bit away from the rest of the vehicles. First that nasty accident, now this… There was a large crowd of people standing in the rain. Flashing lights from an ambulance and several patrol cars and SUVs lit the area. Some white flashes came from behind the bar: crime scene photos, no doubt.

He was greeted by Carlos. "Thanks for coming. Didn't know who else to call."

"Whitney not around with his dog?"

"Oh, Whitney and that dog of his are here, all right…but, well, come and see for yourself. Not bringing Nugget?"

"Not yet, I want to look at the scene first—where the vic is, and so on. I want to avoid as many smells for Nugget as possible before I let him out."

Carlos led Frank behind the building, towards the brow of the hillside below where it met the tree line. Several uniformed officers and a few civilians were there. Two pit bulls lay on the ground, whining loudly and acting very nervous. A man in handcuffs stood there trying to talk to them, an attractive young police woman next to him, frowning deeply. Officer Whitney was trying to calm his German Shepherd, Tango, but his dog also lay on the ground whining. The entire scene seemed absurd, and a bit strange to Frank. "Give me quick summary, Carlos?"

"We think someone might have forgotten to close the back gates, and a bear got inside the fence. The bartender, Joe Halls, had one of the guests kicked out in the back—there's a kind of rest area there with a bench under a porch roof."

"Why would he send out someone there?"

"For the person to sober up, I guess. But in this case, it was Beatrice Mayhaw—you know her?—and she became hysterical when she heard about the death of Noise Clement…you know him, right?"

Frank's eyes widened. "Yeah, who hasn't heard about him and BBB? When did Little Noise die?"

"Guess you haven't heard, but since the cat's out of the bag, I might as well fill you in. My colleagues and I were on our way to the Harris logging site to investigate a report of a dead body when we got involved in the accident where you and that Hollywood star helped us out."

"Was it a bear that killed Noise?"

"Dunno. From the markings, it could very well be, but there's a catch. Someone neatly sliced off his head."

"And you still know it was Noise."

"His size and his tats were confirmed by two witnesses, so yeah, I'm pretty sure it was him. Anyway, Joe had one of his employees take BBB outside so she could get some fresh air and calm down. He left her outside crying, and after a while they heard a horrible scream and the sounds of fighting. They got out here and found BBB bleeding from the neck. Something tore her up but good. Someone claims they saw the back of a bear heading up here into the forest. "There's some type of stink on BBB and on Noise; not sure what it is."

Frank just nodded sadly, staring into the deep dark woods. He felt like something was staring back. "Hell of a note. To be perfectly honest with you, Carlos, if it was a bear, then it's probably long gone, scared away by all the commotion."

"You're right, but what if it *wasn't* a bear?"

"Don't worry. If there's a track, we'll find it."

"Any thoughts about that?" Carlos pointed at the three terrified dogs lying on the ground whining.

"I have no idea what that's all about. Normally those types of dogs would have charged after any animal. It's in their nature, and from the looks of it…is that the owner of the pit bulls?" Frank pointed at the cuffed civilian.

"Yep, he tried to hunt whatever attacked BBB."

"I normally don't judge a person, but something tells me he shouldn't have dogs."

"Right on."

Frank and Carlos went back to his truck, and Frank got Nugget out and put him on a thirty-foot red leash. Nugget was as calm as day, breathing normally with his tongue hanging out.

"You packing?" Carlos asked.

Frank patted the side of his shirt, and lifted the hem, revealing a large revolver in a brown holster. "Need to see my license?"

Carlos shook his head. "Got my own copy of it in my office."

Frank rolled up the long leash, and then headed to where the other dogs were; and just before he reached them, Nugget froze. Inside Nugget's mind, something that had always lain hidden, perhaps a dormant gene somewhere, awakened. Nugget didn't know what it was, but it was something that this particular dog breed had been trained and taught to recognize for hundreds of years: this specific scent. At the first whiff of it, Nugget didn't understand what it was or what was happening, so he stopped. The smell was wrong; and suddenly that hidden little gene that had awakened sent to his brain the signal Nugget needed: the ultimate hunt was on.

The hunt for a lion.

Nugget went ballistic. Frank, who had been holding the line somewhat loosely, reacted too slowly; but the line was attached to his belt. Unlike the other dogs, who were still lying on the ground whining, Nugget was invigorated. The hair on his back stood straight up; he barked extremely aggressively, and when the line attached to his collar forced him to come to a sudden halt, he went even madder, trying to get it off him. Nugget jumped, growled, and barked like he never had before. With a new alpha in place, the natural instincts of the other dogs took over, and suddenly they, too, went mad. Someone had forgotten to put a leash on the pit bulls, and they flew into the forest. The German Shepherd also somehow got loose, and it too ran into the woods, barking in the wake of the silent pits.

"Oh no," Frank moaned, lying on the ground, watching Nugget taking off with the long line dragging behind him. He looked at the attachment to his belt; the metal had broken. "Crap material," he snarled, then got on his feet and took off after the dogs. Behind him, the people watching let out a cheer, and soon many of them were following as well; and some idiot fired off a few rounds into the air.

The hunt was on.

BY THEN, the beast was far from the crime scene, feeling good about himself, having taken care of the second witness. No one must know of his existence. He wasn't sure if the fat bitch had actually seen him the other night, but she had sure enough nailed him with a couple of pellets from the shotgun.

Two-leggeds are lesser beings, and should all die, he thought fiercely. They were ruining Mother Earth, and he was her guardian.

But he had underestimated the local law enforcement. They had been more alert than he expected. He was miles away from the killing ground, but he had to stop now. Far down on the road was a police vehicle with the lights turned off. It had gotten there just as he had, about half an hour after the last kill. The beast had first waited for the vehicle to move on, but it idled there. He followed the tree line and a long curve on the road away from the car, and came to another intersection—and there was another vehicle, this one clearly a Highway Patrol car. Both cars had the road covered, though neither was in the line of sight of the other. Still, not good. This was no highway here, just a small forest road, so this made no sense. Well he was patient, and he could wait; two-leggeds were the direct opposite, and eventually they would leave. He lay there for a while, observing the officer who sat in the car.

Suddenly the beast heard the barking of dogs in the far distance; it came from the direction of the killing ground. He must move, but what animal would dare to challenge him? His odor was formulated to discourage any beast on land, a potion that had taken ages to develop. Something wasn't right, and the beast felt uneasy. The barking grew closer, but the beast more or less ignored it because he was the ultimate killer, handcrafted by Mother Nature. He would rather not kill an animal, but would if or when he felt threatened. He made a decision: another two-legged must die, but then he must lay low for a while. The consequences of killing a uniformed two-legged should not be underestimated. He was far too clever and would, if he could, avoid any more kills or detection for now. After all, he still had the primary prey to deal with.

"ANYTHING, D'LANCY?" Ethan Jones's voiced crackled over the radio.

"Nothing, sir, but should we really be here?"

"Do as you're told, Officer."

"Yessir, but I need to remind you that my shift ended almost two hours ago."

"Yeah, but you're still getting paid, aren't you?"

"Yessir."

"Keep it tight, girl, we'll be replaced soon."

"But why are we parking here?"

"Because I helped Carlos in the past, chasing some troublemakers from the same bar, and they ran into this forest and came out on this road. As of a matter of fact, I ran one of those bastards over with my car." Ethan Jones laughed as he turned off the microphone, thinking back on the event.

Over the radio came Carlos da Silva's voice. "Ethan, you still parked on the northern path?"

"Sure am."

"Good, the hunt is finally on. The dogs are on their way. Make sure you don't shoot any of them—or run any over."

"Roger." Jones hung up the microphone, cursing Carlos. "What the fuck, does that sand wasp think I'm a fucking amateur?" He picked up the microphone again. "You get that, D'Lancy?"

"Roger, sir."

"Good. Lock and load."

"That's a copy, sir."

Ethan Jones stepped out of his car, lighting a thin, long cigar. The rain was still pouring down heavily, but his big hat brim covered his precious cancer stick. He opened the trunk and removed the cover on a sniper rifle, then loaded it with four rounds and waited. Despite his personal character, or lack thereof, he was an excellent officer, fearless and law-abiding. He wasn't afraid or the least concerned; to him, this would be just another check-mark on his perfect record.

Ethan cursed aloud as the fog started rolling in. It was thick.

D'LANCY BUTTONED her raincoat and then paused for a bit, thinking of having to go outside in the rain. It was still warm out there, and she would start sweating in minutes. She unlocked the shotgun between the driver and passenger seats, and checked to make sure it was loaded. When she stepped out of the car, she could hear the barking of the dogs and instantly went on high alert, waiting patiently and watching for any sign of the bear crossing the road.

THE BEAST smiled. Mother had heard his prayer; the fog had rolled in just as he had asked, and it was getting thicker and thicker. He had made his decision, and had worked out a plan to get rid of the dogs without hurting them—poor fellow beasts under the slave yoke of the two-legged as they were. But it came with a price. He observed the next kill, and decided to go for it. The two-legged stood by the car, waiting for him.

JONES LAY over the car, using the hood as support for his rifle. Once in a while, he looked through the scope. The small dot was luminous and enhanced the sights, even though it was dark and foggy. Then he looked down the road, not using the scope, wanting to have a wider view on his surroundings. The barking was very close now; he could hear branches breaking in the forest, and he got ready to fire.

"Hurry! Over here!" someone shouted.

Light from many flashlights splashed through the fog like search-lights from a science fiction film, as distant men shouted and cursed in the forest. All the dogs were far ahead of them, barking loudly now that they had a fearless leader.

A shot rang out, the deep-throated roar of a shotgun, and it made most of the followers stop; but not the dogs, who sensed that their prey was near. The hunt escalated, and everyone turned in the direction of the shot. A moment later came the horrible sound of dogs attacking someone.

"They're on something!" Carlos shouted, encouraging the hunters onward.

Lights from a police vehicle became visible from the narrow dirt road, and then there were more gunshots. Carlos emerged from the woods first, followed by Frank; behind them came the rest. On the ground lay a Highway Patrol officer being literally eaten by the two pit bulls, both going for her neck. Carlos had no choice: he pulled his pistol and fired his weapon twice, killing the dogs.

On the ground lay D'Lancy; next to her was a shotgun and a smoking shell casing. Her throat and neck had been ripped open, and blood pooled on the ground. Further down the road, another Highway Patrol car lay in the ditch, lights flashing. Wordlessly, an officer hurried to D'Lancy's body and crouched over her, opening a first aid kit.

Carlos shook his head and made the call everyone in law enforcement dreads: "Officer down," he screamed into his walkie-talkie. He calmed himself. "Ethan, you there?"

After what seemed a long time, a heavily-breathing Ethan Jones responded over the radio. "Heard a shot from D'Lancy's position…hurried over, saw something, probably a bear…hit the fucker in the ditch with my car. Pursuing the animal and following the dogs, hurry."

Carlos said out loud to himself, "Poor fool don't even know about D'Lancy." He looked to the old man with him. "Frank, why would the pits attack her?"

"They wouldn't, normally, not if they were on something. We couldn't make them stop because none of us were the dogs' master."

"What about Nugget and Tango, why didn't they attack?"

"Nugget is on the primary target, and will stay on that trail until caught. He and Tango are much faster and more sustained than the pit bulls. The pits probably fell behind. Not sure why they attacked D'Lancy…hang on, let me check on something."

He stopped and returned to the Highway Patrol car. He leaned down and sniffed the air. "Hey, Carlos, she's got that stink on her, on her neck I guess…what's left of it."

The officer attending D'Lancy had given up on her. She was dead. There was no way to patch up the wounds she'd sustained, not in the field.

"Shit!" Carlos swore, heart sinking.

"You might want to get some of the scent from it, if it's even possible. Right now I'd like to go after my dog."

Carlos looked at Frank and Whitney, both of whom wanted to go after their dogs. He motioned for them to go on, and they ran hard in the direction of the barking.

The visibility was poor, and several times one of the men fell or got whipped in the face by tree branches. Frank's lungs hurt, but he didn't care, and pushed on.

Shouts and screams from the dogs fighting someone echoed in the forest. The sad sound of a dog yelping sharply in pain made Frank freeze; then he increased his speed, shouting "No, no, no!" over and over.

Another shot from a hunting rifle rang out, and there was more fighting, and another horrible scream from an injured dog. Frank knew it was Nugget, and that he was in danger. His tears poured down, but he didn't care. "Not again, not again!" he shouted.

They came upon a small recess in the terrain, and lying on the ground, whimpering, were Nugget and Tango. Both dogs were bleeding heavily, and when a devastated Frank kneeled next to Nugget, the big dog tried to raise his head while weakly wagging his tail.

He licked Frank's hand, and then Nugget closed his eyes.

Next to a boulder lay Ethan Jones, trying to hold in his entrails with his hands, blood gushing out of his abdomen; next to him lay a broken rifle. He stuttered and moaned in shock; nothing he said made any sense. Whitney kneeled next to Tango's suddenly still, quiet body, while Frank remained next to Nugget. *"WHO DID THIS?"* Frank screamed to Ethan.

Ethan had blood pouring out of his mouth; and the last thing that came out of it before he sagged into stillness was, "A monster…"

Frank lost it, and dropped next to Nugget, crying; and after a moment, Whitney placed a strong hand on his shoulder. "Get up soldier, there's still time. We can take 'em to D&D, they live not far from here. YOU HEAR ME, FRANK? Don't you give up on them!"

Whitney saw Carlos running along the top of the ridge; he paused, and Whitney raised his hand in the direction he thought the bear had gone. Carlos looked down on the mess, but now he was hunting. He shouted to one of his deputies and the others coming up far behind, but he couldn't wait for them. He ran uphill and climbed up on a large rock. He looked over the entire region, holding his rifle ready. A lightning flash lit up the area, and roaring thunder followed. The fog had increased, but now he stood above it, focused on the ridge in the distance, hoping the bear hadn't made it that far yet.

Carlos saw the beast crawling on all four legs in the far distance on a rocky hill; it stopped and turned around, staring back at him. He raised his rifle, got the beast in his scope, and snapped off a round, not knowing if he had hit it or not. He lowered his rifle and looked again, but complete darkness lay like a thick blanket over the land. The rain hit his face hard. There was another flash of lightning, and now the beast was standing on its back legs in another location; to Carlos's surprise, it had moved closer to him. He looked through the scope and was just about to fire when a memory overwhelmed him, and then there was complete darkness again. Another lightning bolt, and this time the monster was gone—but Carlos's memory wasn't.

He had seen that thing before.

Whitney, a former Marine trained to never give up, forced Frank to his feet. Half a dozen men and a couple of women ran down the hill and stopped, looking wide-eyed at the carnage. Whitney ordered, "At least two of you see what you can do for Ethan; the rest assist Carlos, he's over that ridge," he pointed in Carlo's direction, "and tell him Frank and I are heading over to D&D's for help, now MOVE OUT!"

The rest of the hunting party that still dared follow Carlos joined him just after he had fired his rifle, and without any orders or target, all of them emptied their weapons down into the valley. Carlos just stood there, eyes distant, looking scared; but eventually he ordered the madness to stop. The smell of gunpowder lay thick in the fog.

Frank and Whitney scrambled to their feet, picked up their injured partners, and ran toward D&D's. With renewed strength from Whitney's words, Frank ran like a demon with Nugget, only one thought running through his mind: "Not again. Not again!"

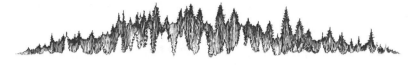

TWELVE

R ohan and Daniela were enjoying a romantic evening alone at last.
Both had been looking forward to spending some quality time together, which would ultimately land them both in awkward and strange
positions later on, for dessert.

They were the most unlikely couple in Skull Creek—or pretty
much anywhere, for that matter. She was a tall, slender Amazon from
South America, with a ravenous beauty that made most men behave
like love-struck idiots in her very presence. She looked more like a run-
way model than a professional physician. He, on the other hand, was
almost a head shorter and was from Sri Lanka—a stocky, short man
who almost always smiled. He was the local dentist. She had a gentle,
soft touch, while he was somewhat clumsy, but his charm was undeni-
able. Both had combined their Doctor and Dentist (D&D) practice in
the same building a mile outside of town, on the opposite side of a lake
deep in the forest. Their log home was rustic and beautiful, with a view
to die for.

Both loved the outdoors, and they had spent many wonderful
times vacationing near Skull Creek while still in school. They loved

camping, climbing in the mountains, and river rafting. Eventually, they had fallen for the place, and several years back had moved here. People were so very friendly, and they loved the environment. The county was pretty much crime-free, with the exception of the past two years, when business had really started booming with the forestry and gold-mining industry. But still, there hadn't been any major crimes. Some tourists had gotten lost and there had been some casualties from accidents, but that was nothing major compared to the big cities.

"So, dearest, are you ready for the perfect burgundy to match the perfect dinner made by your truly perfect husband?"

"Why of course, dear," Daniela purred. "I do look forward to enjoying all the courses you have planned for the evening, and I'm in no hurry whatsoever."

"You're not? But my dear, if you knew what I intend to do to you for dessert, you wouldn't have said that."

Rohan poured the wine very slowly, gently breathing down Daniela's neck. She closed her eyes and enjoyed herself. Then she bit her under lip when he carefully caressed her ear with his own lips, his hot breath raising goosebumps on her—causing him to spill the wine in excitement. Both laughed.

Facing each other, they raised their glasses. Both had been playing their little game for a very long time…too long, perhaps, edging and teasing each other, but work had kept coming between them; so neither had had that special smile on their faces for a while, and both were quite frustrated.

Rohan gave her his infamous charming smile, his mother-of-pearl teeth contrasting against his dark skin. She had an equally sparkling smile on her picture-perfect face, and her golden skin color enhanced her features.

"Cheers, my love." Silence followed, and a patient Rohan held his glass high, waiting for her to respond to his salute.

In the most innocent voice possible, Daniela responded by saying, "I'm not wearing panties."

Rohan's choked on the wine as he drank, and spewed it all over the table. She laughed uproariously, and then he charged her like an av-alanche, taking anything in his way with him. He tossed her onto the table, while tablecloth, candleholder—candle still burning—plates, and wine bottle hit the floor. She laughed even more as he fumbled with his zipper. He wasn't going to have any of that, so he flipped her over and slapped her butt. Daniele giggled like a naughty school girl, and she kept laughing while waiting patiently on her stomach for her clumsy husband, whose zipper got stuck, as he struggled until he finally man-aged to yank it open—

—just as someone knocked on the door.

The pounding on the door quickly grew persistent and harder. Both Rohan and Daniela started to curse, each in their native languag-es, while fixing their clothes. Meanwhile, someone outside shouted over the sounds of the storm, "Open up! Open up, for the love of God open up, Doc, please open up!"

When they opened the door, Frank Hancock charged inside, apol-ogizing almost incoherently. He was carrying a large, bleeding dog in his arms, and was followed by another man, apparently a police officer by his uniform, carrying another dog in even worse shape. "We're tru-ly sorry but the vet is on the other side of town and we knew you guys lived here and—"

"Relax, Frank what do you need?"

"Thank you, Rohan, can you or your wife help us with these poor dogs? They got tore up bad by a bear."

"We're not vets, but…"

"We know, but I don't think they have much time," Whitney shouted.

Daniela joined them in the hallway; at first she was going to pro-test, not because she had a mean streak but because she wasn't a veter-inarian. But when she saw the faces of two grown men with teary eyes and more tears pouring down their faces, she looked the dogs over and nodded her head in consent. "Kitchen, fast, and Rohan, get that plastic tablecloth, please."

Both of them operated on the dogs, helping each other as they went. They used the large kitchen island and the kitchen table as operating theatres. The table, which was made of wood, was stained by all the blood, and was probably ruined; but the kitchen island had the plastic cover on it.

When Daniela and Rohan had done what they could, they made the animals comfortable and spent a long time washing their hands in the kitchen sink. Both dogs lay sleeping soundly, though the rasping sound from their lungs didn't sound good. Whitney stood by Tango, gently touching his fury head, and Frank did the same with Nugget.

"They'll be out for a while from the anesthetic. Can we get you guys anything?"

"I'm fine, Daniela," said Frank.

"I'll have some water, please," Whitney said. "Will they make it?"

Daniela answered in a comfortable tone, making sure she didn't make any promises she couldn't keep. "Only time will tell. We did our best with what we had. They need to be X-rayed and have a professional vet check them over."

"What monster did this?" Rohan demanded.

Both Whitney and Frank looked up, and their expressions made Rohan regret even asking.

"You took the words right out of our mouths. Probably an injured bear that might have gotten hurt by some amateur hunter, who knows?" Whitney said in a low, whispering voice filled with rage. "Got ahold of two highway patrolmen, too. The EMTs are with them by now."

Both Rohan and Danielle knew his anger wasn't directed towards them.

"I don't know about you guys, but I'm going to put on some freshly grounded coffee, might toss in some stronger stuff too. Both of you need it; dentist orders," Rohan said.

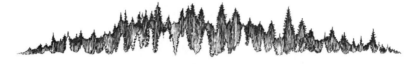

THIRTEEN

The car left a dust cloud behind as it drove away. An arm stretched out on the driver's side, waving good bye. The young boy cried, tears pouring down his face with his hands stretched towards the car; he struggled fiercely, but a strong hand held him back. Standing next to the young boy was an old woman, waving goodbye. The boy struggled and cried out louder, but then out of the blue there hung a nice, sweet chocolate bar in front of his nose. Instantly he smiled and looked up behind him at his grandfather, who smiled back at him. He had to reach for the candy bar a few times, but eventually had it in his own hands. He no longer cried, having completely forgotten about his parents having left him behind, like the traitors they were. Soon his face was covered in chocolate.

Flash.

The kids played in a small creek, while the adults prepared a fiesta on a hill above, next to a large tree. Some berries still attached to a branch floated by, and the little boy picked them up. He put one of the tempting red berries in his mouth. The other kids were splashing water. Everyone was laughing and screaming with happiness.

Flash.

The little boy cried and lay on his stomach, very ill. His grandfather comforted him, while his grandmother leaned over the child with a steaming cup. The grandfather helped him drink. The child closed his eyes and rested.

Flash.

There was music, dancing, laughter, people celebrating, sitting by several long tables eating and cheering. There was a large fire with many people dancing and celebrating around it. The many colorful decorations were lit up brightly, strung all over the place. Kids were chasing each other while grownups clapped their hands. The thunder of fireworks lit the dark, full-moon night, exploding in thousands of colors.

Flash.

Louder explosions, screams, shouts, fire, heat. Gunshots and more explosions.

Flash.

Scared, the little boy crawled out of bed. He moved slowly towards the door, opened it, and peeked outside. Still very frightened, he crouched and looked out carefully.

Flash.

His eyes grew larger and larger. People lay on the ground while houses burned; cars and trucks were ablaze, and some exploded as he watched. His grandmother ran towards him, screaming, waving her hands in the air. His grandfather fought something huge in the background. The boy was too afraid to go outside; he had to hide or run away, but from what?

Flash.

The entire village was engulfed in flames, and from them came a sick, radiating heat and a dense, nauseating smoke that made it difficult to see anything.

Flash.

A man with a rifle fired many times at something huge and hairy rushing him. Another man came up from behind with a revolver, firing at the beast, but it kept attacking. slaughtering the men.

Flash.

He slowly closed the door, and then peeked through the keyhole. His grandmother laid on the porch, and something huge and hairy leaned over her.

Flash.

A large black eye peered into the keyhole and met his.

Flash.

And there was an awful, horrifying stench.

Flash.

Carlos opened his eyes, but he couldn't move, paralyzed by fear. He held his breath for a long while before he managed to move his eyes from one side of the bedroom to the next. He saw his wife hugging her pillow, sleeping calmly, in her typical deep trance. He wanted to smile, but couldn't, because he knew that something was amiss. He turned his head slowly towards the closed bedroom door. He looked at it and re-laxed, and breathed out in relief as he closed his eyes.

The foul stench made his eyes fly open, and move towards the source of the smell. He looked at the keyhole on the bedroom door, and knew that something was looking back at him through it.

Flash.

CARLOS OPENED his eyes, his heart racing as he woke for real. He stared at the ceiling, soaked from having sweat so profusely. It took him a while before he could hear his wife's soft breathing. She had her back turned to him. Good; he hadn't woken her up this time. He slowly got up; the bedroom was dark. He stopped to sniff the air; nothing. He was no longer dreaming, thank the Lord. He touched his pillows and sheet; like him, they were soaking wet. He slowly looked up at the bedroom door and the keyhole, then walked over and opened the door gently, looking back at his wife, making sure he wasn't waking her up.

He trembled as he sneaked down the upstairs hallway, not want-ing to wake his family. He cursed to himself when he heard the wooden floor creak. He stopped several times, making sure everyone still was still asleep. When he reached the stairs, he had to hold onto the railing to make it all the way down. He walked to the guest bathroom, and turned on the light after he had closed the door. He then turned on the water and washed his face.

He didn't like what he saw in the mirror. He was worn out, and looked it. His eyes were bloodshot, and he thought he could hear his own heartbeat, it was pounding that hard. He turned off the light and headed to the basement door. He opened it slowly, and the hinges squeaked loudly, while the old wooden door made a creaking sound. Everything downstairs was very dark, and he fumbled carefully as he descended. Standing right by the staircase, Carlos waved one of his hands in the air until his palm brushed a long cord hanging down. He pulled it, and an old light bulb lit up.

He looked around at his family legacy: hundreds of boxes, with most of their contents forgotten. Many times he had planned to turn this place into a man cave, or something for the kids; his wife already had her own sewing room, so maybe once the kids had left the nest he'll make good on his dream.

He searched all over for a specific box, and after what seemed forever, having made many nice discoveries of missing items, he found what he was looking for. It was perhaps the oldest of all the boxes and crates lying around. He took a deep breath as he reached for it on a shelf. He looked it over and brushed off a lot of dust, which made him sneeze.

He moved some stuff away to make more room, and once he was satisfied, he sat down on an old barstool next to a joiner table. He opened the box—and when he looked inside, it felt like time had stood still.

He remembered vividly when he had opened it last and filled it with its contents. He had been a child then, very young. Inside were some toy soldiers, a few toy cars, and a kid's baseball cap, along with other stuff only a young child would treasure. Then there was the largest item, carefully wrapped in an old newspaper. He slowly removed the old yellowing newsprint, treating the package as if he were handling evidence from a crime scene.

He lifted out a very old child's safe. It had been blue, once, with a red number combination lock on the small safety door. Now it was rusty, with dents in it, and just a few flakes of blue paint left. It was a child's toy that no modern child would ever appreciate. He held it in his hands, and suddenly he started to tremble, and tears fell from his eyes.

"Now, son, we will place all your horrors in your own secret safe, and then you will lock the door. Only you have the combination, no one else. Once you have locked that door, all the horrors and monsters will vanish from your life forever."

"Now do as your father asks, and all will be well. You'll see."

His father's and mother's voices and images flashed in his mind.

He tried to remember the combination, and began spinning the dial. On the second try, he heard a *click*. Before he opened the little safe, he closed his eyes; and once he had gathered his strength, he slowly opened them. There were many folded papers laying neatly stacked inside. One shelf divided the safe in two.

He took out each document or newspaper clipping, one by one, and read them carefully. Anything with a picture he examined intently. The many different headlines from equally as many newspapers read differently, and the headlines flashed one by one. Some were written in Spanish, while a few were in English. *Drug War. Massacre. Slaughtered. Mass grave. No survivors. American witness. FBI. Special Agent Harvey Cole. Perez.*

Carlos looked again into the safe, and found a small, blue plastic bracelet, the kind you wear in the hospital as ID. It only had a number on it.

Words echoed in his mind from his past, a past he had kept long hidden. *"Can't let anyone know he survived…drug cartel might strike again… witness…since he can't testify, there is no need for him to be part of the investigation…we hope your son will get well soon. Good luck. He's witnessed something so horrific his imagination has taken over. Maybe in time he will forget, and then he'll be able to live a normal, productive life, but a trauma this big— who knows if he ever can get well? After all, there are no real monsters."*

It was a bitter Carlos who thought back that night, trying to remember everything, but there were too many bits and pieces missing. Just as he was about to put all the stuff back, he noticed something taped to the ceiling of the toy safe. It was a brown envelope. He carefully removed the envelope and slowly unfolded it, not wanting to ruin the contents; he had no memory whatsoever of placing this in his safe as a child. Maybe he hadn't.

Inside were Mexican and American reports from federal agencies. He eyed them carefully; they were barely legible after all this time. There was also a plastic cover with a faded yellow paper inside that had what seemed to be some greaseproof paper covering it. He saw a sticker, and guessed it was the work of a police artist. He guessed right; it was a portrait gathered from the testimony of a five-year-old boy about something that had happened more than half a century ago. He looked at its blank side; nothing there but the sticker, so he turned it over.

There. There it was.

The monster stared back at him, triggering more flashing images from hidden memories. Again he looked at image, and he remembered the foul odor that came with it. A long-forgotten event started to unfold in Carlos's mind. Parts of it made no sense, and he strained as he tried to remember more.

His wife found Carlos in the basement that morning, sitting there staring at the wall. She approached him, very concerned, and touched him gently on his shoulder. He slowly responded to her call and touch. When he turned towards her, she froze; a cold chill went down her spine when she saw his face. She didn't understand why, but suddenly she was afraid, very afraid.

Carlos smiled tiredly at his beloved Anna-Maria, but his eyes were no longer alive. They looked dead, drained of vitality. She peered at the paper he held in his hand. The drawing was made in pencil, very dark, and she could make out some type of nightmarish monster.

FOURTEEN

Christina woke up with a hellish headache. She slowly moved around in the gargantuan bed, enjoying every square inch of it, and looked around with sleepy eyes. Got up and hit a button on the wall, and the blinds opened on all the windows. She screamed; yep, Mr. Peeping Tom was right outside the window at the end of his branch, staring at her. "Dammit, I need to have Robert remove that fucking branch," she muttered. "Maybe the whole damn tree." She glared at the owl, but it just stared at her, wide-eyed.

She looked around for something to wear. One of her sheets would do. She wrapped it around herself like a Roman toga, went into the bathroom, and when she was done there, she went down to the kitchen, still clad in her toga.

She brewed some coffee and made herself a cheese sandwich, then sat down in a comfortable armchair and enjoyed the view in the back of the house. The weather was sunny and clear, the storm finally past. The sun rose on the opposite side of the house, sending its beautiful rays over the valley without causing her any glare. Water glistered from the leaves and needles on the trees outside.

After finishing her sandwich, she walked barefoot, still wearing her toga and holding her coffee cup, onto the back porch. It smelled fresh and clean outside; birds chirped happily, flitting from tree to tree. It was a very calm, sobering moment, and for the first time in a very long time, Christina felt relaxed. She half-sat and half-lay on a splendid wooden chaise longue. There were matching cushions for all the outside furniture, but they were stored away. It was a bit uncomfortable without the cushions, but she didn't care. She was relaxed and enjoying her morning coffee—

—until all hell broke loose as a civilian helicopter with the words *Skull Creek Sightseeing & Rescue* painted on the side raised itself from the river valley far below and began hovering right in front of her. She dropped her coffee cup, but that wasn't the worst problem. Her toga blew away due to the wind gust coming from the helicopter, to the pilot's and crew's joy; all waved their hands happily at her.

Cool as day, Christina stood up, and did nothing. Her hair flew horizontally like a dark flag while her beautifully tanned body, highlighted by her wiry muscles, was defiantly exposed. She walked confidently towards the bastards in the helicopter, gave them a mischievous smile, then threw them a kiss with her right hand, her middle finger extended. She then turned around and walked slowly and confident back to her seat, peeled off the sheet that lay glued to the patio doors, and then went into her home…and just as she stepped inside she doorway, she bent somewhat sideways and slapped her right buttock.

"Showed those bastards. Must be related to the fucking owl."

The helicopter took off over the house and turned north. She went into the kitchen and made a fruit drink in the blender, then ate one banana. Later, she went upstairs and got dressed in a pair of blue denim shorts and a torn white T-shirt. She put on socks, sneakers, and a headband, then went back downstairs and got her smart-phone. She checked all the missed calls; mostly from her manager, nothing important. She then hooked up some earplugs, and put on a small waist pouch where she put her phone. She checked the fridge, and there were several bottles with water and some chocolate bars inside. She grabbed one water bottle and a chocolate bar, placing them in the adjacent compartment on her pouch.

She went outside and used a tree to push against and stretch her leg muscles. This time, she took off in the direction opposite the one she had gone the previous day. She turned on the music and Kiss's *Heaven's on Fire* came on. She increased her speed as the tempo from the song beat faster. She ran for quite a while, very fast but carefully. The ground was still very wet, but she didn't care if she looked like a dirty troll by the end of the run. She loved working out, especially running; it gave her a sense of freedom.

She ran up and down the hills, through the forest, taking in the fresh, crisp aroma of the surroundings. She reached a cliff edge and stopped to orient herself; she looked behind her and could see her part of her house, far away. She heard the sound of a helicopter and didn't think much about it until she saw not one, but two older military-style Bell helicopters flying in formation. They flew very close to her position, and she could see several weather-beaten soldiers wearing black sunglasses onboard. None smiled at her, or returned her friendly wave. They looked too focused, as if they had a purpose. The helicopters soon split up, going in different directions toward the deep forest, and she noticed, in the far distance, more helicopters flying near the tree line.

Something is definitely up, she thought, and remembered both Frank's and Robert's warnings about people getting lost. Again she looked at the house in the distance, and then she began running again, promising herself she would keep to the trail and the river for now. But when she came to the end of the fence line, she looked down, and a bit further below was a nice, calm pool of water. It was part of the river, but Mother Nature had made it a natural swimming pool. Next to it was the fierce river, with its white rapids.

She half-walked and half-climbed down to the pocket paradise. She loved it, and it lay on her soon-to-be property! What more hidden secrets did this land have in store for her?

Christina stepped into a small clearing and out onto a flat rock, and she looked down about fifteen feet below into the crystal-clear water. She could see the bottom; it was deep here, but she didn't dare dive in yet.

She started her normal morning stretches without a tree this time, but she did find a suitable branch that could take her weight, so she did some pull-ups followed by sit-ups and push-ups. She repeated a few sets until she was exhausted, and her abs and arms could take no more. She was so sweaty, and the water looked just too inviting, so she hurried down to the water line and dipped her hand in. It was cold, very cold. The thundering roar from the nearby river echoed in her ears. She looked around—a natural habit—before removing her clothes and placing them on a rock. She walked slowly into the water, but when her ankles froze, she stopped, took a deep breath, and dove into the cold pool. Instantly, her body reacted with shock, and she almost screamed out her lungful of air. She pushed on underwater, and when she came up for air, she was almost in the center of the pool. She gasped and breathed heavily from the cold, but slowly her body adjusted to the new environment. She laid on her back in the water, kicking a bit with her legs, then combed her hair back while kicking slowly, floating. Indeed, this was paradise.

When she opened her eyes, she saw the cutest and most incredible thing she had ever seen in her life, stunning her into immobility. Two small, cuddly little bears sat on the rock, playing with her clothes! When they found her pouch, she remembered her phone; and without thinking, she swam back to the shore and walked up to the little cuties. She kneeled by them and grabbed her pouch—but one of the little critters wasn't willing to let go. She petted it nicely and it smiled, while making the funniest sounds. Little brother got pissed, though, and shrieked out loud. Christina took out the candy bar and removed the wrapping—

—and suddenly there was Mother Bear.

The huge brown bear charged through the forest, letting out a fearsome roar as she attacked, protecting her cubs. Christina froze for a second, but then she dove back into the pool and swam for her life. The bear dashed into the water and took up chase. Christina swam as fast as she could, and when she took a quick peek behind her, her eyes went wide; the enormous bear was *right there*. She reached the stone on the other edge of the pond and flew up on it, lacerating her knee badly; blood oozed out, and the sharp pain made her scream. She saw the giant's head right where her feet had been, and without thinking, she started to run downstream on the rocky and unfortunately slippery ground. She fell into the powerful river, helpless. The strong currents played with her like she was a straw, tossing her all over the place. She managed to maneuver herself onto her back, as the bear kept running along the side of the river, keeping pace; but as the river pulled her away faster than it could run, the bear stopped, rose onto its back legs, and roared at her defiantly.

A mouthful of water reminded Christina that she was facing another danger. She was freezing, and could barely keep her head above water. More than once, she got more water in her mouth than she could handle; she coughed and screamed as much as her strength allowed her. She was crying and beginning to feel helpless as the current got stronger, and facing her were many dangerous, sharp rocks. Some she missed and others her body hit hard, sending more pain through her body while leaving large black-and-blue marks.

Where's the fucking log? There's always *a fucking* log *sticking out into the river in all the movies to save the fucking* day! she thought morbidly as she started to give up. But with that thought, a surge of power went through her body. She refused to give up. This was not the way Christina Aurora Dawn was going to end her days!

The rapids swept her around a bend, and on the other side she saw her salvation; two older teens, a black boy and a white boy, who were playing by the river with a large brown sack of some sort. One of them hurled it into the water, while the other cheered him on. The white boy had a long branch, hitting the surface of the water or the sack, she couldn't tell.

There were two surprised faces visible when Christina flew by them screaming for help. She grabbed the branch with her last bit of strength and held it hard. The boys looked at each other, surprised, and then they smiled and laughed at her nakedness and predicament. "Looks like we got ourselves a fuckin' mermaid here!" the black one said.

"Come on, hold on to the stick so we can pull you up, lady," cajoled the white boy.

They started pulling her in, but when Christina saw the malice in their faces, she kicked away back into the river.

"Come back here, ho, so we can use our sticks on you, cunt!"

"Don't lose the catch of the day, man, I want her first, she's a pretty li'l bitch!"

Fucking hillbillies, she thought in disgust as the boys ran along the riverside only a few feet from her, screaming and shouting, neither helping her. Instead, the boy with the long stick hit her hard in the head, opening up a gash over her left eyebrow. When they saw the blood pouring out, they got very excited, and it made them start screaming and shouting even more. When the river pulled Christina back towards the center of the river, one of the boys gave her the bird while the other mooned her.

Christina couldn't believe the evil she'd seen in their eyes. The speed of the river left the two boys far behind, and eventually a long turn in the river made them vanish. Christina's lungs hurt now, like thousands of needles had been stabbed through them every time water was forced into her mouth, but instead of fearing the dangerous river or the boys' threats, she got mad—and with a new inner strength, she kicked her bruised legs hard, and swam sideways until she finally reached the shoreline. She had lost all feeling in her arms and legs by then; her skin was bluish, and she trembled so hard it made her muscles hurt. After a moment, she vomited up what seemed like gallons of water, and coughed until her throat and lungs hurt. The bag the boys had hurled into the water floated by, so she reached out and grabbed it; and when she lifted it from the water, there came a horrible yowling screech from inside. Exhausted, she crawled to the rocky shore, where she lay on her side, just staring at the sky in disbelief that she had made it; but the yowling from the bag made her sit up. She opened it, and inside found five small kittens. All but one lay still in the bottom, while the fifth stared up at her in horror, and let out saddest cry for help she'd ever heard.

She lifted the little poor thing up and held it to her chest, while with her other hand she lifted out the rest of the little bodies; but none of them moved. They were dead. Christina started to cry, and her tears poured down as she hid her face in the back of the little kitten who had survived. It stopped screaming but it was still very tense. After a few minutes, the kitten calmed down and rested in her lap, feeling her heart beat. Eventually it meowed, and then actually started purring.

Christina trembled and cried softly as she placed its tiny brothers and sisters back into the bag. She continued to tremble as she stood up, and slowly she walked towards the forest, not caring about the bear or the boys. She guessed she had gone quite some distance down the river. She looked around, but didn't recognize anything. In the far distance came the sound of a helicopter. She looked around carefully, up towards the river toward where the evil boys had been, but she didn't see or hear them. Her nakedness didn't bother her at first, but soon she decided to use the brown sack with its horrible contents for cover, while still holding the live kitten against her chest. She hurt her naked feet on the stony ground more than once, but by then she had so many bruises and cuts that she didn't care; she just pressed on, refusing to give up. She was sad, but at least as angry, and it pushed her onward. She took her bearings and guessed where the road might be, and then she walked into the forest; and once in a while she looked backwards and laid out branches on the ground, just in case she had to double back. Suddenly she heard the sound of a vehicle, and through the tree line she could make out a truck driving by on a ridgeline above. She picked up her pace, and again her feet hurt badly, but with the road so close she ignored the pain and hurried on.

Christina was in shock from the trauma, emotionally as well as physically injured, and she wasn't thinking clearly when she crawled up onto the road. She thought she recognized the truck as the one she and Frank had taken to get to her house. Another truck passed her when she was in the ditch, and she ran up on the road, waving and screaming— but the truck just kept on driving. That's when she remembered she was naked, and at the same time she thought about those boys; they might be coming in a truck, too.

The shriek of rubber grinding on pavement behind her made her jump. The truck swerved around her, almost driving off the road on the opposite side, but the driver managed to gain control as he hit the brakes again.

Christina, even more shaken now after having almost gotten hit by a truck, contemplated running back into the woods. The truck had stopped about fifty yards away from her. Having made up her mind, Christina walked slowly forward. A man looked out the driver's side and shouted to her, "Do you need help, ma'am?" He sounded a bit stressed, yet oddly calm for someone who had barely missed hitting a stranger who had suddenly popped up on the road in front of him.

His voice was powerful and friendly, and he looked at her shyly. He lowered his head and walked towards her, and as he did, he unbuttoned his typical red plaid lumberjack shirt. He stopped several feet away, turned his head away from her, and reached out with his shirt. She carefully took it and put it on; it reached to below her knees. Still with his back turned, he handed her a cellular phone.

"Please, ma'am, call a family member or friend."

She realized that the gesture was made in an effort for her to feel safe around him. The sun was shining in Christina's face, and all she really could make out of the man was a large shadow. She looked him over; another giant. He seemed completely bald, but she wasn't sure. He sounded white with a northern accent, but his arm had a very dark skin tone or tan. When he looked at her, he smiled shyly and pleasantly. Christina was too tired and shaken up to make a phone call, so she handed the phone back wordlessly.

"What happened to you, miss, if you don't mind me asking?"

Christina shuddered, "Cute cubs, but a bear attacked. Fell into the river. Couple of boys killing these kittens wanted to rape me."

She could hear him dialing someone, and she heard him mentioning the bear attack but nothing about the boys or cats. She was too exhausted to focus on the man's conversation and decided to ignore whatever the guy was saying, though she knew that wasn't a good idea. She was just so tired…

"I called 911 and they're sending the paramedics," he said. "Now, where about did you say those boys were, and what did they look like?"

Christina was still very confused and just said, "In their late teens or early twenties, one white and the other black." She made a sloppy gesture with her arms towards the river.

"Wait here and I'll get you something to drink, because I sure need something to calm my own nerves. Girl, you almost caused another accident like the one the other day, when that woman jumped into the road and got herself killed, causing a huge accident with a lotta people hurt. Domino effect, you know? You have to be extra careful with all the mad drivers on the road nowadays. Lucky, I saw you in time."

She sat down by the side of the road and hugged the cat, noticing for the first time that the man had turned on his hazard lights and placed a warning triangle on the road. He returned with a camping canteen; he held it out to her, but Christina just gave it a suspicious glare. Suddenly she heard a helicopter nearby; she looked up, and saw the man taking a sip from the canteen. Again he held it in front of her. She took it with her left hand, still holding onto the sleeping kitten. She drank some, and it tasted like green tea. Almost instantly, she felt a bit stronger, and so she drank some more. He had to stop her, and with mild force, recovered his canteen.

"Trust me, you don't want to drink too much of it, miss. It has coca leaves in it."

She looked at him. frightened.

"Don't worry, it won't be detectable, and you won't become a drug addict. They're very small coca flakes. Makes you feel better, right?"

She smiled effortlessly and nodded. Whatever she had just drank had helped.

"Did you know that in Central and South America, they use these leaves to measure distances?"

She was too tired to answer the nice man, and only shook her head.

The sound of the helicopter increased to a roar, and it suddenly landed on the road beyond the stranger's truck. Another truck was parked on the side of the road behind her, and an old couple stepped out, wondering what was happening. Soon several more vehicles were there, but Christina didn't care. She didn't know how long she'd been on the road, because suddenly she felt very drowsy.

Someone gave her a nudge, and she woke up looking into the eyes of a man with a large white helmet who wore a pair of mirrored sunglasses. "Ma'am, you all right?"

Christina didn't understand what was happening. The man kneeling there wore a typical pilot's outfit with a life vest around his neck.

"Ma'am, can you tell us whereabouts the bear attacked you?"

Someone else said, "Crap, she's passed out."

The man who had helped her took another sip from his canteen while a police officer took down his information. He glanced at the three people who carried a rescue litter with the young woman strapped in to the waiting helicopter down the road. When they passed him and the police officer, he thought, *She looks even prettier* without *that cowboy hat.*

Oh, well. He had bigger fish to fry. There were two young men just dying to meet him.

Fifteen

"S he's waking up, better get the doctor," one nurse said to another as they prepared the hospital bed.

Christina woke up slowly, her vision a blur. There was a very annoying beeping sound in the room. It smelled clean; overly clean, in fact, like alcohol and antiseptic. Another fragrance fought for dominance: she saw several flower bouquets with nice arrangements, and there were some small envelopes and get-well cards attached. No balloons, and with that thought she smiled thankfully. She had something stuck in her nose, and when she turned her head, it was still stuck. She moved her eyes sideways and noticed her bandaged hands. She felt uncomfortable, and her head was spinning, making her feel nauseous.

A moment later, someone peeled back her eyelid and looked at her eye with a bright light, mumbling something to a nurse, who took notes. The doctor then checked on her heartbeat, and made her lean forward and cough, finishing up with checking her throat. Then a cheerful voice greeted Christina: "Hi there. My name is Daniela, and I'll be your doctor for the day."

Christina smiled and whispered back, "Hi, my name is Christina, and I'll be your patient for the day."

"Humor, that's good. How are you feeling?"

"Like a mashed potato."

"Well, Ms. Potato, you'll be glad to know that you've been very fortunate. You have several lacerations and we had to do some stitching, especially over your eye, but fear not; I'm excellent with a thread and needle, and once it's healed it will barely be visible. You're bruised up pretty badly, but with some rest and medication, you should be as good as new in about two weeks."

Christina woke up abruptly. "Two weeks here at the hospital?"

"No, no, not that long, but we do have some important things to discuss."

Christina looked over her body for the first time, and noticed that her head, hands, arms, feet, and chest had been wrapped up. "Why didn't you just wrap me up like a mummy?"

"It can be done," Daniela said drily. "There are quite a few people here to see you. Should I let them in once I'm finished here, or do you want to rest?"

"Any of them reporters?"

"No. They know better."

"Oh. By the way, what time is it?"

"Three o'clock in the afternoon."

"Good, then I'll only been here for a few hours."

Daniela observed her patient thoroughly. "Christina, it's Monday afternoon. You've been asleep for thirty hours."

"But, but…"

"Your body has taken some severe blows, and it needed to rest. You were completely unconscious when you got here. You're very fortunate; and you should also be very proud, because your body overall is in very good condition. Back to one of my first questions; what do you remember? I need to determine if you have amnesia. The MRI didn't show any major damage to your brain, but you do have a minor concussion. Your neck was bruised up pretty badly, and I'll leave your neck brace on until you leave. I'm afraid you'll have to keep all the bandages on, and I would prefer you stayed at least two more days for observation."

Christina thought back for a moment, and then she said, "I went for a jog and found a nice pool...went swimming, and..." She had to think some more, and then she smiled up and continued, "There were bear cubs playing with my clothes. Cute little things. I think they fought over the candy bar I brought with me. I went up and started to pet them."

Daniella's eyes went wide. "You did WHAT?"

An innocent Christina answered, "Petted them. They were so cute."

Daniella was about to lecture her patient about common sense when spending time in the woods, but she wasn't there for that; she bit her tongue instead. "Please continue."

"The mother bear attacked me all of a sudden. I barely escaped, and that's how I ended up in the river."

"Explains why you were naked...some pilots thought you must have dived naked from Frank's and Claire's house, because they claim they saw you there naked earlier...but the idea of diving from that distance is absurd. You wouldn't be able to reach the water anyway."

Christina continued her story, telling Daniela about the boys and what they had done to her, and how she finally managed to reach the shoreline. And then Christina almost shouted, "The kittens! The fuckers murdered the kittens, and...! Wait, there was one alive, where is it!?"

"Okay, you seem to be all right in the memory department, but you need to calm down," Daniela said sternly.

"But what about the kitten?"

"I don't know about any kitten, but relax. I'll find out, but only if you promise to relax."

Daniella never liked using reflexive psychology on her patients, but she knew it worked most of the time. She then went outside and closed the door behind her. Christina could barely hear her warning the people outside about something.

When Dr. Daniela returned, the first visitor entered. He shut the door firmly behind him, keeping whoever was coming up from the rear outside. It was an old man wearing a very expensive suit: Mr. Thomas Billing. Her lawyer. Before he shut the door, he turned in the doorway and snapped something to someone Christina couldn't see, although she caught a glimpse of a uniform. She rolled her eyes at the bobbing balloons he brought with him; definitely didn't match his armor.

"Oh my dear, dear Christina, look at you," he said gloomily. "How are you feeling?"

He was almost like a father or grandfather to her, having taken her under his wings after his only daughter had died from Lupus, SLE at a young age. Anna and Christina had been best friends, but that ended when the disease took her. Tammy had introduced them. The three had been inseparable until death stepped in.

Despite his authoritarian armor, Thomas was one of the sweetest people Christina knew, and she respected him like a parent. However, sometimes he could be a bit of a Mr. Hyde when it came to his work. She knew that when he had raised his voice to the people outside, it had been his paternal instinct speaking, and not the attorney.

"I feel like a mummy," she moaned.

"And I'm afraid you look like one, dear. But don't you worry about a thing. I brought my jet, and we'll have you back in L.A. soon, and have some real experts take care of you."

Christina noticed Dr. Daniella look up sharply from her paperwork.

"Dear Tom, thanks a million for taking the time to fly all the way out here and offer, but I'll stay here. I trust my new physician completely."

He smiled. "A second opinion never hurts." He turned to Daniela. "I respectfully apologize for my poor choice of words. It was never my intention to question your professionalism...it's just that this one," he nodded to Christina, "is like a daughter to me."

Daniella smiled at him. "I'll leave the two of you alone for a while."

"I see you're wearing your armor," she said when they were alone. "A Savile Row suit with tie and all. Long time since I saw you wear one of those."

"I have been in the Big Apple doing big business."

"Another billion?" she asked wryly.

"Two, actually. Are you sure I can't convince you to come back? There have been an awful lot of bad things happening around here lately."

"Hey, you're the one who recommended this place to me."

"Too true."

"Besides, I've decided I want to move here, and I want to buy the place."

Tom sat down next to her and brushed some stray locks of hair from her face. "Yes, I suspected you would fall in love with this place. The house anyway."

"I'll probably have to sell my place in L.A., but it will be worth it."

He looked at her, looking hurt. "Nonsense! I'll help you rent it out. It might not be on the beach, but since it's only two blocks away from one of the world's more popular beaches it won't be a problem finding tenants. Never hurts to earn some extra money. And besides, your back-list has been selling well on DVD and BluRay, and you're getting some tidy royalties lately."

She knew he wanted her to have an anchor near him, so she let it go. She didn't want to hurt him, as he was all alone without Anna. Christina knew very well that if it wasn't for her and Tammy, this man would have no life but his work. It was Tom who had set up Tammy with her new job; not that Tammy wasn't able to do it herself, it was just something he would typically do.

"Like I said…"

"I'll keep it, Tom, don't worry. You'll never get rid of me—or Tammy, for that matter."

"Tammy? That little hellion! I'll never forget when you guys and Anna…" He trailed off.

Christina placed her bandaged left hand on his. "Hey. Come on."

He didn't answer; instead, he took a deep breath, swallowing his tears.

"There's a crowd of people outside who want to see you. I didn't ask you what happened, because I figured you would only want to say it once to everyone, but…did you do anything that might result in questioning in regards to the law?" Mr. Hyde was back.

"If being naïve and stupid is criminal, then yes, guilty as charged."

He never left her side; instead he tapped on something on his wrist, and Christina knew very well that it was some type of radio link to his personal security. The door opened, and in came an avalanche of people. Behind them stood Claire Hancock, waving her hand, but someone shut the door in her face.

Two Highway Patrol officers charged across the room, followed by a park ranger, a soldier, and that rude person who had slammed the door in Claire's face. He was a tall, slender black man wearing a police uniform. Instantly Christina noticed his eyes: clear, intelligent, sad, alert; but there was something very dark about them, and it had nothing to do with his complexion. His eyes reflected experience, a lot of it, and perhaps not the best. For a moment, she thought his eyes were dead. His bluish-black skin, which made him seem more African than African-American, only made his dark stare even more intense. Although he kept to himself in the back of the crowd, he was the one who brought a sense of authority to the room.

Wait—there was one more person in the room, and Christina smiled at herself, because she should have known why she had never noticed him entering the room. It was the legendary and mysterious *Mr. Smith*, the man in charge of Thomas Billing's security. Holding on to his old umbrella -something he always carried with him. He was a very old, odd, and *small* person; Anna had thought he was creepy and never liked him, while Tammy thought the old bugger needed to "get some," as she put it. He was the type of person no one ever noticed in a crowd, and at the same time, if you were in a room with him for more than five minutes, you would feel unease. Christina knew nothing about him and had never asked; it had always seemed a touchy subject. Mr. Smith—or whatever his real name was—never smiled or looked sad. His facial expression was always perfectly neutral. During all the years Christina had known Tom, she could count the words she had heard Mr. Smith utter on the fingers of one hand.

A distinguished older man, wearing what seemed to be a Highway Patrol uniform with patches indicating that he held a high rank, gave her a friendly smile and, in an equally friendly tone, asked Christina to recount what had happened.

She thought back over all the events so that she would get everything in proper order, and then she more or less repeated what she had told Dr. Daniela, but with a few more in-depth details. When she finished, the officer turned to the park ranger, a young woman. "Could it be our bear?"

"No, I doubt it…wait a moment."

The young woman took a map from a side pocket on her pants and started unfolding it. The soldier, an officer with the rank of Major, intervened, and brought up a thin but sturdy-looking computer tablet, which looked like it had been made for use under rough conditions. "May I…?"

Before Christina could answer, he held the tablet in front of her. "This is your home, and this is where they found you, on this road." He pointed at the locations, and it took Christina a minute before she could identify the locations.

"Wow. I must have gone a long way down the river."

"You're lucky you're alive," someone said.

She recognized the small natural pool on the satellite image. The soldier allowed for her to zoom in and point it out. The ranger leaned over and observed. "No, impossible. That can't be the bear we're hunting, not with two cubs and all. I would, respectfully, be grateful if you would inform the hunting parties that's not our bear. The idiots have already killed two black bears for nothing."

The park ranger was very upset, and had no trouble hiding it as she scolded the others in the room. The officers and the soldier quickly related the information to their various people on their smartphones.

Christina almost froze when, suddenly, the black police officer addressed her in a deep, dark voice. "Miss Dawn, my name is Malik Washington. I'm with the Sheriff's Department. Would you recognize the two men who attacked you if you saw them again, perhaps in mugshots?"

"Yes, most definitely. I've never seen such malice in one person before, let alone two."

"I'm somewhat new in these parts, ma'am, but I'll relate what you said to the sheriff."

"Wait, has anyone seen the kitten?"

Everyone looked around the room and then back at Christina, shaking their heads.

"There was a tiny kitten, the only one still alive. I held onto him all the way to the road…" Christina's eyes teared up.

The Major made a call and walked towards a corner in the room, almost colliding with Mr. Smith, who glided silently out of the way. A moment later, he returned with a frown on his face. "It was turned over to an animal shelter, ma'am. I'm afraid it's too young to survive without its mother, and there's no mother cat to wet-nurse it. They say it's going to be euthanized."

Having received this information, Christina tried to get out of her bed, but the stupid torture device that kept her neck in place wouldn't let her. Immediately, people in the room tried to stop her from getting up. Christina cursed them roundly, very upset. Thomas looked at Mr. Smith, who raised his left wrist to his mouth and said something quietly. He then nodded his head towards Thomas, who laid his hand on Christina's arm.

"One of my people is on his way to see if we can find your kitten." He looked at Christina, and then turned his head to Mr. Smith, who just stood there.

With that Christina relaxed. She was stuck in the damned bed anyway.

Someone in the room suddenly burst out to Mr. Smith, "Who are you, and where did you come from?"

Silence. Tom and Christina smiled at each other.

The uniformed party left the room, but not without someone mumbling, "Creepy little bastard," before leaving.

Standing in the doorway, holding some flowers and not knowing if it was her turn to enter yet, stood a very patient but concerned Claire. Christina tried to wave with her left hand for her to come inside, but that didn't work so well, so she called, "Come on in, Claire."

She repeated her story for Claire, and when she reached the part of what the two young men had done, Claire jumped from her seat. "Those no-good-sons of bitches are Anthony Goodney and Eddie Files—both as crazy as their parents! They live way out in the woods with a bunch of other hicks and moonshiners, thinkin' they can do whatever they want! Normally they're hours from here, but now and then they show their ugly faces in town. Not sure why they would be near your property, though."

"Actually they weren't, I think. According to the map, I had river-rafted quite some distance before I saw them." Christina smiled at her own joke.

"How are you feeling, dear?" Claire sounded genuine concerned.

"Like the day after a movie premiere."

"Frank sends his best. Sorry he's not able to come and visit today. There have been some…problems."

From the tone of Claire's voice, Christina suspected that something was wrong. "Is he okay?"

Claire smiled tiredly, "There was an incident, and Nugget was badly hurt. We still don't know if he's going to make it. He's with the vet as we speak."

"Did that happen when they were hunting the grizzly bear?" Tom inquired.

Claire nodded, and filled them in on what had happened.

"Well, Claire, I don't know if this will make you and Frank any happier, because I understand how much you love Nugget…but I'd like to buy the place."

A surprised Claire, "You would? Even after what happened to you?"

"What happened with the mother bear was my own fault, but I can learn, and I want to because I have truly fallen in love with the place. Now, what happened with the two boys…well, that could have happened pretty much anywhere, so that doesn't scare me. I'm tougher than I look. Well, maybe not right now."

Both Claire and Tom laughed at her, but not Mr. Smith. She noticed him doing something again with his wrist, and moments later Malik Washington returned with two more people: Thomas's personal bodyguards, whom Christina knew well.

Deputy Washington got the information he needed about the two suspects, including the names Claire had provided, and related it to Carlos over his radio. He then towered by the bedside. "I'll find them," he vowed.

Christina noticed that even though he had said it to her, he had stared at Tom, who calmly returned the stare from his sitting position, and then at Tom's bodyguards. No more words needed to be said. He had just informed everyone in the room that there would be no vigilantism.

"Don't worry, officer, I won't be the one defending them," Thomas said, his expression as terrifying as Washington's. Both men measured each other, and none gave in to the other. Just as the black man was about to say something, Dr. Daniela entered the room, telling them that visiting hours were over.

Dammit, Christina thought. *I was hoping Robert would show up. That bastard.*

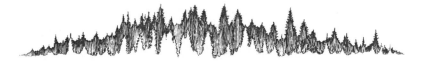

SIXTEEN

He had many names, but in Skull Creek he was Ted Hagglund, though very few people knew him well. He was an outstanding commercial lumberjack, known to travel all over in search of work, with a good reputation for being reliable and sober. The few people who knew of him saw him as being overall friendly, nice and quiet. Not a person who stuck out or demanded attention.

But that was only a façade.

His real name was Tarben Nero Hammond, and he had evolved far beyond what he had begun as. He was no longer one of the weak, inferior *two-leggeds,* as he referred to them. It had taken him a lifetime to achieve the transformation that made him the perfect superior being; born a man, transformed into an animal; and yet he was neither. Any beast with the mind of a human would always be superior to anything else, animal or person.

He had no religion, just one belief; and that was in Mother Nature, and that he was her guardian. The two-leggeds had, for far too long, been the dominant species on Earth; and like the dinosaurs, they rushed towards their own demise. This he knew for a fact: He had been created to help Mother speed up the process for the end of humankind. He was very patient, and a realist, and knew full well that it wouldn't come in his lifetime. That didn't matter, because what needed to be done had to be done. He had to remove the worse enemies of the planet: the ones that actually did direct harm against nature. Going after politicians seemed ridiculous to him; but going after someone littering or harming nature and its creatures directly...that was something different. It was enough for him to do what he did by removing them from the world of the living.

When he had been a simple two-legged, he had never had any sort of sadistic streak in him; nor did he suffer from so-called rape syndrome, or want power and control over other living beings. Weak-minded characters did that, like so many two-legged. What he did was as natural to him as breathing. He felt neither joy nor remorse when taking another life, be it human or animal; however, killing another animal must be avoided at any cost if possible. With his transformation came the learning side; one must always keep learning to become better, and therefore he accepted the fact that he had evolved away from others, but he still had much more to learn about Mother Nature.

Still, there was nothing as thrilling as hunting a two-legged. Using psychological terror on the prey before the kill was euphoria. But he was well aware of the modern technology that advanced law enforcement wielded; it had changed a great deal throughout his life. He knew his limits, and had to be careful. What had happened in Skull Creek had been an embarrassment; then again, in his last hunting ground for the past few years before Skull Creek, the technology had been somewhat limited. He had been careless. These new drones used by rescue and law enforcement presented a major dilemma, much worse than helicopters, because some of them were almost soundless.

He was concerned about but not afraid of the new advancements in technology, and kept himself fairly updated. He understood that all the high-tech bullshit would also speed the two-leggeds' demise. Besides, it had been thanks to technology that he had finally had found the only witness who had gotten away from the cleansing over fifty years ago. Tarben Nero Hammond was very meticulous. He had made a commitment that, once made, he always honored.

Skull Creek had been a disaster so far. First the stupid couple he had come across in the forest, camping and throwing trash around too near his temporary territory, so that it had looked like a dump, not caring where they spewed their garbage. Would it been too much to ask for them to bring a plastic bag and fill it up with their crap? In his evolved mind and body, the rage had taken over, and he had killed the male with ease and then enjoyed hunting the female. The idiot had jumped in front of an upcoming car. *What a loser*, he thought, as he looked out the window upon the beauty of nature while he enjoyed his herbal tea.

Then there was the business with the giant and the bitch who had actually *shot* him. That had been a first. He shook his head, thinking about his own stupidity: crossing a fucking intersection just to save time and in the hope that the cover of the rain and darkness would hide him. Wrong; the giant had seen him. He should have regrouped right there and then, but when the beast took over his mind, it wasn't very controllable, and it was extremely unpredictable.

Locating and killing the giant had been easy. He already knew what crew he worked for, and had heard enough while the idiot had visited the fat cow. Considering his superior skills, strength, and knowledge of human anatomy, not to mention his specially-made bear hide exoskeleton, the kill had been effortless; the big idiot had been afraid when he fell dead on the road. He had left him there next to the woman's truck. What puzzled him most was, who the hell had rigged the body on the yarder and then cut off the head? Could there be *another* witness?

Later, killing the fat cow had been a must; she could have been a witness to the giant's death. The dogs and the police had been a shame; normally he didn't mind people in law enforcement. After all, there were billions of selfish idiots out there destroying the planet who needed his attention before any police, as in this instance. He hadn't used the claws built into the exoskeleton on the dogs, and hoped they would survive. His eyes teared up, thinking about them; and then he got upset at the owners, they should have kept the poor dogs on leashes.

He glanced at the newspaper on the kitchen table, which he had picked up before he'd left Skull Creek. Two headlines blared from the first page. One was about a raving grizzly killing people; the second one was about the homicide. A smaller article on the first page mentioned a huge multi-car accident on Deadman's Curve.

He needed to rest, focus, and meditate, and more so calm down; but he knew that wasn't possible. Soon, he must stop his hunt and hibernate through to next spring. Superior or not, even he had to rest. And then there had been that girl, the one he had planned on taking with him and keeping for a while, to use her as prey for his final hunt this season; but now she didn't fit the criteria of being an enemy to Mother Nature. All two-legged were enemies, make no mistake. But there were billions of them, so killing the ones that were imminent threats was enough. But she had helped the rescue workers repair the mechanical damage to Nature, and she had saved the kitten. Tarben Nero Hammond loved all animals, especially cats.

Now the beautiful young woman was forbidden fruit.

He had no sexual interest in any woman, though he was what people would label as straight; it was just that fornication was only to be done for procuring a child. Animals didn't fornicate for pleasure, only to ensure the future existence of their species. He didn't see or feel any pleasure in fornication; in fact, he found the idea disgusting. After all, who would want to fornicate with a lesser species? He had no urges in that department, as the newly evolved species he was; however, there still was a small part of the human left in him, and like all humans, he was curious. Not so curious that he would rape a woman just so he could satisfy his curiosity; the very thought was repulsive. Rapists and others who committed heinous crimes should be removed from the surface of the Earth. Prison was a waste of time; killing them wasn't.

The only television show Tarben Nero Hammond had ever liked was *Dexter*.

He never collected souvenirs from his own kills, as serial killers do. He didn't regard himself as a such. For him, killing the two-leggeds was a natural act, and that made him very dangerous. He had a perfect record, and several identities created through as many decades. He had learned to become expert in many different professions, but where he stood out were in camouflage and fragrance.

Tarben Nero Hammond was by far nature's perfect killing machine, with over two thousand kills to his name, and he was a virgin.

He took another sip from his cup, and took note of a sound coming from the basement. He placed his cup on the kitchen table and opened an old door leading down to Hell. It was time to play some with Anthony and Eddie.

As he descended the stairs, he turned on the light. On the floor lay two young men: one black, the other white. Both were hogtied, blindfolded, and gagged, and the only thing they wore was their underwear. They had finally woken up. He observed them, watching them struggle in their bonds more and more as they realized their predicament. Terror and fear would soon set in, and they would be in shock; that would be the perfect time to interrogate them, and learn more about the minds of these sadistic criminals who had murdered four kittens and had also hurt the pretty little thing, according to her own testimony. Removing criminals such as murderers and rapists from Earth's surface was something he did from time to time; however, it wasn't really on his life agenda. Perhaps if he was bored or something, he'd do it.

He walked around the prey, hovering over them as they struggled. He estimated both youths to be in their early twenties, or perhaps their late teens. In the old days, the rule had been to never kill a teenager or a child, as they knew not what they did. But as society evolved, youths' increasing lack of respect for their surroundings and elders had caused him to lower that age limit. He had no difficulty killing a ten-year-old if that person committed a heinous crime against Mother Nature or animals. He was disgusted with the way children were raised nowadays by their incompetent parents. In the animal kingdom—and he didn't concider humans animals, because they were inferior to animals—did the cubs disrespect their elder? No, they most certainly did not.

He walked over to the white kid, or young adult, or whatever, and removed his gag. He hushed him some while the prey screamed and shouted and tried to spit, but his throat was too dry. He spoke in a very friendly voice—almost a bit gay, because if the prey was straight, it always freaked them out, and if they were gay it might even freak out Nero some—while combing the prey's hair with his fingers. The kid immediately pulled away, but Tarben Nero Hammond would have none of it and continued petting.

"Relax. Relax, now…would you like some water?"

Not waiting for the answer, he took a bottle and forced water down the kid's throat. Coughing, cursing, and spitting, the prey started to regain some courage. "What's goin' on, man, what the fuck?! Why you doin' this shit?" It went on like that for next five minutes, and the more time went by, the more courage the prey got. "My pop will kill you, you fucker, you hear?"

Silence.

The prey became uneasy. The moaning of his friend finally got to him. "'Zat you, Anthony, he got you too?"

More moaning.

"Fuck, man, we need to get loose and fuck 'im up!"

"Did you think I had left the room?" Nero asked quietly.

"Fucker, I will *end* you, you hear me, slick? I will fucking *kill* you."

"You seem to have forgotten who's tied up here." Nero grabbed the prey hard, and pulled him off the ground by the hair. The reaction was instantaneous: First a howl of pain, and when the prey realized that his blindfold was about to be removed, he became even more frightened, and all his built-up false rage vanished. The prey trembled and pissed himself.

"You will answer my questions," the beast said.

The prey tried to nod while screaming in pain.

Nero asked, "Which one of you came up with the idea of murdering the kittens? What goes through your mind when you harm a tiny, defenseless animal? Is it a way for you to feel power? Is it a sexual thing? What drives a person like you to commit such a heinous act? Don't worry, I'll repeat the questions as we go along…and believe me when I say this: you *will* answer them. One way or another."

He could have added dozens more questions, but he knew that an idiot like this one would take too long in between answers, with its useless blabbering and begging before each question had even been asked.

An hour later, he had received his answers, and all of them were excuses and blame, as always; never once did the prey take responsibility for his own actions.

"So, to summarize: you were high because society has marginalized you, forcing you to become what you are, and therefore you were so mentally incapacitated that you really didn't know what you were doing. In the end, everything was your buddy's idea, and you just went along for the ride."

"Yeah. Yessir. That's how it was."

"So what about the woman?"

"What woman?"

Again Eddie found himself hanging in the air by his hair.

"Should I scalp you, Eddie? Or will you answer?"

"Oh, the mermaid bitch! The one swimming. Yeah, we never hurt her!"

Nero lay the prey back on the ground. He placed a knife on the boy's forehead, and made sure he would feel the cold hard steel; and then he made a small cut along the hairline while pulling on the kid's hair. When Eddie screamed, Nero stopped. For the moment.

"Bitch just swam by, and Anthony hit her on the head, that's all!" Eddie screamed.

"So you guys didn't think she might need saving?"

"From what?"

Nero only shook his head, because that was pretty much all he was going to get from this idiot.

"The river."

"What ya mean?"

"She tried to swim ashore, did she not?"

"Fuck, man, I was so wasted I don't remember!"

"You wanted to fornicate with her, didn't you? Against her will."

"Forni what?"

Nero looked up towards the celling, swearing at his own stupidity at using a word like that with this moron. "I meant you wanted to fuck her, rape her real good. Come on, she's a pretty lady? Hot, right?"

Silence.

"Oh, fuck, now I know," the white boy finally babbled. "You're her pop or boyfriend, aren't you…it was all Anthony! He the one you wanna hurt!"

A long silence from Nero, while Eddie started to tremble and cry like a baby. Once he started to mumble, Nero petted the prey, and then he gagged him again.

Nero repeated the same procedure with Anthony, and now it was Eddie who lay there protesting through his gag while his friend blamed everything on *him*.

Nero started to sound hesitant, and as his two prey finally fell silent, he started to talk to himself, deliberately making himself seem weak. It didn't take long before their body language changed, even though they were tied up. *Finally* he was finished here. It had taken too bloody long anyway, not that Nero wasn't a patient being; it was just that the likes of these sadistic pricks bored him. But what really angered him was that at no time did either prey apologize or show a hint of remorse for their actions.

It's a miracle that the police nowadays have the patience not to shoot shitheads like these, he thought, remembering why he didn't like to harm law enforcement people. *Time to speed things up.*

He quickly removed their blindfolds, under loud protest. After a while, he hushed them, and both lay crying and staring down on the floor. "Raise your heads, or I'll castrate you both," he said harshly.

Slowly, the prey looked up, to stare at a person who sat in a comfortable armchair, his upper body hidden in shadow. When they realized the floor was covered in plastic, they both screamed loudly.

Nero waited for the storm to calm down.

"I'm confused, Anthony and Eddie." He used their names to make it more personal. "Both of you are blaming the other, so I find myself on the horns of a dilemma. You see, that both of you are guilty is a fact; but in the end, I'd rather just deal with the one who originally came up with the idea of killing the kittens, because it had to be only one of you."

Anthony shouted, "You doing all this for some fucking *cats*?"

Nero raised his eyebrows and gave the prey a strange look. Again the blaming started, but now both prey got more and more courage back as they listened to each other's lies. Finally Anthony got some of his wits back, too. Or so he thought. "Hey, man, think you so tough, why don't you just release me and we go man-on-man, you and me. Tough guy cracker motherfucker."

Nero smiled inside, and then he leaned forward and said, in a perfect imitation of Sir Anthony Hopkins in *Silence of the Lambs*, "You're trying to test me. I will eat the guilty one with some fava beans and a nice bottle of Chianti. Now: who's the guilty one?"

Silence, and then both boys looked at each other; and for a moment, their reaction caught Nero off guard. Both looked at him with dead eyes, and then came the threats. *Finally, there they are, their true selves, something that no one can hide from in the end: true psychopathic sadists,* he thought.

Had it been a person with a decent character in their places, he or she would have begged; but never a monster, once unleashed. *Now I have the both of you, guilty as charged.*

Before either victim realized what had happened, Nero had moved swiftly; and with surgical precision, he sliced off the left ear of each, using an old, rusty, but very sharp knife.

Ten minutes later, after much screaming from pain and horror, they calmed down, still breathing heavily and crying some; and before any of the prey could make threats again, Nero spoke to them for the last time.

"I'll have this for dessert, and later I'll come back for some *testicles tartare.*"

He walked towards the stairs; and suddenly he tripped. Nero cursed aloud, and his fall seemed genuine and painful. There was a snapping sound when he hit the ground, and he rolled around, screaming in pain. He rolled back and forth while glancing at the prey. Yes, there was the hope in their eyes again.

"Oh my God, oh my God, I must have broken it." With those words he ran back upstairs, holding his forearm, leaving the knife behind him.

Nero let go of his arm, then walked upstairs and into a room where his second skin was strung up on a scaffold, tossing aside the green twig he'd use to mimic the sound of a broken bone. He looked over the suit.

There was some damage to the bear skin, and even to the inner layer, which was made of Dragon body armor interspersed with Kevlar. The exoskeleton itself, constructed of a high-tech titanium alloy, extremely light and strong, also needed some repair. He would fix everything before he returned to Skull Creek. But would he have the time? There was some serious damage here.

Once in a while he glanced at several images on a computer screen, which displayed the two morons downstairs. He had turned off the volume, tired of listening to their blabber. In between their cries of pain and fright, they lay there blaming and screaming at each other. If it took too long, he would just go down there and snap their necks. Nero didn't torture…well, he might play with his prey like cats do, but he wasn't a sadist like the two downstairs.

Finally, the idiots found the knife; and what did they do when they got loose? Both tried to stand up and take a swing at each other! Nero walked over to the door leading to the basement and rattled the lock, then he bumped into the door a few times.

The prey heard him, and stopped bickering. Even after they cut themselves loose, they fell to the floor several times because neither idiot realized that their hands and feet were useless until the blood flow through them normalized again. Eventually, the boneheads managed to stand up.

They looked around the place for weapons, found some tools, and then, to Nero's surprise, they actually used the stairs. When he turned the key in the lock, both prey ran back down into the basement. They found another door in the back, and entered a room that would remind anyone of a midlevel dungeon, with horrible tools on the walls—sometimes used by Nero to modify and repair his second skin—that inspired them to move faster toward the only entrance leading outside.

Nero opened the basement door and shouted angrily after them. Out they ran, clumsy little pecker-heads clad in only their underwear. Had they surveyed the basement more carefully, they would have found a large, advanced first aid box, and a fridge containing some water and even some food. After all, Nero wanted—or rather, *needed*—a challenge. Probably wouldn't be one now though, he thought sadly. Sometimes life wasn't fair, not at all.

They didn't try to get inside the house and take care of me like they promised, he thought, a little disappointed. However, it was expected: one thing all sadists, rapists, and sociopaths seemed to have in common was that they were all cowards. Had it been three of them, then there would most definitely be an alpha emerging, and they *would* have tried to get inside the house.

Nero tossed the disgusting ears into a trashcan; he would burn them to ash later. Cannibalism was as foreign to him as it was to any other normal person. The idea of it sure scared the hell out of the prey, though.

He suddenly lost interest in the prey outside, running for their lives. They wouldn't be any challenge at all, and he did have to tend to his second skin. Well, he'd done it now, letting them take off into the forest.

He walked over to the kitchen table and prepared his supper, a salad with some bread croutons and vinaigrette. He had baked bread, too, and the steam from it gave the kitchen a nice, homey fragrance. Nero carefully prepared a cheese platter with ten different cheeses, all imported from Europe. With his supper, he would enjoy a bottle of perfectly chilled Alsace.

As the wine was breathing to perfection, he walked outside on the porch and drank some fresh, cold, clear water from a bottle while leaning against the railing. Suddenly, a solution to his problem of hunting down the pray emerged—literally emerged, from the forest. A large black-and-gray wolf regarded him calmly. It was enormous compared to an average wolf, and its sheer size would scare the wits out of just about anyone. Not Nero, of course. He whistled softly, and the beast moved submissively toward him, whining and snarling, with its head bowed and bushy tail between its back legs. Nero scratched the beast behind its ears. It plopped down on the porch, and then lay on its back for him to pet its chest.

Along the tree line were over thirty pair of eyes observing the strange scene.

"You're hungry, aren't you, my dear Alpha wanna-be? I was going to leave them for you and your family...but that isn't what we wants now is it? We wants to hunt, don't we?"

The wolf rolled over and sat up like a trained dog, with its tongue hanging out as it breathed heavily, looking at Nero with eager anticipation.

"What the hell. It's your lair too."

He motioned with his arm and made a growling sound; and with that, the giant wolf took off into the forest, followed by its pack, which had been watching curiously. Nero looked after his pups, smiling; he needed to take care of his second skin after he had eaten, and then focus on a more in-depth plan to take care of the primary prey in Skull Creek.

OUTSIDE, THE forest was dead silent. Ted Hagglund, AKA Tarben Nero Hammond, listened to Beethoven while enjoying his supper outside on the porch, watching the sun set over the mountains. Nero liked Beethoven; it made him calm.

Wolves howled in the far distance.

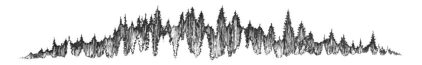

SEVENTEEN

Sally: *"To summarize; the political crisis and the millions of refugees from the Middle East and Africa are splitting a once-unified Europe. More on this during our late news report this evening. Over to you, Richard."*

Richard: *"In South Africa, near the border of Botswana and Zimbabwe, another mass grave has been found containing six to eight bodies. It appears to be similar to the mass grave discovered earlier this year in Namibia, where eleven bodies were found. Two of those bodies have been identified as Americans, and authorities are still keeping their names from the public. Some of the remains appear to be those of local poachers who disappeared a year ago. The FBI has sent representatives to aid in that investigation. Whether or not they will also investigate the latest mass grave we don't yet know; they have yet to comment.*

"Now for some fresh Entertainment News. Believe it or not, we have more to report from the tiny mountain town of Skull Creek. Several days ago, we reported on a possible homicide and a man-eating grizzly bear. Authorities are still searching for the grizzly, which they intend to put down. Your turn, Sally."

Sally: *"You might remember we also mentioned the serious multi-car auto accident that occurred outside Skull Creek at about the same time.*

Well, here's something new. Remember Christina Dawn? As a famous child star, she had several blockbuster movies, but her fortune hasn't been nearly as great as an adult actor, especially these past few years. Now, perhaps, she's a falling star—and when we say falling, we mean it literary. Take a look at these images."

A short clip followed of Christina rappelling down the rescue truck ladder, then falling a few feet. The image froze. Another picture appeared, a glamour shot of Christina.

Richard: Yes, we have confirmed the fallen star really is Christina Dawn. Apparently, she helped save the day with the local fire rescue team. We'll have more on this extraordinary news once we can reach Christina for a comment.

Sally: "Some of these stars must really be desperate—literally trying to hang on to their stardom."

Laughter in the studio.

Richard: "Boy, Sally, Skull Creek really lives up to its name these days."

More laughter.

Sally: "Next we have Paul with the latest weather forecast."

"PLEASE SHUT it off," Christina told the nurse who was helping her get dressed.

"Is that really you?"

"Sadly, yes."

Christina left the hospital that day, but not after she had signed four autographs—her first in Skull Creek.

Outside waited two of Tom Billing's security people, both dressed casually, trying to fit in with the surroundings. The sun shone bright and the sky was clear, the air smelling insanely fresh. *Must be the oxygen emitted by all these huge trees,* she decided, as she glared at the security men.

Holding up his hands in a defensive posture, one declared, "Mr. Billing only wants us here to make sure you're all right. We'll leave soon, or whenever you want us to. He did, however, insist we check out your land and see if the bear is still around."

"Thank you, Peter, I know the old man is a bit protective."

"He only wants the best for the people he cares about."

Christina turned to the second man, "I know, Kevin. By the way, any news about the kitten?"

Kevin answered, "It's too small to be adopted, but the vet has your name unless the real owner shows up. She doubts that anyone will show, so we put your name up for adoption."

"Thanks, guys."

Kevin drove the black Chevy SUV down Main Street and stopped outside Hancock Tool Supply. Peter got out and opened the door for Christina, and then Kevin drove off. At first Christina felt uneasy, looking around because she didn't want to draw any attention to herself. She whispered to Peter, "Please let me get the door next time."

He just nodded and backed away from the main entrance.

"Christina, hey there, they let you out this morning? I thought it was this afternoon? Frank and I were going to pick you up," Claire shouted from across the street, waving.

Christina stopped a moment to take in the strange scene taking place across the street. Claire walked on the sidewalk dragging a cart. At first Christina thought she had grocery bags on it, and she actually *did* have some, but there was also a passenger, sitting high and mighty, staring backwards at the scenery: Winston.

Christina clasped her hands over her mouth, trying to hold back laughter, but she failed utterly when Winston barked and Claire stopped, rolling her eyes at Christina. Winston struggled of the cart, walked over to a fire hydrant, and marked his territory; and then he really struggled while climbing back up into the cart.

Christina remembered that either Frank or Claire had said something about rolling Winston when they first met, but she hadn't put much thought into it until now, and she couldn't hold back her laughter; but she did try to subdue it. From behind and to her side, she heard,

"Go ahead and laugh. Christina, that dog is incorrigible. Met my match with that one."

Frank dried his hands on a cloth while looking at Claire as she patiently let some traffic pass. They honked their horns at Winston, who apparently was a town favorite. Winston ignored everyone, remaining regally on his throne as Claire crossed the street. Frank helped his wife with the cart and groceries, while Winston stepped off and bullied himself into the store. As he entered, he barked, informing everyone that he was back and that no one had better be in his chair.

"You all right, Christina?"

"I'm good. How's Nugget?"

"Sorry I didn't come and visit; been busy and all. Nugget is getting better. He's in the back, hopefully not in Winston's chair."

A flurry of loud barking from the back told them a different story.

"Come on in, Christina. Just have to check on the little ones."

Another loud, protesting bark made Frank hurry.

"Claire, I need to pick up some supplies and such before I go back home," Christina noted.

"No worries, Christina, we'll get you what you need. I can't say how happy we are that you bought the property!"

"I've been looking for a new place for quite some time now, and I know that this is it. It just feels right, despite my misadventures!"

"Well, since you're going to live here, you might want to get to know some of our friends. This weekend there'll be a Hee Haw Party at the Old Red Barn, and it's a good way to meet some of your new neighbors."

Claire bit her tongue, knowing full well that this might not be something Christina would enjoy, given her background, and she held her breath. Christina noticed the tension. She smiled and said, "I'd love to come. I might have to wear a pirate patch over my black eye, though."

"Oh, come now, that bruise is almost gone. Your friend?" Claire nodded her head towards Peter, who stood in the back of the store looking at something. "Saw you come with him and another fella."

"Friends of Mr. Billing, actually, only here for a short while."

As several customers entered the store, Claire said, "Why don't you join Frank in the back, and I'll be with you guys shortly." Claire looked over at Peter. "You're welcome too."

Frank was in the kitchen, putting on some fresh coffee. Christina looked around, and Frank nodded his head towards the living room; and there on Winston's chair lay a patched-up Nugget. Winston lay on the floor nearby, waiting impatiently for his opportunity to reclaim his throne. Hunter showed up from a back room, wagging his tail; Christina kneeled and petted him, while talking that baby-talk people sometimes used when talking to dogs. A pitiful whine from Nugget let her know that he, too, wanted to be petted.

"Is it okay to pet Nugget?" she asked Frank.

"Sure, just don't touch the bandage."

Christina walked over, and Nugget suddenly struggled and got down on the floor. Winston rose immediately and went to stand next to the chair, barking triumphantly.

"Crap, stupid dog," Frank muttered, and hurried across the room, checking on Nugget's bandage.

"I'm sorry, I…"

"Not your fault, hon, he would sooner or later have needed to move anyway. It's just that I'd rather be the one to carry him. Dogs don't realize how much they're hurt sometimes. Their loyalty is overwhelming."

Nugget whined and lay down on the floor on a blanket, and Christina kneeled next to him while carefully stroking his head. Hunter soon joined them, while Winston reminded Frank impatiently that he needed help getting into his armchair.

"What happened?" Christina asked eventually. "Claire said you guys had a brush with a bear or something."

"We think it was a big brown bear or a grizzly, but we're not sure."

"Weren't there two dogs? I thought Hunter was also hurt?"

"No, the other dog was a police K-9, Officer Whitney's German Shepherd, Tango."

"Is he okay?"

There was a pregnant silence, and then Frank shook his head slowly. In a low voice, he replied, "He didn't make it, I'm afraid. He'll be buried this afternoon with honors and all that." Frank had tears in his eyes, but he shook off his somber mood. "So, coffee?" he asked cheerfully.

He poured three cups, and when Claire joined them with Peter, he grabbed a fourth and filled it, too. "We can't say enough how happy we are that you want to buy the lodge, but after everything that's happened, are you really sure?" the older man asked.

"Frank, I'm sure. All these things happening...they're just life, and me learning how to live in Skull Creek. This place is definitely my new home, and even though I don't know that many people in town, what I hear so far is mostly good. Besides, Mr. Billing made me sign the same documents you guys did, so now it's my property like it or not."

"Yeah, well, we do have some shitheads here too. Heard what them boys did to you. Half the town knows, and I doubt we'll be seeing them around here anymore."

"We have that kind back in L.A. too. Those sorts of people are everywhere, I'm afraid."

Claire joined in the conversation. "Afraid you're right, but I see Mr. Billing left you with some of his soldiers."

Frank handed Peter a cup of coffee. He accepted, but never drank from it. Next to Peter sat Hunter, who stared at him. "You're armed," Frank noted.

Peter nodded. "Legally. I can wait outside if you like."

"No, no, any friend of Tom Billing is a friend of ours. Will you be around much?"

"No. My partner and I will check out the property to see if the bear that attacked Christina is still there, and if it's made a den on her property. If it has, we'll consult with the ranger on what to do."

"I think the park ranger and some of the police have been there already. You might want to talk to them, too."

"Will do."

Frank turned to Christina, who was talking with Claire about some furnishings for the house and the company that custom-made them.

"So, you're still shopping for a vehicle?"

"I will, Frank, but not for a few days. Can't drive with my medicine and all. Besides, Peter and his friend will take me around where I need to go. So, are you and Robert coming up to show me the lay of the land?"

"You bet we will. Let me call Robert and see what's on his agenda. I know he's been working overtime, clearing a lot of dangerous trees after the storm for a lot of people. When is a good time for you?"

"This afternoon, if you can. I can't wait."

"It's a date."

Christina took advantage of Peter and Kevin to carry her around town, doing some shopping. Neither Peter nor Kevin helped her with the bags, to some people's surprise, not knowing who they were. Christina, being used to security and having used bodyguards from time to time, didn't think much about it. She purchased food and toiletries at one of the local grocery stores, then walked down the street to a liquor store a block away. She was happily surprised to see the wide selection of wines they had to offer. So far, no one seemed to have recognized her, and she started to relax as she continued her shopping.

After picking out her favorites, she stepped outside; and suddenly her heart jumped. Inside a coffee shop across the street, by the window, sat Robert and a tall, attractive blonde woman, laughing and drinking coffee. She put her hand on his. When he turned his head and saw Christina across the street, he smiled and waved. She immediately turned away, pretending she hadn't seen him. Strange; she hadn't felt this jealous for a long time. She hurried to the waiting SUV, hoping Robert would see Peter opening the door for her.

As they drove past a Western clothing store, she asked Kevin to pull over. She needed some clothes for the barn fest. It was a large, typical Country/Western store filled to the brim with clothing for men, women, and children alike. The place was fairly busy, with over a dozen customers browsing the shelves and racks. Over by a long counter stood several women discussing the big event at the barn, their conversation sprinkled with the normal talk about men. Christina ignored everyone there, focused on what she was looking for. She really didn't have any idea of what to wear, but then again, she'd never been a major player in the fashion league. She glanced at the women her age by the counter and tried to see what they had purchased, and what they wore. Suddenly, her eyes met one woman's, who immediately stopped talking to her friends and then turned back, starting to whisper. All her friends glanced at Christina, who ignored them.

"Hi, my name is Sandra, can I be of any help?" A short, friendly young woman stepped up.

"Yes you can, thanks. I'm going to the party at the Old Red Barn, and I have nothing appropriate to wear."

"Then you came to the right place. Just follow me."

Sandra was very professional, and treated Christina like any other customer. She gave Christina several options for pants and skirts. There was some giggling from the counter, and some stares bordering on the rude.

"Don't mind them," Sandra said in a low voice. "They're all pretty nice but a bit bitchy, and all of them like your friend Robert."

"Robert...? Oh yes, Robert. He's a nice guy...how did you guys know about..." Christina trailed off, realizing this was a very small town.

"Yep, and all the loose skirts around here hunt him like a trophy buck."

Christina bit down on her lower lip, whispering loudly through her teeth, "I'll do my best not to join in on that hunt, then."

"Sorry, I didn't hear you?"

"Oh, nothing important, Sandra. But I have to say it almost feels like being back in high school again, when all the popular girls talked behind my back."

"Yeah, I know what you mean. Most people in town are pretty nice, though, and I'm sure you'll find that out with time."

Christina liked this forthright young woman. With Sandra's help, she bought some matte brown cowboy boots with a matching Stetson, a few blouses, several pairs of jeans, and a couple of skirts—one long, and another short. Very short. She also got a couple of pairs of denim shorts, neither of which her mother would have approved of. As Christina walked up to the counter carrying her purchases, Sandra said goodbye and hurried up to another waiting customer.

The woman Christina took her stuff to might have been Sandra's mother, because they looked very much alike. She scanned the items through the register, giving Christina a friendly smile—then shot a scowl towards Peter, who stood a few yards behind Christina. The talkative women stood further away, still gossiping.

"You don't have to put up with that, you know," the clerk muttered.

Christina gave the woman a very confused look. "The gossiping…?"

"Not that. You know, him hitting you and such."

It took Christina a moment before she realized what the woman was talking about. She *did* have quite a few bruises, though most were covered by bandages and clothes; her former black eye was now more reddish-blue, but still swollen, and was there for all to see. "Oh, no, you don't understand. Peter hasn't hurt me."

The clerk leaned forward, placing her hand over Christina's, and whispered, "Denial, my friend, is the first thing you have to overcome."

Christina tried to get a word in edgewise, but the woman interrupted her by shaking her head firmly. So Christina just rolled her eyes and, after paying for her purchases with her black American Express card, left the store.

Just as they stepped out the door, the clerk shouted, "DENIAL!"

"What was all that about?" Peter asked as they left the store.

"Hah! Well, Peter, she thinks you're my boyfriend, and that you, well, you know." She pointed at her swollen eye. Peter looked calmly back, and then his eyes went round as he realized what the woman had thought of him.

He opened the SUV's door for Christina, muttering, "Stupid old cow, thinking I would hurt women."

They told Kevin what had happened in the store, and he thought it was funny. So did Christina, and soon they were both laughing. Peter wasn't. "Guys, it's not funny. A lot of women and more men than you'd think are hurt by their spouses."

"Not why I'm laughing, partner."

"Then why the hell are you laughing, Kevin?"

"Client laughs, I laugh." He winked at Christina in the rear-view mirror.

"Hey, don't blame it on me, you two. I couldn't get a word in edgewise. I did try and explain to her, but she just kept saying 'denial.' Must have had some bad experiences herself."

"Yeah, well, if we're going to stay over the weekend and go to this fall fest thing, you might want to wear your body armor, Peter. Rumors have a tendency to travel very fast in these small towns."

"Fuck you. I'll be in Africa by then, or down south looking for a nice, peaceful war."

"You guys never change, do you?"

The two men looked at each other and smiled. Christina didn't know for sure, but she suspected that both were more than just working buddies. She kept her thoughts to herself, though, because it wasn't any of her business. Both men were in their mid-fifties, and their eyes reflected hard experience that no one should have, as did their many scars.

When they pulled off the main road into Christina's driveway, Kevin stopped the SUV by the first entrance. Peter jumped out, went to the back of the SUV, and opened the hatch. Moving quickly, he removed his shirt and put on a sand-color combat vest, then locked and loaded what Christina, from a guest-starring role on *Stargate SG-2,* recognized as a P-90 bullpup machine gun with a scope and a few other gizmos. He then altered his pistol holster from a waist to a leg holster, grabbed a bottle of water, and vanished into the forest.

When Kevin continued driving, Christina couldn't help herself, letting out a loud "Wow!" Many more tree branches had been scattered through her property by the renewed storm, and in some cases whole trees had been blown over. She hadn't noticed, since she hadn't been in through the front way during the day since before the incident with the bear and the river. By the second gate entrance, Kevin had to get out and remove a huge branch blocking the road.

"Might want to have the caretaker check out the grounds," he noted. "That branch wasn't here yesterday. I'll drop you off at the main house, and then I'll join Peter. It's a really nice place you have here, by the way."

"You guys have been here before?"

"Come on, you know the Old Man. He doesn't mean to pry, but he *is* very protective, and—"

"Hold it, Kevin, I know. He's like a father to me, so yes, I know. Some people would be pissed off, but I'm not one of them. I'm only sorry for you guys having to babysit me for a while."

"You kiddin'? This is like a vacation for us." They pulled in and parked outside the main entrance, underneath the carport. Kevin leaned back and looked at Christina. "We go way back, don't we, kiddo?"

"We do, Kevin."

"You might have a big bear problem here, and if you ever need anything from us, don't you dare hesitate to call. You mean a lot to both Peter and I. Probably why the Old Man wanted us here."

"Thank you, Kevin, I'll keep that in mind."

"Here, take this." He handed her a necklace and a bracelet. "You can reach us anywhere on this side of the planet with these. I'll show you how they work. It's like the jewelry alarms you get when you go to a major Hollywood function, but these are better, with a much longer reach via satellites. You push the button, and an alarm will go off. Someone will come to your location; they both have a GPS in them."

"Waterproof?"

"Yes, and they're very resilient and durable."

Christina went inside with Kevin, who needed to use the bath-room—at least, that was his diplomatic excuse to check out the place. Later, he joined Peter in the forest, while Christina unpacked the groceries and her new clothing. When she finished, she returned to the kitch-en and made some tuna sandwiches, sour cream dip with a handful of salted pickles, and a pot of fresh coffee made from ground beans. Then she prepared a table on the back porch.

When Peter and Kevin returned, the three of them enjoyed a sim-ple, quiet lunch, listening to the sounds of nature while enjoying the view. "You're planning to get that cat?" Kevin asked.

"Yes I am, unless the real owner shows up."

"Might want to keep it on a leash for a while if you let it outside."

"Why?"

"A lot of predators around these parts. Eagles, hawks, falcons, and I saw the owl in front of the house."

"Oh, you mean my own private peeping tom."

"Your what?"

"The bastard and I have a morning routine. He peeps, and I scream."

Peter changed the subject. "We checked out your security system and it's okay, but we can install a better one if you like."

"I'd like that, if you think it's necessary."

"Well, you know us, a bit paranoid, comes with the job."

Kevin added, "We can go over different options. Some are a bit pri-cy, but I'm sure we can find what you need without going overboard."

"Fine. I just want to be able to be alone in my home without any crazies causing trouble. Then again, I doubt there will be any here."

"True, but there are a few men and women still stalking you, and you might consider getting a guard dog."

"Well, I've always loved having my own dog, but with my work schedule, I'd hate leaving the dog in a kennel."

"Just a thought."

They were interrupted by a loud sound from a speaker inside; it sounded like a doorbell.

"Looks like someone just passed the first entrance. I'll check it out. Kevin, you're with Christina." Peter went inside and examined the monitor by the kitchen, and then he shouted, "Two civilians, and from the looks of it, one is a photographer. I'll be back in a few."

A few minutes later, Kevin touched his earpiece and looked a bit annoyed. "A news reporter with a photographer. Wants to talk to you about you. Not locals."

Christina lowered her head into her hands, leaning on the table. "Oh, no. Tell them to get lost. I really don't want them to see me bruised up. Besides, Peter might get the blame again."

Frank shook his head, grinning, and related the instructions from his wrist microphone. Peter returned a few minutes later. "I told them to please stay away, and that they could contact your manager with an interview request. Don't worry, Christina, I was as nice as I could be."

She frowned and rolled her eyes, knowing very well that Peter and Kevin's "nice" could be a tad less than diplomatic.

There came another knell from the "doorbell."

Peter got up from his comfortable lounge chair. "Now what?" He went back into the kitchen. "Okay. It's a uniform this time, a policewoman."

Kevin asked her, "Want to go greet her?"

"Sure."

"Christina, you might want to get another security entrance that you can open from here."

"I very well could, Kevin, but that would take away the rustic look of the one I have."

"We can get you one that looks almost identical, but that's made of much more durable materials."

They went inside, and soon Peter escorted in a local officer. "Hello, ma'am. My name is Adrianna Vasquez, and I'm with the Sheriff's Department. My boss asked me to drop by. We're asking everyone if they've seen this type of truck." She placed a picture of an older model pickup truck on the kitchen island. "This isn't the actual truck, now. We got this picture off the Internet. But a similar one belonged to a victim or a friend of a victim, and this is the registration number."

She pointed at the picture; below it was the license plate number, written in large, bold letters.

"The color was originally red," Adrianna continued, "but I've been told it was very rusty, and the hood was replaced with a white one. It kinda stands out."

Christina looked at the picture and shook her head. "Sorry, I can't say whether I've seen it or not, because most vehicles here are trucks, and they all look the same to me. I probably would have remembered the white hood, though."

"And what about you guys?"

Peter and Kevin both looked at the picture, and also shook their heads. Neither asked any in-depth questions.

"Well, thank you for your time. Here's my card, in the event you see or remember anything."

Christina walked her to her car, and in that short time she and Adrianna talked as if they had known each other for years. "Nice place you got here, Ms. Dawn."

"Thank you, Deputy Vasquez."

"Please, my name is Adrianna. Small town, everyone knows everyone."

"Well, I'm new, so I've only met a handful so far. But I have to admit, everyone I've come across has been nice, and I feel like I've known them forever. Well, except for the two idiots by the river."

"Yeah, I saw the report. We're looking for them too. Shitheads always comes in pairs. I never met them, because I'm fairly new here myself, but from what I hear and have read about them, they're both bad news."

"Well, I'm not going to let them change my opinion about Skull Creek."

"Don't worry, I think you'll find most folks in these parts really are very nice. There's a get-together this weekend at the Old Red Barn, a fall fiesta. Great chance to meet the locals."

"Yes, I heard, but I'm not sure I'll go." Christina felt a stab of jealousy as she thought about Robert with the tall, attractive blonde.

"Oh…"

Christina noticed the hesitation and body language coming from Adrianna. "Oh, you misunderstand me. I would love to go, but look at me! Covered with bruises." She pointed at her swollen and bruised eye.

Adrianna smiled. "Your call, but I know there are a lot of people who would like to thank you for what you did at the big car accident the other day. Nice job, by the way."

"About the accident—how are all those people doing?"

"Most of them came out well, but there were a few broken arms and legs. The truck driver and…"

"I know. I was sorry to hear about their deaths." Christina thought for a moment. "The woman—did she make it?"

"Which woman?"

"The one that who caused the accident."

Now Adrianna looked puzzled. "No woman caused the accident. It was a reporter in a black Lincoln who was at fault. He was in too much of a hurry to get up to Harris camp to get the story about the body they found. Like so many other people, he forgot about Deadman's Curve."

"Strange. I thought someone told me that it was a women who ran across the road and caused it. Oh well, can't really remember it too well…bumped my head on a few rocks going 'river rafting' the other day." She pointed at her bandaged head with a sarcastic grin.

"No, that's not what happened, but it's so typical of a small community like Skull Creek. Before the truth has left the building, there are hundred rumors floating around. Just be careful when you drive on that curve; they're putting up a huge guard railing for now."

"Yes, I saw that when we passed earlier on."

"Hopefully they'll blast a hole in the mountain next year and widen the road on that part. It's ridiculous how many people get in accidents there. Well, Christina, it was nice talking to you. If you're ever lonely, me and some friends normally hang out now and then, and you're welcome to join us."

"That would be wonderful!"

Adrianna took another one of her business cards and wrote her private number on the back, then handed it to Christina. "Well if you'll excuse me, I have a missing truck to look for."

"Good luck."

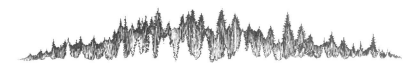

Eighteen

Adrianna had been driving for about an hour now, stopping every now and then at people's homes to ask questions about the missing truck. She looked at her watch, and figured she had time for one more stop before she had to head back and finish her shift, so she followed the mountain road until she came to a three-way intersection. The road to the left would take her to a gold mine almost at the top of a mountain, and the road to the right to another gold mine; that one was a longer ride, while the one to the left was closer, but at a much higher elevation. Both mines would be a problem, given the elevation. She would have difficulty breathing, because she still wasn't used with the high altitude. She chose the left-hand road. One hour later, with no information that could help her, she was back at the same intersection.

Adrianna muttered to herself, "Should I go back and punch out for the day, or…nah, might as well go to the second mine while I'm here. I would hate having to go back this way tomorrow."

She called it in and got the approval for overtime.

The gold mine looked almost identical to the one she had just visited; both of them reminded her of the gold mines from all those reality shows on television. Thinking about the word *mine*, she thought of a hole in the ground and a bunch of dirty dwarfs wobbling around with pickaxes, long beards, large noses, singing stupid shit. This mine and crew, not so much.

She had never been a nature freak, but she did love nature over any concrete desert, and that was why she worked in Skull Creek. However, the devastation to nature from huge bulldozers, semi-trucks, excavators, and dump trucks was just awful. The land was completely ruined, all for a few measly grains of yellow dust.

With narrow roads and huge dump trucks driving very fast back and forth between two large clearings on the mountain plateau, it was a miracle that there were no accidents. More than once she almost got hit, so finally she turned on her light bar, and that worked. The trucks finally slowed down. She looked for an office, and found several trailers and tents. Adrianna parked on a gravel lot occupied only by pickups. She looked over the trucks, but couldn't see the one she was looking for.

A fat fellow greeted her; she turned off the lights and exited the car. A dust cloud from a dump truck slammed grit into her face; she'd left her hat in the car, no reason to get the thing dirty. She coughed some, and could barely hear the guy facing her. He gestured with his hand for her to follow him to a temporary office on top of low hill, half a tent with a wooden front frame, just like in a western film. The sound from below had almost faded away by then, due to the wind.

"Howdy, officer, Bob's the name. What brings you to us, and how can I help?"

Adrianna frowned. The man needed a long shower, but she noticed that he was very calm and not nervous at all, just like the guy at the other mine she had questioned. Good sign. She explained her business, and handed him the picture of the truck. He removed his helmet and ran his fingers through his sparse hair. When she mentioned the white hood he instantly grabbed his enormous goatish beard, squinted, and strained a smile.

Bingo, she thought, and knew that she was on something.

Bob grabbed his shortwave radio. "Harrington, where ya at?"

The radio crackled I return. "I'm out by the *Nugget-Crusher,* Boss. We got a leak—gotta take care of this shit 'fore we lose all our profits."

Bob looked up at Adrianna. "Officer, you mind a short trip?"

"Not at all."

They got in what looked like an electric golf cart's sturdier older brother. Bob drove quickly over a bluff, and then down the side of the mountain to a second dig site. This one was almost twice the size of the first, where Adrianna had parked her car.

Bob shouted, "There's a small wooden road this side of the mountain, you might have missed it, but it's a short cut and it saves you about five minutes. Too small for our larger trucks, excavators, and dump trucks, though."

"Yeah, I must have missed that one."

"You all right, ma'am?"

Adrianna hated the word "ma'am", as it made her feel old and she was only in her mid-twenties, but at least it wasn't "miss." She replied, "Altitude sickness. Having a little problem breathing, that's all."

"I know what you mean. Look at my fat ass, it's a real torture sometimes, but hey—it's worth the gold."

"I bet it is."

They stopped by an enormous machine; Adrianna had seen similar ones on the television shows. Several men were working around a large black hose, making repairs, all wearing hard hats. Bob handed her one. It was pink; his was black.

"Hey, Harrington, can you help us out here?"

An average-sized guy with a perfectly trimmed Amish-style beard joined them; he too needed a shower. Bob explained what Adrianna was looking for. The noise from the machines on this part of the mountain was less than on the other side, and they could talk normally with each other.

"Sounds like Butch or Vern. Neither one of 'em had any vehicle before; we use to pick up them and a couple of other guys every day and give them a ride up the mountain. Either they lost their driver's licenses or didn't own their own vehicle. Pretty sure it's one or both, because they've been driving a truck like you describe for a few days. Never thought much about it. Wait a minute...is it stolen?"

Harrison looked back at his partner, Bob, and both looked upset now. "Ma'am, if it's stolen, we don't want no problems. We'll cooperate with you completely, we don't need no problems with the locals."

"For now, I just need to see the truck, and then talk to them to see if it's the right truck. And no, it hasn't been reported stolen that I know of."

For all she knew, it could have been purchased, but the tingling feeling in her gut told her that she was on the right track. She contemplated contacting her superiors, but decided to get more flesh on the bone before she did.

"Well, I don't know where Butch is, but Vern is down by the 400."

They got back into the little vehicle with Harrington in the back, then drove down a man-made road on the side of an enormous cut. The people behind them had stopped working on the hose to observe them. When they got closer to a huge excavator, the person inside didn't notice them. The top of the giant machine rotated, turned, and with a boom, the bucket dug out the side of the mountain while a large dump truck waited to be loaded. The driver in the dump truck waved, looking bored, not even curious when he saw the police officer. When the top of the excavator turned again, the driver noticed them. He stared in shock at Adrianna, who immediately knew that something was up.

Vern, a very large man, or maybe just very fat, lunged out of the cockpit and started to run. But he tripped and fell hard immediately, before turning his head and starting to crawl. His hard hat rolled away towards Adrianna, who motioned for Bob and Harrington to back off. She walked calmly towards the big blob on the ground; and when he saw the officer he started to crawl on all fours again towards the side of the mountain he had been digging at, screaming and crying like a baby. Adrianna had enough experience to know that whenever anyone ran from the police, something was up.

There was panic in Vern's eyes now when he staggered to his feet and tried to climb the wall facing him. He made it a few feet up, but then slid back down. His shirt lay puddled around his chest and he was filthy and now very dusty. Like all the men on the mountain, he needed a shower. Theirs was a dirty job.

Adrianna's main concern right now was that panic-stricken people could sometimes do very stupid things, and if he was armed, he might end up committing suicide by cop. Vern kept climbing, losing one of his steel-toe boots in the process. But he finally fell back and started to cry, hiding his face behind his surprisingly small hands.

"Man, man, I sorry, I sorry, didn't mean anything by it, I'm so sorry…"

Adriana removed her hand from her revolver's grip and just observed him. If a suspect talked, then the rule was simple: shut the fuck up and let them.

From the blob's blather, she was pretty sure she had scored in this respect, but she needed to know more. She crossed her arms and rested one elbow on her left hand while taking up a thinking gesture with the other, touching her chin. She did gather from the unusual confession that this suspect was most likely not the alpha, but then again she could be wrong; criminals could be very good actors. She was definitely onto something, since there were words like *body*, *truck*, *loose head* and so on.

"Well, sir, why don't you take it again from the beginning?" she said at last.

"I told Butch not to do it, the head and all," Vern blubbered. Then he up and got sick, puking his guts out all over himself.

"Great, now my car will stink from this piece of shit," Adrianna thought, and didn't realize she'd said it aloud until Vern looked up at her voice and started crying, tears cutting through the dust caked on his fat face.

It took twenty minutes before they were back at her car. Adrianna had to use the ankle cuffs *and* her regular cuffs to cuff him. She read him his rights in front of many witnesses, but she wasn't entirely sure what she was going to book him for. She needed to see the truck, but she definitely felt she was on something.

She turned to Bob and Harrington, who were watching open-mouthed and wide-eyed. "Call this number when the other guy is back with the truck. I'd appreciate some discretion, so we can avoid chasing him down or letting him slip away." She gave both a very stern look.

Both men held up their hands in a defensive gesture, and tried to speak at the same time. Bob raised his voice over Harrington's. "I promise we'll hold him here for you guys. We don't want any problems; we got enough problems getting permits mining here as it is, and the other prospectors are after our claim, so trust us—we don't need more problems."

Harrington said, "By the way, what have they done?"

She looked at Harrington. "For now, this one is a suspect in a homicide and possible grand theft auto, at the very least."

Both Bob and Harrington's eyes widened, and they began speaking to each other in low voices, saying something about how it was someone's else's fault for hiring them. Meanwhile, she tried calling it in over her radio, but got nothing but static. Then she tried her cell phone, but there was no reception. "You'd think being up this high, there would be excellent cell reception," she muttered, annoyed.

"Sometimes there is, and sometimes there isn't," Bob said. "Depends on the time of day. We can try and call from the office, if you want."

"Thank you, Bob, please do that. Use the number on the card I gave you, and tell them I'm bringing in a suspect."

She drove away with the big crybaby in the back, wearing his seatbelt. She tried repeatedly to call in to HQ, but to her growing frustration—compounded by the grown man crying in the back—she got nothing. When she almost ran off the road trying, she tossed her cell phone on the passenger seat and focused on her driving. She was about to pass the small wooden road, which was well hidden if you drove up on it from the opposite side, when a reddish-orange rusty pickup truck with a white hood rammed the right front fender of her car, hard, making the car spin. She hit the brakes, and watched as the truck vanished down the road. She never had time to check the plates, but she was one hundred percent sure that this was the truck she was looking for.

Now she was faced with a dilemma. Adrianna couldn't—or rather, shouldn't—take up pursuit on the hit-and-run, because she had a suspect in the back. She had to make a quick decision. She tried radioing and calling her headquarters again, but that still didn't work. She looked in the rearview mirror. The crying had stopped; she looked into the eyes of Vern, who had a very creepy smile on his face. He said nothing, and he didn't have to. He knew that his partner had scared her…or so he thought.

In a squeaky voice, beginning with a short laugh, Vern said, "You in trouble now, bitch!"

She backed up fast, put the gear in drive, and hit the accelerator. Speeding up, Adrianna tried to remember the road ahead, and decided to slow down. The entire time, her passenger kept talking in an unpleasant voice: "Once we catch you, I'm going to come all up on your face, cunt, and then I wanna bust all those perfect little teeth in your mouth."

She glanced in the rearview mirror. "What happened to all the crying, little bitch?"

"You callin' *me* a bitch? Go home south across the border, you fuckin' Mexican whore."

She turned her attention to the road, and hit the brakes hard. The car swirled to the left; the stolen truck was about fifty yards down on the narrow road, and she could see someone leaning over the hood. Her instinct made her pull the hand brake, and the very moment she opened her door she ducked for cover. A shot rang out, followed by the sound of glass exploding from the passenger's side window next to her. Calmly, conditioned by her training, she rolled over on the ground and took cover in the ditch. At first, she didn't realize what had just happened; then another shot rang out, striking her car's door panel, and she understood that the idiot was shooting at her. Adrenaline pumped into her system and she got very nervous, hands trembling and breathing hard. Adrianna had never before used her sidearm against a living person as a police officer; she'd used it for protection, yes, but had never actually fired it at someone.

She peeked over the grassy ditch below on the truck, then pulled out her revolver and aimed. She took one shot at what she thought was a pair of legs, and another shoot at the front right tire of the truck. She missed both; it was hard to hit anything at distance with a handgun. Another shot from the rifle came, hitting the ground nearby, kicking dust and grass into her face. Vern was laughing his ass off now, screaming and shouting with joy. Adrianna emptied her revolver at what she thought was the suspect, but of course it was hard to tell from this angle.

She flipped open the cylinder and dropped the casings from her revolver; some struck her wrist and stung her with the heat, but she didn't care. She was sweating profusely, and her hair lay like glue over her face. She grabbed a speed loader from her belt, fumbled some, and bit down hard on her lower lip, trying to force herself not to tremble as she finally reloaded. She felt dizzy from all the action, and started to feel panic fill her like a dark shadow. She rolled over, and now there were a couple of cowboy boots not too far away, heading towards her. She was shaking by now and emptied her revolver at them. There was a scream of pain and a shot came from the perp; she rolled back down into the ditch and grabbed her last speed loader, reloaded, and crawled further down in the ditch, hurting both elbows and knees, but hardly noticing it. There was the sound of an engine accelerating; she peeked up from the ditch and hurriedly climbed up onto the road, but tripped as she got up. From a kneeling position, she aimed and fired off one more round.

Adrianna got up and ran back to the squad car. She brushed some glass crumbs off her seat, and when she did she cut her hand a bit. She ignored the pain. The fat bastard behind her—who by now reminded her of some fucked-up opera—was howling loudly. She backed up the car, burning rubber, and just as she was about to hit the accelerator, Vern's fat face popped up.

"Told you, bitch! You're fucked! My buddy and I gonna get you!"

Calmly, she turned to face Vern's wide grin, smiling pleasantly. "No talking to the driver while the vehicle is in motion, please." She was about ready to stick the revolver up under his double-chin and pull the trigger.

"What did you say, you crazy fucking cunt? You almost got me killed, you bitch! Ima sue the fuck outta you!"

She smiled again and winked an eye seductively. Vern never saw the stun gun, but he did feel the twenty thousand volts when Adrianna showed it up under his jaw, and he felt the piss when it drained down his leg.

She hit the accelerator, but drove with more caution this time. She noticed a dust cloud down the road and sped up. Suddenly, there was a voice on the radio. The reception was very poor, but she shouted that she was in pursuit of a homicide suspect, and shots had been fired. When she reached the three-way intersection, she could see the truck a bit ahead, but not that far away. There was mist coming up from the hood. She increased her speed, and turned on her lights and sirens. The chase was on.

She lost site of the truck briefly as she came to a long curve, but as she rounded the curve, she could see that it and its billow of steam were getting closer. A huge eighteen-wheeler logging truck pulled out in front of the suspect's truck from a side road , and he had to hit the brakes. She got closer and closer, but the pickup sped up and made a dangerous attempt to pass the logger on the left side of the road. She followed, but to her horror, another eighteen-wheeler faced her. She hit the brakes and saw that the truck with the suspect barely missed the oncoming traffic. The semi in front of her tried to pull to the side and slow down, but that didn't help. The driver motioned with his arm that she could pass. She put the gas pedal to the metal and did. Adrianna noticed in her rear mirror that the driver was a woman, who gave her a thumbs up while honking the horn.

She and the suspect zig-zagged between traffic, and the chase was taking its toll on both drivers and their vehicles. More steam spewed out, from not only the perp's truck, but also from her police car. A few miles before the last intersection, where Deadman's Curve was coming up, the old pickup truck pulled over to the side. Adrianna hit her brakes as Vern woke up screaming. An arm reached out from the driver's side of Vern's truck, holding an automatic pistol, firing several rounds at Adrianna. Then the firing stopped as the gun clicked; either it had misfired or was out of ammo. She got out of her car, aimed carefully, and fired one round. The pistol exploded into a hundred pieces, and she suspected Butch's hand wasn't in much better shape; but he only glared back at her, ignoring her shouts for him to stop and exit his vehicle. He gave her the bird and drove off. She got on her radio, and found that she now had good reception. She related what had happened, as whining cries came from the back seat. When she turned her head, Vern had blood oozing from his shoulder. The crybaby was back; he cried and screamed, tossing in curses and threats once in a while. Suddenly, another police vehicle passed her, moving fast.

Now she could relax some. "Guess your friend doesn't like back-seat driving either. Or maybe he was trying to shut you up," she told Vern.

Reluctantly, Adriana called for a paramedic to meet her further down the road. Another twenty thousand volts, and the fat bastard shut up. She looked over his injury, and then she got a first aid kit from the trunk. She quickly wrapped some gauze over the injured shoulder, just enough to stop the bleeding and for show. She knew she was in trouble already; didn't need to make it worse.

Adrianna was exhausted from the excitement and adrenalin rush when she finished. She brushed off her sweaty forehead, and realized for the first time that there was quite a bit of blood on her forearm. She glanced at the mirror, and noticed that she had a few badly-bleeding lacerations on her face. Her hand had bled too, and now, to her horror, she realized that the steering wheel had become very slippery.

By now there were several civilian cars, trucks, and eighteen-wheelers formed up behind her, keeping their distance. Her lights were long gone, shot to pieces, and the siren made an awful noise. She shut it all off, and started to drive carefully away from there. She reached the intersection before Deadman's Curve and saw that the lane nearest the edge had been cordoned off, and many warning signs had been erected with yellow lights. There were some vehicles there doing road construction and putting up a very sturdy, tall security fence. A worker with a yellow flag motioned for her to advance slowly. He looked very shook up, and Adriana noticed many orange cones rolling around.

"Sorry, officer, but we have to ask you to stop."

Adrianna just lifted her eyebrows.

"Another damn accident—an old truck just flew straight through the new guardrail and fence we're building."

Adrianna, sounding concerned said, "What about the police SUV following it?"

"Fine, just fine—but the other truck…well, it won't make the Indie 500 any time soon."

After some minor commotion, she was allowed to proceed; and during the wait she decided to explain to Carlos the simple truth: she'd taken the suspect into custody and was taking him in when his partner tried to spring him—and kill her in the process.

"Great. Mr. Know-It-All," Adrianna groaned as she slowed her car. A large officer in short sleeves stood before her, flexing his enormous tanned muscles. He wore mirrored aviator glasses, and with a perfect set of bleached, perfect teeth, smiled widely as he walked towards Adrianna while chewing on a giant wad of gum…and yes, here came the fucking bubble. She slowed her car to a stop near the accident site at Deadman's Curve.

"Howdy there, Adrianna. Woman, you seen better days. Looked at yourself in the mirror lately? Heard you been out hunting in the mountains, and I was on my way to assist—and then this shit." He gestured toward the crash site.

"Howdy, Dex. Yeah, our radios are real pieces of shit up here…they need to do something about 'em."

"I know what you mean. You okay? I can take the perp off your hands if you want me too."

"I'm all right; I'll take him from here. Have to meet up with the paramedics down the road, and then make sure someone babysits the thing in the back once he's in the hospital. What about the other guy?"

"Your call. Looking forwarding to reading your report on this one and the guy who went over the cliff; bastard flew straight through the railing."

"Is he alive?"

"Don't know yet. Waiting for back-up before heading down there—rescue workers can't do anything until we say it's okay. By the way, will you be going to the fall party?"

Adrianna licked her lips while undressing Dex in her mind from head to toe. "Oh, yeah."

"Well, let me know if you need to be escorted by a real man."

"Who'd you have in mind, slick?"

He gestured with both hands towards himself, smiling widely.

"In your dreams, cowboy. Well, I have to get going. Think I can hear the ambulance down the road." Adrianna thought for a moment and then said, "What concerns me most for now is whether Carlos will have a shit-fit when he sees my car."

"Relax, I doubt he will. Besides, he ain't in today."

"What you mean?"

"He left town, I guess this morning. Left a note with that old drag-on lady in his office that he'll be back in a day or two."

"He's on vacation *now?*"

"I doubt it's vacation, because his family is still around, but he's sure been acting a bit off ever since that bear hunt last weekend."

CARLOS PARKED his rental car outside the large main building. It was white, with a wraparound porch. The house lay on top of a hill and provided a beautiful panorama for the visitors. There were a few barns and a long, white wooden fence surrounding the typical South Texas ranch. A couple of young girls rode two horses in a large circle, while an instructor stood in the middle, calling out instructions. It was a hot day even though it was fall, definitely nothing like Skull Creek. Instead of cool, damp weather, here it was dry heat. Carlos could see a dust devil in the distance, and some real tumbleweeds skating over the sandy landscape, just like this was some old-time Western movie.

He used the doorbell but didn't hear any ringing, so he knocked on the door instead. After a moment, a woman in her seventies, with a friendly smile and a heavy Mexican accent, greeted him at the door. "Sheriff Carlos da Silva," he announced. "I'm here to meet Special Agent Perez."

"Welcome, sheriff, my name is Penelope, and my husband Anthony is waiting for you in the back."

They walked through the airy home; it was cool, nicely decorated, very clean, and smelled fresh. When they reached the back porch, Penelope pointed towards an old man sitting in a rocking chair with a cowboy hat over his eyes, his legs propped up on the porch rail, ending in cowboy boots. She left Carlos and walked into the kitchen behind them. Carlos could smell fresh coffee being brewed and something baking in the oven, reminding him that he'd skipped breakfast and lunch.

He approached the resting man carefully.

"I'm awake. Just resting my eyes is all." The man gestured for Carlos to seat himself in a similar rocking chair next to him. "Welcome to our home, Carlos da Silva…we meet again. It's been a long time—say, fifty years?"

"You remember?"

"How can I not? It was my first case as a Special Agent across the border—nothing forgettable about it."

Anthony Perez lifted his hat and peered at the surroundings. The two girls were galloping their horses away towards a small lake.

"Nice view and place you got here," Carlos ventured.

Perez just nodded. Carlos was still standing, hesitant.

From his breast pocket, Anthony took out two large Havana cigars and handed one to Carlos. "Guess it's time for celebrating our reunion, huh?"

"No thank you, sir, those things can kill you."

Anthony turned his head and eyed Carlos as he finally stood up, then extended his hand to Carlos, who grabbed it. The old man had a firm grip. He held Carlos's hand tight, and forced Carlos forward; and then he whispered, while staring in the Sheriff's eyes, "And so can monsters."

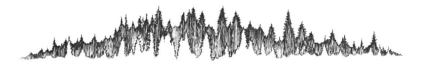

NINETEEN

Please, Malik, I…Carlos needs your help. All I'm asking is for you to take a look at what's down in the basement."

"You said it yourself. He locked the door, and you don't know where the key is. Sorry, Anna-Maria, both of you are my friends, and I don't want to ruin what we have."

"You know, Carlos and I, we don't keep any secrets from each other. I saw some of the drawings, but I really need you to look for yourself."

Malik took a deep breath, and looked up at the ceiling. "Why is it so important? It's probably some old cold case he's been working on. People in law enforcement do it all the time, instead of a hobby, I guess."

"But that's the problem, Malik. In all the years we've been together, he's never brought work home with him. I'm scared."

"Of what?"

"I can feel that something is very wrong, but I just don't know what it is—and Carlos has been like a zombie ever since that bear hunt this past weekend. He hasn't slept since then, and has hardly left the basement; and when he did, he made sure it was locked and he even ordered me and the kids not to go down there."

"Well, there's you answer."

"But please! As our friend, if only you could go down there and check and see what he is doing… I remember seeing some strange picture of… I think it was a werewolf, or something monstrous like you see in the movies."

"You sure he's not just doing something to surprise you guys?"

"Yes, I'm sure, because whatever it is he's doing, it's got him spooked."

Malik scowled. "Bullshit! The Carlos I know is afraid of no man. Listen, I'd love to help, but on this, I can't." Malik put on his hat and walked to the kitchen door.

"Malik, he's not afraid. He's terrified."

Malik held the doorknob; he looked down, and then he turned his head, looking at a desperate Anna-Maria as her tears poured down.

"Whatever we find in the basement must never see daylight if it's as bad as you think. Promise me."

THE OLD man said, "It was the worst case I ever saw in all my time working with the FBI. Thirty-eight people slaughtered, nine of them children, even two infants. All the bodies tossed into a dry riverbed and then set on fire. The village was set on fire, too—miracle, really, that you survived. But from the looks of you, I see you don't remember much, do you?"

Carlos shook his head.

"So what brings you here?"

"Something triggered a memory, one I guess I've been hiding from." Carlos explained what had happened in Skull Creek, and when part of the old memory had returned. He also explained how he had located Special Agent Perez's phone number and address thanks to some newspaper clippings.

"Not hiding, but suppressed," Perez said. "People, especially children, have that ability whenever they've lived through something traumatic. It's quite normal, you know. You were only five years old, and the only witness to a horrible crime. To top it off you were an American citizen, which is why my partner Harvey Cole and I were assigned the job. If I remember correctly, your father was born American and your mother was a legal immigrant from Mexico." Anthony Perez smiled dryly. "If I may ask, what triggered your memory after all these years?"

Carlos looked at the ground. "At first, I thought I saw something, and it reminded me of something I couldn't put my finger on. But that was just a bear, I think. No, what really made me remember was…"

"The smell?"

Carlos looked up abruptly. There had been nothing mentioned about that horrible, bestial smell in any of the newspaper clippings, or anywhere in the few documents he had found. Perez nodded. "We kept that information to ourselves, and as a law enforcement officer yourself, I don't have to explain why."

"Yeah, I know. To keep the idiots out and away from the investigation."

"Yes. Anyway, you were a young child, and the entire case became strictly classified, because drug cartels don't care about the age of a witness. Your testimony made no sense to anyone, and when we went to the site of the former village we found nothing there."

"Nothing?"

"Not at the village. But you see, Carlos, I had a great partner—you know, the old-fashioned kind who never left any loose ends. He always went with what he had, and he eventually became a legend in the FBI. He was my friend and mentor for many years. Anyway, Harvey and I went back and this time he brought a tracker, a Mexican Apache woman, with us."

He motioned his head towards Penelope.

"Yep, she looks a lot younger than I, don't she? But we're the same age, and you did meet her once in the hospital."

"I don't remember that."

"Not surprised." Both looked at Penelope while she was setting a table with a pot of coffee, lemonade, cups, glasses and some homemade cinnamon buns. Steam and fragrance from the fresh-baked buns filled the air. She turned to them and said, "Well, gentlemen, let's eat."

The three of them sat down, and the two young girls rode up and tied their horses to a fence nearby. The instructor was in the far distance, riding another horse.

"Meet our grandkids, Trouble and More Trouble," Perez said.

"Come on, Grandpa, we're your little angels, and you know it!" the older girl said.

The old man almost spit his coffee out.

"'Angels ain't the word I would use to describe you, considering what you guys did at school recently."

"Yeah, well, stupid teachers anyway."

"The one with the mouth is Trudy, and the other one is Trish. Both in high school, and whenever they get in trouble, our son and his wife sends them to us to do chores around the farm. Not entirely a successful enterprise when it comes to punishment, I think."

"Oh, you love it, old man."

"See? The younger one...it mouths off, too. Girls, this is Sheriff Carlos from up north." Perez emphasized the word "sheriff."

All of them enjoyed the afternoon snack. Once they finished. the girls kissed their grandparents goodbye and then hurried back to the horses, laughing aloud.

"I think they get themselves into trouble just so they can have their parents drive fifty miles and drop them off here," Penelope said.

"Point taken, my beautiful wife, and we must never tell our son that."

There was an eerie silence but for the laughter from the girls riding back and forth in the distance.

"Why don't you tell Carlos what you found that day fifty years ago, my dear tracker."

Penelope smiled at his taunt and said, while looking at Carlos, "I will never forget that day, young man. We started tracking in circles around the village, and eventually we found an old truck that had broken down, and some tracks leading north from it. There were three of them, two adults and a child; of course, there was nothing indicating that they were the criminals, but it was all we had, and it seemed that they'd come from the village a couple miles away. The truck had been hidden near some trees and covered with brush. If they hadn't covered it, I guess we wouldn't have thought much about it. Cars and trucks break down in the desert all the time."

Anthony poured some lemonade into three glasses, and all of them drank deeply to combat the region's dry heat.

Anthony continued where his wife had stopped. "Eventually we reached the river, and all the tracks were gone. For two days, we followed the river bank on both sides, but found nothing.

"Dear husband, you forgot the most important thing we found."

"Oh yes. Sorry, it's been a long time, so why don't you fill in the blanks."

"I found some hair on a tree next to a fresh engraving on a border post. It was a strange word…let me think. *Croatoan,* I think it was, but I don't know what it means. Harvey, however, did find out that there has been a native tribe back east that was called that, didn't make much sense though. I didn't pay much attention to it, but I remember a foul smell. Harvey Cole, being very meticulous, immediately bagged the hair, because he remembered that you had mentioned something about a really bad-smelling monster."

"Now let me continue. I'm sure Carlos is in a hurry."

"I'm fine. Just needed to fill in the blanks, but no, I don't want to impose on you guys for too long."

Anthony only waved his hand in the air. "No imposition. Anyway, Harvey took some of the samples and sent them to D.C. Back then, we didn't have all these high-tech gizmos like they do now, but a few months later when the case was more or less cold, unfortunately, we got the results back…unfortunately, I say, because our boss made us stop the investigation."

"What happened?"

"Well, Carlos, turned out the hair came from a lion, of all things. The African kind, *Panthera leo*. That pretty much shut us down, to my partner's despair. Personally, I had just met this beautiful senorita, and my mind wasn't really where it ought to have been. Years went by, and here we are."

Penelope and Anthony smiled at each other.

"No, there *is* one thing more, my love," she said. "You forgot about the box from Harvey Cole, the one his executor sent you."

"Oh yes, the box! As you know, Carlos, many of us in law enforcement never stop investigating the cold cases, not even after retirement. I got this box almost twenty years ago, and I only looked in it once, and guess what case is in the box? Yours, Carlos. I never had any interest in it like my partner must have had. But even as the years went by and we were assigned to different locations, we always kept in contact. Through all that time, he never mentioned that he was still investigated this old case, except for one instance. In the '60s and '70s there were reports of a so-called "skunk ape-man" in Florida, and the description fit your monster. I know Harvey went down there a few times, it's all in his notes; but he found nothing. Later on, back in the mid-nineties when my wife and I were on vacation in Florida, cruising the West Coast and the Everglades, we used to listen to a morning show from Tampa, and they did mention something about the "skunk ape" and interviewed some idiot in the Everglades who claimed to be an expert on the subject."

"You still have it here? The box with the information?" Carlos asked eagerly.

"Of course we do, but before you jump up and down and all over the box, I'm curious. Why now? All this because of a smell?"

"No. The smell helped, but that's not it."

"Then what?"

"You hear what happened at Skull Creek, my home town?"

"Of course. It's been all over the news for days, I think—sure lives up to its name. Homicide and a grizzly bear killing people?"

"No, not a bear," Carlos stated firmly. "It was no bear."

Carlos looked down, trying to hide his teary eyes, and then he looked up at Penelope and Anthony, shaking his head a bit awkwardly. "I'm as sane today as I was fifty years ago, despite what the shrinks must have said back then, and now I remember enough, and I know I've seen it before. The beast is back. At least, one of them."

There was more silence before Perez said, "You are a rational man, it seems, but that story didn't work out for you fifty years ago, and I doubt you'll be keeping your sheriff's star if you say much more about this to anyone." Perez sighed. "Oh, don't look at me like that. I remember the scared but brave kid you were, and now I see the brave lawman you've grown up to be. Your secret is safe with us. You can figure this out if anyone can, Carlos. Keep the box and return it once you're finished, but start thinking rationally, or this whole thing will consume you from the inside. You should have met Harvey. I'll give you this, because it's pretty much what I remember he had written: *species dysphoria*. Study it well, and you might be on to something."

"Never heard of it."

"Few people have, and still, it's something growing in our society. *Species dysphoria* is a type of experience of dysphoria—that is, a profound state of unease or dissatisfaction with what you are. Species dysphoria includes clinical lycanthropy, a delusion of existing as an animal, sometimes even to the point of hallucination. The individual might have an excess concern over his or her body, may feel that their body is wrong and have a desire to be an animal—and of course, there can be some sexual arousal in it."

"Sounds like those 'furries,' the people who dress up in animal suits to have sex. Saw that shit on TV."

Anthony paused and took a sip on his lemonade. "Could be a part of it."

Penelope told him, "Carlos, something scared you when you were a child, but you're an adult now. Whatever scared you back then is still scaring you. Don't let the fright in you take over your reasoning mind.

What my beloved has told you, and what his partner researched, is perhaps the only logical explanation."

"Yes, I understand that…but can either one of you explain why what I saw fifty years ago looks identical now? If it's a person, then that person would be really old by now. It doesn't make any sense." Carlos sounded a little desperate. "And why would I suddenly see it again?"

Anthony Perez's voice took on a lecturing tone. "Let's be rational and go back in time, and walk through to the present. One, you witnessed a horrific act where, according to your testimony, hairy monsters hurt your people, and they smelled bad. Two, A few days ago your memory returned, probably due to post traumatic stress disorder stemming from the event that's has been dormant in the back of your mind. The smell, and what you saw again—let's call it the monster—activated that memory. Three, who was killed in Skull Creek? Was it only one person, or was it more than one? Who were they? Did any of them have any link to what happened in Mexico fifty years ago?"

"No. I can see no connection between the victim in Skull Creek and what I witnessed in Mexico. There *was* a second death, but we think it's a different perp. However, the coroner's report hasn't been submitted yet."

Anthony continued after Carlos's reply, "Four. Out of all places, why has it appeared in Skull Creek, where you happened to reside, Carlos?" He paused. "The official report on the investigation fifty years ago was that it was related to a possible drug war, but neither my partner nor I agreed with that. There were no indications of any drug problems in that village, but having said that, we can't rule out the possibility that a drug lord on some type of vendetta killed them all. Unfortunate as it may be, that could be the reason. However, politics as usual dictated that we close the investigation. The truth is, we didn't really have anything to work with. Nothing rational, anyway. It was almost as if the incident never occurred."

Penelope looked at her husband, confused. "What do you mean? I don't follow."

"Someone involved with drugs might have had relatives in the village, and crossed the wrong people."

"You're saying they would wipe out an entire village for that?"

"I'm afraid so. Mass graves are found now and then, with no explanation of what happened."

Carlos intervened when he sensed tension between Penelope and Anthony. "It's true, ma'am. Those things do occur. At least it seems like the Mexican government is getting things under control nowadays." He turned his attention back to Anthony. "But why would it show up again, and in Skull Creek?"

Penelope walked to the kitchen and got some more coffee for everyone.

"Tell me, is the village still there?" Carlos pressed.

"No, Carlos. The people of the village had actually sold all their land for industrial development just before the…incident. We thought at first that could have been the reason behind the killings, but no; they had all been paid handsomely, and as of a matter of fact were celebrating the fact they would all soon be starting new lives with plenty of money. There's a huge water and power plant there now, operated by the Mexican government. I think that the only problem they had building it was from a few protesters wanting to save the planet and all that."

The sun had dropped low on the horizon, its color deepening to orange as it began setting. The sky was stained with pink fire along the horizon.

Anthony leaned forward and spoke softly. "I think it's you. If it's back, you're the reason this monster is in Skull Creek. You were a witness to a horrific crime—the only witness. Before we had personal computers, finding you would have been next to impossible, but nowadays, with all the information out there, including classified leaks from our government…well, this could very well be some sort of personal vendetta."

"You've got a point there, but again, it doesn't answer the question. If it's a man, then how old is he, assuming it's a he?"

Penelope looked at her grandchildren goofing around with the trainer, while protesting loudly at having to bring the horses to the barn. "He would have to be ancient. Unless…"

Carlos asked, "Unless what?"

Anthony, "Yes, dear, what's on your mind? Because right now, I got nothing for our new friend."

"Unless this has been going on for generations. And is still going on."

"Could be." Anthony stood up and walked over to the railing, where he lit his second cigar, his back turned to the others. "As much as I want to help you, Carlos, because I feel that I owe you somehow… you really don't have much of a case here. There's no evidence, really. For all we know, there might have been a dead animal or a skunk nearby when you saw the victim. You admit that when you saw this thing, the weather conditions were as bad as they could get—rain, darkness, and lightning. You shot at it, but don't know if you hit it at a distance of, what, 50 yards?"

"About that distance, yes."

"Unless you can produce any physical evidence, you have nothing but a horrible memory that returned to you, and as much as I hate to say it, your mind might have played a trick on you."

Anthony turned, facing Carlos. "Don't ruin your career on this, son. In a few years, you can retire. Think about that and your family. Some memories are best kept hidden."

After a short farewell, Anthony and Penelope stood on the front porch and watched as Carlos drove away.

"Do you think he will follow your advice?" Penelope asked in Spanish.

"No, I do not."

"But why?"

"Because I think he believes that he saw something, and he won't let it go, not now. Unsolved mysteries sometime become like a drug for those of us in law enforcement…investigating them can be like an addiction, an irritating itch you can't escape, and Carlos has it. He's afraid, and that itself probably goes against his nature. He'll never stop now, not until he's solved this puzzle or died trying."

"But you insisted that he doesn't have any case."

"That doesn't matter. Carlos believes that he's onto something, and he won't stop his hunt; not now, not ever, I fear."

Anthony hugged her tightly, then let go of his embrace and headed to the main door back to the house. He stopped in the doorway when Penelope said, "But what if he's right? What if it *is* a person?"

Anthony, still standing in the doorway with his back turned, said, "Then he better find it, bag it, and tag it, or he'll ruin his life and his family's. I pray that never happens."

TWENTY

Christina woke up that morning to a buzzing sound, alerting her of someone approaching her home. With her head still buried in the pillow, she turned her head and opened her right eye, looking at the monitor on the wall. There were two vehicles; one SUV and a truck. She closed her eyes and let the medicine take her back to her slumber while hugging her pillow, and then the damn doorbell rang repeatedly, as if someone had found a new toy, and it wouldn't stop.

"Shit!"

She tossed her blanket aside and jumped out of bed, still tired, not noticing that her left foot was caught up in her bed sheet. She hurried to the door and suddenly fell head-first to the floor, like an idiot.

"Fuck! That hurt," she yelled at herself.

She got up and left the master suite, and immediately did a one-eighty back into the bedroom. Opening the door naked wouldn't be good. She walked into the walk-in closet, which was pretty much empty but for some of her clothes she had brought with her and recently bought. She grabbed some shorts and a T-shirt and slipped them on, then looked for her soft slippers, because she didn't like getting her feet dirty. Couldn't find them. The damned doorbell kept ringing, reminding her to hurry. When she left the closet, she glanced at her alarm clock by the side of her bed, and when she saw how early it was, Christina became a fury to be reckoned with. This had better not be some idiot reporter. She hurried downstairs and yanked the door open.

"WHAT!"

Christina was just about to give the morning terrorist a piece of her mind when she was interrupted by a finger wagging in front of her face, leaving her openmouthed. In a lecturing voice, Peter demanded, "Now, before you opened the door, did you check on who was outside?"

Christina stuttered something incoherent.

"Thought not. Well, Missy, you really need to improve on that. I could have been a fan from hell...and we'll just leave it at that."

Some moron honked a horn.

"Congratulations, Mr. Billing sends you his regards. Is the coffee on?"

"What? Who? No, wait..."

Peter headed inside, while Kevin parked a mid-size Mercedes-Benz X-Class, king cab, matte-black pickup with enormous off-road tires. It had an equally humongous red ribbon tied over the trunk. There were all types of extra doodads all over the truck, and there it was again: that annoying sound from the goddamn horn, again and again. She was going to have to rip it out if they didn't stop.

Christina held up both arms, hands curled into claws. "Stop honking the horn, you shithead! I'll do anything, just make it stop!"

A smiling Kevin leaned out the window, having stopped playing with his new toy. "Then do something hot and sexy!"

Christina sighed. "And *it* heard us."

"Show us some skin, toots!" Kevin shouted, and then did a three-sixty burn-out with the truck as dust, sand, small rocks, and wood chips flew all over.

Christina turned one-eighty herself, waving both hands to Kevin, but with only her middle fingers erect. As she went back inside, she bumped into a strong chest.

"There *is* no coffee, did you know that?" Peter complained. She shoved at him and he refused to move; he stood calm as day in the doorway, like an old bouncer blocking the entrance to a bar.

"Yeah, I know. *Someone* just woke up," she snarled.

He patted the top of her head, knowing it would drive her nuts. "Don't you worry about a thing, darlin', in a few minutes there'll be some fresh coffee."

"Well, I'm glad you feel at home."

Someone had the audacity to pinch her left buttock, and Christina turned red as a stoked furnace as she turned around. In her face was a long chain with two high-tech keys hanging from it; she had to cross her eyes to see them. She shook her head to get her vision back to normal, and there stood the other morning terrorist with a smile stretching from ear to ear. Suddenly the brute behind her whisked her off her feet, under wild protest from Christina.

"Wait, you bastards, wait! I don't have any shoes on!"

Peter tossed Christina over her shoulder, and under wild protest from her he slapped her ass, pretty hard. "Spoiled brat. What to do, what to do?"

"We could toss her over the cliff into the river. It's not too high a few hundred yards from here."

"Too far. Wait, what about the nice fountain at the gazebo?"

"Sounds like a plan."

Christina now lay over his shoulder like a sack of potatoes. "You wouldn't dare. This will *not* improve my head injury!"

"Mind over matter, girlie." *Slap.*

She struggled frenetically and punched Peter's back over and over again as he headed for the small structure. "I'll give you a piece of my mind, you fucking matter—wait, wait...no, no, no, No, NO!"

There was a splash from the gazebo, followed by a lot of profane language coming from a very angry little woman.

When Christina found them in the house, drinking coffee, she was soaked and looked like something from out of a horror movie, with leaves and small branches stuck in her messy hair and on her face. "You motherfuckers! You're in so over your heads I'm going to…"

"Make us breakfast, or we'll follow up on a piece of advice your brother gave us last New Year's Eve at Mr. Billing's party."

"And what advice was that, Kevin?" she said dangerously. Christina stood facing them, her fists clenched and planted on her hips, leaning forward; she was so mad she trembled, and then she gave them *The Stare*. Didn't work, though.

"I think he said something about someone having this huge secret of being…what was it, Peter?"

Peter had his head stuck in a newspaper, sitting on one of the bar stools by the kitchen island, drinking coffee.

"Ticklish. I recalled he said she was terribly ticklish. Perhaps the thighs. Hell, all over, I think he said."

Christina suddenly stepped her right foot over her left and in her softest, most loving voice she said, "Scrambled eggs, coming up."

"Yeah, I want some bacon too, and toast. Don't forget the toast."

"Me too."

The two morning terrorists ate their breakfast while Christina sat there, still wet, letting the air dry her off. They had never once reacted in the least to her wet, clingy, semi-transparent top. She had the most mischievous expression as she observed the two men eating like pigs; she didn't eat anything.

"So tell me," she drawled, "how long have you guys been a couple? A year, maybe two?"

Kevin and Peter froze, then looked up from their plates at each other, surprised. With his mouth half-full, Kevin stuttered, "What? We…how did you know?"

Christina got up from her seat and walked up the stairs. "I didn't for sure, but I do now." She turned and waggled her index finger at them.

While she showered and finally got dressed, she thought about Peter and Kevin. She loved them both like family, and had known them for years. Despite their horrible behavior, she felt guilty about outing them, and decided to apologize when she got back downstairs.

Christina went into her bedroom and walked over to the controls on the wall, pushed the button opening the blinds, then screamed when she found herself face-to-face with Mr. Peeping Tom, the owl from hell.

She held her chest and started to laugh at herself. The bloody bird had moved even closer, and was almost right inside; she definitely had to do something about that branch. Suddenly she felt someone behind her; she turned around, and there stood Peter. "You okay, Chris?"

She faced him, remembering one more reason why she loved these two big lugs. "I'm fine." She pointed over her shoulder with her thumb, back turned to the owl. "Just startled by my new boyfriend."

She noticed Peter's hand moving away from his shirt; under it, she knew, he had a weapon. "So, shall we check out your new gift?" he asked brightly.

They went outside and there was Kevin, sweeping her driveway with a push-broom. She said, "Hey guys, I'm sorry for what I said before. I didn't mean to pry, and…"

Peter patted her on her shoulder. "Don't worry about it. Mr. Billing knows."

Kevin smiled at her. "But we'd like to remain in the closet, so to speak, with our work and all."

"Your secret is safe with me."

"And your feet are safe from us," Peter assured her.

"Speak for yourself, Peter—if she acts like a spoiled brat, we just do what her parents once told us many years ago: we bring her back down to earth."

"Wait a minute! I've worked and sacrificed a lot all my life. Everything I have I've earned, so there."

Peter and Kevin raised their eyebrows, looked at her and then at her brand-new truck, and then back at her.

"Okay, so I'm a little spoiled."

They went over the truck meticulously with Christina, and she fell in love with the comfortable seats. Kevin and Christina took the truck for a run, while Peter remained, unpacking many black crates filled with high-tech items.

TED HAGGLUND had returned to Skull Creek to finish up some unfinished business. He had strolled in the forest and mountains for hours, preparing his plan of action. He was dressed like any average jogger out on a run. He pushed himself to the limit, feeling aroused from the tough physical training, and he kept pushing himself. He loved PT, and he could go on for hours without any water or rest, having trained this way ever since he was a young child. He was careful with his footing, and made sure that he stayed as quiet as possible. Now and then, he stopped to take his bearings. Wherever he ran there was silence: no sounds from birds or insects, not even warning sounds. He was used to that, being a superior being and all. Carnivores loved him, while all others feared him. The animal kingdom could sense him for what he was: an angry apex predator.

A light breeze through the terrain brought a faint sound of something that did *not* belong in the forest: engines. He altered his direction and increased his speed; it was a steep uphill run, with many large boulders to navigate. Nero listened to a mix of classics as he ran: Chopin, Mozart, Bach, and of course his favorite, Beethoven, from his left and only earphone.

He had to climb a rocky surface to reach the top of a cliff. There he could look down on the landscape below, at two great plateaus with a narrow line of forest dividing them. Further ahead was the mountaintop, far above where he stood. He wanted to get to the top, but looking down below, he realized that wasn't going to happen today. He looked in horror on the devastation that had been visited on the land by the gold miners. There were huge vehicles driving all over the once-virgin forest, leaving their dreadful marks as deep, rutted tracks. There were bulldozers shoveling away, tearing up the ground, pushing trees to the side, roots and all. Giant machines ate chunks from the land. The fresh, clean air was filled with the stink of diesel engines, the huge gold plant itself making a horrible sound.

He sat down on a large rock and did nothing to keep his tears from pouring down. He just sat there, staring at the devastation caused by man ruining nature, crying like a child, shoulders trembling, holding his face in his hands and once in a while looking up. He was well aware of the gold miners' existence, fighting for land against the many lumberjack crews, but he hadn't been focusing on them; his primary prey for the season had taken all his time, and the fuck-up with the witnesses had stalled him. Unlike the lumberjacks who actually helped nature, despite what a bunch of tree-hugging assholes might think, the miners did not.

Now he was happy he had found this spot, because he had found more prey. The gold miners must die. A message must be sent to the idiots, scaring them so that they would stop their desecration of the land. But sadly, that had to wait until next year. The primary target, once destroyed, would call for more trouble and much investigation. Oh well; he had time, all the time in the world. He smiled sadly at the site below.

"Why are you crying, mister?"

Completely caught off guard, Nero jumped up from his seated position on the rock. Someone being able to sneak up on him was unheard of! He turned, facing a little girl who held some poorly-picked flowers in her hands.

"He cries because he's a pussy, sis, not like our dad, who would never cry. Adults don't cry, just like me."

Nero tilted his head as he turned it towards the new voice, which came from a young boy a few years older than his sister, who stared at him tauntingly.

He blew his nose and said, "So, little children, tell me: who is your father, the one who never cries?"

The little girl looked curiously at him, then she pointed towards one of the gold mines below. "He's down there working."

"Yeah, and he owns the mine, him being the boss, and he ain't no crying sissy like you."

Tarben Nero Hammond, a.k.a. Ted Hagglund, observed the young children, and before they walked away, the little girl handed him her flowers.

"Mister, please don't cry. Take these, maybe it will make you feel better."

"Come on, sis, we ain't allowed to talk to strangers. Let's go kill something."

Nero cleared his throat as he noticed the small rifle on the boy's shoulder. Suddenly, a plan developed in his mind; and it was a very good plan, he thought. He stopped crying and turned his head towards the children. He blinked his eyes while smiling at them very awkwardly, shaking his head side to side; and then the Beast inside of him took over his body, and the Beast was furious.

He said quietly, but in an extremely unpleasant voice, "Little children, I'll bet I can get your father to cry."

The children stopped and looked at him, surprised; and then both of them met the one person all parents warn their children about. The boogeyman.

A shadow covered them, followed by darkness.

SITTING ON a branch on a tree a hundred yards away an owl let out a strange yowl, then took off and flew in a circle, sending out what sounded like a warning cry before it disappeared, flying away towards the valley far below. Hovering far above in the sky, an eagle did the same. A strange silence fell over the land, but no one in the mining camp noticed Mother Nature's sudden mood swing, because they were all too busy tearing her up in search of a dream.

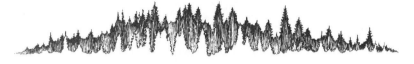

TWENTY-ONE

"Hold it right there, Shaka Zulu. You're no longer in charge. The chief is back, so you just wait your turn."

"What the hell did you call me, woman?"

"Again, the name is Ruth. Better learn it real fast, boy."

Malik stopped in his tracks, staring in disbelief at the unpleasant old woman as she began her morning ritual of walking to Carlos's office with the help of her cane. He shook his head, staring at the old woman, and then his eyeballs practically popped out as she muttered to the man in the office, "Kunta Kinte here to see ya."

"Watch your mouth, Ruth," Carlos said tiredly.

Pointing his thumb over his shoulder at the closed door behind him, Malik demanded, "Where the hell did you dig up the Klan grandmother? She's never uttered a word to me before."

Carlos, his head stuck in a report, only waved his hand for Malik to have a seat. After a moment, he muttered, "Long story. Don't mind her, she's no racist, just likes to push people's buttons is all. And once in a while she brings in a pie or two. Her key lime is the best ever. Probably why I haven't sent her packing already."

Malik observed his best friend with the eyes of a predator, looking for anything out of the ordinary, but when he saw Carlos being himself, he calmed down.

"So, what did you think of my basement?"

Malik froze. Busted.

"I…we did…"

Carlos held up his hand for Malik to stop. "We go back, Malik, don't we?"

Malik nodded. "Way back."

"Seen a lot of shit working in the big cities, yeah?"

Again, Malik nodded.

"So—do you believe in destiny?"

"No. You know I don't, Carlos."

"Do you believe in history?"

"Some of it. I definitely don't believe in everything. The winners have the luxury of writing their own history at their leisure."

"Agreed." Carlos leaned back in his seat and observed his friend; and as usual, he could read nothing from Malik Washington's body language or expression. Carlos smiled. "What about a history that has never been written down by anyone, but has been going on for a long time?" He paused, allowing his words to sink in before he continued. "One thing I never told you. Or anyone. When I was very young, I witnessed something horrible."

It took an hour for Carlos to summarize everything for Malik, who during the entire hour never changed his position in his chair. After a time, he spoke. "Special Agent Perez is right; you don't have any evidence, only a theory. I would be the last person to question what you saw that night, during the storm, through darkness, lightning, and rain…but it could be a form of hallucination, triggered by post-traumatic stress from your past. The shadow of the grizzly and the lightning might have been the cause of it, too."

"True. You're absolutely right, but what if it wasn't a grizzly bear, but a person?"

Malik raised his eyebrows, "Who looks like a bear?"

"Who *dresses* like one."

"But why?"

"Because the person is insane, and thinks he or she really is an animal."

Malik nodded. "I've heard of weirder. But why here in Skull Creek, and why now?"

"Because I was the only witness to that massacre over fifty years ago."

"Carlos, it's a bit farfetched, even for a drug cartel, to go so far in looking for a last witness. And remember, all the cartels from back then have been replaced by new ones, and you also need to take into consideration that Perez and his partner never believed the final official report they were more or less forced to sign. I've worked with what I believe are the best, and that includes you, Carlos. Sometimes there are things that are a challenge to explain, or there's simply no rational explanation at all."

"You're referring to your time with the Air Force, that covert unit you belonged to."

Malik nodded. "At times, even the best of us see things because of the stressful work we do. But if you're right…."

Carlos looked up hopefully.

"Then whatever this thing is will be back. I doubt it, but if it *does* return to our town, Carlos, then I'll be right there by your side to fight it."

"Thank you, Malik."

"Any time. Probably just a grizzly, though."

Carlos leaned back in his chair, knowing that saying any more about his monster theory would be pointless; from now on he was on his own. "So, I read and heard that you guys got two suspects for the homicide at the lumber camp."

"Pretty much Adrianna did that. One hell of a woman; you sure know how to pick 'em. I took her off duty; there are some investigations

Internal Affairs will be doing, and they should be here today from the state capital, talking with her."

"I read her statement, and I think the arrests will hold."

"I agree with you, Carlos. It looks like a rescue attempt, even though it might not have been one, and the suspect who took a shot at Adrianna only tried to get away."

"About the stun gun…?"

Malik smiled.

"Yeah, that might be a tougher nut for her to crack, but to be perfectly honest with you, Adrianna was under a lot of stress, this being her first shoot-out and all. And the fat toad apparently got out of the seatbelt and did disturb her."

"Yeah, well, the testimony from the other gold miners insists that he was a crybaby, and didn't have it in him to taunt any police officer."

Malik just shrugged.

"So, which one of them admitted it first?"

"Butch, and eventually Vern."

"They did all this shit just to scare the lumberjacks so they could prospect gold there?"

"Yeah, and to play a joke by scaring the crap out of them. It worked, too. Some joke. But for the most part, they needed the truck; neither of them had any wheels. We might talk with the park rangers, because we've had a lot of complaints from locals that the miners were on their land, drilling in the ground and looking for new places to dig for gold come next season. Some idiots have even their claim flags inside the national park, and it drives the rangers nuts. By the way, has the medical report gotten back on the homicide victim?"

Carlos grabbed a folder from his desk and handed it to Malik.

"Crap. Says here that the body was dead before the decapitation."

"Yeah, that's what the two morons said; they found him that way. But they'll still go away for a while. A long while, I hope."

Malik kept eyeing the report.

"And they have reliable alibis for that evening. They left their camp, hitchhiking, and then took a shortcut through the wood. Checks out."

"Says in the report that the vic had been hit several times, very hard…scratch marks, lacerations, possible cause of death…a bear attack. Damn."

Malik looked up and glanced at Carlos, who smiled back at him.

"Probably just a grizzly."

Malik didn't fail to notice something dark in Carlos's voice and stare.

TED HAGGLUND had his eyes closed, and he stood on top of a huge boulder lying on the edge of a cliff, with a steep drop to the base hundreds of feet below him. Just like a *Kapellmeister*, Nero moved his hands and head with the music from his earphone; Beethoven's *Ode to Joy*. With his right ear, he could hear the footsteps approaching from behind.

Beethoven was calming him down.

Nero knew that he had gone too far when he had killed the little girl; she didn't fit his profile. The boy, however, did. He also knew that the last thing he had to do before he could no longer control the Beast was to take care of the last witness and follow protocol, but first he had to put his new, perfect plan in motion.

"Say, mister, you seen a couple of kids? A young girl eight years old, and a boy, her brother, going on twelve?"

Ted Hagglund, still with his eyes closed and moving his hands to the sound of the music, nodded his head; and then he pointed below the cliff edge. A few frustrated minutes later, a fat man with a goatee finally manage to climb up next to him. He was out of breath.

"Name's Bob. So, you seen them? They're late for dinner, and…"

Bob paused when he saw into the dead stare of the stranger on the cliff. "Children should be in school during the day."

"Yeah, well, ever hear of homeschooling? What's it to you, anyway?"

Nero inhaled the beautiful music and moved his body in time to it, in ways that would make a ballerina jealous. "And I suppose that you're their father, the tough man who doesn't cry, as they put it."

Bob looked suspiciously at the stranger.

"I decided to test that theory, Man Who Doesn't Cry. Look below, and I suspect you will feel overwhelming and truly horrible sorrow." He stopped dancing around Bob and he waved his finger in the air: no, no. "But you must not cry, oh no, you must not cry…you see?"

A few minutes later, Bob screamed the entire six hundred feet down. He hit the ground face-first and cracked his skull, splattering brain matter all over the bodies of his children, who lay where they had fallen.

Bob's son had been wrong about his father. He had cried like a forlorn child when he saw them down there, twisted and broken.

WHEN CHRISTINA and Kevin returned home several hours later, there were three more trucks parked by her new home. She recognized Frank's and Robert's, but not the third one. They parked Christina's new truck underneath the carport, and there were a few stares—at the truck. Peter was talking to Frank, Robert, and some guy Christina had never met. The moment Christina set foot on the ground, Hunter appeared from nowhere, sitting down while mopping the ground with his tail. She kneeled and let him lick her face, while talking to him in that baby talk dogs are supposed to like. A soft bark made her raise her head, and there was a bandaged Nugget limping towards her, his tail swinging back and forth. He approached slowly and carefully, trying to get between Hunter and Christina. Christina moved and kneeled next to Nugget, who immediately lay on his side, allowing her to carefully pet him.

"Christina, this is Boris, a friend who sometimes he helps me out."

Christina looked up at Robert, and then stood up and shook the giant's hand. Immediately the huge man, who had a full beard and a large, round nose, blushed; it reminded her of a scene from *Snow White.*

"I haven't taken care of your land yet, Christina, you being in the hospital and all…" Robert began.

"Thank you for the flowers," Christina interrupted.

Robert looked bewildered. "Don't think I send you any." He trailed off, looking a bit ashamed.

Christina looked at him seriously and waited.

Robert could sense the hostility in the air, and ignored it. "Anyway, there are still a lot of trees and branches that need to be taken care of from the storm. You still want me to do the job for you?"

"Sure, you do that." She turned to the giant next to Robert. "Nice to meet you, Boris." Again the giant was quiet, and blushed some more.

Christina ignored the two lumberjacks as they picked up their gear and headed along the path. Soon the roar of their chainsaws echoed throughout the forest. Frank walked up next to her, looking in the direction of the sound. "He's a good man, if a bit stubborn."

"All men are stubborn."

Frank just smiled, not wanting to get involved if there was something between Robert and Christina. He handed Christina's old suitcase to her, and nodded for her to open it. Inside were her favorite but very ugly sandals; everything had been cleaned and repaired. She gave Frank a long, hard hug, thanking him.

"I should've called, but figure I'd take Nugget and Hunter for a ride. Nugget needs to work up his muscles again."

"I'm so happy he made it, and at the same time I'm truly sorry for that K-9 that died."

"And that's the reason I'm here."

Christina looked at Frank, questioning. Meanwhile, Hunter and Nugget found the tree with the owl sitting in it, and both stood on their back legs while leaning on the trunk, barking at it once in a while. The owl couldn't care less, apparently.

"Well, Whitney, the police officer that lost his dog in the hunt or attack, whatever, he's gotten himself a new German Shepherd, and it's a cute little guy."

"Yeah? I don't follow, Frank."

"Winter is coming soon, and Claire and I will travel to our place in Florida, as you know."

"Yes, I remembered you guys mentioning that. Or maybe it was Tom Billing, I can't remember."

"Whenever we do go, we only bring Winston, and Whitney usually takes care of Nugget and Hunter. But with him training up a new dog that hopefully will become his next K-9 partner, having Nugget and Hunter around won't do him any favors, so I…"

"I'd love to take care of them for you guys, if you trust me with them."

Frank smiled widely. "Of course we trust you! And the way both of them behave when they're with you is wonderful. Love at first sight."

"And you guys will be gone for how long?"

"Give or take six months, but I'll drop by once or twice in the early spring and check on the store."

"I can do that for you, too."

"Thank you, Christina, but Whitney will take care of that part for us."

"When will you guys leave?"

"At the first snow. Might be in a few weeks, if I believe the weather man. Then again, snow might be early this year."

"I can't wait! I've heard that there are a few nice mountains with ski resorts not too far away from here, and I love downhill skiing."

"Don't break any legs, now."

"Promise, and if I do, then Nugget and Hunter can pull me around on a sled—just the way you do with Winston."

"Oh, you seen that, huh? Yeah, that Winston is a breed apart. By the way, did you know that Hunter is for sale?"

"For sale? No, I had no idea."

"He was trained for another family, who in the end decided to get a poodle instead."

"But do you really want to sell him?"

"No, not really, but both Hunter and Nugget were trained for other owners. Nugget's history is about the same…the family changed their mind. Or I should say, I had my doubts about that particular family."

"If you don't want them, I'll take them!"

"Oh, don't misunderstand me, I love them both dearly…but both my wife and I aren't getting any younger, and these to villains needs a lot of exercise and attention. Think about it, at least. I know your work can take you far away for long periods of time, so you might want to reconsider."

"Let me have them, please, at least until you guys come back, and then we can decide. How's that?"

"Sounds like a plan. Claire and I will keep them until we leave."

"By the way, how are they around cats? I'm thinking of adopting the little one I found in the river."

"If it's a kitten, no problem. If it's an older cat with an attitude, then there might be a Tom and Jerry situation."

Christina laughed with Frank, the sound alerting the dogs, who soon joined them.

"And Nugget's wounds?"

"He should be all right by the time Claire and I leave."

Christina kneeled by the two troublemakers, and let them kiss her all over her face. "I'm going to spoil you guys rotten."

Peter came running up, waving his hands to get their attention. "Got some trouble, I think." He wasn't even out of breath, Christina noticed.

"What's going on?"

"You got some miners drilling holes in your land, Christina."

"What do you mean, drilling?"

Frank explained, "They're prospecting for gold, and then they'll try and make a claim—on your land."

"But can they do that?"

"No, but they don't care, and some of these prospectors are backed financially by some very powerful people, especially the Wicked Witch of the East. Hang on, let me make a call."

Christina turned to Peter. "Whereabouts are they?"

"Down the jogging path. Robert and the big Russian guy are arguing with them now. Well, Robert's arguing; the Russian dude is just standing there looking scary."

"Motherfuckers. Show me the way," Christina ordered, and the two dogs, noticing her mood swing, immediately started to whine while looking at Frank, who was talking on his cell phone. He nodded his head and made a smacking sound. Shortly after, Nugget and Hunter were flanking Christina as she stalked down the jogging trail.

"Thought you guys would chase them off," she said to Peter as they trudged along.

"We would have, but they claim that the owner's given them permission to drill."

"I most certainly have not. Do you think Claire and Frank gave them permission?"

"No, he would have told us."

Frank ran after them and was a bit out of breath when he caught up. "I called the park ranger and the sheriff's office, they're on the way…the ranger almost sounded joyful when I said they'd been caught in the act."

When they arrived at the site, Christina was astonished by the amount of devastation the intruders had created. A strange-looking vehicle with tracks instead of wheels had made its own path to the site, and several large trees had been cut down by the prospectors. The argument was loud, and people were screaming and making threats.

Christina walked over to Robert, who was talking loudly to another man, who was screaming and shouting while waving a document in his hand. It took a while before a dead silence fell over the area.

"I'm the owner of this land, gentlemen," Christina said threateningly, "the land you have ruined with your machines and chainsaws."

"Well, we got city permits, and—"

"Get the fuck off my land! Now! And expect to hear from my lawyer! Go back the way you came, and don't disturb another thing!"

Christina had used *The Tone*, combined with *The Stare*. No one said a word, and eventually the prospectors lost the stare-down.

"You're aware that this part of Ms. Dawn's land is part of a national park?" Frank asked calmly.

"No it's not, and…"

Sirens wailed in the distance.

Someone said threateningly to Christina, "You bitch! You ratted on us and called the fucking pigs?"

Nugget and Hunter lay next to Frank, observing the scene very intently.

The man who had shouted at Robert tried to calm his crew down. His hesitation confirmed what Christina had suspected: that their so-called permit was probably fake.

"You don't know what's coming, you fucking cunt," another person threatened.

Some growling from the dogs.

There were two smacking sounds, and two of the prospectors lay stretched out with broken noses.

Robert turned his head, looking at Boris, who smiled like an innocent child. Well…maybe not that innocent.

The prospectors started to collect their things.

"No. No one moves," Peter said, hand on his pistol.

"You heard my buddy," Robert followed up. They had strategically positioned themselves to stop anyone trying to get away.

A park ranger ran down a long hill toward them, and behind her came Officer Whitney, breathing a bit heavily considering his beer belly. In the ensuing ten minutes, all the prospectors were arrested on the spot, and all the equipment, including the trucks parked on the road, were confiscated. The park ranger, the same woman who had visited Christina at the hospital, was thrilled to death at having finally caught someone in the act, and raging mad when she saw the damage the prospectors had caused.

There was some argument about what Boris had done, but Whitney never arrested him. Boris had muttered something incoherent to the police officer, who had just smiled back. Everyone walked up to the main road. Christina insisted on pressing charges, intending to sue for heavy punitive damages and force them to clean up their mess.

The two-lane mountain road had traffic lined up both ways and Deputy Lucy, a tall woman with short hair, took care of traffic.

"So, what's going on here?" she asked Whitney.

"Some gold prospectors got caught red-handed, trespassing."

"Here? But isn't this part of the national park?"

"Damn right it is."

She waved the truck forward, while making a stop signal towards on-coming traffic. Ted Hagglund touched the tip of his baseball cap towards Robert and Boris, and when he saw Christina, he turned his head away, thinking, *Still a pretty little thing. Maybe me and her…? Nah, disgusting.*

TWENTY-TWO

Christina left the doctor's office after her hopefully last visit for a while, and drove her sporty new truck to the airport to pick up her best friend, Tammy. She smiled as she passed parts of the road she remembered from her long walk. Driving in her truck, it didn't seem that far. She had to be very careful when she drove, though, because there were many big trucks hauling logs to the local mills. Then again, she was used to L.A traffic, and had no real problems. What she wasn't used to was that many roads were only two-lane; she didn't like that, and had decided that no matter how slow the vehicle in front of her was, she would never pass it on the opposite side of the road.

She grabbed a cup of coffee from a vending machine once she was inside the small terminal. The plane was half an hour late. She wore her disguise, avoiding most people; then again, the terminal was almost empty. She didn't want to take any chances if there were any photographers nearby. She still had the L.A. paparazzi scare in her. But she had to admit to herself that most of the locals in Skull Creek didn't give a shit who she was or what she did in the world, because everyone seemed to respect each other's private and professional lives, and most people had been very nice to her. The ones that hadn't weren't local, mostly.

The small passenger plane landed, and of course the first person who stepped out onto the stairway was Tammy. She wore high heels and a tight designer outfit. Over her shoulder she carried a very large purse—or was it a small suitcase? On her head was a typical California straw hat in the latest fashion, with a matching ribbon—Christina hated those hats. It was enormous, and as Tammy tried to wave to her she kept holding the hat with one hand. Eventually she waved both hands like a mad woman to Christina, who stood behind a large window waving back. Then Christina gasped and shielded her mouth with her hands, staring at her friend in horror.

Tammy wasn't just waving to her; she had two very large plastic objects in her hands while doing so—no wonder she had trouble keeping the ugly hat on her head!—and now she was down in front of the plane, signaling to the pilot and copilot, who were both laughing very hard.

The dildos in her hands were abnormally huge.

"And there goes the hat in the wind," Christina mused.

An airport worker ran up to Tammy with her hat, but from the body language the worker was less than amused, and made Tammy move along.

"And yes, she's giving him one of the dildos," Christina said to herself.

She laughed when she saw the reaction of the worker. It was a woman, and now she smiled and waved her hand, not realizing she still held the dildo. The pilots were dying of laughter in the cockpit.

"There goes the idea of remaining in the shadows, right down the drain. So much for not drawing attention to us," Christina muttered.

Christina wasn't upset; instead, she started to laugh herself. The moment Tammy entered the building, she lit it up like a lightning storm with her very presence. She was dressed like a typical professional woman, an independent woman who walked like she talked, with a confidence most people could only envy. They hugged and laughed like only best friends can. They gathered her luggage, and as they left the building, Tammy went by an old man who had been undressing both Christina and Tammy with his eyes, in a futile attempt to conceal it from a very upset wife.

Tammy handed her one of the dildos. "Better than Viagra, rest assured, you horny old toads you."

The couple looked at Tammy questioningly, and then in horror at the large plastic object. After a moment, the man smiled, waving goodbye; and his wife smiled too, but she wasn't looking at the girls.

They got into the truck and drove off. "Yep, you're crazy as hell," Christina drawled.

"Shut up! You love every minute of it. I would never have expected to see you drive one of these Transformers, though. Really going country, aren't ya?"

"Always been a clumsy tomboy."

"Yeah, when it comes to clumsy you sure fit the bill. It's kind of strange when someone with such tiny feet walks and falls like a clown."

"Yeah, well, I'd rather have mine than your giant clogs."

"Oh, Christina, all the boys looooove my feet."

"No, Tammy, they don't. It's what you do with them that they love."

Tammy pouted and stuck her tongue out.

They drove into town, laughing and talking at the same time -- something only women can do. Tammy let out a loud scream when she saw the main road. "Oh my, this is so cool! If not for all the cars, you'd think we were in a Clint Eastwood western. This whole town is so adorable, cuddly, and cute!"

Christina parked at the western store, and like the two professionals they were, they invaded it. Tammy had to update her wardrobe for the Wild West, after all. The people inside never knew what hit them. One hour later, Christina made good use of the back of her truck, grateful that it had a huge lid with a lock on it. She locked the back and started to get in the cab.

"Wait a minute! You said we're going to get something to eat, right?"

Christina, with her back still turned, motioned for Tammy to follow. "Come on, it's just down the street."

"We're walking?"

Christina turned and looked at Tammy's six-inch heels, smiling. She herself had dressed more comfortably; she wore her favorite sandals, faded denim overalls, a T-shirt, and one of her new hats that already looked worn. As they walked on the boardwalk Tammy's shoes got stuck in the cracks more than once, but like the trouper she was, she kept going—a bit wobbly, though.

They stepped into a nice restaurant and waited to be seated. It was lunchtime, and there were a lot of guests in the place. No one reacted to them at first; but when they were escorted to their table, more than one head turned.

"My name is Joseph, and I'll be your waiter," the young man said as he handed them their menus.

As she took hers, Tammy said to Christina, "So, have you had any since you got here, or are you still celibate?"

The waiter blushed. Tammy ignored him, and Christina tried desperately to hide her face in the menu.

"Um, Joseph, could you please give us a few minutes?" Christina asked. He hurried away, having forgotten to ask if they wanted anything to drink.

With a powerful voice, Tammy shouted, "Joseph, two cold ones, and make it snappy."

Later, both ordered the catch of the day, and enjoyed their meal. Tammy was on her second beer by then, but Christina knew her limit whenever she drove a vehicle. They laughed loudly, at times perhaps a little too loudly, but neither cared. Both were happy to be together again. They shared experiences, and Christina talked about everything that had happened to her in Skull Creek, which took a while. More than once she could sense fury from Tammy, but she was a good listener. Eventually, Christina told her about Frank and Claire, and told her they were going to go see them next.

After lunch both walked further down the road, and did a bit more shopping. Once they were back at the truck, they loaded the hoard in the back. Christina drove slowly, and eventually parked outside Hancock Tool Supply. They had to park further down the street than normal, because all the spots in front of the store were taken.

This time when they walked on the wooden sidewalk, Tammy gave up after one of her heels broke off. She picked up the leftovers of her expensive designer shoe and gave it a sad stare. Then they walked inside and were met by a bizarre scene: an argument between Claire and an overdressed older woman. Many patrons around the store had stopped what they were doing to eavesdrop.

"How dare you sell your property to some outsider? I've been wanting to buy it for years, and now you have the audacity to say you *sold* it? How *dare* you?"

"Enough, Mrs. Tulip," Claire snapped. "You know we didn't want to sell it to you. We've told you often enough. Now, if you're not buying anything, then you'll have to leave; this is my final warning."

"No, you listen to me! I pretty much own this town, and you will do as I say, and…and you will tell me how I can get ahold of that fucking porn star. You sold it to a mobster, you all hear me? The Hancocks have sold their land to a famous porn mobster who has a dozen minions, who hurt my son Jesse. You all hear me?"

Tammy leaned in next to the old woman, and suddenly her face was in the old hag's. "Bullies come in all sizes and sexes nowadays, lady, and you're a bully. Bet your son is, too."

"And who the hell are you?"

"No, no, no, old woman. It's never *who* in these scenarios that matters; it's always *what*." Tammy picked up her phone and hit speed dial; after the second tone, someone answered in a bass voice, and Tammy started talking.

"Hi, Goddaddy, it's your little ray of sunshine…what? No, no, I *have* been good…oh. About that. Can we talk later about that? Okay, I promise…yeah, well, they started it."

People moved closer, straining to listen into the conversation. Tammy quickly related what she had overheard the old lady say on the phone. She listened for a moment, and reached her phone out to the mean old bag. "Hey, bitch, it's for you!"

The old woman first stared, flabbergasted at the young woman, and then she snapped the phone from Tammy's hand and started to shout at the person on the other end—but that suddenly stopped. The more she listened, the paler she got. Her voice trailed off, she looked at the Caller ID on the smartphone, and then she started to sweat profusely. She nodded her head more than once, and then said, "Yes. Yessir. I see. Yes sir, yes sir, yes sir…"

She trailed off and looked at the phone in disbelief.

Tammy grabbed the phone back and exchanged a few more words with her godfather, then shut it off.

The old woman cleared her throat and tried to regain some face. "That had better be him for real, or…"

"Want me to call him back, you mean old cunt? Get the fuck out of here and remember: there's always a bigger fish, jackass."

Mrs. Tulip's eyes widened. As the woman left the building, humiliated, some of the watchers cheered and wolf-whistled, while others booed her out. No one stepped aside, so the old bag had to walk around anyone in her way. One man stood in the door way and didn't move until the old hag said please. The only reason he moved, though, was because of another person wanted to go outside, and some guy behind him wanted to get into the store. There was some commotion when one of them hit the sidewalk; either he fell or had been pushed.

"You *had* to call Tom, didn't you?"

"Yes, I most certainly did. You never would, and I respect you for that, but a desperate housewife from hell like that one I've met one time too many. Too much money never translates to class or manners. She can take a step off a fucking cliff wearing a parachute with a hole in it for all I care."

"Her action and your reaction—thank you for that. Hi, I'm Claire Hancock." Claire extended her hand, and Tammy shook it like a man.

"Sorry for my crude language. Never intended to start a scene."

"Don't worry about it, the show was already going on. You're Christina's best friend Tammy, I take it."

"In person. Again, pardon my French."

Behind Tammy stood a typical lumberjack, with one exception: this one was a tad tipsy, evidenced by his big red nose and terrible breath. "(hic) Fuck the French!" he pronounced.

A surprised Tammy turned around and looked at her new fan, inspecting him curiously from head to toe, with a mischievous expression on her face.

Oh no, he's done it now, here we go… Christina thought, trying to hide her face in her hands while leaning on the counter. Tammy smiled devilishly and, with a pitch-perfect tone, said, "*Voulez vous coucher avec moi ce soir?*"

The drunk guy's eyes shone like bright stars and he threw his arms up in the air, shouting back in perfect French, "*Oui, mon ange aimé!*"

Tammy's eyes went wide, and now she even looked hesitant; or perhaps "desperate" might be a better word. Christina, who was also fluent in French, lay on the counter laughing. There were many surprised stares in Hancock Tool Supply that day, and eventually twice as many rumors would soon spread throughout the little community.

The drunk hurried to his new *aimé* with arms extended, ready to embrace Tammy. She, on the other hand, turned quickly to Claire. "Do you sell any guns?!"

"No, dear, that would be across the street."

Ted Hagglund missed the last part of the commotion when he left the store and followed the wicked old lady. He brushed by some idiot in a suit, barely touching him, but the two-legged hit the sidewalk like a drooling drunk. Nero had never really realized his immense physical strength. He stopped on the way by a mailbox and dropped a brown oversized envelope inside, and then he resumed his stalking. *And now there are two pretty little things,* he thought.

Wailing sirens once again filled the idyllic town of Skull Creek, and in the distance came the sound of a low-flying helicopter, all heading towards the mountain range where the gold miners delved for the precious metal. Dozens of people looked on with that questioning expression that meant, *Now what?*

Ted Hagglund ignored the commotion. He knew what that was about, but today he was unusually happy—especially whenever he looked at the woman a block ahead, who was shouting into her phone while gesticulating with her arms as if she were fighting an invisible foe with a sword—and he wasn't even listening to Beethoven.

JOSEPH GREEN was happier than he had ever been, but at the same time he was furious. First, he had seen a real, live Hollywood star walking across the street. He'd read about her in the local paper, which claimed she now lived in Skull Creek; and ever since, he'd tried to locate her. He knew he was everything she needed in a man. However, he was sure she had just seen him being humiliated when that damned stranger made him lose his footing, causing him to fall to the sidewalk.

However, this time there would be an eye for an eye, he decided.

He stalked his perpetrator with the stare he had so often practiced in front of a mirror. He followed him just as they did in the movies; he knew he was the perfect secret agent type, and he did enjoy himself doing it. Even better, he was *finally* going to use the gun he had just picked up, having waited over a week for the stupid permit. He had planned to find the big bully who had embarrassed him his first night in town at the Lumberjack. He had never used a gun before, but he had seen people use them often enough in the movies, and he had played many computer games. He was ready, and he was going to scare the crap out of the rude bastard. He wasn't going to shoot him, just scare him. He had the pistol stuck inside his pants, and the box of cartridges lay in his briefcase with a cleaning kit. What that was used for he had no idea.

He looked over his now-dirty fake Armani suit, and tried to brush some of the dirt off; and then he noticed the greasy stain on his faux silk tie. Now he was *very* upset. He looked at his Rolex replica; there was still time before his next meeting, hopefully the last in this God-forsaken place.

"Good, the idiot is walking to the same parking lot as me," he muttered happily. He had to step aside as a dark blue Jaguar flew by with some old lady screaming at her chauffeur. The lumberjack bastard went to a truck and quickly pulled out of the parking lot.

Joseph Green got into his kit car—it looked like a Ferrari convertible but it had an Audi engine, and the automatic roof didn't work, he really had to struggle to get it attached, so the damn thing was down—and carefully followed the man who had humiliated him. He placed his gun on the passenger seat, then he felt that he needed some motivation and background score, like they had in the movies, as he drove after the lowlife. He cranked up the volume for everyone to hear, and from the speakers blasted *I'm So Beautiful* by Divine.

TED HAGGLUND followed Mrs. Tulip's Jaguar for about twenty minutes. They were heading towards a wealthier part of the county, and he didn't know that region very well. Then again, it didn't matter, because this was only a recon. He already knew the old bag would soon become just another number. He had trouble concentrating on his own thoughts, though, because killing the young girl bothered him, and that was a strange new sensation for him. The boy, not so much. Nits made lice. He'd briefly considered skinning the two kids and displaying their hides to the father to see how hard he cried, but just couldn't do it. And their daddy had responded as expected anyway.

He knew what he had to do, and he'd already put his plan in motion. Removing the two-legged in the Jaguar was a must, but it wouldn't be enough. He had limited time and knew that he was treading on thin ice. He shook his head to clear his mind, then switched on the radio.

"And in other news—and this is sad, folks—another baby dolphin has died on a beach while its mother screamed from the ocean, just so hundreds of people could take selfies with it.

Nero hit the radio so hard he broke it, and at the same time he hit his brakes even harder, coming to a complete stop. He was so enraged by the news on the radio that he didn't even notice something bump into the rear of his truck. He leaned forward over his steering wheel and wept, tears pouring down. He hit the steering wheel over and over again, saying "Purge, purge, purge," and eventually he started yelling the same word over and over again: "PURGE, PURGE, PURGE…"

Joseph Green's car slammed hard into the back of the pickup truck as it came to a sudden stop, and he wasn't wearing his seat belt. He lay over his steering wheel for long moments—he hadn't hooked up the airbags—trying to get his bearings and catch his breath. As the blood seeped out of his nose, his mind gradually returned to reality. When he noticed the devastation to his car, which was stuck in the rear right side of the truck in front of him, he lost it. He slowly got out, having to climb, because the driver door was jammed shut. The entire front of his kit car had dug itself into the right rear tire. Steam poured up from what was left of his engine and hood. The entire front was totaled, being made mostly of plastic and fiberglass.

He grabbed the sides of his head with both hands and pulled his hair. He had teary eyes, and blood oozed out of his nose. He picked up the rearview mirror from the passenger seat, and when he saw himself all black and blue with blood all over, he screamed again. The music from the car speakers worked normally, but that was it. He ran up to the idiot in the truck, and when he realized it was the bonehead he been following, he became outraged.

"Motherfucker! What the hell do you think you're doing, you fucking inbred bastard! You fucking totaled my ride, man, you fucking asshole, what the fuck is wrong with you, man? You fucking crybaby, you hear me, you just fucked me good, motherfucker! Got nothing to say, huh? Think you're some kind of wiseass motherfucker? Yeah, well, I'll show you!"

Even more upset than before he hurried back to his car for the pistol. It lay on the passenger's side floor; he grabbed it and then he headed back to the crying old man. He then realized he had to load the weapon; again he went back to the car. He found his briefcase and took out the box of cartridges. He fumbled with the box, and half of its contents fell onto the driver's seat and the road. He looked at his pistol, having no clue how to load it—he'd never had asked the clerk in the gun shop, because he didn't want to seem like an amateur. Eventually he hit a button or something, because part of the fucking gun broke. He picked up the slim metal case and then realized what it was, a magazine, and he started to load it. "It sure holds a lot of bullets," he muttered as he was loading it. Every now and then he shouted out threats to the fucker who had caused the accident.

Joseph shouted in his best street dialect, just the way they did it in the movies. "You just wait, man, Ima bust a cap in your ass, motherfucker…jeez, how many fucking bullets does this thing take? You hear me, motherfucker, Ima cap yo ass!"

With his tongue sticking out from between his teeth, he loaded the gun magazine as fast as he could, once in a while reaching into the driver's seat for more rounds. The music spurred him on: *You Think You're a Man* by Divine.

He dropped the magazine on the ground and kneeled to pick it up, but someone beat him to it. Joseph looked up at the old man, upset. "Do you like dolphins?" the old man asked as he handed Joseph the loaded magazine.

"What?"

"Do you like dolphins?" There was a sad vibe coming from the old man.

"NO I don't fucking like dolphins, unless they're on my fucking tuna melt sandwich, you fucking mountain-man inbreed! You fucker, you ruined my fucking ride, man!"

The old man's voice changed, sounding more neutral. "You *eat* dolphins?"

"Yeah, motherfucker, I fucking eat dolphins, and now I'm gonna fucking eat your ass! You owe me money for this shit, it's your entire fucking fault, man!" Joseph screeched. He fumbled with his gun and magazine, while the old man observed him with a neutral expression. He finally took the gun and magazine from Joseph's hands and did the job for him. Joseph looked at the old man, surprised and horrified; the old man had taken his spine! But instead of using it on him, he handed the gun back to Joseph.

Joseph took a step back and pointed the gun at the old bastard. "You better have some fucking dough, man, because you're going to pay me for this shit."

"The taste."

"What the fuck?"

"What does dolphin taste like?"

"How the fuck would I know?"

"You said you ate them."

"Oh, you think you're funny now, motherfucker?" He aimed his gun at the ground between them; time to scare the bastard. He pulled the trigger, but nothing happened.

"The safety is on, and you have to chamber a round for it to work."

"What?"

In one agile motion, Nero removed the gun from Joseph's shaking hands with ease. "Look here. I'm holding your courage in my hands. Do you see?"

Joseph swallowed hard; now he was starting to get nervous. He trembled and stuttered, "You, uh, man, I didn't mean anything, man, I was confused from the accident…sir, I most sincerely apologize for my poor behavior."

"I just heard on the news that people on a beach had murdered a baby dolphin because they wanted to take pictures with it. What are your thoughts on that?"

Nero nonchalantly tossed the gun into the car, then looked at his gloved hands as more tears poured down his face.

Joseph started to get some of his courage back. "What's with you and this fucking dolphin?"

One minute later, Nero carefully placed the lifeless body with its broken neck back into the driver's seat. With his truck, he pushed the ugly little fake sports car into the ditch. No one had seen him; then again, he no longer cared. He kept thinking about the little dolphin, and its mother screaming from the water as it dried out and slowly died. How cruel these two-legged creatures were; Nero would never get used to the evil men did.

He was still crying over the loss of the baby dolphin as he drove away.

TWENTY-THREE

Christina shouted in agony, "The bells, the bells, the bells, my head, the fucking bells…you bastards!" She lay in her bed, staring at the nosy owl, and flipped the Peeping Tom off.

"Wakey, wakey, you lazy brats! Get up, breakfast is served, the sun is shining, and the cows need milking!"

Peter and Kevin woke the two vixens up with drumbeats, using whatever they could get their hands on, including pot lids and ladles. Tammy charged out of the guest suite like a tornado; she wasn't going to take this shit from those two clowns. A few minutes later, she dragged herself back into the house, soaking wet. Christina sat like a zombie on one of the barstools by the kitchen island, and from the kitchen came the scent of cooked food.

"I can't believe Dumb and Dumber threw me in the pond," Tammy croaked.

"Yeah, it's a bad habit they have now and then."

"Come now, lassies, what's with the sad faces? Here, have some breakfast."

Peter slammed down two large plates with the works on both: White beans in tomato sauce, crispy traditional bacon, Canadian bacon, scrambled eggs, hash browns, pancakes with sticky maple syrup, and, of course, toast. Each girl took one glance, and then each scrambled to the guest bathroom. Peter slid one plate to Kevin, while starting on the other.

"Yep, they definitely got drunk last night."

"Go figure."

"Check 'em out, they're back."

Both Christina and Tammy just stood in the living room, staring at the two men; both looked like they had just stepped out of some horror movie.

"That's so not fair."

"What, Tammy?"

"You hit me, Kevin, and threw me into the pond."

"Hit you?"

"You slapped my ass!"

"So?"

"I'm just a little girl and you're a big nasty boy. Sexual harassment!"

"Nah, it's okay."

"How's that okay, you idiot!"

"I'm gay, duh. How can I sexually harass you if I'm gay?"

Tammy gave him a bewildered expression, and then she looked at Christina.

Christina patted her on her shoulder and said, "No worries, Tam, I found out about it, and they told me you and Tom already knew."

Peter mused while cleaning up the kitchen that neither of the girls had told the other about his and Kevin's secret, even though they were best friends. Now he respected both even more than he had before, and he knew Kevin would feel the same. He placed two strange, greenish cocktails on the counter, and nodded his head towards the girls for them to take one each.

"Oh shit, Dr. Merlin's fucking magic drink."

"No cursing, Christina," Peter tutted.

"My house, you bas…"

Peter just gave her *The Stare.*

Both girls had to struggle to empty the glasses, and were just setting them down when someone knocked on the open main door. "Anyone home?"

Kevin smiled towards the strangers behind the girls, "Hi there, Robert and Boris, come on in. Coffee?"

Christina's eyeballs practically popped out, and she beat a hasty retreat upstairs.

"What happened to her?" Tammy asked, surprised.

She turned around and stared at Robert, and like a fool, let out a long whistle. "Crap, you weren't supposed to hear that." Suddenly, Tammy too found her wings and flew upstairs.

Robert walked into the kitchen area slowly, pointing his right thumb over his shoulder and frowning. "Anyone?"

Neither Peter nor Kevin answered him, just shaking their heads. Peter poured Robert and Boris two cups of steaming hot coffee.

"Tammy, come and look at this shit!"

"What, Christina?"

The girls were on the second floor, looking down at Robert's truck. Next to it stood a tall blonde in denim shorts, cowboy boots with matching hat, and a shirt tied at her belly button. "The bastard I told you about brought his girlfriend."

"She looks hot."

"Thank you, that's not helping."

"Just go with it. So he has a girlfriend. Move on, silly."

They joined the others in the kitchen, and Christina put on her Hollywood attitude. Kevin lifted his eyebrows when he noticed the cold radiating from Christina when Robert and Boris greeted her. He gave her a suspicious look as he said, "I think Robert has something to ask Your Highness."

Christina shot Kevin a scowl. She turned towards Robert, who held his hat in front of him, thumbing it nervously. "I don't mean to cause any problems, he said, "but there's someone very important to me who has kept bothering me about something lately…so I wonder if it's possible to get your autograph?"

Christina, who had at one time often signed autographs but only reluctantly did so in her home, shrugged and said, "Sure, why not. So who do I make it out to?"

"Wait just a minute, please." Robert hurried outside, and shortly thereafter returned with the blonde.

Christina couldn't hide her fury, and did nothing to conceal it. "You know, normally I'd rather not be bothered by this sort of thing in my home."

"Oh, I'm so sorry!" the other girl said. "I don't want to get my brother into any trouble, so I'll go."

Robert shrugged and said sheepishly, "I told you this was a bad idea, Patty."

Christina raised her eyebrows and immediately felt like an ass. Tammy leaned near her, shaking her head. "Judgmental bonehead," she whispered.

For the first time, Christina noticed that the girl was very young— too young for Robert.

"No, wait, come on in. Welcome, Patty, I'm so sorry for what I said." Christina looked around desperately, but received only blank stares from her friends. Then she looked at Peter and Kevin, and something mischievous came over here. "I apologize for behaving like a jerk, Pat, but you see, my two *much* older brothers here ruined my morning." She turned and faced Pat, pointing over her shoulder.

"Your brothers? They look a lot older than you."

"Yep, they're ancient."

She nodded for Tammy to follow, and then she took Robert's sister with her upstairs. After a while, they returned, and Pat was shining like the sun.

"Robert, Robert! Look what Christina gave me, and she signed it. This T-shirt—she wore it in one of her movies, look!" Robert's little sister's joy was contagious, and soon everyone's mood had improved.

"Thank you, Christina, you didn't have to," Robert said quietly.

Christina waved away Robert's comment. She walked up to him seductively, ignoring everyone else in the room. Tammy was laughing at something the huge Russian said, Peter was on his phone, and Kevin was busy cleaning the kitchen.

"Sorry for being an ass, I…"

"Will you and Tammy be coming to the fall fiesta today?"

"Eh, yes, that's why she came to visit."

"Great, then I'll see you guys there. Now, if you'll excuse me, Boris and I have a few trees to take care of for you."

"What about your sister?"

"Don't worry, she'll help us."

"Dressed like that?"

"Uh, yes."

"Why don't you leave her here with Tammy and I?"

He looked at his sister, who stared back hopefully.

"Sure, why not? we'll be back in an hour. You got a couple of dangerous trees near where you like to go jogging, so we wanted to take care of them today."

"You do that, Robert, while Tammy and I give your sister our best advice on how to deal with a big brother."

"Doubt she needs a lesson for that," he said jokingly, and to Christina's surprise, Robert actually smiled.

Peter laid down his phone and looked at his partner, clearly troubled. Kevin put a towel to the side and walked up to him. "Problems?"

Peter nodded, then shrugged. "I don't know. Could be."

"And I was hoping we'd be back surfing on the West Coast tomorrow."

"Well, it was Frank Hancock who just called—and it seems that there are some more people missing."

"What does that have to do with us? We've finished with the new security installation here, and we both agreed to leave after the party."

"He just wanted for us to know, that's all."

"This place sure lives up from its name. Who's missing now?"

"Some gold-miners—a father and his two kids. Truck's still at the mine, but all three are missing."

Kevin thought for a moment, "Might have gone camping, who knows? Don't give me that look. We're not PIs or superheroes. we're leaving once we finish up here and have gone to that fall thing this afternoon. We're done here; time to move on."

"Yeah, but I have that gut feeling that everything isn't on the up-and-up."

"Oh no, not the gut feeling," Kevin begged, looking alarmed. "Come on, please, not now!"

"Don't worry. Let's stick to the plans. Anyway, Frank is heading up the mountains to the mine with one of his dogs, helping some other K-9 officers from another county. Seems like the local police are running out of people."

HIS GRANDFATHER and father had been right. Ted Hagglund stared at the walls covered with newspaper clippings, diagrams, time-lines, and pictures. Some he recognized. He didn't, however, notice the headings or headlines like most cases under an investigation normally had. There wasn't much to go on, but there *were* a few things that a good investigator might sort out. He was disturbed by how much information the witness had been able to accumulate throughout the years.

He smirked when he read about the skunk ape, and just shook his head. And he had thought his father and grandfather had exaggerated the need for getting rid of any witnesses, especially when they did a purge. He wondered which of the Clan the skunk ape was.

He remembered his first purge to save Mother Earth well, though he'd been only a few years older than the witness. The villagers had sold out, and eventually, huge facilities had been built and ruined the land; but they had sure showed *them*. He'd been hiding by the dry riverbed, and had watched the *bear* and *wolf* wipe out the two-leggeds. He had been afraid, but later he had been raised by his father very strictly, and now he didn't know the meaning of the word fear.

He walked upstairs into the kitchen; it was time to end a fifty-year hunt. He tossed a match into the basement, and the gasoline he'd saturated the place with instantly caught fire. He left the basement door open, along with a few windows. The windows in the basement he had left shut.

He left a note on Carlos's wife's car; it was made to look very amateurish, with letters cut out of different newspapers and magazines, replete with threats and racial slurs about the "spic police" being too incompetent to find missing people. He had left fingerprints from his buddy Anthony's father. Nero never found Eddie's parents. Finding Anthony's father and then taking fingerprints while he was passed out by one of his illegal moonshining stills up in the mountains had been easy, not much of a challenge at all. The fool shouldn't have been allowed to breed. Nero had taken care of that before he had started the run that eventually led him to the gold mine.

The authorities would find the note, and figure out in a day or two who it was supposedly from. The police would visit the moonshiner's home, and then he could deal with the primary target once and for all in the deep, dark forest up in the mountains, where he felt safe.

Nero left the da Silva house burning and walked into the forest at the back of the house, never looking back. In the distance, through the trees, he could see the commotion from the ridiculous fall fiesta; thousands of people had already started to gather at the fairgrounds. He petted his left breast pocket carefully, checking the small glass vial with the stink that would distract any dog. He had changed the ingredients after the mistake with the full-blooded Rhodesian Ridgeback, a breed that had been bred to fight lions.

It was time for him to become what he was, and for that he needed his second skin. He moved fast and stealthy through the forest.

IT WAS the first day of the fall festival, and a beautiful warm sunny day it was, with only a few clouds in the sky—though there was a cloud formation gathering on the horizon in the far distance. More than one person prayed that the clouds would remain where they were. Thousands of people would soon enjoy themselves, and more were showing up by the minute. The fair normally had lasted just two days in the past, but two years back it had doubled in length. The first day was when vendors could start erecting their stands and tents; the big crowds would be there on the following days.

The fresh air intermingled with the various aromas of food being prepared, providing a succulent scent that soon had stomachs growling. Many BBQ pits with as many different meats, recipes, styles, and sauces were already in action. Onion blooms were deep-fried, hotdogs boiled and grilled, and tons of hamburgers were prepared. The food courts were crowded with people creating cotton candy, popcorn, kettle corn, funnel cakes, and all types of other sugar bombs, available for the kids' joy and the parents' horror. There were oceans of soda and ice tea brewing. Beer and wine was available for the adults, with stronger stuff for the real grown-ups.

The fair was huge, drawing in people from several counties, and hundreds of tents and pavilions with equally as many different vendors filled the valley. Some tents were large, though most were quite small. A funfair for kids took up one corner of the field, with many different rides, each looking more frightening than the next. Then there were the ordinary adult rides: the roller-coasters, speedways, helicopter cars, carousels, Ferris wheel, even a haunted house. There were bouncy inflatable castles for the kiddies, of course, and exotic animals in cages and behind fences attracted many visitors.

The most exotic and dangerous animal of all was stalking among them, though, and they had no clue.

Different types of music played across the fairgrounds, pouring from many speakers, from calliope to through country and classic rock 'n roll. In the center of the fairgrounds was an enormous red barn, and it was there that people really began to gather. Several mechanical bull rides had been erected for those willing to test their skills. Bleachers for a rodeo, the evening's main event, were also being erected.

There would be many different competitions throughout the day, for both men and women, most lumberjack-themed: ax-throwing, bow-saw and cross-cut sawing, the underhand standing chop event, pole climbing and cutting, precision cutting with ax, saw, and chainsaw, and so forth. For the non-lumberjacks, there would also be an archery competition and, of course, a pie-eating contest.

Live bands took turns playing on a stage erected on one side of the field. Like a natural-made border, a thin strand of forest separated the huge field in the valley from a smaller field, and on that field were hundreds of tents and campers with trailers and caravans, some looking dirt-poor quality while others looked like they belonged to rock stars. On a third grassy field, the local police had created a temporary parking lot, and many cars had started to fill it up.

Carlos looked up at a helicopter flying overhead, a bit too low, before it headed up towards the mountain range. He had dark bags under his eyes, and gave his wife a tired but friendly smile. Their two daughters, ten-year-old Patricia and Paulina, twelve, chirped like birds about what ride they should go on first. They stared at their parents pleadingly and then Anna-Maria, Carlos's wife, nodded, and the two kids took off laughing. Soon, they met up with several other kids, and all of them headed toward one of the more frightening rides while their parents looked on in horror.

"Never mind them, hon, I'm sure we'll see them again once they run out of tickets," Carlos drawled.

"I know, it's just that I never get used to those rides. Makes me sick just looking at them."

"You and me both, darlin'."

"I'm so happy you can spend some time with us today."

"We got help from the neighboring counties, so I don't have to be everywhere today."

"Any news on the missing people?"

"No, nothing yet. We're following up with the kids' mother; apparently, she and her husband are going through a messy divorce. The kids shouldn't have been hanging around at a gold mine, if you ask me."

"Did they live there with their father?"

"Actually, they had a few days off from school, and they were visiting him. I'm not sure, but from what I gather, the mother might have an issue with alcohol."

"I hope they're fine. How long can you be with us today?"

"All day, I hope."

She kissed him gently on his cheek, and they walked hand-in-hand through the masses, every now and then exchanging greetings with friends or colleagues. In the background came the sound of fire engines in the far distance, and Carlos frowned; just as expected, his phone eventually rang. "Yes Whitney, what you got?" he answered, a bit irritated.

As he listened, his face turned pale.

You're sure…? But you did find them…? God*damm*it. Okay, okay, yeah, get CSI…sure, let me talk to Frank. Good work."

"Hi, it's Frank."

"Carlos here. Thank you for your help. There *is* one thing I must ask…was there anything unusual?"

"Yes. All the dogs acted the same as they did when they chased the bear."

"Meaning that Nugget got a bit upset?"

"You bet, but this time I put him back in my truck. He's still healing."

"Please put Whitney back on… You smelled it too? You're sure? Okay. No, that's all for now, keep up the good work."

Carlos felt a surging sensation through his mind and body, an inchoate, unexplainable sense of fear, anger, and helplessness…goosebumps and nausea followed. He was afraid. He had nothing, no evidence, and *still* he knew he was right: the Beast was back in his life.

His wife looked at him, concerned. "Does that call mean you have to go back to work?"

"No, hon, I promised, remember?"

Another call came in, and he rolled his eyes. Before he answered, he said, "Sorry, love, this one is from Nolan. I have to take it."

Anna-Maria gave him a smile and held his arm hard, looking up at her love of her life. She felt Carlos tense up, and immediately knew something was very wrong. He gave her a concerned expression, and before he had to make an excuse, she saved him.

"Go and do what you have to, but hurry back if you can."

He gave her a smile and walked away, but suddenly he stopped. He turned around, walked back, and in front of God and everyone he grabbed her arms hard and pushed them to her body, and then he kissed her like he never had before.

"Stay here, baby, and take care of our girls. I've gotta go."

She nodded, and with moist eyes she looked into his and saw something infinitely sad. "I'll be back as soon as I can," he vowed before turning away.

As she watched her husband move through the crowd, a cold breeze swept through the valley, and suddenly she had goosebumps; but somehow, she knew it wasn't from the weather.

Carlos hurried through the crowd, and when he saw the long line of cars heading to the parking area, he decided to take a shortcut through the forest. The smoke in the distance urged him on. He called one of his deputies, Bard, and ordered him to meet him on the other side of the forest on the road leading towards the outskirts where his home was. He looked towards his home and saw more black smoke. Carlos hurried his steps; and when he realized not only that he and his family might lose their home with all their memories and possessions, but that everything he had on his fifty-year-old case was in the basement, he started sprinting, leaping over a couple rolling around in the grass. Further ahead sat a typical Rasta-hippie guy, who from the smell had been or was smoking weed; someone next to him seemed sick, puking his or her guts out. He increased his speed as he passed them, and the closer he came to his home, the thicker the smoke became.

Firetrucks continued to wail their way onto his street. He reached a long, narrow ridge, but before he could climb it, he had to turn down a small gorge. He tripped when he reached the top edge of the ridge and pulled himself up with the help of a large root sticking out of an enormous tree. He rounded the large tree and ran into someone.

There was a crackling tinkle of glass breaking.

TED HAGGLUND walked away from the witness' house in deep thought; and when he heard the sound of the fire engines, he took a fast glance behind him, then hurried his steps. Once he had passed a few large trees ahead and was down in the small gully beyond, he would be clear and safe. His sharp senses picked out the sounds of the many people further ahead towards the fairground, but the wailing of the sirens was drowning out some sounds. He stopped and looked around for anyone who might see him, but he saw no one. However, he didn't like the fact that his hearing was disrupted, and sped up; and suddenly he bumped into someone very hard.

He was baffled for a moment, and then, when he looked at the person he just had run into, it all made sense. He was still surprised and taken a bit off guard when he made eye contact with his primary prey. He was so stunned that, too late, he realized that they had maintained eye contact too long.

Worse, he felt something wet in his left breast pocket, and the rising scent betrayed him.

CARLOS IMMEDIATELY stopped, and he was just about to apologize when he noticed the stare of the person he had bumped into. At first he thought nothing of it, and was going to move on…but then he froze. The stink that had triggered his memory weeks before suddenly filled the gully, and as he looked into the eyes of the stranger again, his own eyes widened in horror and surprise. He saw the surprised expression on the stranger, and then Carlos's thirty years of experience as a law enforcement officer took over; he knew full well when he encountered a suspect. The smell told Carlos everything he needed to know, and he went for his gun, but fumbled; and when he looked up, the stranger was gone.

There were sudden sharp blows to his abdomen and then to his face, followed by a third devastating blow to his shoulder, accompanied by the sound of breaking bone. Another blow, and he fell back onto a tree, dazed and confused. Everything was a blur, and the whole time, the pulsing pain from his shoulder jolted through his spine. Carlos felt a painful pressure on his shoulder. He dropped his gun, and the pain of his broken bones was so excruciating that he had to kneel. He lost his footing and fell, hanging onto the root on the large tree. Flashing lights and the pain of thousands of needles shot through his face and body; he didn't think clearly, but he did think. He quickly grabbed his smartphone from his pocket and hit a button. As he started to lose consciousness, he could see a pair of typical lumberjack hard-toed boots. He jammed his phone between two branches, and then rolled back down the small slope.

NERO COULDN'T believe his luck—or un-luck, maybe. Everything had happened so fast. But the bizarre situation was almost too good to be true, and the opportunity was too good to pass up. Alone in the forest with the primary prey? He had to get him off-guard. The prey was armed, so he must be quick. He reacted before thinking.

Nero ignored his primary prey as it held onto a branch; he was more concerned about anyone seeing what was going on, so he looked around carefully around for any witnesses. He heard the moaning from the prey, and then he climbed down confidently after Carlos, who lay on his back, trying to catch his breath, clutching his injured shoulder.

Carlos writhed from the pain and had to bite down hard not to scream, something his pride wouldn't allow him to do. He crawled on his back, using his legs and feet—not away from but to the side of his attacker. He tried reaching his spare gun in his ankle holster, but the man beat him to it.

Nero took a final look at his surroundings. He knew there were people in the forest, but he detected no one nearby. He looked at the small revolver, and then went in for the final blow.

"STOP!"

The fist stopped inches from Carlo's Adam's apple.

Carlos fought against the tears, trying to hold back the excruciating pain throbbing in his shoulder; he realized that the person leaning over him had punched or kicked him with a force to reckoned with. "Why? Just tell me why?" He squirmed from the pain and bit down hard before he whispered, "Why are you doing this?"

Nero hesitated at first, but then he said, standing up, "There can be no witnesses."

Carlos only shook his head, and then said, "But why do you do it at all? All the killings, and why me, now, after all this time?"

Nero backed off for a moment, not being in a very talkative mode, and in a hoarse and very frightening voice, replied, "We purge because, because you and all the others out there," he made a sweeping gesture towards the fairgrounds, and then continued, "...you're our Frankenstein."

Carlos gave him a tired, confused look, and for an instant Nero swore that he had smiled confidently. It made him hesitate for a moment, but finally Nero struck hard with his fist.

Carlos's last thought was of his wife and two daughters. Now he would never take his family to the Caribbean. But before he closed his eyes for the last time, he smiled anyway; he had enough in knowing that he had at last closed the case, revealing who had killed most of his family when he was a child. Carlos da Silva left this life as a loving husband, a dedicated father, and a true police officer.

Nero stared at his primary prey's corpse, with its taunting little smile, feeling disappointed. He wished he had worn his second skin; doing it this way felt a bit off, and just plain wrong.

He was about to leave the forest to enter the melee on the fair-grounds, but before he did, he had one thing more he had to do.

ANNA-MARIA'S PHONE rang while she was talking with the mayor's husband, Phillip.

"One moment, Phillip. Sorry, I don't mean to be rude, but the girls have a phone each and are supposed to call if they're in trouble."

"Now, that's what I'm talking about when it comes to new technology, you see, we need to support it and…"

"Yeah, well, they probably ran out of tickets and need money or something."

"Well, that's the price being a parent. Are you okay?"

Anna-Maria saw that the incoming call was from Carlos's phone and that it was on a Facetime live feed. She smiled and opened it up. It took her several moments before she thought she understood what she was looking at, and then her brain registered everything; but her mind refused to understand it. She passed out, and when she did, her phone slid back into her purse. She hit the ground hard in front of a surprised and shocked Phillip.

NERO STOPPED and engraved one word on the giant tree: *Cro*. He observed his work, and then said, "Grandfather and Father, your purge is complete. Our secret is still safe; you can rest now."

He moved away from the body, following the tracks left by Carlos. An average person wouldn't see them, but Nero was anything but average. Then he froze, realizing he had the stink all over him, and that it would really draw attention to him. He took off his plaid cotton sweater and T-shirt, but the stink was still on him. He had to change his direction, and he had to do it fast; he needed to get away before anyone saw him. This was the reason an evolved being like himself needed a second skin when he hunted: he couldn't be seen like this, naked like a two-legged. Nero changed direction towards one of the huge parking lots.

"Hey man, you seen Little Flower?"

Ted Hagglund stopped in his tracks; he glanced at Carlos's body and then at the hippy idiot who had popped up from nowhere, and then looked up, rolling his eyes, knowing full well that meeting Carlos in the forest had been too good to be true.

The Rasta-hippy guy moved like a drunken fool, wearing typical clothing from the Flower Power era. Three fast steps, and Nero was holding the blabbering idiot by his throat.

"Yo, now hold on, man…"

Nero twisted Rasta-hippy's head sideways and looked at the guy's eyes; yep, high as a kite. No killing required, but he sure needed a new shirt. Moments later, after having to listen to all kind of profound language, he had removed the long shirt with its strange flower print and a T-shirt with Bob Marley on it from the hippy. Both stank of sweat and urine. He gave the guy an elbow under the chin; he dropped like a bad habit. Ted Hagglund was walking away and fixing the shirts when he suddenly rolled his eyes again at the sound of a strident voice.

"Oh no, oh no, what have you done to my Todd, you bastard!"

Nero had his back turned, and could see the woman's position from the side; so he round-kicked her, hitting her in the face. Little Flower dropped like a log next to her Todd. Nero looked at the two idiots, contemplating killing both, but decided against it. He stunk of urine and she of alcohol. He saw a bottle of whiskey lying next to the girl. He took it and rubbed some of the alcohol on his chest, killing most of the stink. After making sure he didn't leave any prints on the glass, he dropped the bottle on the ground. Now he could go back to his original plan and head to the fairgrounds; but before he did, a grin spread over his face.

It took some time, but eventually he got his old T-shirt on the Rasta guy.

For the first time, Nero realized that the forest was too crowded with two-legged idiots, mostly youths, drinking and fornicating. Maybe this hadn't been his best choice of escape route after all. He tried to fit in with the young people partying all around him, but he still had some of the stink on him; the whiskey had only done so much, and whenever he got close to a group of them, he noticed more than one head turning. He wanted to go back to being Ted Hagglund again, but at the same time he knew it was far too late; he was what he had become, and second skin or not, there would be soon be a *purge*. The more he thought of it, the more his mind abandoned the little sanity he had left, as the Beast inside took over.

Sometime later, Todd came to with a splitting headache, still high as a kite; he lifted his head, holding on to his cheek and checking on his jaw. He had no memory whatsoever of what had happened. He shook his head, and then he saw Little Flower lying spread-eagled next to him, her nose bleeding. "Oh, my poor sweet thing!" he wailed. "What have I done to you, my dearest?"

He crawled up next to her and held her head, trying to focus his eyes, shaking his head more than once. He slapped her a few times, but she wouldn't wake up. He looked around and saw the whiskey bottle; there was still some booze in it. Todd did the natural thing that came to his somewhat confused mind, and poured the whiskey onto his girlfriend's face. She coughed and cursed as she came to, spitting and screaming. She saw Todd's happy and enthusiastic expression, and once she got up on a sitting position, she punched him hard in his face.

"Fuck you! Knock me out will ya, asshole?"

"Yo babe, I ain't been touching you."

"Then who did?"

Todd looked around and saw a person lying a few yards away on his back.

"Probably that shithead redneck over there… I must have fucked him up, man, defending you and all. So, wanna do it?"

He gave her a mischievous look, but the normally-peaceful Little Flower was very upset, not feeling peaceful at all. She staggered to her feet and looked at Todd sitting on the ground, trying to light his pipe. "Jeez, man, why do you look like a redneck?"

Todd took a couple of deep drags from the pipe.

"I don't know, man, fucking cool. Smells even cooler."

"Smells like shit to me, man, like cat piss or somethin'. Now gimme some."

Todd got up on his knees and started to unbutton his pants.

"No, fool, not that, gimme the fucking pipe."

Little Flower took a few hits off the pipe, and then Todd grabbed the pipe from her. She walked over to the body and looked it over. "Hey, Todd, we got ourselves a drunk pig over here. Motherfucker wears a fucking star, man, probably one of them fucking Texas Ranger whores, remember the ones that got us busted down near Mexico?"

"Hey, ask him if he got some weed."

Little Flower just rolled her eyes. "I tell you what, man, Ima piss on the law. Wanna join me, Todd?"

"Sure, let's piss on the system and all these fucking SS. Let anarchy rule, man!"

Little Flower pulled down her pants and urinated over Carlos's lifeless body. Todd laughed like a maniac, and fumbled after his phone so he could film the whole thing and put it up on his Facebook page. When he was done, he struggled for a while, getting his own pants down, and then he pissed on both the body and his girlfriend while trying to document everything for all his future children and grandchildren to see.

"You fucking idiot, you just peed all over me, you strung-out fuck!"

"Coolness, babe."

Little Flower rose, very angry now, and pushed Todd away while he was still pissing. He dropped his phone on the ground, then hit his back on the side of the low ridge below the big tree, laughing out loud from the rush. He turned around and pushed away so he could get back up, and when he did, he grabbed onto the root. He looked a bit bewildered when he found a smartphone in his hand. Not giving it a second thought, he put it in one of his pant pockets. Eventually, Todd and his peaceful girlfriend decided to head back to the fairground, and whenever they met someone they knew or liked, judging them from their clothing, they directed them into the woods, because in there lay a drunken cop and anyone could piss on him. Didn't take long before the rumor spread like wildfire.

Nero stood by the edge of a parking lot in a large field, music playing all around him as the crowd of two-legged enjoyed themselves. He stared at some middle-age people working a tailgate BBQ; there were many more people doing the same. Some bikers had built an open fire, and a policewoman was making them put it out. There was some commotion between the police woman and the bikers, so she radioed for assistance while surrounded by half a dozen pissed-off men wearing leather and denim vests with patches on the back. Nero walked by the fire, snagged a medium-size log, and continued his walk. He tossed the log into an open tent. Next to the tent were several motorcycles, and he quickly unscrewed the gas cap on the one nearest the tent. He tore off part of his new shirt and dipped it in. He rubbed the gas on his chest, and as he walked away, a large biker hurried over to him. Nero kneed the biker hard in the groin and, using the biker's own speed and motion, grabbed his jacket and pulled him forward, very hard, sending him headfirst into the two bikes. Both motorcycles fell like dominos, and the one nearest the tent fell on top of it. More smoke came from the tent.

Nero sniffed his chest, and found he could still smell the stink. He really needed to get away from here. A familiar roar made Nero turn around, looking surprised. *That was definitely a big cat*, he thought; and then he saw something that enraged him. At the edge of the parking lot were several large animal crates on wheels, containing wild animals from a circus, lined up in a half-circle. Nero headed to them.

TWENTY-FOUR

So, how long are you going to keep the babysitters?" Tammy pointed over her shoulder with her thumb at Kevin and Peter, who mingled with the crowd.

Christina, attacking her cotton candy like a three-year-old, making sure Tammy wouldn't get any, stopped and licked her fingers. Tammy saw her chance, but Christina moved away the arm holding the stick loaded with spun sugar.

"Hey, you could have gotten your own, but what did you say? *Too much sugar, too much weight.* Tammy dear, I'm totally doing you a favor."

"Hey, look, there's Robert!"

Christina immediately turned her head. "Where?"

And just like that, the cotton candy changed owners.

"You're such a bitch!" Christina cried.

"The bitch with the cotton candy!" Tammy poked her tongue out at Christina.

"I guess they're leaving soon. I think they're pretty much done with the security stuff," Christina said, picking up their previous conversation where they'd dropped it.

"They like it here, especially your guest suite above the three-car garage."

"Funny, I haven't even seen that yet."

"Sure the place isn't too big for you to handle?"

"Of course not. I do have some plans, but they're a secret. You'll see next year. Besides, Robert and the mute Russian are the caretakers, and I'll probably keep them both on."

"So, that's all they be doing—you then, huh?"

Christina just smiled at her friend's trap. "No, they have more properties they work with. Now give me back my sugar rush, you thieving little shit."

"Get your own."

"I *did*." Christina just shook her head, and then she saw something through the crowd and smiled. "Enough of this. Let's ride some humps."

Tammy stood there watching her best friend with eyes the size of golf balls. "Ride what? You horny toad!"

They pushed through a huge crowd full of drunk people about their own age. Everyone was focused on a mechanical bull ride, where people took turns making asses of themselves, while in the background a few professional cowboys smirked at the boneheads—until a hot babe got on top of the bull, whereupon they became the loudest spectators. Robert and Pat stood by a railing, arguing, with him gesturing at her clothing. She was dressed like Tammy and Christina, in Daisy Dukes style.

Christina kicked of her cowboy boots and strolled over on the mechanical bulls barefoot, generating some cheers and wolf whistles. Someone in the crowd shouted out her name, followed by silence; and then came the roar of approval. Peter and Kevin glared at her with irritated expressions, while keeping their eyes on the uproar.

With music thundering from speakers, Christina rode, holding on for dear life, falling off more than once; but stubborn as she was, she never quit. Eventually, when the person in charge of the mechanical bull would only let her ride slow, for her to be sexy and all, she stopped. Tammy and Pat cheered her on and whistled like mad, and before long both found themselves grabbed by the strong hands of overly-friendly cowboys, who encouraged them to take turns on the bull. Robert just shook his head, and didn't look all too happy when his sister mounted the bull. When Pat showed up, Robert stood behind the railing, shouting for her to get back, but she waved him off. She got up on the bull, and not long after she was crowned the winner of all three, both from the applause and by a happy guy screaming at the top of his lungs through a microphone.

Robert gently but firmly escorted her away.

"What's up with him?" Tammy wondered.

Claire showed up from nowhere and said, "He's very protective of her."

Price of being the older brother, I guess, Christina thought, thinking of her own brothers and how protective they could be.

"Especially since he raised her all by his lonesome."

"I didn't know that."

"Christina, both of them are orphans. Their parents died young, and after spending a few years with their grandparents, Robert pretty much raised his sister on his own. Guess she'll be grounded after that little ride."

Christina looked at Robert lecturing his kid sister, and then there were the butterflies. Claire and Tammy noticed Christina's expression, and smiled to each other. "Why don't you go over there and ask him to marry you, silly?" Tammy needled her.

Christina faced Tammy, putting on her sunglasses and correcting them aggressively with her middle finger.

"Hello there, Mr. Hunk, what's your name?" Tammy said, accenting her statement with a whistle.

"Claire, I apologize for my poorly-mannered friend," Christina said.

Claire laughed, "Oh, that's Blake."

Christina turned around, and saw the same man she'd seen at the car accident. She noticed the glare Robert and Blake exchanged. Blake was also attractive, but there was something too serious and sad about his features. "Wow, you can really feel the friction between those two."

"That's an understatement."

Tammy didn't hesitate, walking over to Blake. They started talking, and Blake smiled.

"Come *on*, Claire, you said A, so you might as well say B," Christina insisted.

"Well, Christina, I normally don't spread rumors, but I'll give you girls this one, because I'm sure you'll eventually hear all kinds of crap about those two. Years back, a girl got between them. Until then, they were best friends."

"What happened to the girl?" Christina asked while looking at Robert and Blake?

"She left."

"What, for another guy? Why do they still hate each other?"

"Oh, dear. Well, she left all right, but only after she'd thoroughly and deliberately wrecked their friendship, but it wasn't for another guy. She left for another woman."

Christina looked at Claire, and neither could help laughing a bit. "I guess you guys just have to find out why they don't care for each other yourself," Claire chuckled, "because this jungle drum will drum no more."

Tammy returned, waving a note with a number on it. "This is a real popular celebration, isn't it?"

"Yes, Tammy, we country folks can party too—but you haven't seen anything yet. This is just the pre-party. The real celebration and competitions will be tomorrow and the day after. Then there'll be two or three times as many people here. Frank and I probably won't attend then. We keep the store open, but only for a few hours in the afternoon."

"But where do all these people come from? I'm sure they're not just from Skull Creek," Christina said, while looking around at the ever-increasing crowd.

Claire looked around too. "Of course not. We pull in a lot of people from the surrounding region. Plus, this is the end of the season for all the lumber crews and gold miners; we'll soon have winter coming, and most people will leave and the place will go back to normal. We're lucky we're not a ski resort. There are also a lot of students from the university over in the next county."

"And that's one of the reasons I like this place. Small, calm, and quiet."

"Mostly. Well, I'm heading back to our place with all these bags, and then it's time for supper. I figure my old man will be home soon, and I have to take Winston out on his afternoon roll."

Christina started laughing. "I'm sorry, Claire, but I saw you and Winston once, and it looked really funny."

"Aw, don't worry about it. That dog has a style all his own, and I guess that's we love him and spoil him so much. Well, time for me to go…and if you guys want to catch up with Robert and Blake, you might want to head over to the Red Barn. Soon there'll be line dancing and all, I think."

Claire said goodbye and headed home, while Christina and Tammy headed towards the barn. They passed several cages containing wild circus animals, a few with handlers giving lectures to a crowd of people.

"Lousy way to treat animals. Just look at them, Tammy. The tigers and the mountain lions and all the other animals in those tiny little cages—what a horrible thing to do."

"You're right. They should put the handlers in the cages instead. Come on, let's get away from all this misery."

"Makes you think about the old *Planet of the Apes* movies, where they put people in cages."

"Yeah, you'd like to be put in a cage, wouldn't you? Damn, it stinks here, let's get going. Fuckers should at least clean the cages," Tammy muttered.

"Come on, let's hurry. I think I just felt some rain."

The cloud formation so many had hoped would remain in the distance had appeared overhead as if from nowhere, and with it came a strong wind. The entire region was soon engulfed in darkness.

Nero—no longer Ted Hagglund—had his back turned when he overheard the girls talking. He had seen Christina before they had got too close, and turned away. He nodded, agreeing with what he had overheard; and then he looked at the three handlers talking to the crowd, trying to sell tickets for a circus in the state capital next weekend.

The look on his face wasn't a very friendly one.

Suddenly a giant fireball lit the night in the distance, accompanied a second later by an explosion as much felt as heard. It came from one of the parking lots, and was followed by a thick wreath of smoke blowing in from town. At nearly the same time a lightning bolt struck, lighting up the entire region, followed by rumbling thunder; seconds later, it started to drizzle. A fight became audible in the parking lot, and it soon became obvious that there was some kind of melee occurring in the strip of forest separating the town and the fairgrounds. A good number of civilians tried their best to help the police break up the fighting, but there were too many civilians who seemed to take pleasure in the violence.

Under cover of the distraction, Nero stalked to the temporary railing and climbed over. He went straight for the nearest cage, smashed off the padlock with the hammer in his back pocket, and flung the door open. The puma prowling the limited space looked at him speculatively and sniffed the air, then leaped out. For a long moment, the animal curled up under the moving cage, frightened by all the people and by the one human who smelled so much like a predator; but eventually the big cat gathered his courage and took off into the forest behind the cages, followed by a female puma, who leaped more confidently from the next cage. Nero smiled, then he went on to the third cage as a large, ugly two-legged female shouted to the handlers and pointed at Nero. One handler, a big bald man who thought fat was just as good as muscle, realized what he was doing and hurried towards him, shouting for him to stop. He grabbed Nero's forearm; Nero gave him a bitter smile and then clocked him with the hammer, leaving him unconscious and with a half-dozen fewer teeth. The other two handlers charged Nero, but when they saw he'd opened up the cages containing the matched pair of white tigers, they stopped and turned around, running for their lives. They knew the tigers wouldn't forgive them for the indignities they'd visited upon them over the years. The tigers weren't afraid, unlike the mountain lions, and had no intention of fleeing into the forest for the moment; when they saw the backs of their tormentors, that was all they needed.

Feeding time.

The animals mostly ignored Nero, though one of the huge cats ran his head over Nero's chest in gratitude; and then the hunt was on. Grinning, Nero opened all the rest of the cages and walked casually away as a lion, a pair of timber wolves, and, ironically enough, a grizzly bear charged into the crowd.

A woman screamed, and then, like a tidal wave, people began scattering in all directions, knocking over the elderly, young, and unprepared, and tramping them underfoot. Then there were guns fired in the distance, followed by shouts and screams of terror; and after that, the crowd really panicked, making everything worse. The fighting in the parking lot had escalated into a riot. Civilians, lumberjacks, miners, bikers, hippies; everyone fought everyone. Some people tried to calm the situation, but soon found themselves fighting too. A Swedish exchange student ran around in a blue and yellow T-shirt with the letters *Made in Sweden* on it above the Swedish flag, dancing in the rain, shouting for people to think of peace, love, and understanding. "We are all Muslims!" he shouted, taking some hits on a pipe, dancing with other hippies who did the same.

A dozen or so of the couples fighting—lumberjacks, bikers, and miners, mostly—immediately stopped fighting, turning their heads simultaneously to stare at the confused Swede, who just repeated his words, smiling lovingly with his arms outstretched. On his chest was a patch from his political party, the Green Party. "Stop all the fighting and love everyone, because we are all Muslims here!" he proclaimed.

A bit farther away, a TV reporter, feeling almost deliriously happy at this turn of events, stood in the center of the melee, reporting live on what had once been a boring human interest event -– a punishment after pissing off her manager—and had now become national news. "From what we hear," she said excitedly, "this all began when police shot at several protesters in this stretch of woods." The reporter turned her body, pointing into the forest, which stood out starkly against a backdrop of smoke and flames. The cameraman moved with the reporter, who talked straight into the camera, feeding the public all kinds of misinformation about how the peaceful civilians had been assaulted by local authorities. Three people emerged from the forest; two of them carried a woman between them. She was injured, with blood oozing from her shoulder.

The reporter saw her chance, and hurried to the three people, but had to stop in her track. A young man with a T-shirt proclaiming *Made in Sweden* sprinted past her and the cameraman, pursued by a crowd of some twenty bikers, lumberjacks, and others, all shouting for blood. Once the train of people had passed, she was able to reach the stragglers from the forest.

"So, tell us what's happened here, is it true that the police are shooting unarmed civilians?"

"What the fuck does it look like, man? They're shooting everyone, fucking cops going Terminator on everyone's asses!"

They brushed the reporter away and hurried forward. A shout for them to get the hell out of the way made the reporter and her cameraman turn one-eighty. The people who had chased the confused guy with the Swedish T-shirt ran for their lives back the way they'd come, followed by the Swede, and behind him came over a dozen police officers in many different uniforms, hunting down the civilians. Anyone who got in the way got his or her head mashed, or was wrestled to the ground and arrested on the spot.

"George, tell me you're getting this!"

"Sure am, Amy, sure am… *now* what the fuck?"

George looked away from his camera, still pointing it at the action. "What, George?"

"Just look!… What *is* all this, a fucking Monty Python skit?"

Running back were the police who had just passed them, followed by the confused Swede, and behind him came the lumberjacks, miners, and bikers, all running for their lives. Amy scratched the back of her head, and George only shook his. Amy took her place facing the camera, then suddenly froze.

George looked up from the viewer and said, "Now what?"

Amy's expression made him turn around with the camera, and just then he caught the perfect picture of a huge white tiger with a bloody mouth and long fangs descending from the sky.

The picture, which was still feeding back to the national hub in Atlanta via satellite, went black.

NERO TOSSED a roll of bills and a bottle of whiskey to the young man, who just smiled mischievously. He then took center stage. He raised his arms, looked down with closed eyes, and as the music started to play, he began moving his arms like a professional *Kapellmeister*. The music and lyrics of Ludwig van Beethoven's finest work, *Ode to Joy*, rumbled from the enormous speakers, intermingled with the sound of thunder and powerful ripping roars from the tigers followed by some fireworks; and, as icing on the cake, there came a powerful wind with heavy raindrops falling hard and torrentially.

"OKAY, GUYS, here's our ride, be quick," Peter ordered the girls.

Kevin pulled up to the side of the stage in Christina's new truck. The girls and Peter ran towards the truck, and of course Christina slipped on the muddy ground and fell headfirst—nothing new. She got up with the help of Peter, while her best friend laughed like crazy.

When Christina looked up, she noticed the bizarre event taking place on the stage. She was too far away to see the face of the person who stood there like an idiot, waving his arms as if he were truly conducting Beethoven, but there was something familiar about him. He had at least one fan; a very drunk man stood on the field near where Christina had slipped, shouting, "I love Miley Cyrus! More, baby, more!" He finished by taking a gulp from his moonshine jar.

For a moment, Christina could have sworn the man on the stage had looked at her and made eye contact, and then bowed his head towards her. Peter got ahold on her arm more firmly and almost carried her to her truck, even as she kept looking back. They took off slowly, making sure they didn't hit anyone. In the chaos they saw Robert, Pat, and Blake running through the chaos. "Pick 'em up, Kevin," she shouted.

Kevin laid on the horn and whistled sharply to get their attention, then shouted, "Get in the back!"

All three ran to the truck. A few other guys tried to climb in the back, and Peter had to get outside and pull them off the truck. "You, Pat, get in my seat, and you guys join me here in the back," Peter ordered.

"Robert, tell them about the shortcut, the rabbit trail," Blake shouted, while climbing into the truck bed.

"There's a shortcut through the forest not too far from here," Robert shouted to Peter.

"Right. Try and get in with your sister and show Kevin the way."

But the truck cab was too crowded. "Let me out," Tammy shouted, and forced herself outside. Before Peter could object, Blake lifted her up into the back and deposited her in his lap. Robert got inside, while Peter had to punch a guy to keep him from climbing onto the truck; he then climbed up as Kevin started to drive. Kevin laid on the horn and shouted for people to get back, even as the crowd got increasingly hysterical.

Robert told Kevin where to drive, and after what seemed forever, he turned into the forest behind the stage and pulled away from the town. The truck jumped and jerked all over, and the people on the back of the truck had to hold on for dear life. Tammy and Blake mostly held on to each other. Kevin slammed on the brakes when a huge mountain lion suddenly appeared on the trail before them, its eyes shining like tiny suns in the light of the headlamps. After snarling in their direction, it took off into the deep forest, gunning for freedom. Kevin flipped on the roof spotlights, and the wooded path lit up brightly.

They left the fairgrounds behind them while people continued to panic, shriek, and ran for cover, then running for cover again when their cover was rendered inadequate or invaded by too many other idiots.

It was a historic first day of the Skull Creek Fall Festival.

AFTER DRIVING for quite a while, they reached a clearing; from there, a normal, narrow forest road took them to the outskirts of Skull Creek. By then, the traffic was massive in all directions, and red, blue, and yellow emergency lights flashed everywhere. They went off-road again, behind a large parking lot that was filling up as people pulled over to get out of the traffic and calm their nerves. In the center of the huge parking lot was a large building.

"That's a bar called Lumberjacks, and it'll be jammed-packed by now." Blake pointed at the building.

"So that's where you were going tonight," Tammy shouted innocently over the roar of the engine and the storm.

"No, not tonight. Maybe day after tomorrow, the last night of the fair, it's usually the best night. I'm going with a bunch of friends for the last river rafting of the year tomorrow morning, early."

"Rafting this time of the year?"

"Yes. No tourists. My buddy owns one of the tourist traps up the mountain, and they take tourists rafting all the time. But now the season has ended, so it'll only be us locals; it's a tradition. You and your friend should come."

"I'd love to. Let me talk to Christina." Tammy gave Blake a seductive smile, licking her lips as he looked away.

They parked behind Hancock Tool Supply, and Robert knocked on the back door. Frank opened up and looked at the dirty truck, grinning. "Been mudding, I see."

"Yeah, something like that. Things have been crazy as hell. We'll tell you a little more in a minute. Is it ok for us to hang here until the chaos on the roads calm down?"Frank looked at the crowd gathering outside in the rain, and nodded in consent. Soon everyone was in the living room. A nice, hot fire burned in the large fireplace; Claire handed out towels, and made some coffee and hot chocolate. Nugget and Hunter ran around, doing their best to greet everyone and to steal attention while being petted. Winston, however, lay half sitting on his back, with his fat belly protruding, in his favorite armchair, staring at everyone suspiciously. Since no one bothered to give him any treats, he eventually fell asleep, snoring in front of the fireplace.

As they settled in and Robert spoke to Frank and Claire in concerned tones, Tammy took Christina to the bathroom to freshen up, and told her about the river rafting trip. They agreed to go, but decided they had to get Robert to go with them. The question was, how?

The solution appeared when Pat knocked on the bathroom door.

Later, Pat walked over to her brother and whispered something in his ear. He listened, then he shook his head no. Pat persisted, but Robert was stubborn. More than once he glanced at Blake, who gravely returned the stare.

"So, are you coming with us tomorrow?" Tammy suddenly asked Robert from where she stood next to Blake.

There was an odd tension in the room, and a uncomfortable silence. Christina kept to the back, in the kitchen with Claire; she asked her something, and Claire nodded at a nicely decorated clay pot with a lid. She got a dog treat from the clay pot and walked over to Winston and held the treat under his nose. Suddenly Winston's eyes opened, with a sigh from the king of the house. Finally, a treat. Why he put up with these substandard servants he didn't know, except they had thumbs

and he didn't. Christina waved it in front of him for a while, torment-
ing him, and then to his horror and aggravation, tossed it on the floor.
Why, that woman—!

A normal dog would have gotten up and lunged for it, but Winston was anything but normal. Instead, he let out another put-upon sigh
and leaned back in his seat, shutting his eyes. Nugget, getting attention from Frank and knowing better than to go for the treat, remained
by him, being petted. Hunter, however, seriously wanted the treat, and
went for it. With his eyes still closed, Winston snarled as Hunter got
too close; and when he took it tentatively in his mouth, there was a
loud bark. Winston stood on all fours in his seat, barking ferociously,
until Hunter dropped the treat and slowly backed away, whining, with
his tail between his legs. They all knew who was Alpha here! Winston
then stared at Christina, his eyes boring into hers demandingly. For
some reason, this scenario made the atmosphere lighten up and everyone laughed.

Tammy repeated herself. "So, Robert, you coming too?"

Robert didn't answer.

"Christina wants you to come. Come on, man, what do you say?"

Blake's arm had found itself around Tammy's shoulders, and she
had moved closer to Blake. Christina rolled her eyes, then heard Robert
rumble, "You killed my dog."

Frank said in the background, "Oh jeez, here we go again."

Claire, in a friendly voice but with iron in her tone, "Now boys, if
you're going to fight, do it outside."

"It was an accident…" Blake stopped in the middle of the sentence
and walked straight over to Robert. Hunter and Nugget sensed the tension in the room and sat up, staring in silence; Winston just glared
at Christina, then looked at his treat on the ground. She kneeled and
picked it up. Blake whispered something to Robert, and after a while
they finally shook hands, to everyone's joy—except for Winston, who
didn't give a damn. He was busy staring at the mean woman with his
treat. You just couldn't find good help these days.

"Okay, I'll go," Robert announced.

Christina had her back turned, still kneeling; she smiled and finally gave Winston his treat. He gladly took it from her, crunched it up, and then went back to sleep.

"You're to going need some gear," Frank said happily.

"Yeah, but this time, I'll pay for it, Frank," Christina vowed.

Peter and Kevin knocked on the back door, and after saying said hello to both Nugget and Hunter, they joined the others. Claire handed both a cup each of steaming hot coffee.

"So, girls, time to get to bed, it's getting late," Peter stated.

Both Christina and Tammy scowled at him; Peter just shrugged. Finally Christina admitted, "He's right, Tammy we're going to need some rest before we go rafting tomorrow."

"You're doing what? In this weather? I don't think so!" Kevin protested.

Tammy brushed by him and patted his cheek, hard.

"Oh yes we are, my dear."

"Are you two insane?" A stunned Kevin and Peter stared at the girls when they followed Frank into the store.

THE STORM had returned, and with it, so had Nero. He drove his truck slowly, following a long line of cars and trucks away from Skull Creek and up into the mountains. However, they met as many vehicles going towards the town as there were leaving.

It seemed that the authorities had finally gotten some measure of control over almost everything. Many vehicles from other roads closed in on Skull Creek, and every hotel, bar, salon, and seasonal night club quickly filled up. People hadn't been discouraged from visiting Skull Creek by news of the riot; if anything, the news had encouraged them to join in the party, despite the often-repeated footage of the leaping tiger taking down George the cameraman. Numerous Harleys bearing men either burly and hairy or small and wiry—there seemed to be only two types of bikers—were interspersed among the cars, flashing their club emblems on their jackets. And of course, there were more media trucks.

Nero took a shortcut through the woods, and eventually he reached his current dwelling. He had the perfect opportunity to take care of some final entertainment before he left here and returned to his home far to the north; perhaps he would make it after all? He thought of the letter he had sent to Einar Leeu; perhaps it was a bit premature. Then again, he could always send another. He went inside and picked up a large crate that normally would have taken two people to carry. He placed it in his truck in the hidden compartment where he had once put the two young men, passed out with an oxygen tank between them. He moved the tank; he had refilled it before he returned to Skull Creek, just in case he needed to bring some entertainment with him before he left.

He drove for over an hour, to a preselected area, where he hid his truck. He took a few deep breaths, inhaling the clean air while enjoying the rain showering him. Nero drank some of his homemade herb tea and ate several energy bars. He finished his meal by chewing on a handful of coca leaves. Once he'd finished eating, he removed his body armor and homemade exoskeleton from the truck. He checked on the rigging and the various springs, and finally examined the bear fur with the attached, hollow head. At the moment, it smelled clean; but that would soon change, once he had dosed it with the stink.

Finally, he put on his second skin. Now he could finish this season's hunt in peace. He had to choose between removing the seed—the wealthy landowner, Mrs. Tulip—or returning to the mine and finishing up his work there. Most of the mine workers would be in Skull Creek getting drunk, he figured…well, once the authorities had cleaned up all the mess. He smirked as he thought of it.

He smiled even more when he thought of Christina Dawn and her friend. But they were forbidden fruit. He sighed; something inside him had woken up when he had seen Christina.

That he should stop for now and return home he no longer contemplated; he was too far gone. He wanted to do more; he *had* to do more. It was an inner force that urged him on, and now it was time to destroy the mining operation and hunt down any weak two-leggeds that might still be there.

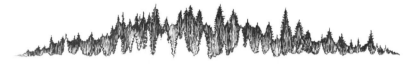

TWENTY-FIVE

I t was still dark outside, with the exception of the streetlights. Malik stood dead calm, waiting outside the Mayor's office, the anger building up inside him like a volcano waiting to erupt. He was sure the politicians behind the closed door were screaming and planning for the next scapegoat to be led towards the altar for sacrifice. If it was him, then be that as it may, because the only thing he had on his mind was the fierce desire to hunt down his best friend's killer. His *only* friend's killer.

Malik had examined the situation, and had come to the conclusion that when his friend had come to him in a time of need and urgency, he had turned his back on him. Carlos's story about a monster chasing him for fifty years…he should have embraced his friend, and said he believed in him and would be by his side. Instead, he had been typical law enforcer Malik Washington. He passed a rough hand over his face and took a deep breath, wanting to do something he had almost forgotten how to do: just give up and cry.

He clutched a folder with a few documents in it, and once in a while hit his leg with it.

The woman had to repeat his name twice before he heard her.

"Sir? Sir? They'll see you now."

The stare he gave the woman made her look at him in horror as he walked toward the mayor's office. She swallowed hard and blurted, "No, not there, sir, that one, they're in the conference room." She nodded at a door further away.

He walked over and grabbed the door knob, looked down at his spit-polished boots, closed his eyes, and took a deep breath; he then opened the door quickly and stepped inside. He found himself in a surprisingly large room, and to his confusion, there were only women inside. That really took him aback. At first, he looked behind himself to check to see if he was in the right place; and when he looked back, some of the women frowned at him. He knew full well that both the Mayor and the Governor were women, but *all* their aides?

About ten women sat going over notes, and when Malik entered, nearly all of them stood up and moved away to the side of the room. Some began talking and laughing while helping themselves to a breakfast buffet.

The Mayor sat at the short end of the large conference table, away from all the commotion, reading some documents through glasses perched on the tip of her nose. Another, much older woman stood with her back turned next to her, her hands behind her back, looking outside into the darkness. He had previously only seen the Governor on television, and he knew the rumors about her obtaining her position only because she was a black woman. Malik didn't give a shit what color her skin was; he harbored a visceral hate towards all politicians.

The Mayor looked up from her papers, nodding to a chair next to her. He ignored it, so she did the same. The Governor said, "You have 24 hours, Undersheriff Washington, and then I'll let the Feds take over. That's the best I'm willing to do."

Malik was hesitant, something he hated, because now he was flabbergasted. "The three deputies who found Carlos da Silvia's body and used their weapons against the perpetrators will be taken off duty…for now," she ground out.

"With pay?" Malik asked.

"Of course."

"Good," he said firmly.

The Mayor, who believed strongly in decorum, looked up at him over her glasses and scowled at him, not just for his tone and smartass answer, but also for not using the Governor's title. "Can the fair go on?" she snapped.

Malik turned to the Mayor. "Yes, Madame Mayor, it can, and I believe it should. We can't let disturbances by the criminal element alter our lifestyle, and we have sufficient help from neighboring counties and the National Guard. They have found and captured the lion and one of the tigers, and there are good leads on the second one. Besides, that one won't be a danger to anyone for a few days."

"It won't?"

"No, Mayor," he said grimly, "not with its belly full and all."

The Mayor just shook her head at Malik's morbid comment. "And what about the other dangerous animals?"

"Almost all the circus animals have been captured except for a couple of mountain lions, and according to the park rangers, they have returned to the wild and are no more dangerous than any other mountain lion in the region. I doubt that the rangers will be looking for them."

"Yeah, I got that impression also last night. For now, Malik, you're the Acting Sheriff."

The Governor, still with her back turned, motioned for him to join her. "Are there any leads regarding Sheriff da Silva's death?"

"Yes, Madame Governor, there are many, but just one solid lead. This." He took a paper from his folder and laid it on the window railing. It was a copy of the drawing of the monster that Carlos's wife had shown him. The Governor tilted her head and looked at it, then looked back outside. "Where did you get that?"

"Carlos's wife gave it to me a few days ago, asking me to help him. He had been acting weird…differently in the last few days."

The Governor continued to study the darkness outside, as the town started to wake up. "Not much to go on. Wouldn't sit right with the people while having their breakfast in the morning, knowing that some monster is running loose killing people, now would it, Sheriff Washington?" She snorted and continued, "Then again, the damned media would love it, I'm sure." She turned her head, staring at him with a neutral expression. "Your thoughts?"

"A human being murdered my frie…" He stopped himself, not wanting to sound to emotionally attached to the case, and then continued, "A human being murdered the Sheriff, and I suspect that from time to time, this madman might dress up like an animal."

"But there were no indications that anyone actually saw something like that." The Governor nodded at the drawing. Malik had nothing to say, because he didn't want to get into any details. Normally, he wouldn't have shown the drawing to her; but in 24 hours, everything would be turned over to the FBI. He had a million and one questions about that soaring through his mind, but decided not to get entangled in a long meeting. Now he was in a hurry.

There was some commotion outside the door, and the Governor turned, facing Malik. "Twenty-four hours, and then the Feds will take over either we like it or not."

"Surprised they haven't already."

The Governor smirked.

"Oh, they tried. But, well, let's say I have a different opinion on how some things should be run in my state. And then there's the media circus."

"You got a call from the big boys in the White House, didn't you?"

The Governor smiled pleasantly at Malik. "I've never liked being told what to do, so I'm not going to tell *you* what to do. With one exception." She turned back toward the window as the door was forced opened and three men wearing suits charged in. "You go and do some hunting now, Sheriff Washington," she continued. "Go and find Carlos da Silva's monster, while I take care of my own."

Malik left the room, ignoring the FBI agent shouting for him to stop. He was a changed man, because he no longer hated politicians…

well, not the ones inside that conference room. *So much for not being judgmental,* he thought, as he hurried back to his new office.

CAL HARRINGTON drove like mad, honking his horn now and then. Once in a while, he pushed hard on the temporary bandage holding back the blood-flow, while steering with his legs. He cried and cursed out loud, screaming at oncoming traffic. He was grateful for the scarce traffic this morning, but whenever he did meet someone, he honked and shouted at them to move aside. Had he looked in the rearview mirror and not been so confused, he would have noticed the patrol car chasing him with lights flashing and sirens wailing.

He finally reached the main street of Skull Creek and hit the accelerator. He had to, because he was getting weaker and weaker; his left side felt ice-cold, and he no could longer move his left arm. Another patrol car tried to intercept him, but failed. When he reached the Sheriff's office, he almost ran over a large black man in the middle of the street. The big man threw himself to the side of the road just in time.

Harrington stopped and stumbled out of the car. He had forgotten to put the car in Park, and it rolled into a stationary police SUV. He himself fell to the ground, bleeding profusely.

Malik heard someone shout "Look out!" and looked up and saw the oncoming threat. He jumped to the side, sliding on the gravel, to avoiding getting hit. Bruised and lacerated, he then scrambled to his feet and drew his gun. *What the hell NOW?* He wondered. Had everyone in Skull Creek gone crazy?

Then he heard the thin wail from the heap next to the mining truck that had barely missed him. "Help! Help us, we're dying! It's killing everyone! Help…"

Malik holstered his gun and ran toward the injured man, who he could now see was bleeding like a stuck hog. From the Sheriff's Department charged two deputies, and behind the truck came two highway patrol cars. A crowd was starting to gather as Malik kneeled next to the bleeding man. "Someone get the paramedics! Nine-One-One!" he shouted.

He leaned over, trying to hold the panicked man on the ground. He kept screaming and crying and squirming, and Malik had to adjust his grip; and when he did, he dropped his folder. A sudden gust of wind flipped it open, and some of his documents flew out. "Hey, hey, c'mon now, relax and just tell me what's going on," he said to the injured man, who was cut up bad and looked like he might yet bleed to death.

The man didn't smell of alcohol, and Malik spoke to him calmly. There were running steps from the direction of the Mayor's office, and Malik looked up and found himself surrounded by uniforms and civilians. The Mayor and the Governor pushed themselves through the small crowd. "Oh my God, Sheriff, you okay? I saw the whole thing from the window!" the Governor exclaimed.

She was interrupted by Harrington, who shouted, "Dead, murdered, they're all dead, help!"

Everyone froze, staring at the injured man, then a deputy stepped forward to turn off the engine of the mining truck.

"Please give them some room," the Mayor ordered.

"Someone get the paramedics," the Governor shouted.

Then Harrington said something that made everyone really stop. "Monsters…monsters…help me!"

"Hey, man, c'mon, try and calm down and tell us who did this to you," Malik said, doing his best to help sooth Harrington as a deputy ran up with a First Aid kit and started working on the man's injured arm.

Harrington sat up with Malik's help, and it seemed like he was just about to say something when his eyes went wide and he suddenly screamed, pointing at Carlos's drawing. Coughing up blood, with his last bit of strength he uttered two words: "The Monster." He then passed out in Malik's arms.

Malik tilted his head up, first looking at the Governor and then at the Mayor. He eased the injured man to the asphalt as the Governor and

Mayor looked back at him with equally frightened expressions. Malik could feel cold chills, followed by goosebumps, and looked down at the injured man.

He let one of his officers begin CPR, but when he realized the size of the blood pool around the man and saw his unusual stillness, he knew it was useless; the man was dead.

Someone shouted, "Look up there! The mountain is burning!"

Thick, dark smoke intermingled with the first rays of the morning sun as the fire on the distant mountain fought for dominance. As everyone stared, Officer Whitney charged out of the police station, interrupting. "Malik! We got a hit! Carlos's cell phone—we got the GPS! We think the killer has it!"

A man in a dark suit stepped up next to Malik; both stared at the burning mountaintop. After a moment, the stranger said, "I'm not going to step on anyone's toes, but for what's it worth, you're going to need my crew and me. Something terrible is happening in this town, and you need as many people fighting it as you can."

"Did you bring many shooters?"

"Enough. I hope."

THE SMALL police station was jam-packed with different flavors of law enforcement officers, all of them focused on Malik, who was giving them a short debrief. Many looked shocked, and there were many doubtful expressions when he related parts of Carlos's story. He finished the meeting by unveiling a large poster, an image of the monster drawn over fifty years ago from the five-year-old Carlos da Silva's testimony. Anna-Maria had made him a copy when she contacted him. Now the rest of the police and feds looked at the strange image, which looked like some hellish mix between a bear and a wolf. The more they looked, the more some of them became concerned; but the majority gagged silently to themselves.

"Like I said, I believe it's a man, or more than one, and they dress up like this."

"Halloween is around the corner, so it makes sense," the leader of the FBI special team joked.

Malik, frustrated and tired, knew full well that he was losing this case. His voice harsh, he said loudly, "I hope you're right, that eventually we can all laugh at this once it's over. Then again, some of us can't, because this *thing* murdered our sheriff—and my friend."

His words made the room fall into silence.

Malik turned to FBI's Special Agent In Charge. He didn't even remember the SAIC's name and couldn't care less. "You wait for ground support before you charge that mine. Do we understand each other?"

In a hostile tone, the FBI agent said, "You worry about your crew, and I'll take care of my own."

When the room cleared out, someone standing behind him cleared her throat. "Yes, Ruth, what is it?"

With the help of her cane, she walked slowly up to Malik. She stared, looking him over from head and toe.

"Don't you do anything stupid and end up like that good man Martin Luther King, you hear me now, Afro? I can't lose two Sheriffs in a day, now can I?"

Her voice failed her. She looked down at the floor, and when she raised her head, her eyes were red, and she did nothing to hold back the stream of tears coming from them.

Malik suddenly had a change of heart when it came to this old woman; there was something motherly happening here. She closed her eyes and shook her head back and forth. She stopped suddenly, and then she gave Malik the deadliest and coldest stare he had ever seen. "Find that motherfucker and bring me his scalp." She turned around and wobbled slowly away from him, and then continued, "Or you can make your own fucking coffee from now on."

"Yes, ma'am."

He smiled when he noticed a cup of fresh-brewed coffee and a mint sitting on the table next to him. He took a gulp of the hot coffee—he sure needed it now—and his eyeballs just about popped out. There was more than just coffee in the cup, and one should definitely not operate any motor vehicles after drinking it.

Ruth looked back and winked at him just as she turned the corner.

"Hey, Ruth, did you ever meet Abe Lincoln?"

An old arm stuck out from around the corner wall, middle finger extended.

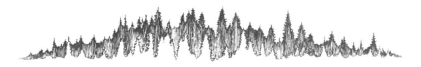

TWENTY-SIX

W ould someone please go get the prima donna?" Peter demanded. "I guess that one was meant for me?" An exhausted Tammy yawned and then dragged herself back upstairs.

Christina was tired from last night's drinking binge, but she wanted this day to be perfect for her and perhaps Robert. She hoped he would make a move, that shy dog. She had braided her hair into one long, thick ponytail. She wore a blue muscle shirt, black shorts, and socks, and now she was tying her black original S.W.A.T. Classic 9 boots. She chose her round blue mirrored sunglasses, then went over to her new backpack and checked that she had all her new equipment and some spare clothing. A sleeping bag and sleeping mat were attached vertically along the back of the backpack. Boy, now she was ready!

She walked into the master bath and closed the door. There was a large mirror attached on the inside, and Christina needed one final inspection. She ignored the hounds snarling downstairs for her to hurry.

Tammy knocked on the door. "You better not be sick, you little wasp. Now hurry your ass up."

Christina looked at herself in the mirror, and then shouted, "Oh NO, no fucking way, what the fuck have I done? What was I *thinking*?"

The door slid open and Tammy peeked inside carefully. When she saw Christina, she gave her a snarky smile. "Well now, that looks great. All you need now is a couple of guns. Come on, Lara Croft, let's go."

"No, no, no, not until I fix myself up, and—!"

"What the hell is keeping the princess this time?" Peter stopped talking when he saw Christina. "Wow, Tomb Raider. Yeah, I didn't see that one coming."

Behind him was Kevin, whistling, who contributed, "I saw that movie. Man, you look even hotter than Angelina Jolie."

"You're supposed to be gay, Kevin."

"I can appreciate feminine beauty."

Tammy taunted, "So, Halloween came early this year."

"Fuck you all! And fuck you, too, Lara Croft," she said, flipping herself off in the mirror.

Peter had to toss Christina over his shoulder, carrying her downstairs under wild protest, while the others laughed. As they left her home, she managed to grab one of her cowboy hats hanging on the wall in the mudroom.

"This is so immature! You know, I'm no longer a little girl, and would everyone please stop slapping my ass!" Christina shouted. Didn't work, though.

Early hours after another night of partying; boy, was that familiar. Christina and Tammy sat in the backseat of Christina's new truck while Peter drove and Kevin navigated. Christina wanted to change her appearance, but for some reason all her so-called friends wouldn't let her.

They waited at a four-way crossing, and after a while Robert's truck showed up. Robert slowed down, and then just winked his hand for them to follow. Next to Robert sat his sister, Pat, with her head leaning on his shoulder; and on the passenger side sat Blake, slumbering. It was still dark outside, but dawn was on the horizon. No one noticed the smoke and fire coming from the distant mountain peak. They drove for some time, and suddenly Robert turned into a well-concealed forest road. Here the driving was more off-road, and anyone who had slept before soon found themselves awake from all the bouncing.

When they reached the campsite, it was almost daylight outside. It was a small clearing containing many cars and trucks, and one minivan bearing the legend *Skull Creek Adventures; Sightseeing, Mountain Climbing & Rafting Tour.* There were three large fire pits, and while some people were erecting tents, others were preparing a fire within a large circle of stones and branches. Another fire pit already contained a fire, mostly smoking coals and glowing embers. Several large logs had been placed as benches around the fire pits. Someone had lit half a dozen tiki torches containing citronella oil and placed them throughout the area. There were also a couple of long park-bench picnic tables.

A bit further away lay the river, and at this location it was quite calm. There was also a natural pool with an entrance to the river—similar to the one on Christina's property—near the camp site. A man directed them where to park, putting them next to several other cars and trucks.

They got out and greeted everyone, who seemed busy erecting the camp, and soon they found themselves helping out. Christina received more than one humorous smile, and she just played along. Before long, a deer carcass was placed on a spit and hung up between two poles. "Oh look! They killed Bambi," Peter joked.

Christina and Tammy glared. "Yeah, well, I'm not eating that, and that's for certain," the latter said.

"Bet you will, Tammy."

"No, Christina, I won't. Look at it, it looks gruesome!"

"Well, if you're not eating Bambi, Tammy, you can always go for Ms. Piggy over there," Kevin motioned with his head as he helped out with Bambi. On the ground, atop a plastic sheet, lay an entire medium-size dead pig.

"Savages! That's it. From now on, I'm vegan. What about you, Ms. Hollywood?"

"Only if bacon is a vegetable."

"I hate you so much right now. No matter how much you stuff yourself, you never get fat."

"Because I'm always training, and so should you. Then again, I guess you do with your boy-toy collection. Oops, here's your next addition." Christina smiled and nodded at Blake as he walked up to Tammy.

"So, guys, you want some breakfast? They're making black-cakes over there. Typical lumberjack food."

"What the hell is that, Blake?"

"I take it you guys have never had any. Come on, you don't want to miss this."

The girls followed Blake to one of the fire pits. On top of the burning coals lay several cast-iron skillets. Each contained a lot of thick, diced bacon squares, building up a greasy surface. Robert, Pat, and a few other people mixed a concoction of half-flour and half-water in plastic containers and then shook them hard, finishing off by pouring the contents into the skillets and letting the batter cook with the bacon and its grease. They tossed in some pepper towards the end. There were a couple more skillets with higher edges on them, and inside there baked some fresh biscuits; and next to them was a large pot with gravy boiling. Two enamel pots on a tipper already had a line of people helping themselves to coffee.

Pat hurried to them with a plate each, and then she ran and got her own. Everyone sat down at one of the picnic tables and ate as if they were starved. "Boy, this is real good," Tammy let out between bites.

"Yeah, and very warm." Christina tried blowing on her plate. They ate with their fingers and cleaned the plates with the biscuits.

A large van, built for tourists, showed up honking. A tall, muscular guy stepped out and introduced himself.

"For all the new guys who don't know me, my name is Gavin and I'll be your tour guide today."

Several people booed him, and Roberts shouted, "Save that speech for the amateurs and tourists."

"Let's get it on," Blake added.

Gavin gathered everyone around and then said, "My partners in crime will meet us up on the mountain, and hopefully we'll make it back here later this afternoon. The river is all right, a bit low in a few places, and we might have to do some dragging and pulling. Except for that, everything should be all right. Now, I hope everyone brought their wet-suits; and if anyone is missing one, we do have some up at the launch pad, as we call it. If you can't swim, you can't come. We'll use our van, and for you guys who will remain here, we'll see you soon. Try and keep the camp neat and clean."

More booing.

Christina whispered to Robert, "Are we just leaving our stuff here?"

"Yes, except for your wet gear."

A honking car horn blared, followed by the thundering roar of a very large, powerful engine. A shiny black Mercedes AMG S 65 pulled up, and it looked a bit out of place next to the rest of the old cars and trucks, with exception of Christina's truck—which might be new, but was very muddy at the moment. Inside sat a short guy in the driver's seat, and on the passenger seat was a tall woman trying to fix her make-up, using the vanity mirror on the back of the visor.

"Finally, the Cuban master chef has arrived!" someone shouted, and hurried to the Mercedes.

Out stepped Rohan and Daniela, both looking a bit flushed. Their clothes were wrinkled and both had leaves in their hair; Rohan's knees were dirty.

"Time to show up? And late as usual, Mr. Cuba?"

"I'm never late, Gavin, and I'm not Cuban. It's my wife's fault—she saw some mushrooms on the side of the road, and she had to pick them."

"Let me guess. She bent over, and…"

Rohan blushed. "Like I said, it's all her fault."

Daniele just rolled her eyes.

"That's great. Did you bring the leaves for the pig?"

"Sure did. Now, where *is* Mr. Porky?"

Rohan removed a bagful of large palm leaves from the back of his car. He and Gavin together wound up the pig in the leaves, then lowered the package onto the hot coals at the bottom of a pre-dug pit. They then covered the hole, shoveling the pile of dirt surrounding it back in with a pair of shovels, ending with a nicely mounded earth oven.

"Hey, Rohan, you forgot the mushrooms," Gavin teased.

"My wife ate them all, fucker."

"Yeah, I'll bet she did."

Gavin gathered everyone around, "Remember, no phones on this trip—and for you guys hanging around here in camp, you can all toss your phones in the box over by the table or simply turn them off. Rohan will take care of the box. Everyone here?"

"No, Adrianna and company haven't shown up yet," someone replied.

Gavin looked around and said, "Not sure they will, after what happened at the fair yesterday."

"Pretty sad business, pissing on a dead cop," Peter said, with a neutral expression. "no wonder the other cops went off the way they did."

An agreeable murmur followed.

"No wonder the place turned into Hollywood," Kevin said, and continued, "If they show up, then I can take them to your office and launch area. Okay with you, Christina?"

Christina nodded. She thought of Peter and Kevin as family, having known them for many years; either one could use her truck whenever they wanted.

While some choose to stay behind and prepare the camp and food, the majority headed up the mountain towards the so-called launch area. They were met there by Sammy, Gavin's business partner, and their wives Megan and Pamela. There was a good-sized parking area there near a log house, used for an office and equipment storage, and a large storage building in the back of the large property, with a paved road leading all the way down to the river. A sizable dock, partially floating on the river, was protected by a natural bend in the waterway, keeping the river somewhat calm by the dock.

Everyone wore their wet-suits with footwear, and anyone without a helmet was given one. Mandatory life jackets and a brief lesson on what to do and what not to do followed. Pamela, Gavin's wife, had one of her legs in a cast, and would lock up and then drive the tour van back to the campsite. She limped around and was a bit shy.

"That one's name is Megan, and the other one is Pamela, and they both look almost like the ones back in Hollywood," Tammy pointed out, nodding her head.

"True, but only if you switch names on them."

"Yeah, but still, what the hell are these people eating? All of them look like models from a fashion catalogue…well, not you, Peter."

"What are you guys whispering and scheming about?"

"What do those two chicks look like to you?"

"Married."

Tammy poked her tongue out at Peter, who said, "No thanks, my boyfriend's is better." Then he looked at something in his hand, and Christina realized that he had his weatherproof cell phone on, and would most likely keep it on, no matter what Gavin had said. Peter walked up to the road, and soon afterward Christina's truck pulled in with Kevin at the wheel. He parked and exchanged a few words with Peter, and then Adrianna and her police partners Lucy and Dex jumped out. Two had been sitting illegally in the back of the pickup.

Adrianna hurried up to Christina and starting chatting with her. Lucy held her girlfriend—Sandra, the same girl who worked in the western clothing store—hard by the hand and they all got introduced, while the big muscular man, Dex, stood back looking jealous with his buddy Chip, who was obviously also a body builder.

Peter walked between them and slapped them both on their backs. "Get over it, mates, the lassies are a bit busy right now, and I wouldn't interrupt."

"What a waste of pussy, dude."

"You got that right, Chip," Dex muttered. "You think Adrianna eats sushi too?"

"For your sake, I hope not."

"Thank you, Chip."

"Hey, guys," Peter said quietly. "So sorry about what happened to your boss."

"Only my boss," Dex said, sighing deeply. "Chip here runs the only gym in town, over next to the medical clinic. Thank you, though. We…reacted badly when we saw what those fuckers were doing to his body. Bad enough that he was dead. We could have gotten suspended, all three of us, for what we did—but I guess even our bosses upstairs draw a line in the sand when someone pisses on a dead man."

"Shitty business. I didn't mean to bring up something that might ruin the mood."

"Peter's your name, right?"

Peter nodded.

"Don't worry about it, Peter. We have very few internal rules back at the office, but one we keep up is to never let a crime ruin our day, no matter how atrocious it might be."

"Good rule. Well, why don't I introduce you two to some friends of mine?"

He brought the two muscle packages to Christina and Tammy and introduced them, knowing full well they wouldn't be interested. He glanced towards Robert and Blake, and neither hid their thoughts very well. Pat, however, got them thinking of something else when she asked them to help her with the zipper on her wet-suit.

Rohan gathered everyone around, standing on top of a rock, waving his hands like schoolteacher drawing the attention of his class. "Time to divide out teams, and of course to name them. First down to the campsite wins! The losers will clean up the place tomorrow."

They quickly divided up into three large groups. The first two called themselves Team Rockies and Team Lumber. When it was time to name the third team, Rohan gave a mischievous look at Christina and announced that her team would henceforth be called Team Croft. Everyone laughed, and Christina turned bright red, edging toward purple.

Daniele sided up to Christina and smiled. "I'm sorry for my husband's behavior. He's a bit mad."

"It's okay. Not sure what I was thinking when I got dressed this morning."

Lucy shouted, "Hey, it looks hot, babe!"

Christina looked at the tall muscular woman, who undressed Christina with her eyes while wetting her lips. Christina gave her a sultry smile and then ran her tongue over her own lips, batting her eyes at Lucy as several of the guys cheered them on. *In your dreams, sweetie,* Christina thought but didn't say aloud.

THE THREE large rafts were lined up as well as they could be, while the crews tried to maintain them on a line in the middle of the river. Pamela fired off a blank, and then the rubber rafts took off. Kevin and Pamela waved them off at the dock, then returned to the log cabin, locking it up. "You guys live here?" he asked her.

"Yes, my husband and I, but we have the business together with Sammy and Megan. We're hoping we can get a B&B license for next year. Business is going great, and we'd like to expand."

"Sounds like a smart plan. If you don't mind me asking, what happened to your leg?"

"We also have mountain climbing, and I fell like a clumsy oaf."

Kevin gave her a horrified expression.

"Don't worry; I fell over there, from the porch, fixing some climbing gear. Not my shiniest moment."

They laughed and went to their respective vehicles, and headed back down the road towards the camp.

The rafts left the dock with about nine people in each. Gavin was in charge of the first and Megan was in the second, followed by her husband Sammy in the third. The water in the river looked almost too calm as they set out, but after the first turn came the first shower—and then the rollercoaster ride was on.

SIX HELICOPTERS—the lead helicopter with Malik was an old Bell UH-1 Iroquois, Huey and it bore the markings of the 7th Air Cavalry - left Skull Creek, and four times as many law enforcement vehicles headed up into the mountains. They split into two groups, one following a road towards the river while the rest headed up towards the burning mountaintop. Behind came several firetrucks and ambulances; last came five park ranger trucks.

Acting Sheriff Malik Washington sat beside the pilot in one of the helicopters, looking out at the beautiful landscape rushing by with a dead man's stare. He closed his eyes, and then he spoke into a microphone. "Eagle One to all Eagles. This one is for Carlos and his family."

Over the next few moments, he got multiple radio returns repeating, "For Carlos."

He finished by thinking aloud, "Let's hunt."

The pilot turned on music—perhaps to ease the tension—Malik didn't care his thoughts was elsewhere but strangely the song playing gave him the chills; Garryowen.

There was a thundering roar when the helicopters flew over Skull Creek, waking anyone who might still be sleeping. Below, on the town square next to the mayor's office, flew American and state flags at half-mast. One neighbor next to Carlos' burned-out home had raised an American flag too, but this one was upside-down—a signal of dire distress in instances of extreme danger to life or property. As they flew by, more flags were raised over the small community, and all of them were upside-down.

Just as they left the city limits, Malik noticed several parked trucks containing many civilians, all armed. Instead of reporting it in, he just leaned back in his seat. If they stayed out of his way, the civvies were welcome to help.

Meanwhile, the most dangerous killer in history stood on top of the burning mountain, waiting patiently. He had trained from childhood for this day, trained to do only two things: protect Mother Earth, and kill its enemies. Nero smiled; he had always enjoyed a challenge whenever he hunted two-leggeds, and something told him that today would be a great day for a hunt. Parked a bit away from the smoldering flames, the only vehicle not burning, was an expensive RV with all its windows open. From its speakers roared Beethoven's Fifth.

TWENTY-SEVEN

The mining camp on the plateau had been demolished. A bulldozer had crashed into the enormous wash plant and forced it down a gorge of its own making. All machines, excavators, and trucks were burning; some had exploded. The entire camp area, with its tents, RVs and camper trailers, had burned down. Part of the forest on the side of the mountain in the direction towards Skull Creek was burning, and the fire was still spreading; however, the many rock formations on the mountainside worked like natural firebreaks. At the actual mining site there was smoke, but it was spread out and minimal.

The bodies lay where they had fallen, most around or near the fire pits where the mining crew had been drinking. Some had been killed in their tents or RVs while sleeping. There had been no children on the site this time, and there were many signs that they were in a process of shutting down the operation. Nero estimated that perhaps ten people had been killed, maybe twelve; then again, he didn't really give a shit about the numbers. No number of dead two-leggeds was ever enough. There had been only two women that he knew of that he had killed, as he surprised them and wiped them out; first one by one, though towards the end, there had been four of them left, four that he had to take care of almost at the same time; but they had scattered like scared mice, and it had been no challenge whatsoever to track them down one by one. He was very disappointed. The fact that most of them had been drunk made the challenge easier, though he supposed their numbers had made up for it. The one who had gotten away in a truck did bother him, because it ruined any further element of surprise; but there was nothing he could do about it now, except hoped that the runaway would die from the wounds he had inflicted on him. The witness, if he survived, would be dealt with in the future, like Carlos da Silva had been. So would anyone he had told.

The road he had fled by was now inaccessible; Nero had seen to that, sawing down several trees in a row and letting them collapse over the road. Whoever tried to scale the mountain would either have to remove the hindrances, or advance on foot…unless of course they had helicopters.

He hustled along quickly atop a ridge, then dropped the heavy chainsaw, the fuel can, and the extra gear for the chainsaw next to a man lying on ground. They were on a huge cliff above the mining camp, with a thin line of trees screening them from view. This man was in his mid-forties, not dead but deeply unconsciousness. He lay in a recovery position concealed by leaves and branches. They were both also well-hidden with thick brush. Between them lay several rifles, two pistols, and a few ammunition boxes. Nero picked out one of the larger caliber rifle with a scope. With the wind at his back and a clear field of fire, but for some smoke, Nero hunkered down and chewed on an energy bar, while sipping some of his herb tea from a canteen. He checked on the man next to him from time to time as he repeatedly went over in his mind the plan of action he had prepared. There had been plenty of weapons in the camp, but none of the miners had any with them when he attacked. He knew full well that miners had rules, just as lumberjacks did, when it came to when a person could carry a weapon; most of the time it was forbidden when in camp, avoiding any accidental shootings.

In the far distance below, he could see a small turn from the road; and that's where he kept his focus, waiting for the flashing lights of the police vehicles. He knew they would come with helicopters in time, and he guessed they would fly around the smoke and circle the place before landing. If they were smart, the police would advance simultaneously from the vehicles and from the air.

Finally, he saw the first police vehicle, followed by many more; and then he heard the helicopters closing in, but he couldn't see them yet. "Guess the idiots from the sky can't wait," he muttered to himself as he prepared his equipment.

He was right: two helicopters flew high towards the mining camp, avoiding the smoke; a third helicopter further away probably had snipers on board, and that was the flying tin can that concerned Nero the most. "Idiots are going to charge in just like Custer did, without even scouting, they're so sure of victory."

Nero leaned over the unconscious man, and broke an ammonia capsule and held it under the man's nose. With the drugs in his system, it would take at least a minute or two before he came to his senses. The man moaned and coughed. Nero ignored him and moved swiftly away, to a point a bit away and above the man. He took cover and aimed at one of the helicopters. It was still too far away, so he waited. As he figured they would, the helicopter rotors made the smoke swirl around like a smoke bomb's output, creating an ideal smoke screen. He aimed the rifle and waited, found the weakest point on the helicopter, and fired one round.

A second later, the helicopter started to twist and turn irregularly as black smoke poured from the engine. A sudden wind gust forced the helicopter towards the ground. The pilot tried to regain control, but failed as the helicopter's rotors brushed a large tree, causing the craft to vault straight down to the ground. The second helicopter landed a bit further away, and several characters dressed in SWAT gear swarmed out. Amateurs. Nero took his time and fired off two more rounds, taking down two of the attackers.

He looked over to where the other man was. The miner sat up, blinking owlishly at the large revolver in his hand, confused as he shook his hand, trying to get rid of it. *Superglue does the trick*, Nero thought, smiling as he crawled carefully away and down the side of the ridge. He could hear the man muttering to himself, and eventually shouting for help. Nero didn't have to look as he hurried away from the first position. He heard the man shouting in the distance, and then there were many gunshots. The man stopped shouting.

Nero got into his second position and waited. It wasn't long before the third helicopter showed up, looking for a place to land. This time Nero hit the pilot dead center between her eyes; as she slumped, the helicopter spiraled down and crashed into the side of the one that had landed.

He moved quickly behind the ridge, staying under cover, then waited and listened for other helicopters; he might have missed one. When he was sure that there had only been three, he decided to advance against the survivors. Most were helping their two gut-shot colleagues, while some tried to help those in the wrecked helicopters. One person stood talking into a radio or walkie-talkie near the dead miner with the revolver glued to his hand.

Wearing his second skin, Nero advanced between the debris and the cover of the smoke until he was feet from the prey; and then he struck. The expression on the man talking on the radio as he died was one of confusion, shock, and then terror. Nero picked up the man's submachine gun and looked toward his team members; most had their backs turned. He chose his weapons quickly, then dropped flat on the ground and tossed a fragmentation grenade with one hand, followed by a phosphorus/magnesium smoke grenade. He rolled behind the cover of a burning vehicle. The explosion was loud and wreaked havoc on the feds. He knew where most of the survivors were, though, and followed up by firing on them from a low position. He emptied the first magazine in seconds, then reloaded with the second clip that was attached to the first. Two SWAT members who stood further away and were unharmed by the explosion instantly turned and fired back, but their aim was too high. Nero rolled to his side and kept shooting until everyone was down. The majority were still alive, saved by their body armor, but they were in shock and/or injured. He used the two large stilettos strapped to one of his forearms to finish off the survivors. One young woman tried crawling away; Nero walked up calmly and imbedded the blades in her neck. All too easy.

He left the bodies and tossed his weapon to the ground next to the dead miner. As he did so, he felt a burning sensation in his lower left side. He had underestimated the two-leggeds; he had been shot. Blood poured down his side, but there was no time to waste. He applied a temporary first-aid dressing, and moved on. He made sure all the two-leggeds were dead, and then he burned the helicopter that had landed, after dousing it with diesel and gasoline.

Nero carefully stretched his back and yawned, unwrapped another energy bar, and drank some water as he ate it. He then headed down the mountain, towards the oncoming convoy of cars and trucks. He could faintly hear the sirens in the far distance.

Stupid. They should have arrived together.

"That takes care of Reno, now it's time for Custer," he said. He found his own words immensely funny and laughed as he walked through the carnage, the sun beams fighting through the smoke casting a ghostly image on the surrounding smoke as he moved away, listening to Beethoven in one ear.

IT WAS a peaceful morning, the storm having long since left the region. The sun shone warmly, making the dew evaporate from the ground and trees, and there were only few clouds in the sky. The normally fresh air was infected by a horrible stench coming from a bundle of clothing lying on a pile of branches that was apparently intended to be a fire, which had never gotten started because of the rain from last night.

Todd finished his beer and tossed the can into the river; then he burped and dropped his pants, pissing into the same stream. Their old

Volkswagen bus was parked on a small flat next to the river; garbage carpeted the ground, from beer cans to fast food bags to plastic cups. Little Flower lay inside their ride, snoring. Todd shook his head, getting his dreadlocks out of his grubby face, and then he lit a joint and stretched his arms into the air. After a moment, he took out his smart-phone and tried dialing, but the battery was dead.

He looked closely at the phone. "Man, this ain't my shit, the fuck you come from, phone? Where the fuck my phone? Yoohoo, Flower, you seen my phone?"

"FUCK OFF! I'm sleeping!"

Suddenly all hell broke loose.

Several helicopters hovered nearby, and one of them came in right over the river, almost at the same level as Todd. From the brush and forest swarmed SWAT teams, surrounding the area. Frightened, Todd dropped the phone into the river.

In less than a minute, both Todd and Little Flower lay face-down on the ground, cuffed, both screaming about their rights. Meanwhile, a couple of officers were kneeling and throwing up their breakfasts.

The first thing Malik noticed as he left his chopper was the foul stink in the air. He did his best to ignore it, but it was highly concentrated. He immediately remembered Carlos's words about a horrible smell, but when he saw the idiots on the ground, he knew they were most likely not his killers.

Whitney walked up to him and whispered, "I recognize these two from the phone we found with that video on it. It was also uploaded on Facebook, and someone else uploaded that on YouTube."

"The one where they urinated on Carlos?"

"Yessir."

"See if you can find more phones."

Todd and Little Flower flat refused to assist the police, and five minutes later one smartphone had been collected. It belonged to Little Flower.

"You're going to be charged with murder," Malik said in his husky but calm baritone.

That shut up both suspects for a moment, and then both started screaming and shouting at the same time.

A SWAT officer approached Malik and Whitney. "Sir, you're going to want to take this," he said, as he handed Malik a phone.

Malik's expression never changed as he listened to the conversation. When he was done, he ordered the SWAT officer, "Get two of those birds on the ground. Whitney, take over here. Find that phone. I'll take two of the squads with me and leave the rest with you. Remember, we still have a tiger and some more shit to find."

Whitney demanded, "What's happening?"

"More deaths at the mine. Many more, from the sound of it. Not sure, it got cut off."

"Sheriff, shouldn't we regroup and try and find out what the hell is going on? Are you really going up there?"

Malik looked around. "I have to go. The thing, the monster it's still up on that peak." He pointed in the direction of the burning mountain.

From several radios came the sounds of people shouting through gunfire, "Officers down, officers down!"

"Fucking great. Let's piss on them, too, you fuc…"

Little Flower caught the butt of a rifle dead center in her mouth, shattering all the perfect white, shining teeth paid for with Daddy's money. She fell backward like a dead tree, unconscious.

"Yeah, try not to do that," Whitney said, without looking at the suspect on the ground or whoever had shut her up. He placed his hand on Malik's forearm and whispered, "Hey man, don't go. I don't think we're ready for this."

"Weren't you a Marine?"

"Yeah, I was—but I also know when to choose my battles. Whoever or whatever is up there is stuck. All we have to do is keep it there and then advance when we're ready."

"That's what you would do?"

"Yes."

Malik shook his head slowly. "I appreciate the advice, but no, I have to go. I have to try. He or they can still get away. We have to go, and we'll go now. You're in charge until I get back." Malik looked Whitney full in the face. "And if I don't come back."

Whitney looked tiredly on as the two helicopters flew towards the burning mountain top. He then turned around, and as he passed Todd, who was screaming about his rights again, he knocked him out cold.

The helicopters landed on the road by the intersection. There were firetrucks and ambulances parked on both sides of the road, paramedics waiting for permission to advance, all looking scared. By the road leading up the mountain were several police cars from different counties, waiting for Malik's leadership. He looked to the officer in charge.

A very nervous middle-aged deputy from the county immediately to the west greeted Malik. "Sir, my name is Duncan. Edge Duncan. We don't know quite what's going on, we haven't been up the mountain yet, but I did send up a scout team."

"Who did you send?"

"Three officers and two rangers, sir. They insisted, and they know the lay of the land."

"When was the last time you heard from them?"

"A while ago. They did, however, report that there are several big trees blocking the access road, so here we are, waiting for you guys."

"No words from the Feds? Their special team?"

"No, nothing. They went ahead of us in the choppers."

"My orders were specific, were they not? To wait for the ground force?"

The officer nodded. "Yessir. I don't know why they went in before we got here. No more signs of the helicopters."

Malik organized the situation at the road crossing, establishing road blocks and consulting the emergency rescue people. It took what seemed like forever, and the SWAT teams he'd brought with him looked at him unhappily; but he didn't care. He wanted everything to be ready before he advanced. Quantity had its own quality when it came to warfare, and he knew in his bones that this was a war. He'd seen it in the streets of New York and Baltimore. Though he'd never expected it here, he would rise to the challenge. He would keep the people who depended on him as safe as possible.

Malik looked up towards the mountain, and then he realized something. "Everyone stop what you're doing and shut up!" he shouted. He had to repeat himself several times before everyone was silent.

There were no sounds from anything except a mild breeze sighing through the pines.

"Strange," he said to Duncan. "There's no sound at all, nothing. Not from animals or anything." He looked at the other man. "How long since the scouts left?"

"Just before you got here, sir, maybe half an hour now."

Malik was furious, and was just about to chew out his colleague when another two police trucks showed up. From the first truck emerged Whitney and Diego, a former Miami SWAT leader. Diego had his old SWAT outfit on, and he still wore a bandage on his head and on one of his arms, and walked stiffly due to his thorax injury.

"Shouldn't you still be in the hospital?"

Diego just frowned as he checked his M24 Sniper Weapons System, then looked up at his Sheriff. "Shouldn't you stop yapping and get hunting?"

Malik just smiled at the smartass remark. He nodded towards Whitney, whom he would normally chew out for leaving his position back at Skull Creek, but their eyes met and no words needed to be said. Whitney carried an old-style Vietnam-era M16 rifle with several magazines attached to an old military west. From the second police truck merged Bard and Takoda. Takoda wore a headband representing his Lakota heritage, two feathers braided into his thick hair—ready to go into battle and count coup with his rifle. Malik ignored Takoda's headband. They were past all formalities; now it was time to hunt, in whichever way made each man most comfortable.

Malik gave some final instructions while checking his weapons. "No one walks alone. Pair up in couples and in groups of four. Half will advance on the south side of the road, and the rest on the north side. Snipers in the back; try and find good cover positions. All rescue workers, stay here until further notice; and highway patrol, remain with the road blocks."

They advanced slowly on both sides of the road in two squads. The two-by-two formations weren't perfect because the terrain was just awful. No one wanted to use the road itself. They went in silence, except for Malik and Whitney occasionally communicating through their radios; each led a squad. Holding back was Diego's squad—the snipers. Changing position constantly, they tried to get a better field of fire covering the advancing squads, once in a while climbing trees or rocks.

The smoke still cloaked parts of the region, and the closer to the mine they got, the thicker it became. The wind was on their side, blowing some smoke away as they advanced. From time to time, someone coughed or a twig snapped, but for all that, they advanced professionally and quickly. Malik noticed that most of the people with him were scared and nervous. Even though all of them tried to conceal it, he had seen enough action and war; he knew full well that the morale of most of his people was scraping bottom.

They reach a long bend in the road; just past the bend, the way was blocked by half a dozen huge logs. As they approached, they saw several bodies lying huddled on the ground: the scout team. Whitney kneeled by one of the park rangers and checked for life signs, then looked at Malik and shook his head. They checked the rest, and all were dead; when they finished, Malik signaled for them to advance.

"Look sharp and check your buddies' backs," he ordered, "Advance carefully."

The smoke thickened, and was soon joined by a horrible stench. Some of the advancing officers tried to use scarfs or parts of their shirts to cover their noses, it was so awful. The only sound was the cracking fire below the road, where it had spread to the trees. They finally reached the mine operation, or what was left of it; there was less smoke here apart from the burning helicopters, which Malik surveyed with a sad shake of his head. The mining camp itself had already burnt out, though there was some smoldering here and there. Someone whistled when they looked over the mess.

"Stay sharp, everyone," Malik barked. "Don't let the fuckers get to you. Check for survivors."

With that said, everyone advanced with extreme caution. "Over here," Whitney shouted suddenly.

Malik hurried over. "What you got?"

Whitney hunkered down by a civilian corpse. "Looks like this could be our monster."

Malik just snorted and motioned for them to advance.

"CONTACT!" someone shouted through the earpiece, followed by shots fired; and suddenly everything turned into a Hollywood shootout. Malik tried to orient himself, looking for any bad guys; the smoke was a hindrance, but here on the mining site it wasn't that bad, more irritating then anything. He moved his head side to side, and there on top of a cliff a good distance away, between a pair of trees, stood something big. He looked through his scope, but he couldn't make out what it was, if it was a bear or not. Many of his people started shooting at the person or animal, but it only stood there staring at them. Diego walked up, calm as day, looked at the target, and then he took steady aim. One shot, and part of the head flew away; and suddenly the thing fell to the ground, out of sight.

Several officers and SWAT team members charged up the hill, shooting and screaming. Malik shouted for them to stop, but naturally no one listened. Diego reloaded and found another spot. Malik took one glance at Diego, who remained where he was, looking through his scope, then hurried after the other officers.

Before more could follow the melee, he turned, facing the others, screaming at the rest to back off and take up covering positions while checking the rear. He then hurried after the group of officers who already charged up the hill. It was a steep hill, and he recognize the place; on the other side, far below, was where the missing father and his two kids had been found. The report had said accidents for the children, and suicide for the father. He had believed that was the case then, but no longer.

He'd just reached the crest on top of the hill, and stood by the large rock. He looked down into a small gorge, and about thirty feet below lay something large and hairy on the ground, surrounded by officers shooting at it. The stench was awful. After they'd settled down, one of the officers reached for the thing on the ground. Malik shouted for him to stop, not to touch it, but it was too late.

The whole world exploded.

THE MAYOR of Skull Creek hung up the phone and stared at it for a while. As she did, the people in the room remained silent. She looked sadly at the Governor, who sat at the opposite side of the conference table. A complete silence fell over the room as the two women stared at each other. No words needed to be said.

Finally, the Governor asked, "How bad?"

The Mayor looked at her, feeling dragged down by exhaustion. "About as bad as it can get," she said quietly.

The Governor looked at a phone next to her. "Leave," she ordered the room. "Not you, Margret."

When they were alone, she picked up the phone and dialed.

"White House Hotline. Governor Barrett, please hold while you're transferred to the President."

TWENTY-EIGHT

The water slammed into Christina's face like a slap from an ex, hitting her hard; but she only laughed, coughed a little, and laughed again, until the next shower hit. The rollercoaster ride on the river was at its peak. The rafts bounced and shook wildly as they slammed swiftly down the torrent, wave after wave splashing everyone onboard. The wetter they got, the more the rafters screamed and laughed. Everyone was soaked, and the cold water made some of them scream even louder. Their arms were tired from all the paddling, but they kept going.

Large rocks sometimes loomed like dangerous fangs in front of the rafts, but the skilled hands of the people in charge of steering made them miss all the dangers. Everyone had to work really hard with the paddles, though, and as the river got wilder, they had to paddle even harder. They made a stop in one of the calmer areas of the river to check on everyone and the gear. Once that was done, they headed back into the whitewater. They competed with each other to see which raft would stay in the lead, and the competition grew fierce. The rafts bumped into each other, and once in a while someone fell overboard; but everything was carefully monitored by the guides, and they were soon hauled aboard.

Peter suddenly motioned for everyone to stop, but no one seemed to care. He turned around and made some type of gesture to Gavin, who immediately turned the raft towards shore. He also got on his radio and ordered the others to follow, to everyone's dismay. Before they reached the shore, Peter jumped off the rubber raft, and waist-deep, hurried to the shore line. He ran up a small hill and stood there listening as the other passengers gave each other puzzled looks.

Someone said, "Wait, listen! You guys hear what I hear?"

There was silence as everyone tried to listen, but the noise of the rapids concealed most sounds. Then, suddenly, a huge explosion echoed through the mountains, rolling in like a tidal wave. In the far distance came the sounds of automatic weapons fire, like someone had started a war. The rafters fell completely silent; Peter looked at the people below, and all of them looked back at him concern. He returned to the raft without a word, said something to Gavin, and then the race was on again.

They went back to paddling and screaming, having the best time of their lives, trying not to worry about what they'd heard, doing more daring moves, challenging each other. They came upon a small but steep waterfall, and one by one, the rafts flew over, making everyone scream and shout for more. They sped up, and the twist and turns got fiercer and faster as they approached a larger and more dangerous waterfall. The pilots on the rafts ordered everyone to sharpen up and stop playing around. The ones who had made this trip before immediately straightened up, and a more serious mood spread among the crews. Just as the first raft headed over the edge, another enormous explosion causing the ground to tremble startled everyone, making them lose their concentration, turning their attention towards the large mountain where the sound had come from. Thick smoke lay over the mountain, as if a dormant volcano just had erupted. The second raft hit the first hard on the side, and both tipped over the edge on the waterfall. The third raft came up too fast and crushed down into the melee below.

The trip had just taken a more serious turn.

Shortly thereafter, everyone lay on the stony side of the river, catching their breaths and spitting out excess water; but still many of them laughed, wanting to do it again. The more experienced guides rolled their eyes. The rest of the journey was under taken a more controlled mood, and quite some time later they saw the camp in the distance; now the competition became fierce. This part of the river looked more like a lake; it was shallow, and the whitewater was more or less gone. They had to paddle hard, and from time to time carry the large rubber rafts between them, running over slippery rocks. Team Croft won; the second raft was Team Lumber, and the last one coming in was Rohan's Team Rockies.

Christina gave Peter a friendly smile. Both knew full well why they had won, considering his background as a former elite soldier. He winked at her and she gratefully winked back.

Working together, everyone helped get the rafts onto a trailer while comparing notes on the best ride of their lives; most stories soon came back to the incident at the second fall. Many of them turned their heads towards the mountain range, wondering what was going on, but that particular mountain could not be seen from where they were.

"Probably the minors using explosives," Gavin suggested.

Peter shook his head and said, "Maybe, but that doesn't explain the shooting."

"Probably having a turkey shoot just for fun, or maybe that loose tiger showed up."

"We should call and check on it," Adrianna suggested.

"No phones," Rohan said emphatically. "No phones or distractions to ruin the best day of the year, thank you."

Many supported his suggestion.

Adrianna looked at her fellow officers, but Lucy and Dex both only shook their heads.

Rohan said, "Perhaps it was a volcano eruption?"

His words were drowned out by laughter, but he took it like the sport he was. Daniele, his wife, walked over to her husband to give him support from the bullies—or maybe not, because she patted him on the top of his head.

"Yes, she patted me on the head," Rohan said defensively. "I'm getting some tonight, YES. Classic head-patting; wonderful foreplay!"

Daniela rolled her eyes. "You're impossible, you know that?"

"Yes, dear, and you love it!"

The few rafters with bruises and cuts were quickly treated by Daniela and Rohan, and then someone shouted "Food! Time to eat!" The tables, prepared by those who had remained in camp, were weighed down with enough dishes to feed an army, and that army quickly dug in, forgetting their table manners along with their cares. The feast was accompanied by music coming from speakers someone had rigged up in the background, which only enhanced the party mood. It was a nice crowd, and the atmosphere was rowdy but happy. In time, some of the attendees who still had the energy headed to the natural pool for swimming and diving; others, deciding that they needed rest, lay down on the ground or in their tents. It was cool and comfortable, the perfect weather for the trip. Two couples bid farewell, having decided to return to the fairgrounds in Skull Creek. No one seemed to care. There were silly adult games to be played, and no matter how silly they might be, everyone participated like happy children.

"MOVE IT, *you lazy little bastard! Or do you want to give up and run home to Mommy and cry in her lap, you disappointing no-good failure? Move it or die."*

The man leaned over the young boy, who lay in the snow crying from the pain and the cold. He had barely any clothes on and his skin was bluish; soon he would freeze to death. A harness was strapped to his thin body, and the harness was attached to a large sled. Where dogs would normally be harnessed, the boy was instead. An old man sat huddled up in the sled, wearing thick winter clothing and a huge bear skin coat. On his head he had a similar fur hat.

"*Told you he was a poor choice. He'll never make it. Be better off if we just leave him here,*" *the old man insisted from his comfortable position.*

"*You hear your grandfather, boy? He thinks of you as dead. Want me to think that about you too, boy? March or die. When you think you're finished, you have 70% left in you! Now don't you dare keep wasting it on tears!*"

The father waved a large bullwhip, but he never whipped his son; verbal abuse was enough, along with the sound of the whip-crack shattering the air. The boy stopped crying and rolled over from his back to his belly. He looked determined. It took him some time before he had the harness straightened out. His limbs were dead tired and numb, and were on the verge of breaking. He closed his eyes and bit down hard, tasting blood in his mouth. He stood, braced himself, and pushed away hard on the snowy ground; he slipped a few times and scraped his knees. His thin undershirt was soaking wet, like his underpants; the blobs of fabric he called shoes almost slipped off his small feet. With a loud roar—at least, as loud as a child can roar — he renewed his efforts and pushed forward. There was no more taunting from his father or grandfather. He knew the sled was frozen to the ground, just as they had warned him would happen if he ever took a rest. Now he was paying the price. He tugged against the harness over and over again, and it cut deep into his flesh and muscles. Suddenly, without any warning, the goddamn sled jerked forward. He fell to the ground, but immediately got to his feet and pushed with all his might.

"*There you go, my true Viking boy, just like our ancestors! Never give up, just push harder! They ran us off from the Old World, but our ancestors were smart—and with the help of Mother Nature's protection, they made it south, through hostile lands and people who wanted to eat them and see them all dead. Ages it took before they found a safe haven!*"

"*Listen to your father, you lazy pup, because you best remember our legacy!*" *the old man in the sled shouted.*

"*Push harder, son, harder! If you're going to protect Mother like she protects us, you must be harder and know your legacy, you must earn the title berserker!*"

"Are you listening, you lazy little shit? Because the two-leggeds will always hate you, and they will always come after you," the old man shouted.

The boy struggled like mad, but he refused to give up; he kept pushing himself, determined to do or die, until finally he saw smoke coming from a chimney in the distance. The sight of it gave him more inner strength, and he pushed more and harder. Father was right; he did have plenty left in him.

He didn't see his father's puzzled and proud expression, because he was far to concentrated on pulling the heavy sled forward. Even his grandfather shut up and looked on with surprise. The little boy just kept going, screaming with pain and anger. He was close to the log cabin now, and he again forced more strength from his frail body — until suddenly, everything went dark.

NERO WOKE up, dizzy and confused. He blinked, trying to focus his eyes and remember what had happened. He had sand and stone-dust in his mouth, and his skin tingled from many small cuts and bruises. A grayish powder covered his entire body, and his lower legs lay under a pile of rocks. His brain registered the pain, but he easily pushed that sensation away. This pain was nothing compared to the pain of his childhood trials. He took a deep breath, only to start coughing. His tongue was swollen and he was very thirsty. He spat heavily, clearing his mouth of dust and dirt, and that made him even thirstier.

He blinked again several times, and felt the rocky powder irritating his eyes and eyelids. His ears rang like bells on a church tower, and he had problems focusing on what had happened to him and what kind of damage he had sustained. He tried moving, but he was stuck. Slowly and carefully, he sat up and began moving rocks off his body and away from him, sliding them to the side. He hoped he didn't make too much noise. He felt exhausted, but something within his mind kept telling him not to give up. The mere thought was enough; and suddenly he could feel the high from his muscles as they began demanding more blood from his heart.

He tried again to remember what had happened, thinking about it for some time as he shoved the rocks away, still a bit confused. He had lured the reinforcements up to the cliffside with his second skin strung up on a framework of cut saplings, and then down into the gorge, where he had left his second skin booby-trapped. He had hurriedly and carefully begun to descend the rocky surface beyond. He had made good progress when he heard voices from above, as people charged down into the gorge. There must have been a crack in the ground, hidden under the moss. Once the trap had gone off, part of the cliff had slid down, missing him by inches as he was descending the mountain side. After that, he remembered only bits and pieces.

He was still alive, though, and any evidence of his second skin and transformation had been obliterated in the explosion; the legacy had been secured. Should the two-leggeds capture him now, at most he would be considered an average mad two-legged murderer. So far, so good; now it was time to leave Skull Creek, but he had to be very careful, because he knew that soon, the entire mountain range would literally crawl with cops and soldiers.

After he cleared his legs, he stood; nothing was broken. He moved slowly away from the mountainside, listening for anything that might jeopardize him, but his hearing was still not 100% after the explosion and the fall. He was bleeding more now and had started feeling weak, but he kept pushing himself. When he had crawled up a hill, he turned around and observed the mountain side he had climbed and fallen down from. Far above came smoke from the mine. He noticed some movement from a few people, who were standing on what was left of the ridge, looking down into the valley. He had made it for now. He crawled slowly backwards, out of sight.

He reached the forest edge, and kept crawling for what seemed forever until he reached a small creek. He rolled into the fresh, cold water and drank gratefully. He then washed off the dust. He checked on his bullet wound, and saw he still had the bandage on, but it was torn. He looked around at the trees; and when he saw a pine with resin oozing onto its trunk, he got up to gather some. He rolled it between his fingers, and when he thought he had enough, he urinated on his hand, mixing the urine and the resin together into a paste. He applied it to his wound, and re-attached the remains of the torn bandage to keep the paste in place. Nero sat down, leaning on the tree, and closed his eyes for a short rest.

He woke up, startled, looking around in confusion. It took him a moment to realize he had fallen asleep, and it was much darker now. Nero cursed himself quietly, and then he got to his feet slowly, did some stretching, and then struggled on toward where had had hidden his truck.

He reached the river and had to walk upstream for some time until he reached the shallows. He waded across in the cold water, holding his bandage in place the entire time. Once he crossed the river, he went downstream; following the forest edge, he would soon reach the place where he had hidden his truck. But as he got closer, he could smell smoke; and then he heard the music.

He stopped, bewildered. What now? He was sure this place had been secluded, the perfect hideout now that rafting season was over. He crept closer towards the sound of guitar music and people singing. He saw many vehicles parked around the campsite, all over and back towards the woods, and a large trailer stacked with rubber rafts. Nero cursed himself silently. He had done his due diligence, and knew full well that the rafting tour had ended the previous week. *Now who are these idiots?* he wondered, as he observed the crowd like the injured and hungry predator he was. It was an older crowd, not teenagers, unfortunately. To his surprise, none of them were fiddling with their damned phones. Instead they ate, drank, sang, and danced. Nor could he smell any pot. This was definitely a strange crowd.

He squinted his eyes, suspicious; no marijuana could mean that there were cops among them. Sadly, they were too far away to tell, and several tents lay in his way, prohibiting him from seeing more. Suddenly he smiled; boy, she sure was a pretty little thing, now wasn't she, dancing around the fire with her friends like a forest nymph?

AN EXHAUSTED Anna-Maria da Silva stared out the hospital window into the early afternoon. She had no more tears to cry, and her dead stare was that of a broken woman. She sensed someone in the room. *Better not be the kids*, she thought. She wasn't ready for that, not yet, but she knew that eventually she would have to gather new strength and face the inevitable. Just the thought of it made her start crying again.

A strong hand fell on her shoulder. "Sorry. Sorry, Anna-Maria, for failing you and Carlos."

She turned, facing Malik Washington. The top of his head was swathed in bandages, and his left arm was in a sling. He was bruised and had several cuts and lacerations on his face, and she guessed his body was covered with them, too. Despite his smoky-dark skin, the big man looked pale. "The bastard is dead—we think," he reported.

"But you don't *know*, do you?"

"We think he blew himself up."

"What if he didn't? Did you see him?"

"Well, I'm pretty sure, and I did see something. Right before the explosion."

She raised her eyebrows. "*Something?* You *think?*" She turned her face away from Malik, who sat himself down next to the hospital bed. "Why don't you make sure of it?"

"There's nothing left of the killer, Anna-Maria. The bastard took most of my colleagues here and in the surrounding counties, and a group of Feds, with him. He killed 12 good men and women in the blast alone."

She looked at him. "Well, I would be grateful if you made sure the person who blew himself up was the same person who murdered my husband."

Malik looked bewildered. "How?"

Anna-Maria sounded a bit more harsh than she wanted to. "Just look at my phone. The man's face is on the last message Carlos send me. He called me, and everything was caught on video, and…"

Malik rushed to his feet, shouting out loud, "Where?! Where is your phone?"

"Over there in my purse. I'm not sure how it got there, but I guess that doesn't matter."

Malik went through her purse. He handed her the phone and she typed in the security code, and then she went through the call list. Once she found the last call, she pushed the play button and handed the phone to Malik.

"I turned off the volume. I don't want to see or hear it ever again."

Malik looked a bit confused, and then he hit the pause button, looking at her inquisitively. She just motioned with her hand for him to leave. She knew he had to listen and watch what she had already seen and heard.

TWENTY-NINE

N ero needed to get away. Normally, he would have waited until
the two-leggeds had left, which would most likely be the next
morning. But right now, he didn't have that luxury; he was injured. He
needed his regular clothes and some food. Everything was in his truck,
and his truck was parked farther away from the small path, near the tree
line. Apparently no one had paid his truck any attention; perhaps they
thought it belonged to one of them. There were, after all, about thirty
people camping. He moved stealthily in the shadows along the tree line
until he reached his truck, then looked over towards the campers and realized that no one was using a phone. Nowadays, that was odd. He soon
found that some idiot had parked a huge Mercedes behind him, blocking his truck. Who drove a Mercedes off-road?

He moved past the large black car; fortunately, it had white leather upholstery, so he could see the large bag and a box with several cell
phones in it on the passenger's seat. He didn't understand why all the
phones were there. Again, he scouted the campsite, and noticed to his
surprise how clean it was. He saw two large black plastic sacks, each
mounted on several wooden poles, used as trash cans.

He was near his own truck, and needed first aid and food; the smell of the barbeque didn't help at all. He decided that there was no need to sneak around, but if he could, he would stay concealed for as long as possible. He unlocked his truck and grabbed his bag. He undressed in a hurry, trying to come up with a plan. He thought, *I can tell them I've been hiking and need to get home. They'll probably invite me to the party; should I stay for a while, or be in a hurry?*

He then got out a plastic bottle containing an alcohol gel mixed with chloride. He rubbed it all over his body as fast as he could. It was the perfect potion to eradicate the stink. He realized he should have done that first, but he was tired and felt weak. His body had taken too many blows, and needed mending and rest before he continued his good work.

Nero took out a more advanced first aid kit and tended to the wound in his side; then he focused on dressing some of the more superficial ones. When he was done, he put on his typical lumberjack clothes; they were dirty and smelled sweaty. He heard more laughter from the partiers. He coughed some, and when he saw the specks of blood on his hand, he knew it was bad.

A GROUP of people sat next to one of the two fires, passing around a tequila bottle, lime, and salt. Others were dancing around the second fire, while several played guitars, bongo drums, and a harmonica.

"All right, who cut one? Man, it really stinks!" someone complained, a few others agreeing. All of them search for the idiot who had dropped the stink bomb.

Parker shouted, "So Rohan and Daniela, tell us…?"

"Tell you what…? You are drunk," Rohan shouted back, while embracing his wife.

"What's your big secret, guys? How do you keep up the perfect marriage?"

Daniela licked up some salt from her upper hand and then she said, "It's quite simple. Happy wife, happy life." She nodded her head towards her new car. "It boils down to three letters: A-M-G." She then went for the bottle of tequila, pushing her husband away a bit so she could drink.

Rohan stood up and gestured with his hands for attention and silence. "Naw, that ain't it."

"What is it, then?" Blake shouted, holding on to Tammy, who was kissing his ear.

Rohan stood in a thinking pose and then he said, "As the good doctor always says, a blowjob a day keeps the wenches away!"

Daniela coughed up her tequila, and the lime shot into the fire like a missile, while the rest of the horde laughed like mad. Rohan finished, "Or was it an apple?"

Blake looked at Tammy, who looked back at him while wetting her lips with her tongue. They were on one of the benches, and she sat on his knees by a table with dozens of platters of food behind them.

Christina, just back from dancing, rolled her eyes at the joke, shaking her head and laughing, only to see her best friend seducing yet another poor man. Tammy stood up and placed her hand in Blake's. A barely noticeable nod of her head, and the two of them wandered away towards the vehicles.

Christina found Robert over by the table, stuffing himself with a mountain of spare ribs. A stack of beer cans sat on the table, empty. *Maybe with some alcohol in him, he'll make a move,* she thought. She grabbed a plate, having no intention of eating more because she was full as it was, and walked over to the food table. She grabbed some homemade bread and a dipping sauce she had tried earlier and liked. She was a little disappointed, because the big lug hadn't made any moves on her at all the entire day; a matter of fact, ever since they had started the journey down the river, he had acted cold and distant toward her. Actually, it had begun just after Peter had introduced the two muscle boys to Tammy and her...

Since there was no place of interest for her to sit on the bench, she walked towards the river and found a flat rock to sit on. Just as

she got settled, she realized to her annoyance that she had forgotten
to grab something to drink. Unlike most of the partiers, she had only
had one beer with supper; after that she'd kept to sodas, iced tea, and
juice. She'd already partied hard for two nights with Tammy, and that
was enough.

"May I join you?" She looked up towards the voice, and was suddenly tongue-tied. The best she could do was nod.

Robert sat next to her, facing the river, and handed her a Coke.
He had brought a spare rib, and chewed on it some. Christina decided
to change her sitting position and get closer, but misjudged her balance
and immediately rolled to the side, right into his lap. *Couldn't play harder to get than that*, she told herself sarcastically as her cheeks burned. She
was grateful for the darkness creeping up on them as the sun set, hiding
her blush. She felt like a naïve little girl in Robert's presence. "Sorry, I'm
a bit clumsy," she apologized.

"Indeed you are."

Christina's eyes went wide; the big oaf wasn't supposed to *agree*,
now was he?

Neither said a word to each other; they just watched the beautiful landscape and river as the sun painted the sky brilliant shades of
orange, red, mauve, and pink, inspired by the smoke pouring from
the mountain.

NERO HAD his back turned, but he could hear the footsteps approaching. "Should I kill them all, or just a few, or none at all?" he
mumbled and half-sung while buttoning his shirt.

Blake faced Tammy, and for a moment they just stared at each
other; and then they started kissing hungrily and a bit clumsily, giv-
en their drinking earlier. It wasn't long before they started fumbling
with each other's clothes, still lip-locked, kicking off shoes and trying
to get pants down.

"Howdy, folks," said a friendly voice.

The kissing stopped instantly. They stared at each other and quickly started fixing their clothes, laughing nervously.

"Howdy, sir. Sorry if you had to see that," Blake said pleasantly, turning to the stranger. He wrinkled his brow, trying to remember the name of the person who stood there looking at him and Tammy.

"Is this your Mercedes?" the man asked. "Sure would appreciate it if you guys could move it. It's blocking in my truck."

"Sure. Well, we can get the owner. Have we met?"

"Not sure. The name's Ted Hagglund." The man extended his hand, and Blake grabbed it thoughtfully.

"I'm Blake, and this is Tammy. Wait, I think I know you; you're one of those precision loggers, right?"

Looking a bit shy, Hagglund replied, "Yeah, well, I'll settle for the term lumberjack."

"I think we might have met here and there. Skull Creek ain't that big."

"Sure isn't."

"I guess you know Robert, then."

"Precision guy who helped the firemen at the accident, right?"

"That's him. I was there too, taking care of the electricity poles."

"Nasty business, all that."

"Sure was. So what are you doing in these parts?"

Tammy interrupted with, "I'm not sure it's any of our business, Blake."

He looked down into the glistening eyes demanding his attention. "Yeah, you're right Tammy."

"No big deal. I've been hiking all day. Love the forest, that's all."

The wind changed direction, and Nero cursed himself. He'd forgotten to put his clothes from the fight in a plastic bag; they still stank.

"Holy shit, that stinks something awful," Tammy said, screwing up her face. "What is that, Blake?"

"Not sure. Could be a dead skunk."

Nero intervened, "Sorry guys, my bad—truth is, I slipped on the trail and fell on, you guessed it, a dead skunk. That's why I smell like detergent right now—had to clean it off myself. The smell's from my darn clothes. I expect I'll have to wash them in tomato juice. Hang on, and I'll put them into a bag."

He hurried to his truck, found the filthy outfit, and tossed it into a thick garbage bag. He tied it closed, and then put the closed bag into one more bag, making sure the stink was taken care of. He then went back to Blake and Tammy.

"So sorry about that, ma'am," he said to Tammy. Tammy smiled at him, then grabbed Blake's hand. "So about the car…?" Nero gestured towards the Mercedes.

Tammy was feeling a bit frustrated, but kept her cool. "I'll get the owner. I'll be right back." As she strolled away she suddenly turned and said, "Hey Ted, would you like to join us? It's a great party with a lot of food and booze!"

Nero did a quick calculation and decided it would look better if he joined them and became one of the gang, so to speak. After all, he *was* very hungry. "Well, ma'am, I don't want to impose."

"Stop the 'ma'am' shit and come on over. We got enough food for an army."

He gave Tammy and Blake a bland smile and joined them. He got introduced to only a few people around the table, and that was good, Nero thought. He grabbed a beer, and instantly he blended in.

Tammy pointed over at a couple making out like teenagers on the end of one of the benches. Suddenly the guy, a short, stocky fellow, fell on his ass on the ground. The tall, slender woman put her hands over her face and laughed hysterically. "Keep it up, lady, and you'll be sleeping alone for a month!" the little guy declared.

"You wouldn't last a month without it!" the woman giggled. Then she laughed even harder, more like a man would.

"Ted, the one laughing at her husband is the person you're looking for. Her name is…"

"Daniela. Yes, I know of her—one of the doctors in town," Nero finished her sentence.

Nero took a paper plate and piled it high with coleslaw and bread. The chicken wings and the ribs smelled wonderful; and even though he mostly avoided meat, he did eat it from time to time, and now was as good as time as any.

But while he ate, he started to feel faint, and his appetite suddenly vanished.

CHRISTINA FELT completely satisfied…well, almost. Without thinking, she leaned her head onto Robert's broad, muscular shoulder. He smelled manly. He trembled a little, so she moved a bit closer, snuggling up to him; and finally there was his arm, coming around her—and just as it touched her shoulder, there was a scream and laughter.

"Hey, bro, there you are. Can I please have one more beer? Please?" Pat stood there with two other girls about her age, both holding a beer each.

Robert stood up, facing his sister. "This is the last one, all right? That goes for all of you."

Christina stared at the river sadly. What the hell, she needed to use the little girl's tree anyway. As she rose, she said, "I'll be right back, Robert…"

She trailed off as she saw him walking away, apparently lecturing his sister and her friends.

Irritated, Christina looked around for a decent spot to relieve herself. She realized she had to head back past the camp to do that. She hurried past one of the tables, where a few people were still eating. She wasn't sure how they could still be hungry, but maybe she'd just found out why most men in Skull Creek were giants. As she passed the table heading into the forest, she sensed eyes on her. She was used to that, but since she had gotten here, almost no one had treated her as Ms. Hollywood; they just treated her like everyone else, so this seemed a little strange.

She turned toward the table, and the man staring at her immediately turned away. Whatever. Christina hurried away, because now she *really* needed to empty her bladder, but she recognized that acquired stare so characteristic of paparazzi and stalkers, and she couldn't keep it out of her mind.

NERO HAD to hurry; apparently, she had recognized him. He didn't understand *why* he had to hurry, but something was amiss—something he had done or said, perhaps. He didn't know, but he knew he needed to move on. That the pretty little thing was here was one thing, but for some reason it had raised red flags in his mind. He went back in his head to the time he first had seen her, then on to the one time they had met on the road, and what he had said to her. But he drew a blank on that, and it bothered him. His intuition for danger was superior to anyone else's because he had evolved to be far superior to these weak two-legged creatures.

No matter. Time to move on.

"Excuse me, ma'am," he said to Daniela, "but I would be grateful if you could move your car. It's blocking my truck."

Daniela gave the stranger a friendly smile. "No problem. Let me get my keys, and I'll meet you over there."

Christina returned from the little girl's tree, and to her dismay found that almost everyone had moved over to the fire near the river, where they sang and kept on partying—including Robert, his sister, and her friends. Her annoyance was displaced by her subconscious mind offering her something it had worked out, as it dawned on her where she remembered the new guy from. He was the man who had helped her on the road after she'd fallen into the river. She looked around for him; the very least she could do was to thank him. She saw Daniela walk to her car and fire it up, and in her headlights she recognized the man who had saved her. She walked over to them.

When Daniela turned on her baby and all twelve cylinders woke up with a thundering roar, so did her in-dash TV, which was still on from earlier when she'd been watching CNN as Rohan drove. As she maneuvered around the truck belonging to the man she knew only as Ted and started to roll the car forward to park in a new spot, the picture popped up with a news bulletin about Skull Creek. She stopped short when she heard the name of her hometown, providing updates on the massacre earlier that day. Being a bit under the influence, she had to really concentrate on the newswoman to get what she was saying.

"Authorities still aren't saying anything about the massacre, but we've learned from our own sources that all the terrorists died in a suicide explosion that caused at least another three officers' deaths. These images were taken by hikers, and if you watch closely, you can see part of the mountain sliding away right after the detonation. Homeland Security…"

Daniela stopped listening, because in one corner of the screen popped up a tiny image of a man. It suddenly filled the screen.

"Authorities are also searching for this man, and want to question him about the murder of Sheriff Carlos da Silva. Ted Hagglund is to be considered armed and extremely dangerous. Should you…"

NERO LOOKED in his rearview mirror as the big Mercedes backed up, then started to pull around him, only to stop suddenly. Well, he could get out now. He backed up, and as he pulled next to the car he lifted his hand towards his forehead, nodding a thank you—and that's when he saw himself on the TV screen on the dash. Daniella had frozen, staring dead ahead. She slowly turned her eyes toward him, and Nero looked back at her calmly. She, however, looked anything but calm. He removed a hidden cover on his door and removed a Glock handgun with a SilencerCo Osprey Suppressor attached. Too bad about the woman, but she was just another two-legged, and he would do what he had to in order to survive.

"THERE YOU are, Christina!" Adrianna shouted. She hurried up to Christina, who was heading over to the parking area. "We were wondering where you took off to. Are you leaving?"

"Me? No, but I just saw the guy who told me about the car accident—you know, the bad one? Anyway, he's the guy who saved me, and I thought I'd say thank you."

"Oh, you mean the guy who said that a woman caused the accident."

"Yeah, that's him."

Adrianna stopped for a moment, and then her cop-brain took over. "How did he know about *that* accident?" she said out loud to herself, looking at Christina.

"What do you mean?"

"We hadn't released much information at the time about that accident, because it was new to us. You discovered it, actually—the truck on the cliff, remember? That was an earlier accident than the big one. A least a day older."

Both girls looked at each other suspiciously, and then headed together to the parking area.

Daniela was sweating profusely. She couldn't move, and tears streamed down her face; she was shaking uncontrollably, and suddenly her entire life flashed before her eyes. When she saw the man walking behind her car and up to her side, she noticed the long, dark object in his hand; and now she cried out loud, and slammed her hands on the controls in the center of the steering wheel. The radio blared to life as she hit the accelerator, flooring it. The engine's 621 horsepower decided to go for a walk in the woods.

Adrianna reacted instantly, tackling Christina to the ground; the Mercedes missed them by inches. The car jetted away like a dark monster, engine roaring, horn howling. It reached a tilted rock that lay on the ground like a launch pad, then the car flew right into a tree, smashing the passenger side. But that didn't stop the car; the impact only altered its direction, and now it headed into camp. It flew over the first campfire, scattering flames and burning logs all over, and then it wobbled and rolled on two wheels while the other two brushed the table with all the food, jetting it in all directions.

Rohan, sitting on the opposite side of the food table, just stared in disbelief, still holding a chicken wing in his hand as the car passed by, a foot away. Then he stood up and yelled, with his fists clenched overhead, "Woohoo! Go baby go!"

People threw themselves to the sides as the car tumbled back onto all four wheels and raced into the second fire, nearer the river. It struck the fire pit like a missile, scattering more burning debris. The car passed between two of the several large logs that had been used as benches as it roared by, and went straight into the river. It was a miracle no one got hit. People just stared in disbelief at the Mercedes when it spun in circles in the water; and then the river started to get ahold on the car.

Sammy and Gavin reacted instantly, diving into the water toward the Mercedes. They reached it quickly, while it was stuck for the moment on the river bottom. Sammy got a rock in his hand and smashed the window, and with the help of Gavin, they pulled out an unconscious Daniela. People screamed and panicked, not understanding what they had just witnessed; some tried to calm everyone down, but the chaos was inevitable. More than two dozen people stared in disbelief at the floating car from the safety of the shore. The lights were still on when the car pulled lose from the river bottom and started on its own rafting tour downstream, ironically as Paul Robeson's *Ol' Man River* wafted from the radio.

Adrianna lay on top of Christina, and both were coughing up dust. After a moment, the policewoman rolled to the side, and she and Christina sat up, looking around, bewildered. Part of the tree line had caught fire, the bright headlights from a pickup forcing its rays through the rapidly-building smoke. They saw a shadow of a man walking towards them, and then, suddenly, Adrianna was yanked to her feet.

Christina dragged herself backwards, still lying on the ground. The man who held Adrianna had a gun to her head. When Christina saw the weapon, a new spike of adrenaline hit her bloodstream, and she began breathing faster. Adrianna resisted briefly, but stopped after the person holding her whispered something in her ear.

Christina, having had her share of dangerous encounters with stalkers, reacted instantly. Without any hesitation, her hand went for her necklace, and she turned it on as she squeezed it lightly. As she had been taught, she then scratched her neck, as if she were doing something normal.

Nero sensed someone behind him; he turned to the side, and fired one round at his attacker.

"Blake! NO!" Tammy screamed as her date went down, bleeding from his forehead. She ran up next to him and kneeled, in shock and screaming hysterically. Then, suddenly, she went utterly, eerily silent. She rose to her feet and charged Nero, who backhanded her in the face, sending her crashing to the ground next to Blake.

Nero focused on Christina and said in a low, friendly voice, almost whispering: "You. Yes, you, the pretty one. You make sure all your friends keep away, now. You make sure you tell them, or I'll kill all of them. Nod your head if you understand."

Christina couldn't really grasp what had happened—she was in a state of shock. Nero knew this, knew he had to act fast; hence his calm voice. Unless she complied, he would have to make one more kill, maybe two, to instill a paralyzing fear into the crowd.

It wasn't long before the crowd on the riverbank noticed that something was going on over by the parking area. Gavin and Sammy tried to organize parties to stamp out the scattered fires before they spread. Dex and Lucy, however, sneaked away towards the tents.

Rohan shouted, "That man has a gun, and I think he just shot someone!"

Sammy and Gavin, along with the rest, walked slowly towards what seemed to be a few people standing and lying near a truck with its engine running and lights on. But as they got closer, Christina intercepted them and shouted for them to stop. She had to raise her voice more than once.

"If you don't stop, he'll kill someone else. Don't move! Please!" She was crying and trembling; she wanted to run away, but she didn't dare; she could sense the killer's eyes on her back.

"C'mon, Christina, what the fuck is going on?"

The rest had stopped, except for Sammy, who had a strange expression on his face. It was anything but afraid; it was more a curious or perhaps a longing expression, something very few would understand. Christina knew that Peter suspected that Sammy and Gavin were former Navy SEALs, and that thought did give Christina some measure of comfort; but she had just witnessed a man murdered in cold blood. She didn't know what to do. She just stood there, turning her upper body, while crying almost silently. Sammy took a step closer, but when she raised her hand, Sammy stopped.

Gavin suddenly appeared next to his partner and lay a hand on his shoulder, whispering something to him. Sammy glanced towards the tent area and calmed down. Gavin mouthed, *How many?* Christina held up one finger halfway, still shaking uncontrollably.

Meanwhile, the crowd had gathered in a half circle facing Christina, who kept telling them not to move forward any more. Suddenly, she got help from both Gavin and Sammy, who spread to the sides. Their normally friendly faces had suddenly changed into something frightening, almost taunting. She felt a pang of worry and repeated, "Please, please, don't come any closer. Don't try anything. He killed Blake and he has Adrianna, and I think Tammy is injured too."

Through the smoke, two people moved in unison, only a few feet; Nero held Adrianna hard by her neck and long hair, making sure the gun with the sound suppressor was easily visible.

"Okay, pretty one, come on over here," he said calmly.

Gavin gestured for her to do as she was told. The tension in the air was thick as a cloud, and no one noticed the drizzle that had started falling. Christina moved slowly towards Nero.

"Tell me, Christina Dawn, what do you think of animals?" Nero asked, like they were having a friendly conversation over coffee.

She looked at him, surprised, and then she said truthfully, "I love animals. I'm in the process of adopting a kitten, and I'm dog-sitting this winter."

"Really? How wonderful. And what about our Mother?"

"Mother?"

Nero smiled. "Mother Nature?"

"I love her, too. I'm sorry to say that nature is being ruined by greed, though. I had to force some prospectors off my land recently under threat of legal action."

Nero chuckled as he motioned for her to move closer. "What's your friend's name?" he asked, gesturing with the pistol.

"Adrianna."

"Adrianna. Lovely. Adrianna, I want you to take a few steps over to my truck and look in the back, under the big green plastic cover, and then I want you tell everyone what you see."

Adrianna did as she was told, as he kept his gun trained on Christina; and when she returned, she looked pale and more frightened that ever. "He's got enough C-4 rigged up back there to crack the world open. Back off, everyone."

Nero ordered everyone to their knees. When Christina started to kneel, he reached out and pulled her to her feet, as easily as a child might lift a building block. "No, not you, my pretty little one; you must never kneel for anyone. You're different, you see. You might not know it, but you are. No harm must ever come to one of our females, or it will be the end. Fear not. Now: please tell those two guards of yours to lower their weapons. One is by my truck, and the other behind a tree near what's left of the table over there."

Christina called oud loudly, "He knows you're there, and Adrianna says there are a lot of explosives in the truck."

Peter shouted from back of the truck, "Hope you don't mind me getting a second opinion."

Nero smiled, knowing full well he had won. "By all means. Take your time."

After a few moments, there was a low whistle from Peter. He carefully approached Nero and tossed his gun on the ground, shaking his head towards Kevin, who remained hidden. Peter then turned towards the tents, and shouted for Dex and Lucy to back off too.

Peter looked around; then, with his back towards the crowd, he faced Nero. Something in Nero's expression changed, and Peter noticed Robert walking straight towards Christina. Peter reached out with his right arm and slammed it into Robert's chest, hard. "Don't. Just stay by my side."

Robert shot him an angry glare, but settled back. Christina reacted, though, and Nero noticed it. He squinted at Robert and then Christina, and felt a stab of something alien to him. For the first time in his life, Nero was in love; and with that most wonderful sensation any human can feel came a more morbid reality, the sensation of feeling jealous. Nero was unfamiliar with these two new emotions, even though the first one had crept over him slowly these past weeks. But being jealous; that was something awful. *Should I just kill the bastard and take the pretty one? No, then she would hate me,* he thought.

Nero shook his head a bit wildly, trying to rid himself of this new sensation; but it wasn't that easy. Worse, he had become hesitant, and he didn't like that at all. Would this be his Greasy Grass, his Little Bighorn, his final stand where he would honor his berserker ancestors and go wild?

No, not yet. He had secured the secret, the legacy, when his second skin was vaporized in the blast. Now he was a man on the run; but that didn't matter. There had been no surviving witnesses to his other actions, except for Carlos's murder, evidently. Now he was glad he hadn't had his second skin on that day. No; this would not be his end, not here. He wanted a better challenge; and besides, killing himself wasn't an idea he cared for. He would if he had to, but he would rather go out fighting Mother's enemies, just like his ancestors had.

"You two, over here," he ordered Robert and Peter, who both reluctantly complied. Nero looked at Adrianna and tossed her some plastic

Cobra Cuffs. "Put these on them." Then he said, "No, not on the pretty one or yourself, stupid girl, on *them*." He pointed on Robert and Peter. Now everyone looked surprised.

"Wait!"

Kevin suddenly appeared next to Nero, pointing his gun at the berserker's head. Nero smiled at Kevin and aimed his gun at Christina, and for an instant, Kevin hesitated. The gun changed direction instantly, and discharged with a muffled *thump*. Peter fell to the ground, bleeding from his abdomen; two more shoots lashed out, hitting both Lucy and Dex in the legs. All three were injured but not killed. Nero wanted to delay them; hurt a few, and take out the entire unit. Adrianna stepped quickly between Kevin and Nero with her hands held high. "Don't, you'll kill us all! He has enough C-4 to wipe us all out. Please, Kevin, don't!"

Kevin shook his head, and finally lowered his gun. He took one step closer to Nero, who aimed his gun at Christina's head, his cold, hard stare boring into Kevin's eyes. He leaned close to Adrianna and whispered something.

"Robert, Kevin, you guys have to go with him. If you do, we live; and if you don't, we all die right now." Adrianna stopped talking, trying to hold back her tears, feeling completely helpless.

In less than a minute, both Kevin and Robert lay inside the secret compartment of Nero's truck, equipped with a breather each, unconscious. Nero had injected both with a powerful tranquilizer. Meanwhile, no one dared to even move except Pat, who screamed for her brother; but strong hands held her back as she snarled and called them all gutless cowards, and after Gavin clipped her on the jaw to shut her up, a strange silence fell over the campground.

Nero walked up to Christina, and tilted her jaw up some. He smiled and said, "Boy howdy, you sure are a pretty one, aren't ya."

Christina had stopped trembling and crying. She steadied herself and looked into the killer's eyes, and then she said something that surprised everyone: "Hurt them, and I'll hunt you down until I find you, and then I will *kill* you."

Nero knew from past experience that whenever an average two-legged threatened to kill someone, it was always bullshit talk; no normal individual lacking experience from having killed a person in self-defense or in a war would ever say such thing. He doubted that the pretty little girl had ever killed anything in her life; but looking in her eyes, he also knew that she had told him the truth. She would hunt him to the end of his days if he hurt his hostages.

He looked seriously at Christina, who had taken center stage in his drama. But this wasn't a film, where one could rehearse or re-take the scene over and over again until it was perfect; this was real life, her facing a monster with only one take. Nero could do nothing other than admire her. Nodding thoughtfully, he turned and walked to his truck, where he grabbed a case from behind the seats. It was made out of ancient cracked leather, carrying an equally old Winchester rifle and a very old ammunition belt. He walked towards Christina, and extended the weapon to her until she took it.

"That's the spirit, little girl. Use this gun when you come for me. It was once Long Hair's, and he carried it with him when he invaded the *Paha Sapa* of the Lakota, to force them to give up their gold. The Son of the Morning Star who attacks at dawn, they called him; but remember too who the Christians call the Morning Star. He was an evil man, and no matter what anyone else might say otherwise, this rifle was his. You see, my great-grandfather was the man who killed him and took this trophy.

"You come find me, now. Alone, you hear? You and only you."

He turned his back on her and walked towards his truck.

"Why me?"

Nero looked back, eyes hooded and blank as a lizard's. "You earned it. You are my Croatoan."

"Your what?"

"Sorry; that's the old forgotten language from across the great sea far to the north. A purge," Nero started coughing, and after a moment continued, "for a group, or a demise for one person. The lesser is used for an entire tribe, the full name for the one."

Christina thought that part of what he'd said made no sense.

"Then why don't we just end it here and now?"

Nero got in his truck and pulled up next to Christina.

"To do a Cro, one must earn it."

Christina, feeling more desperate at losing one of her oldest friends and perhaps her new love, swallowed hard. "How do I find you?"

"You already have." Nero lowered his eyes towards the rifle case, and then he drove off slowly. As the bed of the truck passed Christina, she stepped up and slid her activated necklace inside the back. As the truck left, Nero turned up the music: *O Fortuna* by Carl Orff.

Christina watched the bright embers of the taillights as the truck vanished amongst the trees. "Fuck your riddles and welcome to the twenty-first fucking century, you caveman motherfucker," she growled.

NERO STOPPED the truck at the nearest intersection, got out, and walked to the back, where he used a flashlight to find the necklace. He picked it up and looked at the jewelry, touching it gently until the golden face slid to the side and he saw the transmitter within. He smiled. "That's my girl."

His eyes watered as he tilted his head and looked up at the dark sky. The moon fought for dominance against the thick, rushing clouds.

After driving for a while, he passed another truck; he tossed the necklace into the back. Then he pulled into a remote side road, and removed all the camouflage from the sides, hood, and roof of the truck. The entire truck had large magnetized stickers covering it, giving the appearance of a rusty white color. Once they were removed, the truck was bright red. He then altered his appearance with a razor and a few cosmetics so it matched another driver's license with a different name. He reloaded his Glock just in case, and then he drove away towards his lair, listening to Vangelis's *Conquest of Paradise*.

Presently, he drove over a bridge and followed the serpentine road along the mountain ridge; the road bent and actually headed back towards the camping area on the other side of the river. Nero parked his truck on the side of the road opposite the camp. It was several miles away, but from this elevation he could see several of the fires from it.

He knew the pretty one would bring with her all kinds of entertainment. She would have kept her promise to come alone if he had made her do so, but the other, weaker two-leggeds never would. He was done for the day. He had helped his Mother, he had kept the legacy a secret, and now all he had to do was to wait for the two-leggeds and all the entertainment they would bring with them.

They thought they were hunting a regular, old-fashioned serial killer. His days were numbered, but the legacy would never die; all the secrets would die with him.

In Nero's mind, he had lost the battle but won the war, and for him, that was a good day indeed.

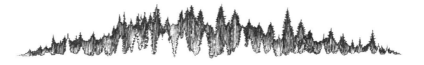

THIRTY

Rohan and Daniela, aided by a few of the less-rattled campers, were busy applying first aid to the injured persons. Christina held Tammy in a tight embrace, kneeling by her side. Tammy was silent, staring, bewildered, dead ahead. Most of the people remaining in camp were in serious shock. Sammy and Gavin patched up each other with the help of their wives, Megan and Pamela. Unlike the rest, except for Peter, their faces were hard as steel; and no matter how much their wives tried talking sense into them, they wanted to handle things the way they had in a life before they met their loved ones. Their wives begged for both to calm down, but they might as well have been talking to a pair of trees. More than once, the two former SEALs exchanged silent glances with Peter.

Daniela moved over to Peter and started to patch him up while he talked on his phone.

"It's done. Paramedics are on the way."

"Did you tell them what happened?" Adrianna wanted to know.

He shook his head.

"Hey, tough guy, we have a major crime scene here, with one person murdered!"

Suddenly a very upset Rohan ran up to them, looking very serious.

"Wait a minute, hold on there! What's that?"

Peter looked skeptically at Rohan, questioningly, "What?"

"That!" Rohan pointed accusingly at his phone.

"My phone. Now if you'll excuse me, we have an emergency, in case you missed it, and I need to make a call."

"But, but, that's cheating! We were all told to put our phones in the box!"

Everyone near Rohan stopped what they were doing and turned their heads towards him in disbelief, including his wife Daniela. "Sorry, guys, his mother dropped him on his head several times as a child," Daniela muttered.

Peter just smiled and said, "Hey, Doc, great comeback after that flight with your car."

Daniela looked up at Peter with glistering eyes, holding her own tears back. "It's what I do."

"And you do it well," Peter comforted her.

"No, she does it best," Rohan said holding back his own tears. He supported his wife by gently embracing her, and then her floodgates opened up. She shook her upper body for her husband to stop and move on, not wanting to cry in front of everyone. But he wouldn't have it; instead he embraced her harder, and made her work on Peter a bit more difficult.

Daniela stopped crying and cleared her throat. "By the way, dear, do tell me that you mailed all the letters before we left, like I asked."

Rohan got a suspicious look on his face. "What? Why?"

Daniela turned facing her husband and smiled, "You know, our bills…like the car insurance?"

The size of Rohan's eyes and expression confirmed that he hadn't. There was some laughter from a few people nearby. Daniela just shook her head sadly, and suddenly Rohan decided that Christina needed a bandage whether she wanted one or not.

Peter smiled to himself, despite his own nagging worry. It was important that everyone kept their spirits up, and jokes never hurt anyone.

"If we call it in, guys, then I believe this guy Ted Hagglund will be
true to his word, and our friends will die," Adrianna pointed out loudly.

"We don't have much of a choice, now do we?" Dex said, checking
on his own bandage. "We're cops, not vigilantes."

Lucy lay very calmly on a blanket, sweating profusely. Her injury had come uncomfortably close to the femoral artery of her left leg,
and she felt awful. In a trembling voice, she stated, "Whatever you
guys are going to do, you need to hurry, before the shithead gets away.
But I agree with Adrianna: if we call in the cavalry now, I doubt it will
end well."

"It's not going to end well no matter what happens!" Dex yelled.

Tammy whispered to Christina between her sobs, "Don't lose him,
fool. I've never seen you like this with any guy before, ever. You know
what you have to do."

Christina looked at her best friend and then at Peter, who looked
at her and gave a tiny nod.

"His love is gone, too. You just go now and save your knight in
shining armor, you hear me, sister?" Tammy hissed.

"But what about you and the others?"

"Oh, Christina, you're such a dear, always thinking about everyone
else but yourself—which is exactly why you never get laid anymore."

The old Tammy was back, but Christina saw that it took tremen-
dous effort; Tammy might be able to put on a macho act, but her tears
gave it all away. "Just go!" Tammy begged.

Before Christina could object again, Tammy placed her finger on
her lips for her to be silent.

"Now, go and get me that bloody phone from Peter. I have a call to
make to our godfather."

They embraced, and then Christina walked up to Peter. Now that
she was closer, she could see the lines of pain on his face, and the hurt in
his eyes. Even though there had been no tears she knew he was hurting,

and not from the gunshot wound. She looked him dead in the eyes and extended her hand. "My keys."

He looked at her for a moment. "This ain't one of your movies, girl. This is for real."

"Guess I only get one shot at getting this right, then."

"One shot will do it," he agreed.

She motioned with her hand again. Peter looked up towards the moon, which seemed to scud through a cloudy sea. Thin snowflakes started to fall. "I'll probably get fired for this."

"I doubt it."

He smirked and sighed. "I'm coming with you."

"You're hurt."

"Want your keys back or not?"

TURNED OUT Tammy had a plan. There was a reason why she had become a top executive at her young age, and it wasn't because of her godfather's influence: when it came to tactics and strategy, her mind would be the envy of any General in the field. She went over her plan with Christina and Peter.

"Could work," Peter mused. "Just make sure he keeps everyone away until we signal."

"You'll need back-up," Adrianna intervened from behind them.

"Shouldn't sneak up on people like that," Peter said pleasantly.

"Now, I don't know who this Tom guy is, but from the sound of it, he might have some juice?"

"You could say that," Peter said, sounding a bit aggravated. "Your point is?"

"That this man you're going after has killed God only knows how many people, and nothing has stopped him so far. That being the case, may I add something to you plan?"

Sammy and Gavin wobbled over to them, leaning on their wives for support. Not having much choice, Tammy and Christina allowed Adrianna to speak; and within seconds, Tammy was nodding eagerly as she listened. When she was finished, Tammy suggested a few minor changes, and finally they had what they thought was a good plan for now.

"I only have a flesh wound," Sammy insisted. "I'm coming along whether you like it or not. Someone wants to dance, I'll dance. We found bin Laden and took him out; we can do the same with this bastard." He looked at his wife, Megan, who looked back with worried but supportive eyes.

"Sorry, fellas, as much as I want to, the fucker got me good." Gavin looked at Pamela, who held him up and kept her head turned away. Her body was shaking.

"Pussy," Sammy joked.

The two men grabbed each other's arms and hands in an arm-wrestling shake, and gave each other deadly stares.

Gavin said, "Don't run to your death."

Sammy nodded his head and then replied, "The only easy day was yesterday, bro."

He nodded towards his wife, and Gavin blinked his eyes slowly; unfortunately, Megan saw and heard everything, but she stood tall and held back her emotions. Megan's voice was calm as day, "Try to get back before the first heavy snowfall. A lot of firewood still need to be chopped."

"Let's saddle up," Peter shouted.

"Wait for me! I need to get something," Adrianna called as she dashed towards her tent.

Lucy looked a bit unhappy. "Oh no."

"What?" Peter wondered.

"Some women like shoes, but Adrianna has a thing for…"

"What now?" Sammy demanded impatiently.

Adrianna came running back, something large flashing silver in her hand. "Can't go without Dirty Harriet."

Lucy continued, "… very large guns. Holy-moly, is that a .44 caliber?"

Peter leaned towards Lucy and whispered, "Is she really old enough to have one of those?"

"Afraid so. That one must be new. They confiscated the guns we used in the riot."

"I need to get my own kit," Sammy insisted.

"Sorry, frogman, no time," Peter said. "I have two kits in the back of Christina's truck. We'll use those."

"You do?" Christina asked, surprised.

"Yeah, we always bring our kits, kiddo. You never know when you're going to run into a fucking boogeyman in the boondocks."

Christina said thoughtfully, "Maybe it's better if I go alone. You're all a bunch of maniacs."

Rohan joined them, a large tree branch propped on his shoulder as a weapon. Christina just tossed her arms in the air and walked towards her truck.

"I might just be a dentist," Rohan vowed, "but I'm going with you fellas. Time to kick some ass!"

Everyone looked at him in disbelief, but before anyone had a chance to say anything, Daniela came up from behind Rohan, grabbed him by his ear, and dragged him away under wild protest. Daniela's angry voice overrode his, saying something about insurance papers and her car.

"Guess that's our cue to go," Peter said grimly.

NERO PEERED through his binoculars, looking down on them from a bend on the road higher in the mountains. He couldn't see much this far away, but he smiled when only one truck left the camp. He remained there briefly, watching as the rest of the campers loaded up the injured on a few vehicles while the rest started to break camp. In the distance, the flashing lights of rescue vehicles approached. He was too far away to hear the sirens.

He got into his truck and drove away.

PETER TURNED up the volume on the radio so they could listen to the news of what had happened earlier outside Skull Creek. According to authorities, there had been a terrorist attack on one of the mines; and later, when authorities had raided Ted Hagglund's house, a bomb had exploded, causing widespread damage. They had found a charred male body inside, and the media presumed it was the man who had killed Carlos.

Adrianna muttered, "Wonder how he got through all these road blocks?"

"Stop, Christina!" Peter said urgently.

She hit the brakes. "What? You told me to follow the dot on the GPS!"

Peter raised his hand. "One moment." He got out of the truck and peered at the ground. The snowflakes were larger, and a thin layer of white was accumulating over the land. With the snow came a cold breeze. Peter scrutinized the tracks in the thin snow cover, and after a long moment, he got back into the truck.

"You told me to follow the blip precisely, and here's where he turned south," Christina said, confused.

Peter signed. "Yes, that's right—but the only vehicle we met was that other truck, and there are no signs that he made a three point turn here." Peter nodded at the ground in front of the truck. "See? One track leading north and one south."

"Meaning?"

"Meaning he must have found the transmitter. If I had my own truck, then the computer in it could show us a better picture. But for now, we have to make do with my phone hooked up to your truck. Keep going north."

They left the second police checkpoint and roadblock behind them; there had been no problems passing through either. They kept driving for what seemed like hours, until suddenly Peter's phone went off. He answered and listened for a long time, then said, "Okay, under-stood, will do."

"Who was it?"

"It was Tammy; everyone is safe and sound, the police and the mil-itary are on the crime scene now, and she's about to call Tom."

"You're sure we're going the right way?"

"I sure hope so…yeah, I'm sure." Peter pointed towards the far distance.

Sammy leaned between them and said, "Looks like a hell of a fire."

"He wants us to find him," Adrianna said calmly.

They passed a burning gas station, where fire and explosions were still erupting. Several firetrucks and cop cars had their lights flashing on the opposite side on the road as they raced past.

After another half hour, they switched seats; Adrianna drove, and Sammy rode shotgun. Christina and Peter sat in the back, and Peter fell asleep instantly. Christina, however, did not. Instead she was looking at the rifle case leaning on the side of the truck wall next to her. It was very old, and had leather engravings and imprints; *7ʰ Cavalry, To G.A.C with love, Libbie.* She turned the case around and saw a large leather patch on it, as if someone had repaired it. It was a bit cramped in the back of her truck, so she leaned the rifle case back to the side, trying not to disturb Peter, who was out cold. She noticed that Sammy was asleep too.

She said quietly, "Stop the truck, Adrianna, we need to check on their wounds."

Christina had been right: both men were bleeding, and despite their protests, she and Adrianna knew that they were risking their lives. Just as Daniela had warned before they left, in the end they had to ar-gue with two big babies. There was no point in arguing further, so after re-dressing their wounds, they split some food between them that they had salvaged from the picnic. Meanwhile, the road kept taking them north, and soon the mountain range was far behind them. It was snow-ing more here; the traffic was scarce, as by now it was very late. Christina was glad for the huge, knobby mud-tires on the truck, which provided a necessary measure of traction.

They had entered a different terrain of high bluffs and hills dressed with thick forest. They passed several places where Ted Hagglund had left his mark, from burning buildings to cars driven off the road. They learned from two different couples that the maniac who did it had been driving a red truck that looked almost new. Their description of Hagglund more or less matched. Sammy thought that he might have ditched the other vehicle and stolen a truck somewhere, and no one challenged his suggestion. As they drove on, Peter kept reading and typing on his phone.

Eventually, they reached a fork in the road and had to stop; unlike earlier, where there had been signs for them to follow, here there were none. A new day was approaching as dawn crept over the land. They paused and walked over the entire area, looking for signs, but found nothing. Christina returned to the truck after she did her business behind a tree on the side of the road. While Adrianna remained guarding the truck and the guys searched for signs on both sides of the fork, Christina decided to see if she could figure out if the rifle was loaded.

"Adrianna, can you help me with this old Winchester?" Christina held up the rifle.

Adrianna hurried to her aid. "That's not a Winchester, it's a Remington .50-caliber sporting rifle with an octagonal barrel." She whistled appreciatively as she eyed the old rifle. "Wow, this is really old, and still in great shape." She checked the rifle and tested the aim. "Got the ammo?"

Christina handed her an ancient ammo belt with cartridges snugged into its many leather loops. "Is the ammunition too old?" she asked Adrianna.

Adrianna took out some of the rounds from the belt and looked them over.

"Actually, they're not as old as they look. These are reloads on old brass, but the lead looks pretty new, and the bullets themselves are very well made. Probably used an original mold."

Adrianna showed Christina how to load, eject, and reload the weapon, then set the sight at two hundred meters and explained how she should use it. Christina had some experience with modern weapons—having been taught by several experts how to use them whenever she'd made action movies—but didn't want to rain on Adrianna's parade, and listened to her lecture. When she finished, Christina put the rifle back in the leather case. Now she could take her time to appreciate the fine craftsmanship. She gently let her fingers touch the old leather.

"Who was 'Long Hair?' Or…something about a morning star?"

Adrianna looked at her for a moment, and then said, "Both Long Hair and the Son of the Morning Star were Indian names for George Armstrong Custer, the officer famous for dying at the battle of Little Bighorn. Why?"

"That Ted guy claimed this was his weapon from that battle."

The policewoman's eyes went wide. "Who knows? It could be, but I doubt it. It's probably in some museum or lost somewhere."

Adrianna stroked her large revolver like it was a baby, checking the aim. Christina, meanwhile, looked at the large patch on the leather gun case. It took her a while before she realized what it was she was looking at. "I think I know which way we should take," she said slowly.

Peter and Sammy hurried back to the truck after hearing Adrianna's whistle. "Look, guys. The Tomb Raider solved the riddle," Adrianna joked, smiling to Christina, who just rolled her eyes.

"I found a map, right here on the rifle case. *Now* I understand what he meant when he said I'd already found him."

They stood around the case, looking at the map tooled into the leather while Peter held it, comparing their surroundings with the map. They chose the left road, a dirt track, and headed into a deep forest.

Peter drove slowly; the windows on the doors were down, and Sammy held an automatic rifle ready out his side. They drove up a steady incline and came to the top of a hill, where the road made a wide right turn down into a valley. From their position, they could see quite a distance down below. There was a red truck parked where the road ended.

Sammy got out of the truck and crawled to the edge of the road, so he could see down into the valley better while maintaining a low profile. Peter kept watch on the opposite side, while Adrianna kept watch in front of the truck, leaving Christina to cover the rear.

Sammy made a pre-arranged bird call, and the rest joined him quickly. All took up cover positions while he crawled through the snowy grass, descending the hill. As he approached the red truck, he stopped and peered through the scope on his automatic rifle.

"You think they're still in the truck?" Christina asked Peter hopefully.

"Don't know. Doubt it."

Sammy returned and said, "I think I could hear something coming from the truck, but I don't want to get to close in case the bastard is watching and waiting for us to make a move so he can kill us all."

"You're right. The fucker's probably still loaded with explosives."

Adrianna asked, "What did you hear?"

"Sounded like music, but there are tracks in the snow, the little that's left, leading into the forest."

Adrianna intervened, "I can see it's the same or a similar truck, but how did he change the color like that? If it hadn't been for all the stuff in the back of the truck, I wouldn't think twice about this one, but I do recognize some of it."

"Me too," Peter agreed.

"Well, if this is the truck, then we need to save Robert and Kevin if they're still locked up in the back," Christina stated.

"Not until we know where the bastard is," Peter said firmly. "No, this is far too easy."

Christina insisted, "Come on, Sammy said he heard something, and…"

The truck exploded.

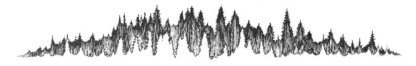

THIRTY-ONE

The searing heat swept them off their feet—which was fortunate, because shrapnel followed in its wake. When they looked up, there was a giant charred hole in the landscape where there once had been a truck.

"Well, I guess we just rang the doorbell," Sammy chuckled.

Peter smiled. "Let's hunt."

"You're fucking *laughing*? They could be dead!" Christina screamed, grabbing and holding up a smoldering cowboy boot. "This was Robert's!"

"Calm yourself, Christina, or you'll stay here," Peter snapped. "Did you or did you not hear Sammy say there were tracks leading *away* from the truck in the snow? Besides, look inside the boot." She did. "Do you see any flesh or blood?"

She shook her head, trying to stop sobbing.

Sammy said, "He made them walk barefoot. Pretty standard when moving prisoners in the bush. Makes them less mobile, less likely to run."

"But they'll freeze!"

Peter nodded. "The cold is the least of their problems, though. Now, let's move out as soon as we can—I figure the prick has a lead of at least two hours."

Adrianna looked down at the crater. "Wonder what set off the explosives?"

Sammy gave her a dead stare. "Who cares? You can always ask him when we find him."

Christina drove slowly down to the valley floor, while the others hovered around her truck like the Secret Service around the President, looking in all directions. She parked and got out of the truck, and for the first time realized that she was very cold. It had stopped snowing, but dark clouds fought the sun on the horizon, and more clouds hurried in their direction on a cold northern wind. She still wore her Lara Croft outfit, less the sunglasses. Peter noticed her predicament and gave her his jacket.

Then they went over their arsenal and split the weapons between them. Peter put the gun belt from his kit on Christina, and when he'd finished, he leaned back and inspected his work. He tilted his head "If I had a double holster and two guns, you really would make a picture-perfect Lara Croft."

Sammy tossed his belt strap with gun to Adrianna, who immediately slipped it on. Both Christina and she were given two spare magazines each. Adrianna checked on her giant .44, and placed the spare ammo in her breast pockets, making her chest even bigger. Christina took the ancient rifle case and strapped it over her back so that it poked up over her left shoulder. With her right hand, she reached back and pulled out Custer's rifle, loading it with the ammo from the strap crisscrossing the rifle's strap. In addition to their pistols, Sammy and Peter each strapped on a large, very nasty-looking black knife that looked Asian.

They split the remaining food amongst them, as well as a few water bottles. "In case you don't know, do *not* eat any of the snow, no matter how thirsty you get," Sammy advised them. "It will cool down your body and could cause hypothermia."

Sammy began to search the outskirts of the blast radius; it took a while before he could find their quarry's tracks in the snow. Once their trail ahead was clear, he took the lead with Christina following and then

Adrianna, while Peter took up the rear. They advanced slow and carefully, in single-file, following the tracks leading into the forest. Everyone was on their toes, and the calmness of the men, with their greater experience, was soon reflected in the women. The walked a long way, over hills and bluffs, down valleys and gorges. At one point they passed a small creek, and eventually a small river with a quaint little waterfall. The entire time they remained tense and alert. There were no sounds in the forest from any animals, not even birds, and it made the atmosphere very eerie.

Although it was getting colder and new snow had started to fall, they were all sweating.

When they had walked for well over two hours, Sammy ordered a halt to rest. He then inspected everyone's feet. Peter didn't object, thought the girls didn't care for it; but they let him check on them.

"I knew it. The bastard is into feet," Adrianna whispered to Christina, as the two of them put their boots back on.

"Hold it, Adrianna, you need a bandage," Sammy said calmly, removing a first aid kit from his backpack. He taped up her foot while she glared at him. "That blistered heel could ruin yours and everyone's day," he explained.

"It's standard procedure to check marching soldiers' feet. Take it like man, officer," Peter joked.

Before getting underway again, Sammy had them eat some of their food and drink some water. "Not sure how he can move so bloody fast with two barefoot prisoners," Sammy noted.

"Yeah, I thought about that as well," Peter agreed, and then turned to Christina. "Let's look at the map again."

She handed him her rifle case, with the rifle inside. Peter and Sammy peered at the map, trying to understand it better. "We need to get to higher ground and see if we can see that place there," Sammy said, tapping the map. "I think it's a mountain." He passed the gun case to the others so they could share their thoughts.

"Why bother, since we're just following their tracks?"

"Because, Adrianna, if we know where exactly they're heading, then I can try a short-cut and maybe ambush the fucker," Sammy said through gritted teeth. He was frustrated, and didn't bother to hide it.

After the rest, they moved on; and now they hurried faster, because the snow started to fall more intensely, and they didn't want to lose the tracks. When they came to a clearing, they stopped at the edge to reconnoiter. There was a small hill before them, and Sammy crawled to the top. After a while he waved for the others to join him. They did, walking along the tree line to avoid crossing the clearing. All of them could still see the tracks, but the snow didn't help at all. Christina felt as if they were being watched, and so did the others, she suspected, because of the way they moved with weapons at the ready, looking in all directions.

"Oh shit," Sammy said in a low voice as they reached him. He kneeled, raising his hand for everyone to stop. Peter hurried to him in a crouch.

"What've you got?"

"We're being watched, but that's not the bad thing. Look." Sammy pointed towards the clearing, and to the sides of the surrounding trees, at the hills and bluffs. They were covered with animal bones. "It's a den, a wolf den—and it's awful big."

Just as he uttered the words, a single howl split the air; soon it was answered by another a little farther to the west, and another and another.

"Defensive square formation on me, move to the clearing and make it fast!" Sammy ordered loudly.

Something dark and swift moved between the trees, like a giant shadow; and there was more movement all around them.

"And the fucker just walked through this place," Peter said bitterly, as he aimed his weapon towards the forest.

A large gray wolf appeared atop a nearby hill, peering down at them with its tongue lolling out of its mouth. Soon it was joined by another dozen wolves, all of which appeared enormous. "Look for the alpha!" Sammy shouted. "Take that one out, and the pack will be confused and run!"

Adrianna smiled like a demon. "Go ahead, punk, make my day." She pulled out her enormous revolver and aimed at the first wolf on top of the hill. "Bet that's the fucker in charge," she said, and then pulled the trigger. The wolf's head dissolved into a red mist.

"Nope, that wasn't the one," Peter shouted.

From all sides charged some fifty wolves, howling and snarling. Peter fired single controlled shots, killing three of them, while Adrianna emptied her giant hand cannon, killing at least one more. Then she dropped her artillery piece and used her other sidearm. Sammy killed several of the beasts, while Christina was in shock at first, fumbling with her handgun. A fanged maw only feet from her made her raise her eyes and scream while pulling the trigger as fast as she could. Seconds later, the four humans lay struggling on the ground, wrestling the giant canines that were trying to kill them.

Sammy rolled to his side and pulled his knife, stabbing one wolf in the neck several times, very quickly, as another bit down on his left boot. He thrust his knife into the monster's head. The wolf fell like a rock, but the knife was jammed in its skull. Another wolf jumped at him, going for his throat; it fell dead over him as a shot rang out. Adrianna kneeled next to him and fired single shots against the attackers. Peter struggled to his feet and stood tall, having reloaded somehow, aiming and firing while Christina lay on the ground between his legs, firing behind him. When Peter ran out of rounds, having no time to reload he pulled his knife and stabbed fast as a demon at any animal near him, standing over Christina and protecting her. He wielded his weapon like a samurai, and soon the blade was dripping red.

Adrianna screamed in pain as one animal bit down on her ankle. Peter spun around and quickly dispatched the wolf with a pair of jabs to its chest.

Christina's pistol clicked as the slide locked back, and she realized she had to reload quickly. She'd trained with a weapon just like this one a couple of years ago, but this wasn't a movie set. She fumbled with one of her spare magazines and dropped it; as she was scrambling to retrieve it, she heard a threatening snarl, and looked up at a yellow-eyed beast preparing to leap at her. But that's as far as it got. Suddenly all the wolves stopped attacking, instead backing off to circle them, yelping and snarling.

There came the faint sound of a horn in the distance. Not a car horn; something more like a bugle. As Christina snapped up the dropped magazine and reloaded her gun, she looked up at a sheer cliff face; and on top of it was the largest, blackest wolf she had ever seen. It stood there staring down at the carnage with its pitch-black eyes, not moving. At a second blast from a horn, all the wolves that could still run took off in the direction of the cliff where the giant stood.

It blinked its eyes slowly, then turned and moved away regally.

They counted eleven wolves on the ground, though a few weren't completely dead. Peter put them out of their misery with his knife. Meanwhile, Sammy struggled to get his own knife lose from the last wolf he had killed.

"Fucker controls the fucking *animals*," he snarled, while gritting his teeth and pulling the knife free.

They stumbled away from the wolf den as fast as they could support each other, and didn't stop until they felt somewhat secure on top of a large hill. The entire time, they could *feel* the presence of the wolf pack following them through the forest. There were several large rocks on top of the hill, forming a loose circle, and they helped each other to the center. "We'll be safe here for now, I hope. Check your weapons and do an ammo count. How bad is everyone hurt?" Sammy said, checking his weapon.

They chimed in with their conditions. Only Adrianna had been seriously injured during the wolf fight.

They remained on the rock for some time, catching their breath and trying to decide what to do next. Christina walked a few steps away from the others, to the edge of a rock on the opposite side of the circle. The view she saw took her breath away; the enormous hidden valley was beautiful. It almost looked like a park, with hardly any undergrowth or deadwood at all, as if someone had taken care of this part of the forest. In the distance, a stream flowed into a river, leading to a lake with a small but very wide waterfall; and on the opposite side of the lake was a lovely log home on top of a hill, looking like a child's toy in the distance.

The entire scenario was incredible, but the lack of bird song and animal sounds reminded her that this was anything but a paradise. As she watched, smoke began to drift from the chimney of the house, as the wolves raised a howl in the distance. Christina squinted her eyes, and could have sworn there was a man sitting on the porch of the house, waving at her, but she wasn't sure; the distance was far too great.

"Use this," Sammy said, and handed her a small pair of binoculars Peter had lent him earlier.

"He's there, waiting for me. He's waving now."

She handed the binoculars back to Sammy, but Peter was there to intercept. Next to him stood Adrianna. After a good look, Peter eventually handed the binoculars to her.

"What's he waiting for?" Adrianna asked of no one in particular. She continued, "Can anyone of you guys hit him from here?"

"Not with these scopes, I think," Peter said, looking at Sammy.

"We might, but do we want to? We don't know the location of the hostages."

Christina didn't like the fact that Sammy had called her friends hostages—it sounded a bit too impersonal and professional—but she kept her thoughts to herself. "I'll go alone," she said.

"No fucking way," Peter replied harshly.

"It's the only way I can think of."

"I *said* no fucking *way*."

Adrianna asked, "What about the wolves?"

"He controls them somehow, at least that's what I think, and he won't let them harm me. He wants me, and only me."

Sammy looked at her. "How do you know?"

"He's not my first mad stalker," Christina tried to joke.

"What part of *no fucking way* don't you understand!?"

"Peter, I understand that the fates of Robert and Kevin lie in that madman's hands. I also firmly believe he's in love with me, and that's why I should go. Besides, look at you guys: you're all injured. Adrianna can barely walk, and neither can either of you men."

They all fell silent, thinking of what Christina had said, until Peter muttered, "Cavalry should be here soon."

"Won't that make things worse?"

He looked tiredly at Christina, and then he sat down heavily on the hard, rocky surface, looking very tired.

From across the lake suddenly floated the strains of Beethoven's *Ode To Joy (Vocal)* from *Symphony No. 9 in D-Minor*. The song echoed loudly across the lake's surface, and the valley's natural acoustics enhanced the sound nicely. They all stared in disbelief at the man sitting on his porch, waving.

"Yeah, that does it. You aren't going—that fucker's completely lost it."

"Peter, please, I *have* to go. If there's the slightest chance of saving our men, then we have to explore it."

"At the price of your life? Never! No matter what my feelings are for Kevin, he would never let you risk your life for his!"

"Kevin isn't here now, is he, Peter? And then there's Robert."

No one said a word. The darkness started to creep up on them as the music changed: *The Last of the Mohicans. The Gael. Royal Scots Dragoon Guards. The Promontory Main Theme.*

"He sure knows how to put on a dramatic show for you, now don't he?"

Peter looked at Christina. He stood up and placed both his hands on her shoulders, looking down at her; and she looked back with neither hesitation nor fear in her eyes. His own eyes watered as he nodded. "Time to earn your Oscar, kiddo. Get going."

They watched as Christina removed her jacket and dropped it on the ground, together with the rifle case. Sammy handed her his knife. "For the ropes...or the madman. Your choice."

Christina gave him a shy smile.

With Lt. Colonel George Armstrong Custer's rifle in hand, she headed towards the house in the far distance. A horn sounded, and all the wolves took off into the woods. The man they knew as Ted Hagglund was no longer on his porch, but the music kept playing: Clannad's *I will Find You. Love Theme from Last of the Mohicans.*

Christina disappeared over a rise, and they held their breath, looking for her to reappear. "Look, there she is, she's back! Wait, the wolves are back too," Sammy shouted desperately.

"Fuck this, let me see."

Peter took the binoculars away from Sammy and looked down into the valley. Christina was walking straight towards the lake, and following behind her were what looked like over a hundred wolves, keeping their distance. Their leader was a gigantic black beast. Peter gave back the binoculars to Sammy, who handed them to Adrianna.

"She got some big *cojones* on her, don't she," the other woman muttered.

"Tom, it's me. Key on my phone's GPS coordinates. Send in the cavalry." Sammy and Adrianna both turned their heads sharply, looking at Peter as he pocketed his phone and picked up his rifle. "The wolves are down there where Christina is," he explained, "and I'm going to join her."

No more words needed to be said. The three of them began to trek toward Christina. They had to support each other due to their injuries at times, but not one of them ever complained. Soon the full moon had risen above the horizon, and the wolves began their eerie song.

Christina walked as fast as she dared through the lovingly tended, deadly landscape. It reminded her of an enormous botanical garden. The darkness came swiftly here in the mountains, and so did the full moon. The lighting was adequate for her needs, though she could have done without the howling. She couldn't explain where she got her confidence from, but strangely enough, she wasn't afraid—not even when she heard the panting of the monsters behind her. Ted wouldn't allow them to hurt her; of that she was certain. She glanced behind her and saw a giant of a wolf, a darker blot in the night, gleaming yellow eyes focusing on her.

She hastened her steps.

Christina soon reached the edge of the lake, and realized it would be a very long walk going around it from either side. She headed away from the waterfall side; and as she did, she noticed something shiny under the surface. She moved closer to the water's edge, and she saw a rock just beneath the surface. Another lay beyond it, and others beyond that one. Someone had created a path across the lake. She moved carefully, checking to see if the rocks were slippery; they were, but not too bad, thanks to her boots. She started to walk, and with every step she grew more confident. When she reached halfway, she dared to turn her head, and saw that the wolves had stopped at the edge of the water.

"Pussies! Don't like to get your feet wet, huh?" she snickered, and then she slipped and fell on her ass.

She considered her own situation in disbelief, and then she started laughing at herself and her own clumsiness. She got up and looked towards the hill with the rocky circle, but couldn't make out her friends standing there; it was too dark. She turned and continued walking towards the log cabin, and as she approached, she realized it was actually a very large house.

"GREAT, NOW she walks on water. What else is she going to do? Yep, she fell on her ass." Peter handed the binoculars back to Sammy and continued, "She's so small, and still the clumsiest girl I've ever met."

"She's like family, isn't she?" Adrianna asked, already knowing the answer.

"That and more, and I guess after this round of sight-seeing, you two are, too."

Sammy and Adrianna nodded, and continued following after Christina. "So, Peter, did it ever occur you should have called in the backup *before* the fucking wolves attacked us?"

"What would be the sport in that, Adrianna?"

"SPORT? Are you insane?"

"Maybe," Peter admitted.

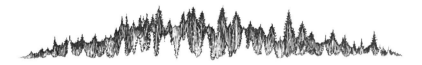

THIRTY-TWO

Nero stood on a cliff looking down at his house as the smoke started to build up. He held a torch in his hand, and the fire reflected onto his face. He wore his final skin; The Coyote. The head gear was made from a coyote's head, and his great-grandfather had worn it at the battle of Little Big Horn. It included no armor, like his bearskin exoskeleton had. Instead, he wore old-style buffalo trousers and moccasins, and around his neck and shoulder hung a centuries-old Viking horn. His weapons were two axes, one long and one short, also dating from the Viking era; the blades were very old, but as sharp as they had been when made ages ago. They were both beautifully engraved, and many museum would have paid a mint to have them. The shafts were newer than the blades, of course, but they also had beautiful inscriptions and patterns, including sigils from six Indian nations and runic letters from Scandinavia.

Patiently, he waited for the love of his life.

Christina smelled the smoke before she saw it, and she started running across the bridge of stepping stones; and of course she fell on her ass twice more. But that only pissed her off and urged her on. When she finally reached the other side of the lake, she tore off part of her shirt, and suddenly she wore a muscle shirt showing off her midriff. She dunked the torn part into the water, and tied it around her face before running straight towards the house.

More smoke was building up, and now she could see the naked flames. The music had stopped. She shouted for Robert and Kevin, but there was no answer. She held her rifle at the ready as she entered the lodge. It was snug and well-built inside. She tried to shout their names again, only to choke on the thick smoke. She made it into the kitchen and saw the door to the basement; it was open, and lights shone from below. She slowly descended the stairs and let out a whoop of joy when she found Robert and Kevin trussed up like hogs, lying on the floor unconscious.

Christina removed the smoke filter from her mouth, as there was less smoke down here. She shouted both men's names, but got no response. Drugged, then. She hustled over to a sink and grabbed a bucket to the side, filled it with water, and then showered the sleeping beauties until they decided to wake up. It took a while. She used the knife to cut them free, as both stared at her, dazed and confused. As she was about to toss a third bucket on them, Kevin held up his hand for her not to. "That's okay, kid, I think we're awake now. What took you so long?"

"No time to explain, but we have to get going. The place is on fire. You guys better be able to walk, because I sure as hell won't be carrying you."

"Wait Robert, don't stand up just yet. Massage your ankles and wrists, or you'll only end up straining or breaking them," Kevin warned.

Suddenly Christina was a masseuse, rubbing Roberts's ankles franticly.

"Guess I'll do my own by myself," Kevin muttered. Few minutes later, he stumbled to the door letting out into the next room, where Nero repaired his second skin. He placed his hand on the door and immediately pulled it away. "Can't go that way, door's too hot," he reported. "We open it and we'll get cooked."

Robert said, "Guess we have to go upstairs. Christina, please grab those blankets over there and get them wet. We'll use them for cover against the flames."

Draped in wet blankets, they struggled upstairs and found that most of the interior was ablaze now. The only way out was through the dining room, which led to a large grand room. By then, burning debris was falling from the ceiling. Christina suddenly stopped, while the guys hurried towards a door. There was a strange painting in a frame that drew her attention—a drawing with many pictures superimposed atop a large map. On one of the bigger pictures was old lettering: *Roanoke Colony established 1585; Croatoan 1590.* There was an old colony fortress in the center, and all around the main drawing were miniature pictures displaying a history of some sort, where people were fighting large animals like bears, wolves, and panthers.

"What the hell are you doing! This is no time to admire the artwork!" Robert shouted at Christina.

"But wait, wait—that word, Croatoan! He said that to me, wait!"

Robert would have none of it, tossing her over his shoulder when Christina reached for the painting on the wall. Robert followed Kevin outside onto the large wraparound porch. They got clear and huddled in front of the house, away from the lake side, where the main entrance was. All of them fell onto a nicely mowed grass lawn, coughing and gathering their strength.

Nero watched them from far above on his cliff. Smiling, he walked over to a thick rope and attacked it with his shorter ax. When the rope was sliced through, a large rock teetered and tumbled down the slope, starting a domino effect and opening up several gashes in the side of the mountain. Out poured oil, mixed with gasoline and detergent. It ran like small rivers in multiple directions, soon surrounding his home in an enormous circle of homemade napalm. Face now solemn, he lit a torch, then tossed it onto the flowing fuel.

The flames spread fast, sprinting along the circle in a wall of fire until it looked as if the entire mountain was burning, with several other bright snakes crawling through the landscape. He lifted his Viking horn and blew a long blast, then howled loudly, wolf-like. His call was answered by over a hundred other wolves, which hurried across the lake on the stepping-stone bridge, coming to their alpha's aid.

As he watched and waited, Nero ate some special dried mushrooms, and finished them off with a large wooden cup full of sweet, warm mead, made with an ancestral recipe and aged to perfection for several years. He descended from the cliff, and landed between Christina, Robert, and Kevin. Behind him was the road to safety.

"Now, my love, come and earn your Cro. There can only be one Alpha," he crooned.

Nero swung his axes dangerously while dancing in circles. The wolves kept their distance, staying clear of the fire, though it did not frighten them at all. Nero did.

Suddenly, the ground started to tremble, and the sound of many horses' hooves and wild shouts came soaring down into the valley. Nero looked up, confused. Hundreds of riders charged the clearing, many firing weapons into the air.

"Hey, lover boy," Christina taunted.

Furious, Nero turned and stared at the .50 rifle pointing at him. He sneered, "Go ahead, love, fire that weapon, and my pets will devour all of you. Now what?"

Christina tilted her head, looking at Nero. Robert and Kevin watched nervously, glancing frequently at the wolves waiting on the other side of the firewall. "Ever seen any of the Indiana Jones movies?" she asked Nero.

"Hey, didn't you hear him? You fire and we're done for," Kevin murmured.

"Trust me on this one, Kev."

Christina fired one round, striking Nero in his right leg. He hit the ground like a rock.

"Come on, let's go," Christina ordered, and started backing away carefully from Nero and the wolves. Robert and Kevin followed.

The giant black wolf stood between them and freedom. First it glared at them; then it ignored them, eyes focused on the injured Alpha on the ground, breathing raggedly. It sensed that it was weak, and the Alpha could not be weak. There could only be one Alpha, and it must be the strongest.

Taking a .50 bullet to the leg at close range guarantees that the leg will be lost. The hydrostatic shock was enough to nearly kill Nero. He barely clung to consciousness, barely believing that she had pulled the trigger.

Christina and her friends broke into a sprint, passing through the thinnest part of the inferno, gaining a few more nasty burns and patting out clothing that had caught fire; and the last thing they heard over the crackle of the flames was Nero's weak scream before the wolf tore his throat out.

A few wolves decided to follow them. One leaped onto Robert's back, and he hit the ground as Christina tried to club it away with the rifle butt. But suddenly a black shadow and a brown one flew through the air: Hunter and Nugget, both at least the size of their feral cousin, tore into the beast viciously; and from behind charged hundreds of riders, firing at the wolves, screaming and shouting wildly. They appeared to be Native Americans, some wearing tribal police uniforms.

Frank rode up and extended his hand to Christina; and soon Malik, Takoda, Whitney, and many more familiar faces had shown up. Sitting behind three of the riders were Peter, Adrianna, and Sammy. From the air descended a handful of helicopters with spotlights. The black wolf, now the pack's new Alpha, led the surviving pack members back into the dark forest, running flat out, to escape to fight another day.

THIRTY-THREE

Hundreds of people had gathered in a large mesa on top of a bluff. The area was surrounded by forest and fields; the night sky was clear, and there were no clouds. Most of the snow had melted, but everyone knew that soon, true winter would come, altering the scene. A cold wind blew in from the north. In the far distance came the sound of wolves howling.

Several fires burned, and natives danced and sang about the end of the *Yee Naaldlooshii:* The Skinwalker, an old Navajo folk tale that other tribes had also adopted.

Lights flashing from emergency vehicles spoiled the effect. A tent camp had been erected; several RVs were parked in one area, and behind them on an adjacent field were five helicopters. One stood out, larger and gleaming, corporate rather than utilitarian.

A line of people stood by a few truck tailgates, being served food; the savor aroma of outdoor cooking lay like a blanket over the area.

"And when Daniela walked over to confirm that Blake was really dead, she removed the blanket Pat had placed over him, and suddenly the corpse sat up," Whitney reported.

"Blake! He's alive?" Robert shouted, leaping to his feet.

"Wait, there's more. Instead of penetrating his forehead, the bullet hit at just the right angle to be deflected *around* the skull before it exited over his ear. It happens sometimes; I saw it once in the service. They call it a 'flexible bullet.' But what with all the blood, we thought he was dead."

"Well, that's great," Sammy said, as paramedics forced him back onto a stretcher.

"Tell that to Daniela. I think her professional pride got hit a bit hard."

"What happened next?" Peter wanted to know; he too lay on a stretcher, next to Adrianna, who was fighting Takoda over her hand cannon.

"Silly girl!" shouted the Lakota man. "You have to turn it in, you hear me?" Takoda finally stripped her of her gun, as she responded by insulting both him and his parentage.

Takoda turned to the crowd, holding the gun in his hand. "Malik and I followed the paramedics after we heard the call on the radio, suspecting something. Most of the Feds and military thought the ordeal was over, but we didn't. As a matter of fact, they still think it was a terrorist group behind everything."

"Idiots." Malik stepped up, drinking coffee from a huge mug. "When we heard what had happened at the hiking camp, I called Frank and begged him to bring that brown dog of his. Once I mentioned Christina, he and Claire got in their RV and we used it for a mobile HQ. We all knew we'd over stepped our boundaries when we left the state, but I guess that'll be something we'll have to deal with in the near future."

"Don't worry. If you need an attorney, you got one," Tom Billing said calmly.

They all laughed.

Takoda continued, "When we realized that you guys were near the rez, I called for help, avoiding all the red tape, but the problem was that this entire region has been taboo for centuries. No one ever ventured into those forests over there." He pointed at the dark forest in the distance, where a fire could be seen as what remained of Nero's home continued to burn. Helicopters kept flying over it, and lights from several emergency vehicles flashed nearby.

"Eventually, the tribal elders agreed to muster the local police and militia from the reservation, but for what it's worth it wasn't easy. We keep our traditions tight up here."

Malik continued, "So far, the CSI and the police have found several sets of human remains, mostly skeletal, over by the wolf den, but they can't do any more work there until daylight. Too dangerous right now."

Takoda turned, facing Tom. "So where are your goddaughters? My people want to thank them both."

"Tammy is in Skull Creek with Blake, and as for Christina, I think she's over at Frank and Claire's RV."

CHRISTINA HUNG up the phone, smiling, knowing that both Tammy and Blake would be fine. She then put on a more serious expression as she read from the computer screen; *"The Roanoke Colony, also known as the Lost Colony. Established in 1585, abandoned before August 1590. The colonists disappeared during the Anglo-Spanish War. There is no conclusive evidence as to what happened to the colonists."*

"Some things are better kept secret," said a quiet voice.

Christina jumped about three feet. "HOLY SHIT! Oh, it's you, Mr. Smith. You really need to stop spooking people like that. If I still had Custer's gun with me, there'd be a huge hole in you right now."

Mr. Smith barely smiled. He placed his old umbrella next to the desk as he leaned over Christina's shoulder, reading from the computer screen. Thank goodness for the wireless hotspots that most smartphones came with these days. As he paged through the document, she said, "Why are some things best kept secret?"

"Well…take your rifle, for example, the one that was given to you. How long do you think you can keep it once the authorities find out about it? Or his descendants, if he has any."

"They'll probably take it away from me."

"And still, you earned it, and it was given to you. It will probably end up in a museum; or worse, bagged as evidence in storage for ages to come, until someone wealthy buys it at an auction."

"Maybe it belongs in a museum."

"Maybe it does, and then wouldn't it be more right and proper if you were the one donating your property?"

"You scared me only to tell me this?"

"No, ma'am. The others would like to see you, whenever you're ready. But if that comes out…" He nodded at the screen.

"What comes out?"

"What you might know of that. Imagine what it might do. A secret society murdering people who they think are enemies of nature, who have been doing it for centuries? One that explains the skinwalker and berserker legends, who knows maybe even bigfoot? Just imagine all the copycat killings that will follow."

"But how do you *know* that?"

Mr. Smith smiled and said, "Who says I do?" He just stared at the computer screen, then watched as Christina walked over and petted a gray kitten sleeping in a lounge chair. On the floor in front of it lay Winston the bulldog, moaning sadly as he stared at his chair, giving the little intruder a very sad expression. Christina petted the old dog, and he just rolled his eyes at her and then back to his chair. Christina laughed, then headed outside.

Mr. Smith looked at the Croatoan files Christina had downloaded, then turned off the computer. He looked at the rifle and then on the umbrella with a sad expression.

When Christina exited the vehicle, she found Claire sitting in a lawn chair, looking like a concerned mother; next to her sat Christina's new dogs, Hunter and Nugget, both wagging their tails. She petted them and exchanged pleasantries with Claire, but her mind wasn't focused on anything in particular.

"He's over by the horses, talking to his sister on a phone, I think," Claire said pleasantly.

Christina found Robert standing by a line of horses, petting one of them. She walked up to him and cleared her throat. He slowly turned, facing her. Suddenly she blushed; but then she got her act together, and walked right up to him, only inches separating them. She looked up at him, and he looked back, both trembling a little.

"So tell me, how does a girl get to know a guy like you?" she asked after a long, quiet moment.

"She has to answer my question."

Christina looked at him suspiciously and mischievously. "What's the question?"

He smiled and looked like he was about to say something, when suddenly he leaned forward. He smelled wonderful. Christina stood on her tip-toes and closed her eyes; again she felt his stubble on her cheek as it brushed her face. But the expected kiss never came; instead he leaned to her side, breathed into her ear, and then he asked her his question: "What does a man have to do to keep a girl like you around?"

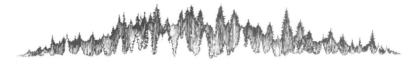

EPILOGUE

SOUTH AFRICA

Einar Leeu stood on top of a hill by a river bank, watching the vultures and hyenas fighting over the spoils left behind by illegal poachers—local scouts and several wealthy overseas tourists.

Two large male lions lay next to him, licking their bloody paws, their bellies full. One of the giant cats moved up to Einar and pushed his massive, bloody head and mane into his human's chest, just like any cat wanting affection. He petted it lovingly, and buried his head in the thick mane. The cat purred with happiness; soon the second giant joined them.

A moment later, he looked on fondly as the two cats walked down to the river as if they owned it and began lapping up water. Nearby stood a gazelle, drinking delicately from the river, but the two lions couldn't care less; and the gazelle knew it.

Einar walked over to his Land Rover, an older model 4x4, a vintage vehicle without a hard-top. He slid into the driver's seat and taking an open brown envelope from his breast pocket, he looked at it for some time; and then he took out the letter and read it again and again, and as he did, his eyes watered. But there were no tears. Facing him was the hot, reddish African sun, setting on the horizon, heat-mirages dancing in the air.

By now, his adoptive father would have made his exit. No doubt it would be all over CNN when he returned to civilization.

He started his vehicle, and made a one-eighty turn before driving away, leaving his cats behind. Absently, he turned on the CD player; AC/DC's *Thunderstruck* roared out. Dead eyes stared into the rearview mirror at the setting sun.

Whereas some people like to have large plush dice hanging from the rearview mirror, Einar Leeu, a.k.a. Tala Caligula Butler, had two shrunken heads—and they weren't made of plastic.

THE END

CPSIA information can be obtained
at www.ICGtesting.com
Printed in the USA
LVOW11*1702210218
567416LV00008B/50/P